$\mathscr{T}$UPPENCE

TO

$\mathscr{P}$ASS

Sara Powter

Bible Quotes from the King James Version

ISBN: 9781923097070
Paperback Edition

Pacific Wanderland Publications
ABN 99 768 734 831

Kincumber NSW 2251

saragpowter@gmail.com
www.sarapowter.com.au

1st edition 2025 printed by Amazon/ Kindle
an Amazon Company; available on Kindle Unlimited & KDP
Produced by Pacific Wanderland Publications
Also available in eBook and large print paperback.

Graphic Acknowledgements

Cover

Joseph Lycett

https://digital.sl.nsw.gov.au/delivery/DeliveryManagerServlet?
*embedded=true&toolbar=false&dps_pid=IE3143665&_gl=1*gppeno*_ga*MT*
*Q2NDM5NDA2NC4xNzQxOTTkwODM0M0*_ga_CYHFMM592Q*MTc0M*
jI2MzAzMi44LjEuMTc0MjI2NDU2Ny41MC4wLjg3NzYzNTg1Mw

https://dictionaryofsydney.org/media/67811
ML55

Inset

https://www.bonhams.com/auction/27485/lot/146/heywood-hardy-
british-1843-1933-saddling-up/

Chapter graphics in the Public Domain

Cover by Beckon Creative
beck@beckoncreative.biz

In England.
Turnpikes and Tolls.

They originated in the 17th century because local governments, specifically parishes, were unwilling or unable to invest in roads. This money kept the roads in reasonable order.

In Australia.
Toll roads in New South Wales were started by Governor Lachlan Macquarie in 1811.

Australia's first toll road was a newly constructed turnpike road from Sydney to Parramatta. It opened on 10 April 1811 with one toll bar in George Street, Haymarket, and soon afterwards, another at the Pitt Road near the cemetery at the end of Parramatta, with a third on the road to Windsor. This was a successful arrangement, as a profit of £930 was made in 1815 alone from the tolls on the Sydney to Parramatta Road. There was a toll for an earlier road, but it was for the ferry crossing.

Major General Lachlan Macquarie, the 5th governor, left the colony a much better place than he found it. He returned home to face the false accusations. Unfortunately, he died before the verdict was given. He was posthumously acquitted of all charges and is affectionately called the "Father of Australia." He is buried on the Isle of Mull in his beloved Scotland, and this epitaph is written on his tomb.

While my character, Josh, and his family are fictional, the works of Lachlan Macquarie and Chief Ruatara are historically accurate.

Thanks to my husband,
Steve, for all your support in my writing.
He's my **Alpha** reader.

To Roby Aiken
for your patience in correcting my punctuation.

and to my **Beta** readers
Noreen Robertson, Linda Upcroft,
& Anna Marie Leffew for doing the final read-throughs.

Also to
Rebekah Robinson for my cover.
Cover by Beckon Creative
beck@beckoncreative.biz

Table of Contents

*The grammar and language in this book are
Australian English spelling*

~ *- time passing*

 *- different location*

Chapter 1   Only Worth Tuppence

*T*he leaves of the neatly trimmed hedge snapped back into place.

Flo Lawrence, the laundry lady, could hear the sniggers of the local lads who had just cut across the grass. The three boys were well known to her and usually did not annoy her so much, but today had not started well. She was sick to death of the naughty wretches messing up her clean washing. She had just finished hanging her master's freshly washed linen shirts when she realised two were missing.

Mrs Lawrence was fully aware that the naughty lads were still within earshot. She called, "Joshua, Andy, Micky, put those shirts back this minute. I'll count to three, and they had better be returned! One... Two..." She didn't need to count further as the two, now dirty, oversized shirts were thrown back over the hedge.

The laundry maid followed the action with a verbal tirade. She told them how she felt as she realised both shirts needed to be rewashed. Her blue language made the three boys chuckle.

They heard her shout, "I'll get you blasted little rascals one day; you mark my words!" She gripped one of the long poles from the laundry line and poked it through the hedge.

She aimed for where she heard the giggle and shoved.

"Ouch!" came a cry.

The overweight laundry lady felt that she had struck something soft. "Ha! Got one of you! I told you, you young blighters, stay clear of me, or you'll know the feeling of a paddy-whack on your backsides if you come near me again. Do you hear my words?"

She heard the rustle of the leaves on the hedge, then the sound of running footsteps.

When far enough away, they stopped.

The three lads had escaped, but Andy had a scrape across his stomach where the pole had jabbed him.

Josh and Micky fell to the ground, laughing at his misfortune.

Andy was angry. Not just at being caught, but by his friends' laughter. "Quit it, you two! It hurts." He lifted his shirt again and saw blood trickling down his stomach. What was worse, he knew he could not admit to his mama how he got the injury.

Micky came to his rescue. "Pa has a bottle of potent grog at home. Come on, and we'll clean you up."

Josh chuckled at his friend again. "Sorry, Andy, I know I shouldn't laugh, but she was so angry this time. I think we'd better lay off her for a while."

Andy shot him a filthy look and said, "I'll get you back, Josh. This hurts like hell. It was your blooming idea this time. Now I have to hide this from Mama."

Micky stayed silent. He knew his young friend could hold a grudge and wondered what he would do to get back at the older boy.

Micky was somewhat in awe of Josh, but was never game to say anything against him. He dropped his head and kept walking. Josh was usually the one halting their pranks, not starting them. Today had been a rare occurrence.

~

Six months later, in early 1809

A trembling voice replied shakily, "Not guilty, Your Honour!" The lad was shaking and had been doing so since he was arrested with these two friends a month ago. Andy and Micky had named him for stealing the fat Post Master's linen shirt. He had not even been with them on this outing, and now he was likely to be transported for something he had not even done.

Josh was livid. This was Andy's way of getting back at him for his injury. He had hardly seen the two younger boys since the day Mrs Lawrence had poked at them, as his father had been killed shortly afterwards. He needed to help his mama at home, and he was surprised that the two younger boys had not been around much.

The last time he saw them was when the local theatre caught fire just after Christmas. He had seen them scampering away like scalded rabbits. He wondered if they had been responsible for starting it.

He knew Andy loved playing with fire, and he would not put it past them. However, he would not say anything about that. He knew they had been at the Covent Garden Theatre when the fire started. It had been a couple of weeks after his papa had been killed, and he had taken over Papa's soap and cologne stall at the markets. He had to collect the rents from the other stallholders to ensure they had a proper income. It supplemented his mother's sewing income from making costumes for the stage. However, when the Royal Theatre in Drury Lane was also destroyed, her income ceased completely. His job at the market was all they now had. That income only just covered the rent. His mother and sister, Jenny, made the soaps and colognes he sold.

They had sold all their father's possessions as well as their furniture and moved into a tiny attic room at the Rookery. Their old rooms had been part of his papa's payment, which ended when he died. Their new place was a hovel, but at least it was a roof over their head.

Life stank, and Josh missed his papa. He sniffed and turned his attention back to the present.

The judge's booming voice made him step back in shock. "What do you mean, not guilty? Your friends admitted that you had previously played pranks on the laundry lady and taken some of the washing, and now you deny you did it?"

Josh was petrified. "No, I mean yes, sir."

The white-wigged judge shook his gavel at Josh. "Make up your mind, boy. You can't have it both ways. You either did or didn't steal these shirts."

Josh was horrified as a tear trickled down his cheek. Brushing it away angrily, he sniffed and then replied, "I admit that we have played tricks on Mrs Lawrence before, but we never stole nuffin'. I've done nuffin' to her for months. We would take the shirts off the hedge, mess them up a bit, and then throw them back. Ask her, Your Lordship; we did it often. But I haven't been since my papa died, sir."

Josh's eyes sought out the accusing woman. "Isn't that right, Missus? We never kept nuffin', just mussed them up on you. Last time I did it, you dug us with the pole."

The judge bellowed at Josh's attempt to appeal to his accuser. "Speak only when spoken to, boy, and leave her out of this." He rubbed his reddened bulbous nose, and his lips twisted as though thinking.

Josh knew that he had to follow the man's rules, as he was known to be mean. He fell silent, but if looks could kill, Mrs Lawrence would be dead, as would his two supposed friends, whom he saw sitting in the visitors' gallery. Her face was flushed red, and she was angry. How had they escaped punishment? Then he realised Andy and Micky laid the blame solely at his feet.

He should dob on them for burning down both theatres if he were mean. Only he knew they would probably say he was with them.

Although he was angry at them all, he really only had himself to blame. He was the eldest of the three and should have known better. His papa had taught him to behave.

Mrs Lawrence had become the target when she verbally abused his mother after church one day. She called her a streetwalker. She was a nasty person with an evil temper and a worse tongue.

Josh had not been with his friends when whatever crime they had committed was the cause of him standing here now, because after he had closed his stall, he had picked the pocket of a particular noble gentleman as he left the markets. This man had run over his father and hardly paused.

The fifteen pounds that Josh had stolen would see his family through for more than five years if they were careful. It would cover rent and food for that long. He had managed to pass the money to his little sister, Jenny, then run away.

The fat man did not even realise his wallet had been picked. Josh grabbed a few notes, shoved the billfold back into the man's overcoat pocket, and fled. As he ran past, he grabbed an apple from Mr Pendergast's fruit stall from the box of bruised fruit. It was at the end of the street that the Bow Street Runner had caught him for this petty crime. He saw him take the fruit, and Josh had taken a big bite of the rosy apple.

Josh had not seen the Runner waiting for him, as he had slowed to check that Jenny had managed to escape with their ill-gotten goods.

They had targeted this peer before, as he showed no remorse when he had run over and killed their papa. A judge had ordered him to pay a fine, then pocketed it himself. They received nothing.

Josh released a sigh of relief and ran smack bang into the arms of the roughly dressed red-vested Runner.

Josh wondered how long he would be locked up for this time. It was not the first time he had been caught taking bruised fruit from Mr Pendergast's stall, but it was never the man himself who complained.

Usually, three weeks in the magistrates' lock-up was the term, but linen shirts cost a lot more than damaged food. If the judge knew about the stolen money, he would be a goner. Josh was resigned to serve more time in gaol.

Josh met the judge's gaze and tried hard to look innocent. He wasn't sure how to achieve that facial expression, but at thirteen, he had fooled most of the adults he knew. It wasn't that he was intentionally naughty, but the only way his mother and sister had to survive was by thieving from the rich toff who all but murdered his parent. The pranks they played on the laundry woman were just that.

Josh stood waiting. He watched the judge pull an oversized handkerchief from his pocket and blow his swollen, ruddy nose. His bloated face was a testament to his overindulgence in both spirits and fine food. Josh wondered if he had gout, as he knew by reputation that people with that condition were often cranky.

Stuffing the used kerchief back into his pocket, the judge pursed his lips. "Boy, how many times have you been before me?"

Josh timidly answered, "Three times, Your Honour, and once before a magistrate."

This time, the judge's brows knitted. "I thought I remembered you. All for petty theft, I suppose? Well, this time, you're not getting off so easily." He scribbled a few notes, then looked up again. "Joshua James Callan, I sentence you to three years to be served in the hulks."

Josh reeled, "Three years, but sir, I weren't even there. Ask Mr Pendergast; he saw me take a bruised apple from his market stall when this was supposed to have happened. It was not even worth tuppence. He has a basket of the bruised fruit that he gives to us street urchins. He would not have reported me for taking a bit o' fruit." He took a deep breath, then added, "I didn't do it, Mr, I mean Sir, I mean, Your Honour. It wasn't me. I didn't steal no shirts from no one. Why would I want that man's stuff? It is so big that they would be on the ground on me because he was your size, sir."

The angry judge rounded on him. Pointing out his oversized girth did not assist Josh's plea. "I told you to speak only when spoken to, boy! So you admit that you stole an apple, did you? Is that not theft? You have obviously not mended your ways. Tuppence indeed! You are a street rat and not worth that much. I will lock you away for a longer period if you continue to speak insolently. It's time you learned to respect your betters. By the time you have completed your term, you hopefully will have learned to do so."

Josh opened his mouth and said, "But, I…"

The judge was fuming that his order not to speak had been ignored. "I said, *Silence!* Reconsidering, I shall make your term seven years and you shall serve it in New South Wales."

With a huff, the man banged his gavel. "Next case!"

The judge then muttered none too softly for a second time, just in case Josh had not heard the first utterance. "Street rats like you are not worth even tuppence. You'll never amount to anything, boy." He glared at Josh and angrily waved his hand to dismiss him.

Josh heard him and gasped. Before he could make any reply, he was manhandled out of the dock by the guards. His eyes stung with unshed tears. How dare he? He was convicted of something not even worth two pence. The judge's words cut deep. He dared not cry, but the words hurt.

He muttered, "I'll show him! I'll amount to something one day! I'll do my time and make the best of my life. Seven years, my foot!" He caught sight of his sister and mother watching, but he dared not call out again.

However, his mother shouted at him. "We love you, Joshy. We'll be all right." He saw Jenny weeping, but there was no way he could do more than blow them a kiss. Knowing he could not make a noise, he mouthed the words back to them. "I love you."

The God that Mama was on about endlessly was now the only one they had to rely on. Josh hoped that her God would do better for them than He had over the last year. Since Papa died the previous year, life had been tough. Up until then, he had believed that God did care for them. But the rich driver had hardly paused when Papa had been run over on the way back from work. Others reported him, so the man got a fine.

Josh discovered who it was and targeted his father's murderer whenever he saw him. He took a pound here and there, but nothing else. The fifteen pounds that Josh had stolen from the murderer would keep his family alive for some time. He was thankful Jenny had not been captured.

Two burly court attendants all but dragged him back to the cells. They hooked their arms through his and, at places, carried him down the dark corridor of the prison complex.

Josh had tried to get regular work and had worked as a pure collector for the tanner, a street sweeper for the wealthy, and any other job he could find, but it was never enough.

After the fires, he and Jenny had taken to working together as a pickpocket team and were good at it. They only targeted wealthy individuals who cheated the stallholders or abused the children in the area.

More often than not, Josh kept some of his bounty from his sister and handed it to the storekeeper who had been short-changed. It was why none had turned him in for theft. Even Mr Pendergast benefited from Josh's light-handed skills. Josh knew he would not have reported him over a single apple.

As Josh was pushed into the cell, he realised he would not see his family again for seven long years, if not longer. He didn't want to weep, but the judge's comment hit him hard. He adored his family. Everything he did was for them.

Life had been fun until last year; now it stank.

The court attendants shoved him inside, and he fell to his knees.

He crawled to the side of the cramped room and wept. He thought of the small room he had found for his family when they had been thrown out of the rooms that came with his father's work at Covent Garden.

The attic loft they lived in was in the Rookery, as the slums were known, and was barely habitable. Gone was the nice food, the clean clothing and the security of the rooms that had been at Red Lyon Street, Whitechapel, where he was born.

Now, thanks to his friends' lies, he had lost access to his family. He was alone and had to make the best of what was before him. He was thirteen and would be twenty when his term finished.

He groaned. "I'll be an old man." Sitting on the stone floor of the squalid cell with his back to the other occupants, his tears finally fell. The stench of the room assailed his nostrils.

The slop bucket had not been emptied and was now overflowing. Unable to move further away from it, he hid his nose in the lapel of his tweed jacket. This coat was the last thing his father had bought for him, and he had nearly grown out of it. At least it was warm and sopped up his cascading tears.

In previous years, due to his age, he had been detained at the nearby watch house. He wondered if that was where he would be returned to. He should only have appeared in front of a magistrate rather than a judge. He shrugged. He now had seven years to serve because he opened his big mouth.

Josh remained alone and huddled in a corner, trying not to notice what was happening around him. All the prisoners who had to appear before the magistrates or the angry judge were locked in one big room.

The women arrested for drunkenness were obviously streetwalkers as they continued to ply their trade in the cells. Their bodices were open, and their breasts bared. It was hard not to watch as they enticed any man or youth who had a penny spare to use them where they stood. Some had sores on their lips, and most were filthy. They were here because they had stolen things, not because of their profession.

Josh had not been intimate with a woman, but his older friends often boasted about their conquests. Josh's parents had taught him about finding someone he cared about before slaking his lusts.

The debauchery was occurring in various spots around him, leaving little to his imagination. He knew what went where, but had never succumbed to his carnal urges. He hid his head in his arms, trying not to hear or watch. His sleeves became damp from his anguished tears.

When all the cases for the day were over, those who had received harsh sentences were loaded into various wagons and taken to Newgate prison. Thankfully, that included most of the immoral women.

Josh sighed with relief. With only thirty of the youngest lads left in the cell, they were shackled, led through the streets, and taken to the much smaller Giltspur Street Compter gaol. This was a small gaol controlled by a sheriff. He knew that this place was a feeder prison for Newgate, but it was intended for those less hardened and the young. Thankfully, he still qualified to be held with these boys.

Unfortunately, other than those in individual cells, it was for mixed genders, and there was nowhere that he could hide from the activities of the few cavorting couples around him. Although most of the other occupants were children, a few of the older felons were in their twenties. It was these men who accepted the offering of the loose women.

He discovered from some long-term occupants that the debtors were in another building, but the night watch rooms were nearby.

Josh had heard of something called the clap; his mother had explained that loose women's activities spread it to the immoral men they cavorted with. Although this lock-up was nowhere near as bad as Newgate Prison or even the court cells, Josh found that sitting near the cell doors gave him some respite from the activities towards the back of the large dungeon.

Other young boys joined him throughout the afternoon.

Overcrowding meant they had no beds or bunks, so sleeping on the cell floor was the only option.

Rats were a constant problem, but they usually made their way to the slop buckets.

Lying down, Josh flung his arms over his ears and eyes, then slept.

~

Josh was shaken awake by a warder. His bleary eyes took some time to focus properly. A uniformed arm reached through the bars and held tight.

"Come on, laddie; your mama is waiting. Shh!"

The older warder, Matthew Gilks, didn't usually permit visitors, but he knew this lady and her past. He remembered her from her youth. She had been arrested for a petty crime when about Josh's age and locked up here for a week. He had needed to pull off the men who tried to rape her. She was bruised and battered, but he managed to transfer her to the cells with the very young children. There, she had cared for the little ones, which brought her to his notice.

On meeting her recently, he discovered that Cathy had been able to leave that part of her life behind and was pleased to hear she had married. He did what he could for the young ones, and occasionally, a face here or there would be burned into his memory. Cathy had been one of those faces. She was known as Kat back then, as she fought like a kitten. He knew what she did was not her choice. Her story was of being sold by a parent. He had learned that this was all too common for many young girls.

Matthew had never mentioned that he was aware of her past, but she knew. He and his wife met her in St John's church in Hackney last week and discovered that she was now widowed. Then she mentioned that her son was in prison. He was delighted to discover that it was in the area where he worked.

Josh woke. "What? Mama has been permitted in?" Josh rubbed his eyes and was quickly on his feet. He whispered, "What time is it?

The warder put a finger to his lips. "Two in the morning. Yes, shh. Come." He unlocked the cell door quietly.

Josh followed the warder out and was in his mother's arms in minutes. The emotions of the past weeks bubbled out of his eyes.

Her loving arms comforted him in a way no other means could. He realised that after a few moments, she was whispering to him. He concentrated on her caring words.

What she said sank in. "Josh, we will follow you. Actually, we may even beat you there. We've purchased a passage and will be on the next ship that will take us. Jenny can travel for free. I have learned that you may be assigned to me once you arrive. We will leave now, so we won't be able to come again."

He was now wide awake. Noting that the warder had left them alone in the room, Josh pumped her for information. "Mama, what do you mean you are coming? How can I be assigned to you?"

Cathy pushed him away and motioned for Jenny to come over and give him a hug. "We needed to leave our room, and we returned to the church where Papa lived in Hackney. We are safe, but we need to leave."

Josh had not even seen his little sister in the room, but he tousled her hair and kissed her cheek. "I missed you, sis," was all he said. Jenny knew he adored her.

Cathy pointed to a bench seat, and the three sat down. Keeping her voice down, she said, "Joshy, the money you took means that I can pay for a steerage ticket, which is £5. As we have nothing here, we're coming too. I've been asking around, and things are better there than here in the Rookery. We left the flat and are staying in the crypt at the church. If you leave, then I will be forced to…" She didn't want to voice what she would be forced to resort to. She would have few options to make money if she remained.

Josh looked at his sister and shook his head. "Mama, that is amazing, but what would you do there?"

Cathy didn't know and said as much. "Josh, there's not much I can do here now that your papa has gone, or since the theatres burned down. So I may as well do nothing there. I may even be able to find a good man and remarry. I heard that wives are in short supply. Over there, I should be able to take in sewing to support us."

Both her children glanced at her in stunned surprise.

Cathy smiled. "Well, why should I not remarry? You will both soon be independent, then who will care for me?" She gave a happy laugh. "Jenny and I are booked on the *Hindostan,* and it leaves in May. The warder told me you will be on the *Ann,* though they don't have a departure date yet. Joshy, keep your head down and stay out of trouble. Trust that God will get the glory from this."

Josh grunted. "I don't see how! You have no idea what it's like in here, Mama."

Cathy swept the lock of hair from her son's forehead. "Don't be so sure about that, son. I had to survive on the streets before I met your papa. Matthew Gilks, your warder, saved me more than once. I only told him on Sunday that I knew he recognised me. Back then, life was not good, son. You know what it's like in here. It was worse for me on the streets before I met your father."

Josh's astonished gaze caught hers over his sister's head, shock etched on his face.

Cathy put her finger to her lips and glanced at her ten-year-old daughter.

Josh was reeling. Had his mother indulged in the same behaviour as the women in his cell?

The look on his face brought tears to Cathy's eyes. Her life before her marriage was not of her choosing. Her father had sold her to a man who resold her after he deflowered her. He sold her to a madam, and she had finally run away from the brothel madam she had lived with since she reached maturity. For two years, she had been used and abused by filthy peers like the Earl of Oxenborough-Thorpe and Baron George Mortonford. The only blessing was that the peers were usually clean and disease-free, and she did not contract the clap. Although she escaped those particular men's attention, their friends were as bad. Then James Callan had met her while selling both flowers and herself in Covent Garden.

Within a week, James had hidden her at the preacher's home in Hackney, where he lived, and then married her as soon as she turned fifteen. Josh was born the following year.

Cathy had changed her name and appearance and stayed out of sight. She had previously worked with or for the filthy, lustful peers who haunted the ghettos and streets of the less desirable areas of London.

When Josh was two, her madam was killed by another of her clients, and finally, Cathy was free. By then, she had perfected the cologne that James adored. It was made from sandalwood and orange peels. With little access to water for bathing, the scent masked the worst of the body odours.

James loved it and wore it daily. Even their minister, Reverend Phineas Brackenridge, who sheltered them, wore it occasionally. She smiled at the thought that something she made from waste was so enjoyed.

Josh saw a smile flick across his mother's lips. His brow wrinkled. He watched as her face relived those years.

Then the memory of those two years made her shudder. "Josh, when we get to Sydney, I shall tell you my story, but you now know why I loved your father more than you will ever realise. He gave me a reason to live and explained that with God's forgiveness, nothing is beyond Him to wipe completely clean. Nothing, Josh! My old life was washed away. I have been forgiven. It's why I dragged you both to church. I need you to hear how God can help us when no one else can. It is not God who is to blame for our sins and wilful lives, but Satan. God will forgive you if you mean it when you ask, but as I have said before, you must try to be good."

Josh knew she had realised he had been pickpocketing. He sighed and acknowledged their thieving activities to her: "Mama, I only ever took what we needed, and normally only from Lord Wiskhamford. He didn't even deny hitting Papa, yet he received no punishment other than a stupid fine the judge pocketed. We got no compensation, so I took money when we needed it. The last time, his billfold was so full of notes that I could have taken ten more, and he would not have missed them. He must have had over a hundred pounds in it; however, I took what we needed to survive and no more. To use his money to start a new life is apt justice."

Cathy grinned and nodded. She had always known the source of the funds that Josh and Jenny brought home. She didn't mind as she, too, knew how James's death had affected them even more than her. "Joshy, I have always known what you two have been up to. You took from the rich thieves, and I know you repaid the stallholders. They told me. We could not have lived without this stolen money. Now, we will use it to start a new life."

She turned as she heard approaching footsteps. "Joshy, keep the faith, son."

Jenny hugged her brother again, and then Cathy took him in her arms. "I love you. We shall see you in Sydney Cove, son," she said, kissing his forehead.

The warder returned.

Josh heard his mother thank the man. "Matthew, thank you so much for permitting our entry. I won't see you again as we are leaving for the colony. Thank you for everything. Will you let Marjory know how much I appreciate her help? But for you, I may well be dead."

Matthew smiled and told her to wait for his return. He took Josh back to his overcrowded cell before he returned and escorted Cathy and Jenny out of the gaol. Marjory would be pleased that one more girl would be out of the horrid life she had been forced to live. He knew they were living in the crypt again and would be safe until they boarded.

He was off duty and would walk them home, such as it was. His wife, Marjory, awaited him at home, and it was she who had drawn his attention to Cathy's unfortunate situation.

~

Dawn came all too soon. Another warder woke everyone by walking along the bars with a metal spoon and yelling, "Wakey, wakey, people. Your banquet awaits."

As Josh had not eaten since the morning before, he was famished. He had missed his midday meal because of the trial. He was sleepy, but that was worth it. He now had something to look forward to. Even the thin porridge served in the quadrangle was better than nothing. It was thin, but at least it was hot. Having been held in the magistrates' lock-up for the months before his trial, he was thankful he had not been moved to Newgate. He hoped the food here at Giltspur Street Compter was the same, if not better, than the first place he had been held. After the scant breakfast the day before, he was hungry. They had given him only water while he was in the court cells.

Floor by floor and cell by cell, the prisoners were given bowls of lumpy porridge. It was thankfully hot, warming him as he ate. Josh had never liked noise, and the cacophony of voices echoing around the eating area was almost overwhelming.

The small amount of food he was served was what Jenny would eat if not hungry; he, however, was ravenous. He wondered if he dared ask if there were seconds. He waited until the queue had finished, and rather than ask for more, he offered to assist in the cleanup. Being short of stature, the same head warder gave him a curt nod. He was told to collect the bowls and spoons and ensure everyone returned them to the basket.

Josh circled the room, ensuring every spoon and their licked-clean bowls were put in the basket by the convicts.

One nasty-looking, older chap tried to trick him and keep his spoon. Josh didn't fall for his sleight of hand. "Give it up, mister. None of us will get more nosh until them's all put in the basket."

The man glared at him and slammed the spoon in with the others. "There, brat, now clear off!"

Josh did just that. He followed the warder back to the kitchen.

The filthy cook accepted the basket and counted its contents. "Good lad, they are all here. Do you think you can fit in another bowl full of grub?"

Josh felt like punching the air with delight. He gave her the biggest smile. He replied and tried to sound like his uneducated friends: "Aw gee, thanks, ma'am," as she handed him a large bowl filled to the top, then added a dollop of thick cream from a bowl behind her.

Her odour was worse than his cell, but he intended to butter her up for all his worth. Extra food was worth the effort.

~

Over the following weeks, Josh offered to clean up after every meal. He kept his nose out of other people's business and stayed out of trouble. He learned to suck up to the warders as well as the cook, and he was given all the best offcuts of the warders' meals, as well as their leftovers from their roast dinners or hearty stews.

~

By the time Josh had been incarcerated for four months, he was used to the routine. He had put on a little weight and, surprisingly, looked healthy.

After a breakfast cleanup, Matthew came into the kitchen and said, "Hey, laddie, I've got news for you. They are coming to get you today at noon."

Josh swung around and stared at him open-mouthed. "They are really shipping me out?" He was excited, but he felt ill because the cook stank even worse today. He wondered if she had pooped her drawers. She kept coming to his side. Overwhelmed, his face had drained of blood, and he felt dizzy. "Cor, mister, I don't feel good." Josh sank to the floor, feeling ill.

The cook came to his side, and before he knew it, Josh was hoisted up like a rag doll and scooped into the immense woman's lap. "Cummon, laddie, you'll be all right. Go see if the laddie's mama can come for a visit, Maffew."

Matthew replied, "She's gone, ma'am. She left London."

Josh felt really ill now as the woman reeked. She was bad enough on the other side of the room, but in close proximity, she stank.

Bile hit the roof of his mouth.

She kept speaking, and he could smell that her breath smelled like rotting fish, and her body odour was far more than nauseating up close.

He pulled himself from her arms and threw up on the floor at her feet. "I'm so sorry, missus. I'll clean it up, but…"

The cook gave him a grin that showed how black her teeth were. "… but no need, laddie; you go and get washed up, and I'll mop up the mess."

She reached for the filthy rag she had cleaned the table with. He knew it was never properly washed.

Bile again filled his mouth.

Josh ran out to the muddy courtyard, threw up, then scrubbed himself in the bucket of water that sat under the pump. His vomit didn't smell too bad in comparison. He was desperate to wash off the woman's stench. He would be so pleased to leave this hellhole. He could hardly wipe the smile from his lips. It had been her odour that had made him feel ill.

On his way back, Josh bypassed the kitchen and walked to where Matthew was waiting. The warder returned him to a solitary cell this time.

Matthew told him to remain quiet.

Voices approached.

Matthew said in a stern voice so the others could hear, "Remain here, and I will come and collect you later." He pulled out a six-inch-long key and locked Josh inside. In a whisper, Matthew said, "Sleep while you can, lad."

Josh had nothing whatsoever to pack and take with him. Even the blanket he had been allocated must stay at the prison. He sat on the slab bed and waited. Hopefully, his mother would be well on her way to Sydney with Jenny. He was excited as it was only hours now until he was collected for transportation, and then, hopefully, he would see them again soon.

With a long sigh, he flopped back onto his hard bed.

The noises of the gaol had become familiar. Numerous conversations floated around him, and he had become immune to the goings-on of the women prisoners. Amongst the noise, he drifted off and slept.

~

Matthew returned to Josh's cell some hours later. "Sorry, laddie, time's up. The wagon is waiting for you. I hope you had a good nap, as you have a long trip ahead of you." He had come to like this boy and given him far more leeway than most other prisoners. Mostly this was for Cathy's sake, but Marjory asked after the lad frequently.

Josh was in a far better frame of mind now than he had been earlier. As he walked towards his transport to the ship, he smiled at Matthew. "Thanks for everything, sir."

Matthew tussled his hair. "Stay out of trouble for your mama's sake, will you?"

Josh nodded.

Rather than locking Josh in leg irons, as a warder was supposed to do, he slung his arm around the lad's shoulders and walked him out to the waiting wagon. The other prisoners were already shackled onto the prison transport.

Matthew said, "Up you go, laddie, and good luck. Keep your nose clean, as your mama told you. And so you know, Cathy and your sister got away just fine on the *Hindoostan,* I think they called it. I made sure of that myself. Marjory and I escorted them to the dock. We ensured they were safe and settled before we left them."

Josh thanked him as the wagon jerked away to begin its long journey.

The driver had hardly waited for Josh to settle Billy from the floor above before it headed off towards the dockland.

Billy had only arrived the week before, but they quickly became friends. As he had been locked in a cell after his incident in the kitchen, he was amazed to discover Billy on the cart beside him.

The life he knew up until now was soon to be his past. Like those on the transport with him, they drank in the city sights around them.

No one spoke, and many of them dodged the occasional bits of rodent food or excrement thrown at them from the locals as the prison wagon passed them by.

Only Josh was somewhat excited and was smiling. With him joining his family in Sydney, he had something to look forward to. Josh's happiness came from deep within him. This was the first time since his father died that he genuinely felt happy. He would try to do what his mother asked and avoid trouble. He had already worked out how to make himself useful and would attempt to do this on board if given a chance. Arriving unshackled boded well.

As the vehicle drew closer to the river, the smell of the filthy water assaulted them. The stench worsened as the tide receded, exposing the mudflats.

The vessel that awaited them was tied to the wharf rather than anchored in the river, which meant they were quickly loaded and the ship was prepared for the tide change.

Because Josh had been working in the kitchen, he was cleaner than most prisoners. Billy hadn't become as dirty as he had not been in prison for as long.

Chapter 2   The Hindostan
London, May 1809

Wen Josh was arrested, Cathy and Jenny packed up their tiny room and fled to the church crypt—now, they readied their scant possessions to board their ship to leave for New South Wales.

In a thick London fog, the warder Matthew and his wife escorted them to the wharf and waved them farewell. The *Hindostan* was due to leave London in a few days. As the vessel was tied to a jetty, Cathy and Jenny realised they could disembark and purchase a few required items to make their trip more comfortable. However, Cathy was horrified to discover she was the only female in a deck filled with soldiers. Two men had already made abhorrent suggestions to her, and she wished another option were open to them.

The steerage bunks were six-foot by eighteen-inch wooden pallet berths serving as sleeping spaces for each person, but since Jenny was under twelve, she had a free passage; therefore, they didn't get a second allocation of space. Cathy was aghast when she discovered that a soldier occupied the other half of her pallet bunk. He was one of the men who had already made a pass at her.

Having already spent £5 on the tiny space, Cathy realised that for another £5, they could upgrade to a small servant's cabin for them both. It would use most of their money, but they would be safe.

Before she reached the upper deck, Cathy had already been vilely propositioned twice more. She did not want Jenny to have to fend off the unwanted advances of the foul-mouthed soldiers they were supposed to share her accommodation with.

Men such as these were not fussy about using young girls for their carnal relief. She knew that all too well. The first thing Cathy did once on deck was disembark and try to upgrade their ticket.

At twenty-nine, Cathy knew she was young enough to remarry and possibly even have children. She was only sixteen when Josh was born. None of the men below would be a candidate for her future husband. Because James was such a wonderful man, she was determined to have a choice of partners. If she decided to remarry, any future husband would need to be a man of faith.

James and Josh had fallen ill just before Jenny was born. James had been very sick, and his private parts and face had been severely swollen for some time. The doctor called it *epidemic parotitis*, but Reverend Josiah Winchester, the minister's new assistant, said it was known as the mumps. It swept through the Rookery, followed by measles. Cathy had not conceived again after James recovered, and she presumed that his illness had something to do with that.

Cathy visited the shipping agent and paid an additional £5 of Josh's stolen money to upgrade their passage. They moved their scant possessions into the tiny one-bed servant's cabin, but here they could lock their door and sleep safely.

Two days after they changed their booking, they were standing at the railing on the main deck when an assortment of wagons arrived.

Red-coated soldiers started oozing from the various vehicles. Luggage wagons followed, and each was unloaded. The soldiers then carried their possessions on board. A few blue-coated senior officers watched what their men were doing, but none assisted.

Cathy was holding Jenny close when two men walked towards them. One was in a senior uniform with numerous gold braids. He stopped at her side. He bowed on arrival. "Captain John Pasco, at your service, ma'am. I believe you have upgraded to a cabin?"

Cathy nervously glanced at the two men. She gave a servant's bob to them both and introduced herself and then Jenny.

The second man gave an elegant bow and said, "I am also pleased to meet you, ma'am. I am Surgeon Joseph Arnold, and I will be in charge of the health of all the passengers and crew." Rather than wait for an answer, he knelt and spoke to Jenny. "Miss Callan, should you need my services, I have packed some boiled sweets. Do you like peppermint?"

As Jenny had never had a boiled lolly before, she had no idea if she did or did not. While not trying to be rude, she moved closer to her mother, but she didn't answer. Cathy drew her close.

The doctor stood and met Cathy's gaze. Cathy said, "Sir, she has never had such a treat before. Sweets were not something they ever had money for. "Every penny we have went towards a better life that was hopefully to come."

Rather than think she was rude, the doctor smiled. "Madam, miss, I would be honoured if you would walk with me, and I shall show you the ship's sickbay. I hope you will never need it, but you will know where to find me should you require my services."

He realised that this woman had seen more than a female of her age should. She had initially shied away from them when they approached, and he noticed her quick, very telling action. "Captain, if you are not busy, would you care to escort us?"

As Cathy looked at Jenny, Doctor Arnold nodded his request to John over their heads. Cathy had been about to return to their cabin before the soldiers boarded, so she accepted their offer: "Thank you, sirs, we would be honoured to view the ship's hospital."

The captain led the way, and the doctor waved for them to follow him. Cathy and Jenny went hand in hand down the narrow steps and followed the uniformed man as he led the way through the depths of his ship. As he walked, John said, "Mrs Callan, Miss Callan, there are some terms on a ship that are strange to a landlubber. We have not just come down steps, but a ladder. The walls are called bulkheads, the kitchen is the galley, the rooms are cabins, and the sails above us are called sheets. There are many more, but you will hear many such strange words over the next months. Do not hesitate to ask their meaning."

Cathy was too timid to reply, but Jenny said, "Do you mean sheets like on a bed, Captain?"

It was the first time either man had heard the child speak. She didn't have the same cockney drawl as her mother. Jenny had spent many days with her father at Covent Garden. She noticed the surprise on the men's faces and again shrank closer to her mother.

Cathy said, "Jenny spent much time with her father at Covent Garden Markets until he was killed in a hit-and-run carriage accident last year. He managed much of the market activity there." She didn't want to talk about James as the memory always made her weep. Even that mention had made her eyes water. She brushed a tear away before it escaped.

Both men witnessed the display of emotion. They wondered how they had managed to cope through those months.

They reached the sick bay, and the captain stepped aside to let the doctor pass. The small room had a central table and a series of narrow pallet bunks around the side of the room. There was a locked, glass-fronted cupboard containing an assortment of bottles. A wall nearby had a variety of surgical implements hanging on it. The room reeked of brandy.

The captain inhaled deeply. "I smell that you have been cleaning again, Doctor."

The doctor chuckled. "Yes, Captain, I have been preparing for the unfortunate eventuality of injury. Hopefully, I will not be needed on this journey."

Cathy nervously spoke up. "Should my help be required, I have some nursing ability. Being a mother of two, the children and their friends often needed attention." She bit her lip. Surely, they would ask about her other child. She caught a covert glance between them, but they asked no further questions. There was certainly no way she would admit that her son was a convict.

The doctor accepted her offer. "Ma'am, should that be required, I would willingly accept any help I can get. Now, Miss Callan, I promised you your first taste of a sweetie." He reached over and picked up a large jar. Inside was about one pound of boiled red and white striped sweets. Having emptied the bag of lollies into the jar, some fragments of cracked toffee were sitting on top. "Miss, as a taste, just take a chipped one. If you like it, then you can have a whole one. These are the peppermint ones. You won't like the black and white ones as they have an aniseed flavour. As we will be at sea some months, I will need to eke them out, but today's will be a treat."

Jenny did as she was told, took a shard of lolly, and delicately popped it in her mouth. The three adults watched the child's face. The explosion of sweetness and flavour hit her palate. As expected, her face lit up with delight. "Oh, Mama, this is yummy!"

The doctor grinned. "Then, as I promised, have a whole one, dear." He held the jar open for her.

Jenny delicately took the one promised sweet. Rather than put it in her mouth, she wrapped it in her clean handkerchief for later. She curtsied a thank you to both men and returned to her mother's side.

Overhead, the sound of many footsteps sounded. The captain needed to return to his post. The men escorted her to her cabin and suggested that while the regiment and their wives boarded, they should remain in the safety of their room.

Cathy pushed Jenny into their cabin and thanked the men. She already knew that no convicts would be on this ship, but she had not realised many coarse soldiers would be travelling with them. She wondered if any of them were men of faith looking for a wife. She smiled as she closed the door after watching the two men depart to return to their duty.

~

The passage from London to Portsmouth took over a week.

Cathy saw another ship similar to theirs leave London at the same time.

During that short journey, the English Channel's seas were rough. The waves bucked and bounced, but both passengers remained unaffected by the sickness from the angry sea. Cathy discovered that neither Jenny nor she was susceptible to seasickness. They sailed between the Isle of Wight and the mainland, then through a bay's narrow entrance, pulled into the calm waters of the protected harbour, and slowly moved towards the Portsmouth naval dockyard.

On May 16th, they tied up to the naval jetty. Mother and daughter were on deck to watch their entry into the harbour and sail towards the main navy base. The doctor pointed out places of interest.

The line of convict hulks they passed reeked of the effluent of the many bodies held in custody there. Would Josh be moved to one of these?

The girls held perfumed handkerchiefs over their noses until the ship moored at the naval jetty.

~

Over the next three days, more of the 73rd regiment came and went until noon on the third day. Another vessel had drawn up behind them. This vessel was the *Dromedary.*

There were now hundreds of men in red coats and more than a few senior officers mulling around the dock. More men from different regiments were busy onshore. A few were garbed in blue uniforms, but the majority wore red of differing shades.

A fuss on the pier drew her attention to those on shore. Cathy and Jenny were doing a circuit of the decks and saw the hasty departure of the captain, quickly followed by the doctor. The *Dromedary* was also being loaded with hundreds of soldiers and supplies. The doctor said they were to travel in tandem with this other vessel. Cathy saw many women waiting to board.

When the doctor returned on the first day, he explained that many of the women were the regiment's wives and family. They would share the soldiers' deck and were a rough lot. The colourful language emanating from their lips was enough to draw Jenny away from the railing.

Today, the doctor returned to the *Hindostan* a worried man. He sought out Cathy and said, "Madam, I am in a fluster. I can now inform you of who will be travelling on the *Dromedary.* Colonel Macquarie is to be the next Governor of New South Wales. He and his wife will be passengers. They have sorted the soldiers so that those of a rougher nature will travel with us rather than them." He paused, looking worried.

Cathy gasped but knew the doctor well enough to know he hesitated to continue. "Doctor Arnold, I can tell you are anxious to say more."

The doctor nodded. "Madam, Mrs Callan, the colonel has insisted that many of the regiment and poorer families are to board our ship. Our ship will now be mostly men and fifty lower-class women whom Colonel Macquarie asked to be transferred to us instead of travelling with them. The women on their ship are the wives of the higher-ranking soldiers. If you consent to transfer to the other ship, you would find it far more congenial to your safety and, dare I say, a more pleasant journey, as there are other ladies present."

The doctor had already chastised some of the soldiers who had given the young, attractive widow a whistle as she walked on deck. He had reported the incident to the captain, and three soldiers, Robert Young, Thomas Kelly and James Frazier, had already been chastised by their superior officer.

Cathy frowned, "You wish us to travel with Colonel Macquarie and his wife?"

Doctor Joseph nodded. "Would you mind, madam?" He swallowed. He had grown fond of the petite woman and her daughter in the few days they had been on board. He would be sad to see them leave.

Cathy checked to see who was within earshot. "Doctor, I am not a suitable woman to be in the presence of such an esteemed person. I was… I was…" She wiped her eyes, unable to finish.

The doctor raised his hand and placed it carefully on her arm. Instead, with a lowered voice, he said, "Whatever you once were is in your past, ma'am. You are now a widow, and a new life awaits you. Use this journey to create a fresh start. I have arranged a cabin for you, and if you are interested, the ship's captain has his wife and young son travelling with him. You could be of assistance to them."

Jenny's eyes lit up. She nodded at her mother. "Can we go, Mama?"

Cathy shuddered. "Do they know about us?"

The doctor nodded. "Yes. Mrs Callan, I truly believe you will be better off there. Otherwise, I would not have suggested it." He looked at the lovely young girl. "Ma'am, you must think of your daughter. This ship and the lot below decks here is no place for her."

Jenny's pleading face made Cathy caress her cheek. "For you, my darling. I would do anything to keep you safe. It's why we are here."

The doctor released a long sigh of relief. "I will collect you in half an hour. Is that long enough to arrange your things?"

Jenny danced with delight. "We don't have much, sir. We can be packed in about ten minutes." She grasped her mother's hand and pulled her towards their tiny cabin. Cathy followed, stunned at the unexpected transfer.

Within two hours, they were packed, and their scant possessions had been transferred onto the *Dromedary*. Officers from both vessels carried their belongings, including Josh's things, and the doctor took Jenny's hand as they disembarked down the narrow gangplank. He stayed with them until they were shown their new cabin.

Rather than a tiny six-foot-wide box bed, their new cabin was twice that size, with an opening porthole. Cathy turned to say something when she saw the doctor put his finger to his lips. The soldiers placed their possessions on the wide box bed, leaving them to sort things out. The doctor stood waiting at the door, and once they were gone, he said softly, "I just mentioned that you were in a cabin on our vessel; I did not say how big it was. Make this a new start in your life, Mrs Callan. The Lord has supplied this opportunity; grasp it." He and Cathy had spent a few evenings at the railings discussing the past that each had experienced. He had come straight out and asked her about her early life. "Ma'am, I noticed various actions that were all too familiar. You do not trust any male, and this is wise."

Her gasp and silence prompted him to share some of his early experiences assisting the less fortunate. She had all the signs of not trusting men. For him, that spoke volumes. He realised that she had either been abused or worse. Cathy had opened up about her early days, although she had left her two sordid years unvoiced. No matter what he imagined, it could not have been worse than what she had lived through. Now, she was being given a fresh start.

Chapter 3 Illustrious Passengers
The Dromedary

*C*athy thanked the doctor as he escorted them onto the new ship. She would miss his counsel and the evening chats.

Jenny was already trying out their new large box bed while Cathy put away their clothing. They owned one small, old carpet bag of possessions, which included two spare shirts for Josh and James's old tweed coat.

The doctor called the child over and pulled something out of his pocket. "Miss Jenny, as you are not going to be with me on this journey, I would not wish that you miss the joys of the peppermint sweets." He handed her a small paper bag of peppermint humbugs. "Eke them out, lassie, and I'll see if any are left in my jar if we cross paths on the journey."

Jenny ran to him and hugged him. "Thank you, Doctor Joseph." He bowed to them and departed.

Jenny and Cathy set about unpacking and sorting their new cabin. The cost of this cabin would have been far more than the £10 she had paid for her passage. They had just finished when there was a knock at their door.

Cathy opened it to a tall gentleman with a waxed moustache. His naval uniform was the same as Captain Pasco's, so she presumed this must be her new captain. She curtseyed as she saw him. "Good afternoon, sir."

The man bowed. "Good afternoon, madam. I am your new captain, Samuel Prichard. I wish to welcome you aboard and thank you for accommodating our change of cabins. To compensate you for your inconvenience, the Navy is refunding you the cost of your passage." He held out an envelope, "My wife is keen to meet you and your daughter, madam." He bowed as Cathy took the proffered envelope.

She gracefully accepted the money. Cathy felt like cheering. Their fare had been refunded. It was more than three years' wages. They had gone from a pallet berth in steerage, shared with over a hundred soldiers, to a large cabin, and they would be travelling with the future governor of the colony they were to live in. Hopefully, they may even get to meet them.

After the captain had gone, she carefully put the money with the remainder of her funds. She stored her money with her monthly rags. No man would willingly place his hands on such a vile item.

Prior to being refunded their fare, she only had two pounds left of the cash Josh had stolen. James had only made three pounds a year, so this money should be enough to keep them going until Josh arrived. She had no idea what was ahead of them, but it could not have been worse than London. She knew what her only option would have been there, and she refused ever to sell her body again.

~

Over the following days at port, they settled in and made themselves as comfortable as possible. Jenny was bouncing with excitement at the forthcoming trip. Cathy realised she had not brought anything to occupy her time on the voyage. With the return of the money, she and Jenny disembarked and purchased lengths of fabric, notions, scissors, and a small sewing kit. She also wished to see if there were any second-hand books and a slate and chalk she could purchase. She would continue their writing lessons. James had taught his entire family to read and write, telling them it was a path out of poverty.

Cathy only had three old gowns, none of which were suitable for anything more than menial work. Jenny also needed clothing. She purchased some yards of fine cotton to make some shirts for Josh. All of them would need new underclothing. She had managed to keep her tattered work gowns covered with her dark blue redingote, but she could not always wear that. They were soon to leave the chill of England, and then her lack of suitable clothing would be exposed. James had given the coat to her shortly before he died.

In the years since they married, James and Cathy had scrimped and saved to reuse items found left around the Covent Garden. A search through the extensive gardens after the evening festivities was often rewarding. Many discarded items of clothing were claimed and redesigned. Since the fire that burned the Theatre in Drury Lane in February, Covent Garden had become a place of ill repute. It also meant that Cathy's only source of income had quite literally gone up in flames.

The day before sailing, Cathy, Jenny, and Mrs Jones took another opportunity to go ashore on a final shopping expedition. Shopping with Mrs Jones meant they were permitted to use a naval carriage. This meant they were shown more fabrics than she had dreamed about. Most of it was far too expensive for them, but there was a fabric table in the marketplace just outside the shop. Here, Cathy found a stall that sold watermarked lengths of the most beautiful lightweight fabrics, and she carefully chose some delightful material. She purchased a large quantity of cheap printed cotton lengths to make up during the voyage. The store owner added a long length of water-stained linen for undergarments.

In the years since James rescued her, Cathy worked from home sewing costumes primarily for the Royal Theatre in Drury Lane, but occasionally for the Covent Garden Theatre company until they burned down, not long before the Drury Lane one. Her sewing skills had improved immensely since her first job of sewing the backdrop blanks. She could now cut out a gown without a pattern, and once completed, it looked as good as one from Bond Street. Her gowns did not have accessories like pearls and beading, but she could embroider beautifully. Jenny also loved sewing and would do the hemming of all the items Cathy made. One of the treats she purchased for herself was a bundle of used embroidery silks. An unknown rich woman had discarded the unused skeins of thread after completing a project. Cathy purchased some fine embroidery needles so she could embellish her new gowns.

With the comings and goings of the many soldiers, Cathy only wandered around when necessary. From what she could see, the setup of the eating facilities was similar to that of the *Hindostan*. That meant she would need to eat her meals with the illustrious couple at the long dining table in the mess area. It was here that all their meals had been served to date.

She wondered if the couple would eat alone in their cabin. On the previous vessel, she and Jenny had dined at the first sitting, then retired to the privacy of their minute cabin to stay away from the rabble of the soldiers.

Having stowed the new items from their latest shopping trip, Cathy and Jenny donned their bonnets again and went outside to watch the activity on the shore. On exiting their cabin, Cathy had to step back quickly.

A red-coated officer was making his way past with an armload of wooden boxes. He had not seen her.

Cathy was not quite fast enough to move back. Her gasp and an involuntary "Ouch" made him stop mid-step.

The soldier had been looking around the far side of his load, and Cathy had been out of his line of view. The exclamation made him check the other side. He saw a beautiful woman and a child standing in the doorway. She had a red slash on her cheek and a frown on her lovely brow. "Oh, ma'am, I'm so sorry I did not see you there." He moved slightly so he could get a better look at the woman. He did a quick inhalation. She was stunning. "If you permit me, I will deliver these; then I shall return in a moment."

Cathy could hardly see his face, but he had a similar accent to her own. "Of course, sir. I am well. It was but a glancing blow."

He gave a nod and continued down the narrow section of the corridor. Wherever he had to go, it was obviously not far. He returned less than a minute later.

The wound on Cathy's cheek now showed a trickle of blood, and once again, she was escorted to the sick bay.

Jenny clung tightly to her mother's hand but she wore a frown.

Captain Mark Duffy was profusely apologetic for causing her an injury.

After the doctor treated the small cut with brandy, the soldier offered to escort her up on deck and introduce them to the various staff that she would be travelling with.

Cathy and Jenny followed the contrite soldier to where a group of well-dressed travellers stood.

One by one, he introduced them. The first was the captain's wife, Mrs Prichard and their two-year-old son. The boy was on a leather harness held by a smiling negro servant who was introduced as just Tom.

Cathy greeted them with a bob curtsy and a smile. She included the child's minder in her greeting. She also gave him a grin and a bob of her head.

Captain Mark saw that small action and inwardly cheered. Not many would acknowledge any staff of foreign descent. Who was this lady?

Standing nearby was Mrs Jones, Mrs Macquarie's maid. She had just finished arranging the luggage and was exhausted. She was waiting for the exalted couple to arrive. As Mrs Jones had already met Cathy, she beckoned her to stand close.

Cathy nodded that she would.

Next, the captain introduced Cathy to Deputy Judge-Advocate Ellis Bent, Mrs Bent, and their son. Beside them stood Captain Henry Antill, a fellow officer and a friend of Captain Duffy's. Captain Duffy explained, "Ma'am, Captain Antill is the head of the new governor's security detail. Behind him is Ensign Alexander Huey, and the other young man is Ensign John Maclaine." All received the same bob and smile from the lovely lady.

Mark explained that Ensign Maclaine was Mrs Macquarie's nephew. To each, Cathy and Jenny gave the same degree of subservience as to Tom. Although having seen how Mrs Bent curtsied, Cathy curtsied a little lower than her average servant's bob to that lady. She had no idea the degree one should curtsy. She had never met any such exalted people before, and she was out of her depth.

Mrs Bent and Mrs Prichard invited Cathy and Jenny to stand near them. Cathy accepted, although she gave Mrs Jones a panicked look. Her new friend smiled and nodded. Cathy realised she understood her hesitation.

The activity on the dock was interesting, but she had yet to learn what was occurring.

Captain Duffy saw her knitted brow and explained what was about to happen. "Ma'am, the Macquaries are about to embark. The guard of honour is forming, and Colonel Macquarie's entourage will follow them. They are his Indian manservant, George Jarvis. He's the young, dark-skinned man at the back, and Robert Fopp is their butler. Mrs Jones, you have obviously met, as I saw you shop together earlier today. Joseph Bigg is their coachman, but he is already on board, having come with the horses, as is Mrs Ovens. She is appropriately named as she is their personal cook. It was her cooking utensils that I was carrying when I bumped you."

Cathy nodded her thanks to his explanation.

The contrite soldier's brow creased with concern. "Ma'am, I really am sorry, and I hate to point out that your cut is again bleeding." Mark again apologised and proffered a handkerchief.

Cathy took the proffered kerchief and dabbed at the blood where the cut was. She missed the trickle that had reached her chin.

Mark said, "May I?" He retrieved the cloth and gently dabbed at the trickle of blood down her cheek.

Mrs Prichard saw the almost affectionate action of the supposedly tough soldier and asked about Cathy's injury.

Before Cathy could say anything, the captain explained. "I accept full responsibility, ma'am. I was distracted and not paying attention to where I was going. Unfortunately, I hit Mrs Callan with the load I was carrying."

Mrs Prichard gasped and said, "Oh, my dear, how unfortunate."

The captain caught Cathy's eye and smiled at her. He knew he should return to duty, but having wounded the lovely young lady, he knew others would complete the loading of the wagon full of food. The young girl beside her clung tightly to her mother. He had hardly noticed her, but she was well behaved and that at least was a relief. He abhorred misbehaving children.

After cleaning up the blood, he pocketed the dirtied cloth, and they turned to watch the arrival of the guests of honour. He was aware of the young girl's stare, which was disconcerting. She kept trying to sniff his clothing.

Jenny was still clinging tightly to her mother. When the black man, Tom, lifted the little boy so he could see better, she looked at Mark and wondered if she was too big to do the same. Her father would have easily lifted her. A wave of sadness engulfed her, and it was as though she could almost smell that he was near them. The ship's railing was high, and she couldn't see much. She wiped away an errant tear.

Mark saw the girl's sadness and asked permission to lift her.

Cathy replied with a nod. "Thank you, Captain Duffy. Even if you could lift her for a little while, I think she would like that."

Mark quickly hoisted the child into his arms. He was surprised that Jenny gazed at him rather than look at the activities onshore.

She wrapped her arm around his neck and breathed in his cologne. "You smell just like Papa used to." She took another deep breath. "Mama and I would make his orange peel and sandalwood cologne." She rested her head on Mark's shoulder and whispered. "I loved his smell. I miss him so much."

Mark smiled at the unexpected affection the girl showed him, but her words had a far greater impact on him than he expected. He missed his mother, even though they had never been close. She did what she could for him, but his stepfather hated him. After collecting his thoughts, he chuckled and said, "My mama bought this for me at Covent Garden over the summer last year. She told me a man was selling bottles of it, and she liked the scent."

He noticed Jenny tear up again and gaze at her mother. "What's up, miss? Did I say something wrong?"

Jenny's head shook, but she didn't answer. Her tears continued.

Cathy overheard the interchange. She, too, had gasped and teared up. She replied, "My husband, James, was the market manager at Covent Garden, sir. He would sell my homemade cologne at a stall there. He was killed in September last year on the way home. He was hit by a carriage that did not stop to assist him. It paused, and when the man inside saw they had hit someone, he ordered the carriage to drive on."

Mrs Bent and Mrs Prichard overheard her explanation. Although they said nothing, each placed a caring hand on her arm.

Mark was gutted. The cologne had been gifted to him the month before his mother died unexpectedly in early August. It had become his favourite, but now he would not wear it while they were on board. James Callan and his mother must have died within weeks of each other.

Ignoring what was occurring on shore, Jenny sniffed his neck again. "I love that you smell like Papa. I miss him so much."

Mark wrapped his other arm around her protectively and gently squeezed her affectionately. "I shall wash it off if you wish."

In unison, both teary-eyed Callan ladies said, "Please don't!"

He was somewhat surprised by their dogmatic reply, but nodded in agreement.

Cathy said softly, "I'm honoured that you like it, sir."

During this short interchange, things on shore had changed. The new viceregal couple were now making their way up the gangplank.

Cathy realised the captain would need to return to duty. The other military personnel who had been with them had already departed. "Jenny dear, the captain will need to put you down as he must attend to his duty, sweetheart."

Jenny smiled, took another deep inhalation of his scent and then released her hold on him. "Thank you, Captain Duffy."

He knuckled her cheek affectionately and said, "Anytime, Miss Jennifer. Come for a hug when you wish." He bowed to the collective group and moved to the top of the gangplank behind Captain Prichard. He had met his new commander-in-chief onshore several times since their arrival from London. He had given the orders to remove the excess soldiers onto the *Hindostan* and then convert the lower accommodation decks on the *Dromedary* from sleeping pallets to hammocks. This allowed them far more space, and although the intimacies of the fifty married couples would be more challenging, they found a way to have some privacy with the erection of dividers. He had left some of the upper pallets for storing luggage. The work had been completed, and the ships were nearly ready to sail.

~

The official party came and went for the following three days before finally settling in. Once they were settled, the two ships had moved away from the dock and were anchored just offshore.

On May 22nd, the crew marched around the vast capstan and hauled anchors aboard. The ropes were pulled onto the deck, and two ships set sail with the tide. Their journey to a new life had started in earnest.

Jenny found the remaining children in the hold far too boisterous and loud. However, Captain Prichard's little boy was a delight, and Jenny gravitated to him whenever possible. Initially, this was during meal times, as they were fed at the same time as the captain's son, the servants, and the junior officers. Captain Duffy typically oversaw proceedings for this mess, so the Callans saw him daily.

Now at sea, Cathy and Mrs Jones undertook to sit and sew together.

For the first week, Cathy and Jenny were content to eat in the first sitting with the children and servants.

Captain Duffy seemed to gravitate to her side, but he did not stop wearing the cologne that she had made for James.

Cathy was pleased that the staff welcomed her presence. Of the viceregal couple, Cathy saw nothing.

Jenny had taken to giving Captain Mark a big hug each morning and breathing in his scent while it was fresh.

Having had little to do with children, Mark found this unusual. However, this child was quite adorable. She would ask to be released and wander off to occupy her two-year-old friend at the other end of the room.

Cathy and Mark's friendship blossomed.

Both were Londoners and unattached.

Having lost his mother in August, Mark had changed regiments after time spent in too many bloody battles. He was over war and hated fighting. With no ties to hold him to England, he was thrilled when he discovered that his new regiment had been reassigned to accompany Colonel Macquarie to New South Wales. Mark had worked his way up to be a captain in the 42nd regiment, and he transferred to the 73rd in December. All his new men already trusted him. Knowledge of his heroic deeds had gone before him, though he never mentioned them. Whispers of heroism spread, but he refused to discuss his past.

After a slip of the tongue by Jenny, it opened the door for Mark to ask Cathy about her son.

Realising that it was best that Mark find out about Josh early in any possible relationship, she decided to reveal the reason for their journey.

Standing at the poop deck railing one dark evening, Cathy told Mark about life after James's death and the fire that destroyed her only source of income. She expected to be shunned, but Mark reached out and placed his hand on hers in such a way that it was comforting.

He said little, but mentioned that he had grown up in the same precinct. "I can read between the lines, Mrs Callan; please say no more. I know what life in that area is like."

She shook her head. The story had taken some time to relate, and the moon had just popped its head above the water. In the dim, moonlit night, she saw compassion etched on his face.

~

The following morning, Mrs Macquarie emerged from their cabin when Cathy did.

Cathy dropped into a deep curtsy, and Mrs Macquarie chuckled. "My dear Mrs Callan, I am a commoner like you. I am a soldier's wife, and as we will be in constant company for the next months, please don't." She gave a quick gurgle of delight before continuing, "So, no more of that." She motioned that she meant the curtsy. "In a moving vessel, you need two feet on the ground lest you fall over."

Cathy loved the lady's Scottish accent and smiled at the petite lady with a riot of light brown curls. Her eyes sparkled with fun, and her chuckle and lack of protocol boded well for an enjoyable journey. Cathy noticed that she carried a book, an inkwell, and a quill.

Mrs Macquarie said, "Mrs Jones mentioned that you sit together and sew. Would you mind very much if I joined you in writing my journal? As you know, the cabins are somewhat claustrophobic."

Cathy was about to curtsy again, but said, "Ma'am, we would be delighted. At least I would; I should not answer for Mrs Jones."

The brown eyes danced with delight. "Fiddle-faddle, my dear. She won't mind in the least." Elizabeth Macquarie led the way to the long table near the galley.

Jenny was already there, entertaining the captain's child and teaching him how to hold chalk. The Prichards' servant, Tom, was watching the children.

After an hour of sewing, Cathy felt she was being watched. She lifted her head to find Elizabeth Macquarie staring at her.

Cathy had not realised that the other women and children had gone.

Elizabeth said, "Mrs Callan, we had the windows of our cabin open last evening, and without intending to do so, I overheard your conversation with Captain Duffy."

Cathy was aghast. Tears welled immediately. It had not occurred to her that anyone would ever know Josh's status, but now they knew all. Her eyes watered with the news. "Oh, ma'am, I am so sorry. I shall leave at once." Cathy started to gather her possessions.

Elizabeth replied almost instantly. "Mrs Callan, stop that this instant."

Cathy froze.

Elizabeth said, "We are going to govern a penal colony. I want to ask you about your life in London, and if you don't mind, I would also like to inquire about your son and his conviction. I know your husband died, and you have already told Mrs Jones about the fire at the Drury Lane Theatre and its impact, but I do not like hearing things second-hand. I consider that gossip."

Cathy brushed aside a wayward tear. She seated herself again and asked, "Are you sure, ma'am?"

Elizabeth nodded.

Cathy checked that no one else was within earshot. The children had been taken outdoors by the adorable Mrs Jones. Cathy's story from her marriage at fifteen to James poured out. She spoke of their poverty, hunger, and the lack of dignity of any sort in their squalid and impoverished home, but they were happy.

Elizabeth sat, absorbing it all. Occasionally, she would ask a question to clarify something, but otherwise, she let Cathy talk. The death of her beloved James in September the year before had seen her pause to weep.

With Cathy's head on her arms, sobbing, Elizabeth came to her side and embraced her. "We, too, know grief such as this, my dear. We lost our only child, Jane, shortly before we sailed. She was only two months old. So I know such hurt."

Cathy's teary face lifted to the regal lady beside her. "Oh, my lady, I'm so sorry. We lost a child between our two, but she only lived a matter of hours." Visions of the limp body and the death of the tiny babe still made Cathy smart. Another tear oozed from her eye, and she brushed it away.

Elizabeth heard the anguish in her voice. "I'm told that the hurt never leaves, but it gets a little easier each day. You said your husband died nearly a year ago?"

Cathy nodded. "Yes, I was just fifteen when we married, and we had fourteen happy years together."

Elizabeth's lips twitched in a partial smile. "You are young, dear; look forward to the new life ahead."

Cathy gave her a wan reply. "I shall only remarry if I find a God-fearing man like James. He lived by what he believed, which was why we had few luxuries. Our world was surrounded by poverty, and so many were less fortunate than ourselves. We at least had food and shelter, so we were happy to share what we had with those who had absolutely nothing. Poverty in London was dire, m'lady."

Elizabeth smiled. She, too, looked around to make sure they were not overheard. "I married for love, dear, and even though I am not Mr M's first wife, he is dear to me. He is also my cousin." She paused and glanced at Cathy. "It makes the marriage bed nice when one loves one's man."

Cathy gave the lady a genuine grin and nodded. James took delight in pleasuring her. Having been used by men over the preceding two years, she understood that far more than an ordinary wife would. James turned her sordid acts for work into ones of love and adoration. Cathy would never settle for less. The two sat in companionable silence for some time. Both were deep in thought about their past losses.

Elizabeth delicately blew her nose. She drew a long breath and said, "The past is behind you, dear, and a new future is to be made. With so few ladies on board, and yes, I do include you as a lady, for you have more decorum than many titled peers I have met. I feel we shall become friends. I grew up in the wilds of Scotland, my dear. May I call you by name?" She didn't pause. "Cathy, friends there were few and far between, and I need everyone I can find."

Cathy caught a flash of a smile.

Elizabeth said, "Now, while we are alone, I will interfere so far as to say that handsome Captain Mark Duffy is a man of faith and would suit you perfectly. Were I not married to my heart's desire, I may have even set my cap at him." Her chuckle was met by Cathy's gasp.

The twinkle in her eye made Cathy blush. Cathy said, "Would he not need permission, though, ma'am? He has already asked me for evening walks."

Elizabeth chuckled again, "He would indeed... from my husband." Her cocked eyebrow made both ladies giggle.

Chapter 4   Transported
The Ann.

Billy Green had been on a different gaol floor, but Josh had met him during meals. The boys were much the same age and had struck up a discreet friendship while eating. Billy was so skinny that Josh always ensured he got a bigger serving. He knew what it was like to be a growing boy and very hungry. Although conversation had not been permitted, the initial astonished look Billy had given him when Josh filled his bowl with gruel had been enough to forge a bond. His toothy grin won Josh over.

When that had been repeated daily, Billy soon realised he had a sympathetic friend. As they rode on the wagon to the dockland, he noticed that Josh was not chained.

When Josh had hopped up beside him on the transport, they were finally freed from the prison rules, and they chattered.

Josh could have run away, but with his family now going to Sydney, his conviction would provide him with free passage to a new life. He had worked out that by the time he arrived, he would only have about six years to serve.

Josh asked, "Got any family, Billy?"

Billy shook his head. "Mama died just before I got nabbed."

Josh realised the poor kid had lived on the street as best he could. Prison slops and porridge were far better than he had ever had before. "Okay, then stick close."

Billy nodded and drew closer. Thankfully, Billy didn't smell much as he had not been in gaol long.

Josh was surprised that only thirty convicts were on the wagon. He presumed others would join them on their journey, but they hadn't.

~

Josh helped Billy from the back of the wagon, and they stood together, waiting for instructions. "Stick with me, Billy; we might be able to share a bunk."

Billy nodded nervously.

As the boys walked towards the ship, a man in a blue naval uniform adorned with gold braid stood with his feet apart and hands behind his back. He motioned for them all to stand in line, and he would address the new arrivals. When all were assembled, he introduced himself. "I am Captain Clark and the skipper for your cruise to a new life." He chuckled. "As you are the supposedly better-behaved prisoners from Giltspur Street Compter, you have been collected here, in London, rather than in Portsmouth, where we will load our supplies and get the remainder of our human cargo. I will choose one or two of you to serve as cabin boys for our passengers." His eyes fell on Josh and the boy beside him. They were young but cleaner than the rest.

When everyone was finally lined up, the uniformed man walked among the convicts. The captain pointed to the two boys. "You and you stand over there." Not daring to disobey, the two boys moved to the spot where he had pointed.

The captain continued to address the new arrivals. "I have no intention of dealing with misbehaviour on board. As we will be travelling with a large detachment of the 73rd Regiment, I don't imagine you will have any wiggle room for disobedience." The captain sniggered at his own joke.

No one thought it was funny.

Josh was unsure whether this man was serious or attempting to make them laugh. One by one, a soldier unshackled the convicts. Once all their feet were out of chains, the captain motioned for everyone to board the ship. Motioning for the two lads to follow, he said the boys were to stand apart once on deck.

With no further words to the group, the captain waved off the other felons. They were the last to board, and once on the ship's deck, they were told to wait near the central mast.

The captain watched as the other convicts were escorted below.

Billy's hand shackles were unlocked as he waited with Josh. He stood rubbing his chafed wrists. Thankfully, the irons had not broken the skin.

Soon, the two soldiers, the captain, and the two boys were all that remained on the main deck.

Once the noise from the departing convicts diminished, the captain turned to the boys. "I don't suppose either of you can read?"

Josh nodded but remained silent.

The captain's eyes opened wide. "You can read? Really?"

Again, Josh nodded. He still had not been given permission to speak.

"Speak up, lad," the captain finally said.

Josh swallowed. He wondered where this would lead. "I can, and count, sir; I mean, Captain. My papa taught me, as he had a stall at Covent Garden, and I would have taken it over, but he was killed." The man didn't need to know his story.

The captain motioned for Josh to spin around to be inspected.

He did and wondered what this was about.

The uniformed man said, "Fine, you will do. One of the passengers who has just come aboard is a reverend gentleman with his wife and a new, um, special friend. He requested that a cabin boy be at his beck and call for the guest. You must tidy their cabins and carry their things as the minister goes about his work on board. You seem reasonably clean, so you will do for him. What's your name?"

Josh was proud of his name. He stood slightly erect before replying, "Joshua Callan, sir."

The captain nodded. "Well, young Josh… I presume that is what you are called?"

Josh nodded.

Seeing the affirmation, the captain continued, "The reverend's name is Samuel Marsden. However, you will specifically be at his friend Chief Ruatara's beck and call, meaning you must be in the servant's cabin on his deck."

Josh grinned and nodded acceptance of his role. "Thank you, sir."

The captain's attention turned to Billy. "Can't read?"

Billy shook his head.

The captain frowned. "Oh, well, never mind. You are to be the cook's helper, anyway, so you won't need that skill." He saw the boy's face brighten markedly. He smiled as he looked at the skinny boy, wondering if he had ever had enough food. When he saw the skinny lad's face light up, he said, "Don't get too excited, lad. Once you are at sea, I doubt you will keep much down until you get your sea legs. However, you two will be sharing one tiny airless cabin." He huffed. "As I said, Reverend Marsden has brought an important man on board, and this person is of foreign descent." He swallowed nervously. "He's, um, he is very different."

The captain was unsure how the oddly garbed, dark-skinned man coped in London's cold climate. However, he had only been asked to supply a servant for the passenger. He frowned, then said, "Josh, you will only speak when spoken to and obey every request you possibly can. Do you understand?"

Josh nodded vigorously. He was delighted as he didn't have to travel in the convict decks and could share a half-decent cabin with his new friend. Oh, he understood all right, and he was thrilled. He replied, "Yes, sir. I will do my very best, Captain."

The captain had one more warning for the boys. "As you will both see the reverend's guest soon, I must warn you; his face is fully tattooed, and what isn't, is dark skinned. He is what is called a Maori warrior. I tell you only so neither of you stares at him, mouths agape." The raised eyebrow by the captain elicited the response of another vigorous nod from both boys.

They quickly glanced at each other. Both were thrilled to have been chosen to help this man and foresaw a great adventure ahead of them.

Billy was over the moon that he would be in the galley. That meant food.

The captain waved over one of the crew to take watch as he took them to their cabin. Two guarding soldiers followed them below deck.

The six-foot-wide room had a double bunk of narrow cots, a washstand, and some built-in furniture. Neither owned anything, so the drawers and wardrobe would remain empty. However, they noticed there were horsehair mattresses on the bunks and a folded sheet on each bed. They gasped in delight. This room was better than either had ever slept in before.

The captain said, "Someone will bring you clean clothing and a blanket each. Those will be standard convict issue, so you are entitled to them."

Even in Whitechapel, where Josh's family had lived, their beds only had one blanket. Admittedly, they had nice mattresses, but everything had to be left behind when his father was killed. Another man moved into the apartment when he took over the job. Here, there was a water ewer and a chamberpot under the bed. They only had time to determine who would have which bunk before their door opened again.

A doctor had come to give them a health check before they met Reverend Marsden, his wife, and his friend. Other passengers had yet to arrive, but the doctor checked the convicts as they descended the stairs.

He greeted them cheerily. "Hello, lads, I'm the acting ship's surgeon for this trip. Martin's the name, well, George Martin actually, but you had better call me just Doctor or Doc." He gave them the once-over, checking their temperature with his hand, inspecting their teeth and throat, then their chest, and had them lift their shirts to check for rashes, among other things. With a clean bill of health, the boys were told to follow him. All the while, he gave a running commentary of what they saw.

The doctor led the boys and pointed to a group sitting around some tables fixed to the floor in the middle of the deck. One by one, he introduced the passengers.

"Joshua, you will ultimately answer to Reverend and Mrs Marsden; however, this is Reverend Robert Cartwright and his family and this, young Josh, is Reverend Marsden's special guest, Chief Ruatara. Billy, although you will probably be in the galley with Clive, you will answer to the military Captain Archibald John Maclaine, Lieutenant John Purcell, and Lieutenant Robert Drurie of the 73rd Regiment. Of course, both of you will also answer to me, as well as to Captain Clark. He is a naval captain rather than a soldier. I will give you a quick tour of the ship so you will not get lost when you are sent on an errand."

Although all eyes had turned to them when they entered, most of the group had barely acknowledged the boys after their introduction and had already returned to their conversation. However, the chief's eyes held Josh's gaze.

The boys found it hard not to stare at the heavily tattooed man. He wore clothing similar to what could be seen in any poor London street, but his entire face was covered in intricately swirling geometric tattoos. His big brown eyes met Josh's, and he smiled. His perfect white teeth glistened in the beam of afternoon sun that came through the porthole. His eyebrows lifted in unison, followed by a slight head lift. He quietly mouthed, "Hello."

Josh grinned. Relief flooded over him. The man looked kind. He was going to like working for this man, and he returned the smile. He mouthed "Hello" back.

The boys followed the doctor as he progressed further down the deck. He pointed out the captain's cabin and said that his own cabin was opposite. The door to his room was open, and someone was making his bed.

The doctor followed their gaze. "Sadly, the steward won't attend to me unless I fall ill, which, God forbid, won't occur. So I may call on you two to fetch and carry for me. Savvy?" He saw both boys frown at the strange word. "Savvy means, 'Do you understand?'. It is West Indian slang with a Latin root meaning."

Again, they nodded. Excitement was building in both boys. They had reached the bow of the ship. The bulkheads narrowed as they walked. He opened a small door, and a strange contraption was revealed. It was built into the sides of the vessel.

The doctor continued his tour. "That's the water closet, only on a ship of any sort; it's called the head. One of your duties will be to empty the cabin passengers' chamber pots into here. That is where you put the contents. Savvy?" The doctor lifted the square lid, and they saw that it covered a hole where one sat to do one's smelly business.

The boys grinned in understanding. Neither had seen a contraption like this before. They had both had to empty the chamberpots at home anyway, so it was not an arduous task. The main 'head' drained directly into the sea.

The doctor's eyes twinkled. "A word of warning about using this facility in a big sea. The sea is where this drains, but in heavy weather, the waves also wash up through here. Keep the lid down and the door shut."

A throaty chuckle emanated from both boys as they could imagine the mess that would be made if someone were on it when a wave hit.

The doctor grinned, nodded and then continued the tour past the other cabins. He spoke nonstop as he walked. He pointed out who was in which rooms, and then they followed him down a narrow staircase. "On a ship, rooms are cabins, stairs are called ladders, walls are called bulkheads, and the railings on the main deck are called gunnels. The drain holes up there are called the scuppers. You will learn about their use when we experience bad weather. Trust me, if we get 'rocked to the scuppers', you will know about it."

On the lower deck, they discovered the regiment's quarters. Some of the soldiers were married and had been allocated smaller curtained areas. Very few were in there at the moment. Many hammocks were slung from the rafters, but the officer's ones had bars at the head and foot with a mattress in them. They had much more room, but still little privacy.

They passed through the section with some soldiers and arrived at another area that housed the crew. At the end of this was a door. "I wish to show you in here, as I may need you to get things for me. This is the hospital room. If I send for you, I will need you to bring supplies, so listen well and remember where everything is."

The medical cabin, such as it was, was similar in size to two of their cabins. It had six narrow bunks and an empty table in the middle of the room. The doctor called their attention to the emergency bag and various other items. "This is the sick bay, lads."

Both listened attentively, trying to remember all he told them. "If I have to do surgery on anyone, I will possibly need you two to scrub the operating table when I'm done. While other doctors don't believe in cleanliness, I was taught it was next to Godliness. Hence, I scrub everything in a heavy saline solution, which is essentially concentrated seawater, and then give everything a thorough wipe over with a clean cloth soaked in spirits of some sort. I've seen startling results of no infections if the treating physician has doused their hands and instruments in strong spirits before treatment."

The doctor looked at the two blank faces. "Well, that was a bit of useless information, wasn't it?"

Neither boy replied, but Josh shook his head. He would remember that.

With an exasperated sigh, the doctor asked, "Don't either of you ever say anything?"

Josh nodded. "Of course, we do, sir, but we were told not to speak unless required to do so."

Billy followed the example of his friend and said, "Me too, sir."

With a cheery smile, the doctor said, "Ahh, with me, you may chat away and ask me any questions that you wish. We'll lock up here and go below. I'll show you where the spare key is. Even the crew do not know, so keep that information under your hat. You two are both too young to drink, and that's what they want. Your companions will have settled by now, and you will see where you will go if you misbehave. Savvy?" He slipped the key into a narrow beam with a small gap behind it. Then put his finger to his lips. "The crew drink my brandy and rum, so say nothing."

"Yes, sir," was echoed from his young shadows.

Heading past the crew's dining area, the doctor said, "Don't ask why, but cover one eye as we walk through here."

The boys did as requested but had no idea why the unusual order had been issued. With a hand still covering an eye, they descended another narrow staircase, and the doctor told them to remove their hands. With the eyes they had covered, they could see well, even though it was almost pitch-black.

Standing on the lowest deck, the doctor said, "When you cover one eye, it adjusts to the darkness before the other one, so that when you enter somewhere that you know will have little natural light, covering your eye prepares you so you can immediately see. Have you ever seen a sailor with an eye patch flipped up?"

Both nodded enthusiastically.

The doctor chuckled at their enthusiasm. "Well, now you know why. Most have both eyes. I'm pleased you both obeyed without question. I won't always have time to explain my reason, but let this be a lesson learned, eh? Instant obedience, hey, what?"

"Oh!" was echoed by the boys, who both nodded.

They walked along the darkened deck and saw convicts spread out through the various cells.

The doctor knew that once they reached Portsmouth, they would collect one hundred and seventy more convicts. He said to the felons below, "Chaps, if you have friends, make the most of your space. We are leaving on the receding tide and heading to Portsmouth. We will collect more roommates for you. Stay where you are until we reach port, but the next lot will be a rough bunch, and many are lifers from Newgate Prison, if that means anything to you. I have been told that over one hundred and thirty fellows in the next lot are serving life sentences. If I were you, I would cluster at the foot of the steps, as they will wish to be back in the dark corners."

Usually, most of the convicts would have been in irons or at least locked in their cells, but with a guard at each exit and so few on the deck, they had been permitted free range of their quarters. These were from Compter cells rather than a proper prison, so they were given a little more freedom. All had less than seven years to serve, and most would be given the privileges of mess captains and similar before they reached Portsmouth.

The groans that the trio heard were followed by one or two thanking the doctor. He was known to them already, as he had given each of them a quick health check as they entered the deck.

As the doctor turned to leave, he said, "You two, follow me."

With the most critical areas of the vessel now viewed, the doctor explained, "Okay, lads, up to your cabin. I don't think you'll stay there long once we're at sea. However, as we are still tied up, you must remain in your cabin unless one of us calls for you. Savvy?"

The dual echo of "Savvy, sir" followed.

They moved towards their cabin through the galley. The doctor asked, "When did you last eat?"

Josh knew that they had both missed the noon gruel. He said, "Early this morning, sir, we missed the noon meal of thin soup." The bowl of thin gruel was hardly filling, but it was better than not eating at all.

The doctor gave a nod and said, "Follow me. I have not introduced you to the cook. Billy, you will be working for him."

Neither argued if it meant the possibility of food coming their way.

The cook was a giant of a man with a long beard, and he wore a filthy apron. He grunted at the appearance of the trio.

Rather than being put off by his attitude, the doctor introduced them to each other. "Clive, this is Billy and Josh. Billy will be your *gofer*."

Josh's brows knitted together. "Gopher, sir? What's that?"

Clive roared with laughter. "Go fer this or go fer that, laddie." He eyed Billy up. "Skinny little runt, aren't ya! Well, you'll be able to clean up whatever's left from the soldiers' tucker, so that'll fatten ya up quick like, laddie." He had been slicing loaves of bread, and he slopped a dollop of congealed gravy onto the crust, then dipped it into the juicy dripping again. He did this to another crust end, and the bread sat on his hands temptingly. "Eat up, lads."

The boys' mouths were salivating. They took the delicious treats and bit into them with glee. Bread and dripping had been a treat rarely given by Josh's parents, and Billy had never had such a thing before.

Both boys adored the greasy food.

The doctor watched as they ate. His heart went out to these two lads. He had never known hunger or poverty, but he had seen it often enough in his work. He was beginning to like this boy, Josh. He chewed with his mouth closed and seemed to have some education. He wiped his mouth with his thumb and licked it. Billy cleaned his mouth on what remained of his sleeve. He saw a glob of gravy-filled dripping stuck to Josh's lip and touched his own.

Josh licked the lump into his mouth and grinned. "Sorry, sir," he said. "I haven't enjoyed that treat since my papa died."

Billy stayed silent but was eyeing more ends of the loaves. He dearly wanted more but dared not ask.

Clive watched his frown. "The cabin class won't eat crusts, so boys, finish it orf. There are plenty of meaty juices in the pan. Scoop off the congealed fat, or you'll get sick. Bread and drippin' should really be called bread and juices. There are the end bits of their roast pork under the cup. Dig in, as it will save me from gettin' fatter!" He roared with laughter.

The boys didn't need to be asked twice. They each took three more crusts and pushed back some of the congealed dripping to soak their bread in the delicious meaty juices.

By the time the crusts were gone, they were both full for the first time in a long time.

The doctor remembered doing much the same when he was a growing lad. He waited until they had finished and said, "Come on, boys, I'd better get you back to your cabin in case you are needed. Eat like that once at sea, and you will lose the lot."

By the time the doctor arrived at the cabin door, the sound of the ropes being hauled aboard was audible through the ship. He had already felt the tide lift the ship and heard it bump against the pier.

Josh knew the tide had been coming in when they boarded, and in the hours that passed, it had reached its zenith and was now on the ebb.

The *Ann* was not the only ship to now go with the river's tide flow and head towards the open sea. Only one small sail was permitted to be hoisted on the seaward passage.

The doctor said that the trip to the ocean could take up to four days if there were a headwind. As there was a tailwind, it could be overnight.

Few vessels were heading out to sea, and with the wind behind them, the journey was relatively quick. The boy's faces were glued to their small sealed cabin porthole. They were thrilled even to be permitted to have a view of any sort, as they knew they should be locked below deck. Down below, the gun ports were the only view outside, and the doctor said most of them were nailed shut. They were in the only servants' cabin with a glass porthole.

Two days after setting sail, the ship's rolling showed they had reached the open sea at Sheerness.

Billy lay on the floor, vomiting into the chamberpot. The stench of the enclosed room nearly made Josh ill, but thankfully, he had been busy attending to the needs of the senior passengers. He had thrown up a few times, but keeping busy helped.

Of the Marsdens, Josh saw little, but he was asked to attend to the needs of the Maori chief as a priority. Josh found that the man's needs were for companionship, and Josh was willing to provide that in abundance.

It meant he was to stay with him on deck, and he felt the salty sea spray on his face for the first time in his life. Rather than being frightening or standoffish, Chief Ruatara was an absolute delight to be with. His cheerful grin was accompanied by a belly laugh that Josh could not help but enjoy.

On the journey to Portsmouth, Ruatara, as he insisted on being called, had twice knocked on the boys' cabin to get Josh at night and said, "*Kia ora.* Come, little *pakepakeha*; we're going outdoors."

Josh learned that *pakepakeha* was what the Maori people called a white person. The chief later shortened that to *pākehā*. Josh also learned that *Kia ora* was a universal greeting that could mean hello, welcome, and also good day, depending on the circumstance. It was a friendly greeting. Josh would follow the man onto the deck at night, and the pair would find a nook out of the breeze and watch the stars. There, Josh's education truly began.

The chief said, "Joshua, the stars, or *whetū*, are your friends. Wherever you are, learn their path, for then you will never be lost. These are different from the ones at home, yet they are still the same."

Ruatara told Josh how he had arrived in England on a whaling boat and had only been there for two weeks when the reverend came across him. "Josh, the stars called me far from home, and I wanted to see where the white men came from. We saw their boats with white cloud sails like this one. Those big ships catch the whales, which we call *ika moana*, and as it was the easiest way to find a passage, I worked on a whaling ship, but they only took me as far as Sydney Cove."

Josh looked surprised. "Where did you learn English, sir? If you don't mind me asking."

The man chuckled. "The whaling ships have called into our bays for many years. I first picked up bits from them. On the boat to England, the *Santa Anna*, I had to learn quickly. Before that, I was in Sydney Cove for over a year, and I fast or starved. All that time, the stars were with me. I looked up at night in Sydney Cove and saw the same star configurations that I saw at home. That was comforting."

They sat silently for a while, and Josh shivered.

Ruatara drew him close. "Body warmth will keep you warm."

Josh knew that, as he and his sister huddled under the blankets with their mother to stave off the cold. They sat gazing skyward, and Josh asked, "Will you teach me your ways, sir? I have always loved being outdoors, but in London, it's so foggy you can barely see the sky, let alone the stars."

Ruatara smiled at the lad under his arm. "Josh, I'd be delighted, and Billy, too, if he's interested. I'm out of place with the soldiers and the reverend, but we shall be friends; hey, what?"

Josh chuckled. The English euphemism sounded out of place, coming from the mouth of the heavily tattooed Maori man. "I'd be honoured, sir, but I'm here to serve you. I'm a convict, sir."

The chief laughed. "And I'm a Maori Chief who has worked his way halfway around the world on a whaling vessel, and I have seen sights too mighty to behold. Although I only spent a few weeks in England, I saw many great things. I want to take these things and that knowledge back to my people. I saw how these people grow crops and harvest bountiful things. Our hunger can be kept at bay with this knowledge. We grow yams and other root foods, but not grains. Oh, yes, Joshua, I wish to take those skills home and teach my people." He fell silent for a while. "Yes, Josh Callan, I will teach you about the stars and the water currents that are the home of the *Moana;* that is the ebb and flow of the ocean. It's part of the sharing of information that we need to have. You will teach me a great deal, too. Even as a convict, can you help me with my English?"

Josh nodded. "Absolutely, sir. I'd be honoured, but I won't be a very good teacher."

Ruatara chuckled. "You speak well enough for my purposes."

The pair watched the stars for some time until the chill penetrated through even the body warmth of the chieftain's enormous tattooed arm.

After another shiver, Ruatara said, "Bedtime for us both, I think, lad. Portsmouth tomorrow, where you will be locked up again. As we head south, we'll start our lessons for real. As we approach the equator, the temperature increases. We might even sleep on deck some evenings when it's too hot in the cabins. Rio de Janeiro is two months away, but we'll have some magical evenings before then."

Chapter 5   Rolling Emotions
The Dromedary

*T*he *Hindostan* and the *Dromedary* remained in reasonable proximity so they could signal to each other with flags. There were bouts of calm weather, but on the whole, the stormy seas rolled and crashed with great regularity. By early August, they were nearing Rio de Janeiro. The *Hindostan* was stricken with many illnesses, and Colonel Macquarie called for an extended stay in the famous port.

This long stop had not been part of the planned trip, but the supply of crew on board the *Hindostan* had dwindled to such an extent that it would not have made it to the Cape in Africa.

Dysentery had swept through everyone on the *Hindostan*, and many of the hundreds on board were ill.

Elizabeth admitted to Cathy that her husband had been severely afflicted with *mal-de-mer*, and he would be thankful for the calmer waters of the Brazilian harbour.

The planned stay in port of a few days was extended to nearly a month. More than one hundred were so debilitated that they were taken to the hospital on shore.

During one of the onboard sewing sessions, while anchored, Cathy offered to transfer back on board the *Hindostan* and offered to assist Doctor Arnold.

Mark had just descended from the upper deck and was horrified to overhear her words. Unable to stop himself, he said, "Mrs Callan, I cannot permit you to risk the life and limb of both yourself and your daughter and leave us." He looked stricken.

Cathy rose and said, "Captain, the doctor on board was kind to us. He is overwhelmed and understaffed. I could be useful."

Mark didn't know what to say. He had no right to stop her, no claim on her at all, and he didn't like that situation. He wished he could ask her to marry him, but as a soldier, he needed permission to court, let alone marry, and he didn't have it. He could not even approach her until he had that. He had not made any progress in their relationship, as he refused to lead her on. He would not condone any other sort of liaison.

With her standing in front of him, he mouthed softly, "Don't go! Don't leave me, please, Cathy." He had not used her name before, though he knew it well. He dreamed of her each night, and his cologne now reminded him of the love she had for her lost husband rather than him. He kept himself at arm's length from her, but his face was now an open book of loving concern for her.

Cathy saw him blanch, and she was worried he would clasp her before Mrs Macquarie. She was unsure of what to do or say.

Elizabeth Macquarie witnessed their interchange. Both were frozen into immobility and unable to speak; she said, "Captain, I will not permit her to leave. Jenny has already lost her father. If her mother attends to the sick, she could also catch it. No, Mrs Callan, you will remain here with me and stay safe, for Jenny's sake, if nothing else."

Mark heaved a long sigh of relief. His heart rate slowly returned to its normal rhythm.

Elizabeth noticed his face relax.

When Lachlan Macquarie returned from the mainland, he came bearing news that some of the perpetrators from the coup in Sydney Cove had recently been in port on the way to London. Their ship had left a few days earlier. On board was George Johnston, who had taken over the colony after Bligh was arrested, and one John Macarthur. It was the arrest of six of his friends that sparked the insurrection. On board were also a dozen or more of the New South Wales Corps who had been involved. The colony had been left in the hands of Major Joseph Foveaux while Lieutenant Colonel Paterson remained in Port Dalrymple in Van Diemen's Land. These men were going to plead their case to the Naval authority.

Lachlan huffed in utter frustration. The position as governor, to which Lachlan Macquarie was being sent, came about due to this particular uprising, but few details had been uncovered. A visit to a previous governor had forewarned Lachlan of the coup *en route*. John Hunter, in Portsmouth, had more information than Admiralty House in London.

Lachlan read Crispin Milroy's lengthy screed to Admiral Hunter and was determined to look up this chap and thank him. He smiled, knowing he knew far more than his orders contained.

The Macquaries had not expected to hear any more about the colony's situation until they reached the shores of the distant land. However, Colonel Macquarie was handed a proclamation addressed to Edward Harrison, Master of the *Admiral Gambier*. The document explained that the state of affairs in Sydney Cove was dire and detailed some of the grievances, but it still did not explain the root cause. Was it as John's letter said? Was Macarthur's squabble the cause? He knew that Governor Bligh had initially been under house arrest by the militia, but had been released on the promise of his return to England. The letter he now held said that rather than keep that promise, Bligh had fled to Van Diemen's Land, where he was still holed up. Lachlan groaned as he read. Sydney Cove was now under the control of Colonel Paterson.

With his commanding officer's attention occupied by the recent news, it was two more days before Mark sought permission to court Cathy. He had written his request and handed it over.

Lachlan opened it, read it, and said, "Yes, yes, whatever!" It was not quite the reply Mark had wished for, but approval was given nonetheless. Before parting company in Rio de Janeiro, extensive discussion took place about the colony.

~

On August 23rd, 1809, they finally weighed anchor and set sail from Rio de Janeiro. It had been a year since Mark's mother died. Over one hundred of the 73rd regiment and their families were left behind and instructed to catch the *Ann* or one of the other troop ships or convict transports that followed.

Once at sea, the ships experienced more than their fair share of bad weather, but this night was calm, and the breeze was enough to need a warm coat. Mark knew she did not have any warm clothing.

When in Rio, he had purchased an oilskin overcoat for Cathy's use for the trip. Jenny received a smaller coat. These garments would keep both ladies warm and dry. He was already protective of them, and even if Cathy refused him, he would do everything in his power to keep them safe. He had been in denial about his deep feelings until Cathy offered to leave the ship. His heart had crashed. Mark waited until they were at sea before he approached Cathy. Once again, they stood at the poop deck railing in the fading twilight. "Mrs Callan, would you care for a turn around the deck?"

Considering how small the poop deck was, she smiled at his offer. "Thank you, Captain." She took his proffered arm, and they strolled around the small elevated poop deck.

The sea was already building for another gale, but for tonight, the stars were out. The sails overhead were full, and the ropes and brasses clinked in the steady breeze.

After some minutes of circling the tiny upper deck, Mark paused at the centre of the back railing. They were invisible to all but anyone above them in the rigging. "Mrs Callan, Cathy, is it too soon after your tragic loss to declare my interest and intent?"

Cathy had been hoping the handsome captain was not toying with her feelings. He had not said anything prior to today. "Captain, it is nearly a year since James was killed. Having said that, a great deal has happened since then. I never expected to leave everything I know behind and move halfway around the globe to chase my son."

She dropped her head and thought about the last eleven months. So much had happened to her over her short life, but she had survived. When James died, she had prayed that she would die too, but her children needed her. She struggled to regain her will to live. Josh had stolen to help the family survive, but she knew that he and Jenny had targeted the man who had made them fatherless and her a widow. Lord Wiskhamford was a disgusting, debauched pig. She knew far too much about his carnal activities to let the peer realise she had a ten-year-old daughter. He was known for his penchant for girls and liked them to be young, innocent, and inexperienced. He also liked his carnal liaisons rough. She had managed to escape his notice in the two years she had worked the streets, but she knew the man's reputation well. He had vilely violated her friends. The more the girls fought, the more he liked it. She blanched at the memories and stumbled as the ship rolled down the side of a big wave.

Mark caught her and cupped her cheek. As she had not replied, he addressed her formally, "Mrs Callan, are you well?"

Cathy's glassy eyes lifted to him. "Yes, Captain. My life was not always easy, and before I answer your question, I need to tell you about the years before I married James."

Mark's thumb moved to her lips to silence her. "No, Cathy, your silence about these few years speaks volumes. I know what life was like in this area and what one needed to do to survive. One day, you can tell me all, but I want you as you are. That means with your background, children, and all. I want to care for you, protect you, and be your rock. You are who you are now because of James and your life before him. His faith and belief in you made you strong. I have no desire to take that from you. If our Lord can forgive my sins, then who am I to criticise someone else?" He thumbed a tear from her cheek.

Cathy grabbed his hand and pressed her cheek into his palm. She kissed his thumb, which had sat on her lips, and softly replied, "Yes, Captain. My answer is yes; enough time has passed." Her voice dropped. She whispered, "But I insist I tell you of those horrible two years after my father sold me to a madam."

He gasped. The knowledge that her father had sold her into working the street cut into his heart, but he knew such men existed. Mark's heart was beating twenty to the dozen. "If you must, but you truly mean it? Will you allow me to court you? It will be an unusual situation, as I won't be able to give you flowers or take you on drives in the park. We shall have to make do with the sound of the sea and the stars to shine upon your face." Mark felt like twirling her around. He was unsure of what to do, but Cathy wasn't.

Cathy's voice was like music to his ears. She said, "You have given us warm coats, and that is worth more than flowers."

He hardly heard her words over the rush of blood to his ears. She had agreed.

She continued. "All I want, sir, is a faithful, caring man. Captain, it's been a long time since I was held close, and I crave the loving touch. Will you hold me?"

Mark's hand slid from her cheek to around her neck, then down her back. She was in his arms, fitting so well. "Oh, Cathy, I have wanted to hold you so since we met. Will you not call me by my given name of Mark?"

She nodded against his chest.

Although not one to weep often, her emotions overwhelmed her.

She broke down. She had been strong for so long and so alone. No more, her sobs made him draw her closer. Her past hurts were indeed healing. God had answered her prayers and brought another Godly man into her life. She felt safe, cradled in his strong arms. She rested against him as she relaxed into his embrace.

Mark felt her melt against him. "Cathy, are you all right?" He had felt the dampness of her tears seep through his linen shirt.

She took a few moments to answer before lifting her face and saying, "Yes, Mark. I am, but I never expected to feel this way again." She sniffed. "While you are holding me so close, I will tell you of those two horrible years. I will not hold you to your request after you hear my background."

Knowing she had been overheard before, she gave him a very brief outline of what happened when her father had sold her for a handful of gold coins so he could get another drink.

She pulled back a little but stayed in his arms. After her story unfolded, he couldn't resist and dropped a light kiss onto her lips. He would wait for a few weeks before asking for more. He replied by saying, "The past is behind us both. We are who we are because of that. Christ washed our pasts clean; we must learn to believe that and move on. My feelings for you are unchanged. I know what life was like for us all when living there. Cathy, I will not claim more than my quick kiss yet, but know that I wish to and will kiss you properly soon."

Cathy rested her cheek against his chest again. "I'm not going anywhere, Mark."

He smiled. "Nor am I."

Their courtship was indeed strange.

Mark was all that was polite. Even James had not treated her like a duchess, but she knew full well that she was no lady.

Cathy felt uncomfortable; she kept saying that Mark deserved better. Their evenings on the upper deck were special. He had still not kissed her properly, but he would occasionally kiss her hand or cheek or drop a peck on her upturned lips.

~

One day in early September, Cathy didn't appear at the luncheon. Mark had not seen her all morning, and he became worried.

Jenny had come for her regular morning hug, but she had said nothing about her mother's absence. Eventually, he saw Mrs Macquarie sewing alone and dared to ask her. "Ma'am, I was wondering if you had seen Mrs Callan today?"

Rather than answer immediately, Elizabeth patted the seat beside her.

Mark sat somewhat uncomfortably. He felt like the bench seat was lined with sharp pins.

Elizabeth put aside her work and turned to gaze directly at him. "Captain, today is the anniversary of her husband's passing. Today, she puts off her mourning officially and…and…" She was surprisingly lost for words. She had watched the growing relationship between these two people. "… and Captain, from tomorrow, she shall be free and able to marry without society's condemnation. Give her today, and then let tomorrow look after itself."

He closed his eyes and gave a brief prayer of thanksgiving. Mark nodded his understanding. "Will you give her a message for me?"

Elizabeth nodded.

Mark met her honest gaze. "Would you tell her I will pray for her today and hope to see her tomorrow?"

She nodded with a smile. "Thank you, Captain. Your sensitivity does you justice. Please be assured that your feelings are reciprocated. If the opportunity arose in Cape Town, I wondered if it would be too soon to require a church service." She gave a twisted smile while biting her bottom lip. Was she overstepping her interference?

Mark's face lit with excitement. "Would that be permitted, though, ma'am?"

Elizabeth was relieved. She had read his intent correctly. "I shall ask Colonel Macquarie, then, shall I?"

Mark stood and bowed. "Ma'am, that would be wonderful, but should I not request his permission in person?" His beaming smile belied the sadness he felt at not being able to see Cathy today. However, he was fully aware that Cape Town was only a little under three weeks away. He had asked to court her just after the anniversary of his mother's passing. He knew that the end of her official bereavement was close at hand. In a few weeks, Cathy may well be his wife. Three wonderful weeks! He would know tomorrow if she would marry him. She may wish to wait until Sydney, so Josh could be part of their happiness. That, of course, was if she said yes. He would let her choose.

Mark was about to head up to the main deck when he met his commander-in-chief descending the stairs. He saluted and stood aside.

Lachlan Macquarie saw who it was, paused and frowned. "Captain, walk with me."

Mark fell into step behind his superior officer.

Lachlan led the way into his small office, located adjacent to their cabin. They reached the Macquaries' suite of rooms, if the two small cabins could be called that. The colonel said, "Come sit in my ready room, Captain."

He pointed to a chair, and Mark sat nervously.

Lachlan stood with his hands behind his back. "Captain, tell me about your lady friend."

His abrupt question left Mark stunned. "Um, what exactly, sir? She is a widow with two children."

Lachlan slowly paced the small room. "Yes, yes, I know about that, but where is her second child? Has she told you about him?"

Mark nodded. "Yes, sir."

Lachlan spun around and faced him. "So you know he is on the *Ann* as a convict?"

Mark felt he was walking on thin ice. He had not yet met the boy, but his colonel obviously knew more than he let on. "Yes, sir, that's why Mrs Callan and Miss Jennifer are moving to New South Wales. Sir, the lad was only thirteen when arrested."

Lachlan nodded that he knew that. "Go on."

Mark decided to spill what he knew. "Sir, the boy was convicted of stealing linen shirts. Of that, he was innocent, although he had frequently teased a laundry lady. Mrs Callan knows that as a fact because she knew he was elsewhere." He paused and swallowed nervously. He saw his boss's eyebrow raise questioningly.

"Which was?" Lachlan rolled his hand, inferring he was to continue.

Mark nodded and did. "Joshua was picking the pocket of the man who had run down and killed his father. After initially pausing, the man drove off without even stopping to help." With hardly a breath, he continued. "Sewing costumes for the Drury Lane Theatre was the only means of Mrs Callan making money, and when it burned down earlier this year, her only source of income was gone. Josh did the only thing he could justify." He paused again, wondering if he should say more.

Lachlan circled his hand again for Mark to continue his story. He paced the small cabin as he listened.

Mark took a deep breath and did as requested. "Sir, Joshua, that is the lad's name, would only pick Lord Wiskhamford's pocket, help himself to some money and hand back the billfold as though the man had dropped it. He was often rewarded with another coin or more. This money kept the family alive."

Mark swallowed nervously. Knowing his colonel had seen the seedy side of life in India and Egypt, he continued. "Sir, I grew up in this area, and I know the foul reputation of this particular man, plus others of his disgusting kind. He has a penchant for little girls, and I mean very, very young girls, sir. Miss Jennifer is at that age, and Mrs Callan could no longer protect her."

Lachlan spun around, stunned. "The girl is what, eight?" His mouth sagged open with shock.

Mark shook his head. "Ten, sir. Mrs Callan knew she needed to get her away from the area. The last time Josh picked the man's pocket, he took fifteen pounds, as the billfold had so much in it that he probably wouldn't miss that. He passed the money off to an assistant and ran."

The colonel's eyebrows lifted. "Miss Jennifer, I presume? Continue…"

Mark's single nod confirmed the statement. "Yes, sir. With Mrs Callan's permission, I asked Jenny to tell me her version of that day, and their stories tally. Miss Jennifer took the money from Josh, then watched as he took an apple from a stall. Without watching where he was running, he ran straight into the arms of a Bow Street Runner. He had no idea his so-called friends had dropped his name as a shirt thief. Therefore, he was given three years for theft, which was later lengthened to seven because Josh objected." His boss's frown worried Mark. Was he going to withdraw his permission? He added, "Sir, I have not yet met Josh."

Lachlan paced across the room a few times before turning to his officer. "Captain, all that information tallies with what I know of the story."

He saw the look of surprise on his captain's face and laughed. "Did you really think I would not have found out who the strange woman was travelling with us? I personally knew everyone else in the cabins. Mrs Callan has been honest with you. I received a court transcript and one from the Bow Street Runners. Mind you, there is nothing about Lord Wiskhamford and his part in the boy's file." His brows knitted. "Both children truly lost their father because of that man? The girl was truly in danger of drawing his attention?"

Mark nodded. "Yes, sir."

Lachlan blew out his cheeks and said, "If the girl assures you that only that man's pocket was picked, then I will not take that matter further."

Mark sighed with relief.

But Lachlan wasn't finished yet. "Captain, I presume you are about to propose?"

Mark affirmed that supposition with, "Yes, sir, if you approve."

Twice, Lachlan turned to speak, and then kept pacing. Finally, he asked, "Captain, did Mrs Callan mention her childhood?"

Mark swallowed nervously, wondering how to phrase what he knew in such a way that Cathy would not be shunned. "Mrs Callan told me everything, sir, including being sold by her father when she was thirteen, but I had already guessed her background. As I said, I grew up in that area and knew the various professions of the residents and the lack of options available." He was relieved that he would not have to say more.

His colonel was not so subtle. "So you know of her occupation for the years prior to her marriage?"

Mark nodded. How did his boss know about Cathy? Mark cleared his throat and said, "I do, sir. I told her she did not need to let me know, but she insisted. Her father sold her when she reached maturity. I am sad to say this was not uncommon in this area. It is frequented by unscrupulous peers such as Wiskhamford. Mrs Callan's husband, James Callan, rescued her when she was only fourteen and married her as soon as he could. Josh was born a year later. She lost a daughter at a few hours old before Jenny came along."

Lachlan was happy with what he was hearing. He took a seat and leaned on his elbows. He stood again and moved to the porthole. After a while, he said, "Good! I wanted to know if she was honest with you. As such, I have no opposition to her as your wife, should she agree. However, I have read that Sydney has no married officers' quarters. If my extensive report is correct, the facilities are scant, to say the least. I have no idea what the buildings are like or if any are available to rent. When I met Admiral John Hunter, he gave me an outline of the place, but admittedly, that was eight years ago. I read letters from friends he had there, but those sorts of details were absent. Having escaped her London life, it is not likely that she will want to bunk in with the rabble below decks. She's had enough of that."

Mark was wondering why his colonel was so concerned. His worry must have been obvious. Perspiration beaded on his brow.

Lachlan had been looking out the porthole. He now turned and sat down again. "Settle down, Captain. Mrs Macquarie has taken a liking to your young lady and is determined to see her safely situated. As you have only recently transferred into my regiment, I do not know you as well as Henry Antill. I wanted to know about your plans and whether you might be interested in joining our personal security detail with Henry. This means you would live at Government House with us, and the lad could be assigned to either me or you."

Mark was stunned. "You want me as part of your personal detail, sir?"

Lachlan gave one of his very rare broad grins. "Why not? You are a man of faith; you don't drink to excess, and you care about your men."

Mark gasped.

Lachlan smiled. "Yes, yes, I checked into your background before you transferred into my regiment. I read of the many heroic deeds that you never mention. As I said, Mrs Macquarie likes the woman who, hopefully, will one day be your wife. Having said that, the offer stands, even if Mrs Callan does not accept your proposal. Captain Antill has already accepted my offer. As you are aware, it's why he is here with me." He released a long sigh. "Recent revelations in Rio suggest I should increase my security detail."

Mark's chin shot up. "Is there trouble brewing out there, sir?"

Lachlan reclined in his chair and said, "From what I have both read and heard, I have little doubt about that. I intend to arrive with a strong presence." His brow cleared, then he said, "No need to answer straight away."

Lachlan once again waved his hand to show Mark that he was dismissed.

Mark stood and saluted. "Sir, I am honoured and will accept your offer immediately. I am quite sure she will accept my troth."

Lachlan had already turned his concentration to the paperwork on his desk. "Good, let me know when you get an official reply from her. I do hope she says yes, for your sake. A happy union is a joy to behold. I should know, as I've had two."

Mark smiled and took his leave. He knew about his superior officer's first wife, Jane, and the sadness after her passing. Henry had filled him in on the anniversary of the first Mrs Macquarie's death. Mark closed the cabin door quietly and bowed his head in a prayer of thanks. He now had a secure future to offer Cathy. He had not wished her to live with the rowdy soldiers' wives, but he knew she would not have complained.

Chapter 6   Crossing the Equator
The Ann

*O*nly weeks after leaving Portsmouth, the zero horizontal point on the map was reached. The seas at the equator were relatively flat, but it was raining. However, a sail-sheet had been hauled over a rope, and a large chair was placed at the base of the central mast. Josh's face crinkled in a frown. H e watched the proceedings for some time until he was grabbed, stripped of his shirt, and tied to a bollard. When the captain approached, he pleaded with him, saying, "Sir, what have I done wrong? I'm sorry for whatever it was."

The skipper roared with laughter before replying, "Nothing, lad, but this is the first time you have crossed the equator. Today, we are celebrating this event, and you will be introduced to King Neptune."

Josh watched from the side as a long trident-like fork was placed beside the captain's chair. Now, a crown of seaweed was ceremoniously placed on the captain's head, and a box sat at the man's feet.

People emerged from various points around the ship, and the crew and passengers stood at a distance, obviously to watch the strange ceremony.

Billy was nowhere in sight. Josh saw Ruatara leaning against a railing with his arms folded and a massive grin on his tattooed lips. He obviously had something he was hiding behind his back, but Josh couldn't catch a glimpse of what it was.

Josh was petrified at what the crew would do to him. He watched the dumping of more seaweed around the captain's chair and was horrified to feel some draped around his neck from behind.

A screech from the other side of the ship showed Josh that Billy was receiving similar treatment, but he was out of sight.

With the long blast from a conch shell that Ruatara produced from behind his back, the captain called all to attention. "Hear ye, hear ye! King Neptune, be it known on this day Joshua Callan and William Green are crossing the line for the first time, as well as those held below decks."

Cheers and wolf whistles from the crew followed the proclamation.

Someone started a slow clap, to which everyone else followed suit. Soon, the irregular clapping was followed by the beating of some drums, and the crew and soldiers started stomping on the deck with their feet.

Josh saw the Marsden's group of missionaries join Chief Ruatara off to the side. All were grinning, and Josh knew that the very pious Reverend Marsden would not have condoned anything that went against his religion, so he relaxed a little. Ruatara winked at Josh, and his heart lightened.

This was obviously some ritual for the passengers' enjoyment. He just wished he wasn't the centre of attention. He had lived his life trying to be invisible. That was unsuccessful today. When the many crewmen started stomping rhythmically, Josh wondered what it would sound like in the decks below. He was trying to watch the various activities going on around him. He leaned forward to see if Billy was visible when a blindfold was placed over his eyes from behind. He released a shout of surprise, but with his hands still tied behind his back, he could not resist.

As soon as the blindfold was on, he was manhandled by the crew and passed overhead by many hands until he was carried horizontally up the steps towards the captain on the quarterdeck. He was placed unceremoniously on the stool he had seen in front of the captain.

In a sonorous voice, the captain, now dressed as Neptune, read a long screed about King Neptune's rights and the dues required to pass the invisible line in the water.

The blindfold was tightly tied around his eyes, and it also dulled his hearing. However, he heard his name questioned.

The captain asked, "Are you Joshua Callan?"

Josh nodded, then whispered huskily, "I am."

The skipper's booming voice said, "Speak up, boy, so that King Neptune can hear you."

Josh cleared his throat and said loudly, "I am, sir, and it's a name to be proud of." He sat up straighter on the stool and tried to be brave. He wiggled his nose, and it moved the blindfold slightly. He could not see much, but saw a section of a bilge pump hose lying on the deck. The oiled leather hose slowly filled, and soon, he was doused with a cascade of water. Thankfully, it was not the filthy bilge water but the clean, salty water. He was soon drenched, but unharmed. In the stifling heat of the day, the water was refreshing.

More seaweed was thrown at him, and he was surrounded by the sound of laughter from everyone watching.

He heard the surgeon, Doctor George Martin's voice above the rest. "Captain, I forbid you to throw the lad overboard, sir. The last vessel I travelled on had that done to the lad, and the boy drowned. Haze him if you must, but nothing harmful. I forbid it, sir."

The captain must have replied in the affirmative as Josh was placed on his stomach on the deck and flayed with lengths of the flat seaweed that had bubbly lumps on the side. It stung but didn't cut him.

After another drenching of salty water, it was Billy's turn for hazing.

Ruatara came and claimed his cabin boy, removing his blindfold. He whispered, "Are you unharmed, lad?"

Josh nodded. "Yes, thanks, sir."

Ruatara smiled and put his finger to his lips. "Shh!"

A stumbling Billy was brought forward for his treatment. He, too, was blindfolded and had been unable to see what had been done to Josh. He had no idea what was before him.

Josh was about to call out to encourage his friend when Ruatara's fingers tightened painfully on his shoulder. "I said, shh."

Josh fell silent and watched.

The process was repeated, but Billy screamed as one of the lengths of seaweed had a few barnacles on it, and he received some deep cuts across his back. He was so skinny that it cut to his ribs. His blood dribbled onto the deck.

The ceremony was quickly over, and Josh was handed his shirt.

Although Ruatara had motioned for Josh to remain silent after his return, Josh called to his friend. "Billy, are you okay?"

Billy nodded. He was still tied and blindfolded. Once released, Clive shushed his assistant as they moved to stand near Ruatara and Josh.

Josh saw a lot of blood flowing down Billy's back and saw that the doctor had also noticed it and had moved closer to see if he needed treatment. He did. The seaweed that he had been flayed with had barnacles on it. Some were now embedded in the cuts. The gashes were deep and required immediate treatment. The doctor could see bits of grit in the wound. He tapped Clive on the shoulder, pointed to Billy, and the trio slunk away silently. Clive's bloated face showed he was worried.

Reverend Marsden read a lengthy passage from the Bible.

When it was over, Josh looked around to speak to his friend, only to find that both he and the cook had vanished, as had the doctor. Josh was now pleased that he had not squealed through the process and was congratulated by many soldiers and crew for his forbearance. He watched as the seaweed and hose were moved aside and tables were set up on deck. The seaweed was placed down the centre of the tables as decoration, and soon, food was brought up from the galley. A King Neptune banquet was being served.

The crew had caught two giant tuna the day before, and Josh had been surprised that they had not had any to eat that night. Now he found out why. The fish had been prepared in various ways, plus there were large bowls of rice mixed with dried peas to accompany it.

Ruatara dragged Josh to the table and said, "This is how we eat these big fish at home. I have used the last of my coconuts and lime to make this, so enjoy it, lad. A treat I learned from the islanders in the Pacific Ocean when on the whaling boat."

The dish had white cubes in a creamy sauce. Josh gingerly took a small square and nibbled at a cube with his fingers. He expected it to be revolting, but the flavours that hit his tongue were incredible. Having never tasted either lime or coconut, the tart but creamy sauce was heavenly. "Oh, sir, this is… this is… Well, sir, I've never tasted anything like it before." Josh ladled more onto his plate. "It's delicious."

Ruatara did the same, but others were a little more standoffish.

The captain arrived at their side, and Ruatara greeted him as usual. "*Kia ora*, captain, please try this. It's a dish from home, and as you can see, young Josh likes it."

The officer smiled, replying, "The boys have hollow legs. They will eat anything." The captain knew what it was and was hesitant. He did not like raw fish, but he took a single cube and nibbled on it.

The chief's eyes never left the captain as he tasted the dish. A simple word queried the flavour. With an eyebrow lifted, he asked, "Well?"

The captain's action was enough of an answer. He scooped a large spoonful onto his plate. After eating two large mouthfuls of the dish, he said, "This truly is raw tuna? I never would have guessed. It tastes just like lobster. Actually, even better than that. I have eaten crayfish, crabs, prawns, and oysters, but this is the king of all those kinds of seafood."

With the captain's words being overheard, the Marsdens' group, then the soldiers and crew, soon emptied the enormous bowl.

Josh sat silently, enjoying his delicious repast. He had had enough of being the centre of attention for the day.

Ruatara's following conversation with the captain was overheard by many. He explained, "Captain, my people are seafarers of old. However, they don't have ships like this; they have large… um," he turned to Josh. "What was that word for *waka* you used, my young friend ?"

Josh replied between mouthfuls. "Canoe or skinny long boat, sir. But you said that your canoes have a tall front with carvings on them."

The chief's face lit up. He turned back to the captain and continued, "Yes, canoe, only some of ours have outriggers on the sides. In these, we store the food. We can travel many miles across the sea. We know the currents, and we use the stars. We can journey from land to land, but must carry our food in such a way that it will not perish. This dish prevents tooth and gum decay, and I believe you call it scurvy. We call this dish *papaka* if it's made from crab, or *iki mata* if it's made from fish. This dish is delicious and needs no cooking. We do not often light fires on our wooden canoes, and with this dish, we do not need to do so."

The conversation was eye-opening for the very British captain. He had not thought of other cultures traversing the seas. On starry evenings, he had seen the unusual pair sitting on the deck and gazing skyward. They had even slept on the deck on the calm, warm nights. "Your people came across the seas? When?"

While grinning, Ruatara said, "The Maori people's oral history takes a long time to tell, so I will give you the short version." He saw a few others had drawn closer to listen, so he lifted his voice a little. "A long time ago, over generations, my ancestors came from islands in the middle of what you call the Pacific Ocean. Before that, I'm not sure. They traversed from island to island, settling on many of them; we ended up in *Aotearoa*. This is what we call our new land. It means *'Land of the Long White Cloud'*. My people navigate by the stars and currents, and it is this that I am teaching Joshua. We have stories, but no written words."

The captain was still eating, but he turned and looked at the convict cabin boy. "You are interested in learning all this?"

Josh grinned. "Too right, sir. I never got to see many stars in London, but my papa pointed out some to me when we could see them." He didn't elaborate further as the captain's attention had already turned back to his unusual passenger.

The captain realised he had finished his fish dish and turned to get more, only to find the bowl was empty. With an exasperated sigh, he said, "Well, in Rio, we shall load up with more, um,..." He licked the creamy dressing and asked, "What exactly is in it?"

Ruatara grinned again. "I would like to say it's a secret, but there are only two other things besides the fish. The raw, diced flesh is soaked in fresh lime juice, which turns it white, and then the cream of the coconut is mixed in. Normally, we drain off some of the lime juice, but I like the extra tartness of the lime, so I left it in as it is sad to throw it away. It can be seasoned with salt and some hot spice, but it's unnecessary."

The captain turned to Clive and said, "Cook, in Rio, add coconuts to your order and let the chief tell you what sort to get. Also, limes you say, sir?"

The tattooed head nodded before he said, "Clive, the coconuts are to be green, not ripe. I shall come with you to purchase them. They must be just right to make the cream. We need lots of limes as they have many purposes. Billy will tell you I squeezed some on the cuts on his back. It will stop them from infecting."

With the remainder of the feast to consume, the captain moved on to speak to others.

Clive and Billy had yet to serve the fish stew to the convicts below decks. None of them was hazed, but the special meal was made from the carcass of the two tunas. There was plenty of flesh on it to make the fish stew delicious. Clive added brown rice, onion, and dried peas to thicken the tasty concoction.

Having never had much to eat before, Billy was delighted to experiment with food and flavours he had never seen or tasted. He had tried the stew and added some cracked pepper to the dish. Even the porridge was salted and made with excess milk from the ship's goats. He was becoming a dab hand at cooking, and the convicts, soldiers, and crew ate well.

Two weeks after their hazing, the boys were permitted to watch the ship enter the harbour at Rio de Janeiro.

They had sailed steadily southwest until they turned a headland. The breeze dropped, and by the time they sailed into the wide bay, the sun was not far from setting.

Billy had gone to the cabin to wash up before serving dinner for the convicts. Ruatara kept Josh up on deck and pointed out some of the plants visible to the London boy. "That one with a feathery branch is a coconut palm tree, and the flat leaf one near it is a banana tree."

Josh had never seen a banana before, so he had no idea what it was. But Ruatara waxed lyrical about the bent yellow fruit of this plant.

The captain joined them at the railing as the sun hit the horizon. "Chief, Captain Maclaine insists that both lads are to be locked in their cabin once we drop anchor. We will be here for a week, and in that time, the boys are to stay below deck unless you or a soldier is with them."

The chief frowned. "Sir, they have proved their trustworthiness; are they not to be trusted now?"

The captain shrugged. "Naval rules, sorry, Chief. If we give in to one convict, it sets a precedent for the others."

Josh had not been asked for input but said, "That's fine, sirs. Billy and I were expecting this. Neither of us can believe that we even have a cabin and are not locked up in chains. However, may I ask that you see if you can find me a slate and some chalk while we are here? I wish to teach Billy to at least write his name."

The captain looked at the gangly lad beside the chief. The boy didn't want anything personally, but if the opportunity arose, he wished to teach his friend to write. "I think we can manage that, lad." He smiled at the fact that Josh asked for nothing for himself. This boy was not what he expected when he pulled him aside. He wondered how many more below deck would thrive like this lad if given an opportunity. He asked Josh, "Do you read books?"

The direct question took Josh aback. He nodded. "I learned to read from the Bible, sir, but I had another book when I was a boy. We had to sell it after Papa died. It was called '*The Keeper's Travels in Search of His Master*'. It was about a dog who had become lost and sought to find his way home."

The captain chuckled. "I remember that one. If I remember correctly, it's written like the dog is telling the story?"

Josh nodded with a grin. "I loved it."

Ruatara's head was switching from side to side following their conversation. "The dog talked?" The tattooed man's face showed surprise.

They explained the plot of the children's story, and he laughed. "Ahh, I would need to learn to read your English better before I attempted that. I can speak it well enough, but reading is another matter." He shook his head in confusion. "Your written word is a hard thing to master."

The dinner bell clanged, and they retreated to the mess room below. The evening meal was much later than usual because the vessel arrived in the harbour. The convicts below had been served as usual, but the crew, soldiers, and passengers didn't eat until the ship had anchored and set up for the time in the harbour. It was dark by the time the crew had prepared the ship for a week anchored in the bay.

As the captain had left Ruatara to go about his duties, Josh excused himself and went to assist with the convict meal. When not required elsewhere, Josh had got into the habit of helping Billy and Clive in serving the meals. He took up his position, and as they served the food, he told Billy of their enforced confinement for the following week.

After their meal had been consumed and cleaned up, the captain of the 73rd regiment made a noisy fuss of escorting both boys to their cabin.

They carried two jugs of water and had both used the head before their enforced confinement. They would need to use chamberpots while the ship remained in port.

Captain Maclaine followed them into their cabin and said, "Sorry, lads, rules say I must keep you under lock and key while anchored." He shut the door behind him and quietly said, "I will unlock it shortly, but I wish you to stay in your cabin unless escorted out. Savvy?"

They nodded and replied in unison, "Yes, sir." They laughed at how many had picked up the doctor's slang word.

The captain continued, "I will have to be seen to follow the letter of the law, but don't ruin this for yourselves. Stay indoors unless Captain Clark or I say otherwise. You may clean Ruatara's cabin, as he will be on shore all day, but you will wait until you are escorted before you do your work."

The two stunned boys nodded gleefully. They had a week to loll about doing nothing but resting. Not that either had had an arduous journey, but both were pleased to be able to sleep in rather than be up at sunrise.

Captain Maclaine left the cabin, and they heard the key turn in the lock. They did a hand bump and then settled down for the night. Both would miss their freedom on board, but it was only for a week. They lay down to rest, and both fell asleep.

Neither heard the door get unlocked half an hour later.

Dawn came with the ship swinging at anchor. The calm waters and silence from above were strange. Expecting to sleep in, both boys were soon clambering out of their bunks when they heard a longboat being launched. They saw the splash but could see little until it came alongside, and they saw Ruatara and the Marsdens climbing on board.

Ruatara saw the boys' faces at their tiny porthole and waved to them.

The boys watched the longboat pulling away from the ship from their tiny vantage point. The crew had long, even strokes and the boat made its way towards shore quickly. Over the next hour, three more longboats were launched, each loaded with empty barrels, hessian bags, and empty cases.

Clive also waved to the boys as he climbed down the rope ladder. Halfway down, he paused and called up to a crew member on board. He had forgotten to send the boys food or refill their water jugs.

Before that boat reached shore, the cabin door opened, and two bowls of tepid congealed porridge were brought in, but the man didn't bring any more water.

They ate their scant meal, and the door opened again as they finished. Lieutenant Robert Drurie stood there. "Morning, lads; while the passengers are gone, I'll supervise you while cleaning their cabins."

The boys pulled on their now-tight trousers and tucked in the tattered shirts they had slept in.

Robert noticed that neither had underclothing, and they smelled. After the Lieutenant flicked his finger to tell them they needed to tidy their beds first, he noticed there were no blankets on them either. Their sheets were unwashed and crumpled. He escorted them to the nearby cabins and stood guard while they emptied the bowls and cleaned the various chamberpots. Then, they refilled the water ewers.

Josh carried their nearly full chamberpot and emptied it in the head. He used a bucket of seawater to rinse the porcelain bowl before returning it to their cabin. Josh did Ruatara's cabin, while Billy did Marsden's suite. The other cabins were soon clean and tidy.

After completing a few more small chores, the lieutenant handed each of them a large handful of ship biscuits, known as hard tack. "These are just in case we forget to feed you again."

As the Lieutenant ushered them back into their cabin, he said, "You've both filled out a little. Do either of you have anything else to wear?"

The boys shook their heads in unison.

Josh, however, blushed. He had split his trousers while doing the chief's cabin that morning. He now had a huge slit up the back of his pants.

The lieutenant had seen his predicament. The convicts below decks had been issued with prison clothing when they boarded. He knew a store of prison garb was in the hold, but it would all be too big for them. "I figured you two had been overlooked. Hang tight, boys." He locked the door as he left.

They settled down to gaze out the sealed porthole, but they realised the tide had turned, and the ship was now facing the opposite direction. The sun now beat down on their side of the ship. Rather than see the sugar-cone-shaped mountain and verdant hills, they could now see the farms and valleys surrounding the town. They watched various canoes and triangle-sailed skiffs fishing in the bay, and there was spiralling smoke from fires onshore. The land was strange to them, but they drank it all in.

Josh pointed out the different trees to Billy that the chief had shown him.

Half an hour after the lieutenant departed, he unlocked the door and entered again. He carried an armload of clothing and blankets. "This is what they each received below decks; you should have been allocated them too. Mind you, those clothes would have hung on you when you boarded. As you have each filled out a bit and both shot up some inches or so, I think these can be adjusted to fit." The large bundle also included two new blankets.

Rather than leave the boys to dress, he figured they may never have seen linen under clothing before, and he was correct. After separating the piles, he showed them how to wear undergarments. "Boys, these are called drawers. They are what gentlemen wear under their breeches. I noticed that neither of you had any on, and you will find them much more comfortable than just your woollen trousers."

The linen drawers were initially too big, but with some pulling, adjusting, and tightening of the laces, both managed to work out how to wear them.

Next came the trousers. Again, both were too long, but they rolled up the hems, and the lieutenant tightened Josh's laces at the back until they fitted snugly around his waist. These trousers had a front flap, and neither boy had owned proper flapped breeches before. There were no shoes, but neither boy had ever owned a pair of shoes either.

Billy was so excited. He said, "Cor, Josh, by the time I get to Sydney Cove, I'll be a real gentl'man like, 'nd wiv you teaching me to write my name and speak proper-like 'nd all, I'll almos' be a toff." He was holding his new trousers up as if he let go; they would fall off. He strutted around the tiny cabin and made the other two laugh. The oversized clothes made him look even skinnier than he had before. He would never be handsome, but he looked much better than when he left London. What was better was that Josh and he got along very well.

The lieutenant stifled his chuckle. "Come here, lad, and I'll lace them properly. They will fall off you if you mince about like that."

Billy stood with his back to the soldier while the officer pulled and tightened the various fastenings on the back of his clothing.

The lieutenant then showed them how to undo the front fastenings to use the facilities and how to dress again quickly.

Lieutenant Drurie was pleased he had discovered the oversight of the guards. The boys must have frozen in the weeks since they left London. Now decently clad, he realised that the chief had been wearing only two sets of attire. Neither of which was clean. The offensive smell of the boys' garments had first alerted him to their predicament. He had not been into Ruatara's cabin before that morning, and he noticed today that there was virtually nothing in there either. Before dropping off the boys' apparel, he had deposited a larger armload of better-quality attire on the chief's bunk, including two new blankets.

When any passengers or crew had died on previous voyages, their clothing had been stored in a large case. The captain had shown him a chest containing assorted attire items that were available for use if required. It was from this that he had sourced the new outfits. Rather than take the offending old clothes with him, the boys were told to wash them and hang them to dry. They could keep their shirts, but the old trousers would be handed to the sailmaker and repaired. They would then return the clothes to the trunk in case another child ever needed them. He would also ask the two captains about obtaining another set of clothing or two for each of the lads while in port. Some of the younger felons below were in a similar predicament.

He left them in their cabin and returned to his duties.

The boys spent the remainder of the day in their quarters. With the arrival of their clothes, they had forgotten to refill their water jug, and both were thirsty. The sun continued to beat down on their side of the ship. The temperature rose in the small sealed room as the afternoon heated up.

Around noon, Josh tested the door and realised it was unlocked. "They only said we had to stay in our cabin, Billy. They said nothing about whether we could have the door open. We'll close it when we hear the boats arrive."

They lay on their bunks and enjoyed the slightly cooler air circulating from the corridor. Both were very thirsty but would not leave the cabin to fill their jugs. As the heat of the confined room eased slightly, the boys drifted off to sleep.

Neither heard the first of the long boats draw alongside, and they missed the unloading of many interesting food items.

The boat departed for another load, and its position was taken by a second; then a third long boat came alongside.

The fourth boat contained some returning passengers for the evening. Ruatara and Captain Clark returned to the ship after completing some shopping.

The boys were oblivious to it all and totally unaware of the looming danger they were in.

Chapter 7   Rio de Janeiro
The Ann

$\mathcal{R}$uatara and Captain Clark shook the boys until they woke.

"Oh, thank goodness, I thought you were both dead," Ruatara said shakily as Josh's eyes opened blearily.

Captain Maclaine looked equally concerned from the doorway. He had ensured the convicts below deck had at least the hatches and gun ports open, and the hot tropical air was cooled by the sea breezes blowing overhead. He had been told of other convict ships that had left the hatches closed when in this port, and the convicts had nearly cooked. Although the felons were not permitted on deck, the crew had doused any who wished with buckets full of seawater. The crossbar covers over the hatches meant that the convicts only had to shout, and a bucket of water could be poured over the men below. A spare sail slung over a rope had provided shade on the deck. The heat up there was stifling. Then he remembered that he had ordered the boys to stay in their cabin.

The boys were eventually awake enough to sit up. They could not believe they had missed the returning ships; now they had been caught with their door open. Were they in trouble?

Ruatara had dropped a wrapped parcel at the end of Josh's bed when he found them unresponsive. He said, "It looks like you may not need these after all." He fingered the clean shirt and pointed to Josh's new breeches.

Josh was now more alert. He jumped out of his bunk and onto the cabin floor, an effort that nearly made him pass out. "Sorry, sirs. It was so hot in here earlier that we needed to open the door. We didn't leave except when the lieutenant had us clean the cabins. Honest, sirs!"

Billy was still groggy and trying to sit up.

The guilty look on Josh's face made the captain feel his forehead.

Captain Clark said, "Cor, you two are burning up. You need to cool down and fast."

Josh certainly didn't feel too good. He wobbled where he stood and grasped the wall to steady himself. He would have collapsed had not Ruatara caught him. The chief said, "Quick, get them out on deck now. They have had too much heat. We need to cool their bodies down fast."

The captain called in two soldiers, and soon, the boys were being settled on the deck in the shade. Compared to the temperature in the cabins, the evening breezes were a delight. However, Josh barely made it on deck before he needed to throw up. Having been on the top bunk, he was most affected by the heat. He was thirsty but too lightheaded to stand, and there was nothing left to drink. He just wanted to lie down and die.

Ruatara had not followed them on deck. He had turned and gone to the galley. He took a pitcher and added some cooled, boiled water, squeezed in some lime, a large spoonful of honey, and then half a spoonful of salt. Next, he had Clive bring up three green coconuts from the hold, and he took his large machete, sliced off the tops of two of them, and poured the coconut water into the pitcher to top it up. He took two mugs and carried them upstairs to the boys. Pouring each a full cup, he said, "Drink, but not too fast, or you will get cramps!" The full pitcher was empty in minutes.

Carrying the empty jug, Ruatara returned to the galley again. This time, the pitcher had the same mixture but was sweeter, and he finely diced some ginger and added it as well. When he took this one to the boys, he told them to drink it more slowly.

The boys were feeling much better by the time the second jug was empty.

When the chief was getting the drink, the boys had both been doused with buckets of cool seawater. They sat looking bedraggled in their new but now drenched apparel. They didn't care. Over the next hour, they consumed more fluid and received additional seawater poured over them.

By the time the sun set, they were both feeling much better. Ruatara brought them an unusual, curved yellow thing and told them to eat it. Billy bit into his and cringed. He pulled a face.

Ruatara chuckled and explained, "No, Billy, peel it first. This is a banana." He showed them how to peel the fruit and then watched as they took a bite of the delicious treat.

Josh tentatively nibbled the peeled fruit. Its consistency was like set cold porridge, but the flavour was like honey-sweetened custard. The next bite was larger, and the fruit was easy on his stomach. However, he set it aside for a while before taking another nibble. Nausea washed over him again, and he rested against the bulkhead, feeling the deck move and wishing to sink into oblivion.

Ruatara realised that Josh was still suffering from heat exhaustion and needed to be immersed in the water to cool his entire body. Knowing the boy could not get down a rope ladder to dip in the sea, he asked the captain if they could bring out Mrs Marsden's hip bath. Making sure the good lady was in her quarters and aware of the situation, Josh was stripped completely and assisted into the tub. His overheated body was soon immersed in the cool seawater. Billy had more water poured over him. By the time Clive had prepared the evening meal, the boys were feeling much better.

Neither lad was permitted to do any work that night, and both ate while sitting on the deck. They were unaware of what had been happening around them. Josh had finished his banana whilst still in the bath and ate some seafood *paella* that Clive and the chief had prepared. The spicy fish and rice dish was quick to make and could be cooked in bulk. However, the cook cheated and made it with boiled rice as he had no time to make the *paella* properly.

Billy's stomach roiled at the spices, so Clive gave him a plain rice dish. Josh found that the banana and bath had settled his stomach, and he enjoyed the aroma of the spicy dish. The flavour was divine, and he hoped there would be seconds. There was.

That night, the boys were allowed to sleep on deck under the watch of the night guard. Neither felt Ruatara's hand check their temperature as they slept. The other cabins had their portholes and windows open, but the porthole in the boys' cabin was fixed. With no ventilation, the heat in their room was still overwhelming, even with the door open.

The following morning, before setting off on the day's shore trip, Captain Clark sought out Josh. "Lad, I didn't get to give this to you last night, but I found something that might interest you both." He handed Josh a small cloth-bound parcel tied with a string.

Josh was overwhelmed. "Thank you, sir." He unwrapped the gift and saw not only a slate and some chalk, but also a book. He read the title, *Travels into the Interior of Africa,* by Anthony Sattin. Josh's heart was pumping. He had seen a copy of this in a shop window and had stood gazing at it. "Oh, Captain! Thank you so much. I will have a wonderful time reading this to Billy."

"And me too, Joshua." Ruatara had walked up behind him. "That is, if are you happy to do so?" His eyebrows raised questioningly, as was his habit.

Josh swung around. "Oh, yes, sir, of course!" Josh realised he held not one, but two slates, and a bag full of chalk sticks. He was to become a teacher. He laughed. He had fought hard about learning to read, but his father had insisted. Now, he had reason to think back on those evenings with happiness. Facing the two men who should, by rights, not even know he existed, he grinned. "I'll do my very best, sirs, and thank you ever so much."

The heat in Rio de Janeiro remained constant. The next night, the boys slept on the galley floor. The larger portholes in this area were open, and the evening breeze swept down the corridor past the cabins. Everyone else slept with the cabin doors open. Later that day, new soldiers joined the ship. Their presence caused Josh some distress as they brought news about illness on his mother's vessel.

By the end of the week, new produce had been purchased and loaded onto the wagon. At Ruatara's insistence, huge bunches of green bananas now hung in the storage hold, along with colossal string bags full of green coconuts and wooden boxes full of limes and other citrus fruit. Many other tropical fruits, a large pile of pineapples, and vegetables were added to the menu. Clive purchased the spices from the market at Ruatara's suggestion. The cook had drawn the line at buying mutton birds for the cabin class dinner. He had eaten that before and thought it tasted like rancid oil.

Captain Clark had purchased some piglets, and Clive had despatched one for dinner the following day. The roast suckling pig would be a special meal before leaving port. Ruatara bemoaned the lack of an underground earth oven, which he called a *hangi,* until he sank his teeth into the salt-covered crackling of the roasted pork skin. It crunched delightfully when he bit into it. For once, he agreed that this was an area where the English excelled.

Josh and Billy were back on duty after their heatstroke, so they were no longer confined to their cabin. However, they were only permitted above deck when escorted. As this was no hardship, Josh settled at the mess table and started teaching Billy to write his name.

The week passed quickly, and soon, the ship was readying to set sail on the next leg of their journey. Once the land had faded from view, Ruatara joined the boys at the tables, and they set about their lessons. On rough days, the Marsdens and officers joined them, and after their hour of writing practice, one or other of the men read Josh's new book aloud to all who wished to listen. The beginning of the book listed many foreign words with their meanings, showing that this was not a novel. The journal was the diary of two men and their travels through Africa. With months ahead of them, they teased out the time spent reading, and the listeners would spend equal time discussing the passages they had just heard. The captain produced a map from his cabin, and they followed the route mentioned.

Josh and Billy sat listening, spellbound by the stories. Both were learning, and they were permitted to sit at the table with such learned people.

The soldiers should be guarding them rather than reading them stories.

Billy glanced at his friend. Josh was often seen sitting and listening with a grin on his lips. Billy wiggled with happiness. Being a convict wasn't so bad after all. It was better than living on the streets with nothing.

Reverend Marsden was often seen staring at the lads. He disapproved of his friend conversing with the convict cabin boy. However, his complaints subsided in the weeks that followed. Now, he watched the growing young man with a frown on his brow but remained silent.

Josh knew he was the focus of the dour, rotund minister's attention, but he ignored him, lest he be dismissed and banished to the rabble below. He decided it was best not to poke a bee's nest and left the man to gaze at him at will.

Soon after landing in Rio, Clive, Ruatara, and a team of helpers restocked their fresh supplies and ordered hundreds of green coconuts, limes, and other items their Maori passenger had recommended. Small barrels of blended curry powder were another addition that Ruatara added to the cook's pantry. He had grown fond of this dish on the voyage to England.

When they arrived in Rio de Janeiro, it was to find that the *Hindostan* and *Dromedary* had spent nearly four weeks in the harbour and had left only eight weeks earlier. This was due to a significant outbreak of illness on the troop ship. The two vessels had sailed from Rio only two days before the *Ann* had left Portsmouth. The *Ann* had taken only fifty-six days to traverse the distance.

Before permitting them to board, Captain Clark and the doctor conducted medical checks on the remaining soldiers of the 73rd regiment who had remained in Rio recovering from their sicknesses. They now had to find room on the already overcrowded soldiers' deck.

The majority of the sick *Hindostan* crew and passengers were now fit and well and ready to return to active duty. The *Ann* stayed in port to rearrange the sleeping area and restock before they continued their journey. They purchased a few more goats and some cages of chickens.

On their return from their first day ashore, the captain and doctor were shocked to find the two young lads in a state of severe heat exhaustion. Captain Clark handed over the reassignment of quarters to Captain Maclaine while dealing with the critical case of reviving the cabin boys.

The new soldiers and their families were settled by the time the lads were well enough to return to their work. It wasn't until the day after their incident that they returned to orderly duty in the galley. A third mess sitting was now required to feed the hungry men of the 73rd regiment.

When serving the meals on their third day in port, Josh overheard the men explaining their sickness. He knew his mother and sister had been on the *Hindostan* and was horrified to hear that dysentery had ravaged the vessel.

He had initially panicked until one of the new officers said, "Hey, lad, you said your mother and sister were on board our vessel?"

Josh nodded. "Yes, sir, she told me she was booked on that ship."

The lieutenant who had just boarded said, "Ahh, then I know what occurred, laddie. Is she petite, dark-headed, and very pretty, and has a young girl with her?"

Josh nodded. He had not thought of his mother as very pretty or young, but he supposed she was. She was just his mama.

The lieutenant explained the shuffling of passengers in Portsmouth. "Laddie, Mrs and Miss Callan were moved into a cabin on the new governor's vessel."

Josh sank onto the bench seat in relief. He thanked him and was now greatly relieved that they were safe. However, he was amazed that his mother had been allocated a cabin not far from the new governor's quarters.

The lieutenant had been one of the officers who had assisted in moving their possessions.

Knowing they were safe, Josh went back to work.

Having reshuffled the occupants of the soldiers' deck, the *Ann* set sail again. This time, they were headed to Cape Town in Africa.

Once at sea, the convicts below were released from their shackles and had the run of the lowest deck. The space they previously enjoyed was a thing of the past.

With the extra one hundred soldiers, the convicts were now all confined to the lowest gun deck, and the soldiers entirely filled the upper one. Canvas hammocks had been slung for the extra men and their families.

Evenings were again spent on deck with Ruatara teaching the boys about the stars.

Chapter 8   Cape Town and Beyond
The Dromedary

$\mathcal{T}$he *Dromedary* sailed into the harbour at Cape Town at eleven o'clock in the morning on September 23rd and moored with enough room for the *Hindostan* to anchor nearby when she arrived. Contact had been lost with her sister ship some days before. There must be enough room left for the various vessels to swing with the ebb and rise of the tide. The majestic mountain, aptly named Table Mountain, sat proudly over the wide bay, drawing the eye of all visitors. A special event was planned whilst at this port of call. Mark and Cathy were to be married. Cathy wished Josh could be there, but she did not wish to wait as she was keen to share her bed with a husband again. She missed snuggling to keep warm; sleeping with a ten-year-old daughter was a different experience.

When Mark proposed on the day after the anniversary of James's death, he shared the colonel's conversation, which included the plan for both children to live with them. Then, he dropped to one knee and asked for her hand in marriage. Cathy pulled away from him slightly and said, "You really want us all? For I am a package deal. I am all my children have left."

He replied lovingly. "Yes, Cathy. Take one, take all. I never doubted that for a moment. But I will never replace James. I will be a father figure for them if they wish, but never their Papa. I never expect them to call me that either." She nodded her acceptance, as she was too happy for words. Mark finally drew her into his arms and kissed her. While still holding her, he quietly related Lachlan Macquarie's offer of a position at Government House as part of the governor's security detail. Josh would need to work as a houseboy-cum-groomsman, but he would get to live with his family.

Rather than her expected excitement, Cathy wept on his shoulder. After a few moments of tears, she pulled back a little and shaking her head, she whispered, "Mark, I am not a fit person to live in such an exalted place. You know my past. But I…"

Mark pulled her back into his arms and silenced her with his lips. When he lifted his head, he drew away a little. Keeping her within his arms for her security, he said, "My darling love, if the future governor does not mind, why should we? He knows everything, my sweet, and it was not I who told him. He knew before you came aboard in Portsmouth. His lovely wife has also known from the outset. It will be a new start for us both. Our pasts have been washed clean by God, and the Macquaries will see that society accepts us as well. The children will grow up with a life far removed from the filthy surroundings on the fetid London streets of the Rookery that we knew far too well. And my darling love, I will love them as if they were my own children. As I said, I will never replace James, but I can be there for them and for you." He paused while he kissed her, then added, "God has opened this door for us both; who are we to refuse that?" The chill of the evening began to seep through their clothing. Mark knew their time together was over for that evening, but it was merely the beginning of what was to come.

~

The day after arriving in Cape Town, Mark went shopping and found a lovely diamond ring set in gold. It was not ostentatious, but perfect for Cathy. On return to the ship, Mark once again escorted her to the poop deck. However, this time, it was noon, and kneeling before her, he offered her his heart. She nodded her acceptance again, and he held out his ring of troth. The difference this time was that, as it was daylight, all the crew saw their action. He proposed with nearly all the crew watching from the rigging. Up until then, their engagement was known by few. Cheers erupted from above them when she nodded, making her seek shelter in his arms. Their hug was followed by the cry from above them, "Kiss her, kiss her," which sounded through the masts and rigging. Mark slid his ring onto her finger and did just that.

With no Church of England building in Cape Town, their wedding was held in the minister's residence. On September 26th, they were pronounced husband and wife. They could have been married in the Dutch Church, as an English service was offered there, but that would have meant waiting four more days. They chose the simple service at the rectory.

The Macquaries and Mark's friend, Captain Henry Antill, witnessed the ceremony. Jenny, of course, was included and carried a posy of flowers purchased by Mark from a street hawker on their way to the ceremony.

Mark was given leave for the duration of their stay in Cape Town. Mrs Prichard suggested that Jenny be moved into their son's cabin and share the remainder of the journey with him. The lad's room was a little further down the corridor, and this would give the newlyweds some much-needed privacy.

They saw little of the Macquaries during their stay, as the viceregal couple seemed to be ashore most days and were gone the following morning before the honeymoon couple rose.

Each revealed their entire history to the other, aware that the governor likely knew more about them than he had revealed. They did not wish for any surprises later. Unlike most men, Mark had not sown his seed in his youth, and Cathy took great pleasure in instructing him in the joys of marriage. To say he was delighted was an understatement. He had embarked on this voyage as a single man who stood apart from his lustful and somewhat earthy men. In his youth, the spark of his faith had been sown by a street preacher one dark night in London. Aged only nine, he had just been thrown out of his home in the Rookery. Mark had wondered what life would bring when his father died. Having little option to do otherwise, his mother quickly remarried.

After being thrown out of his home, the preacher had seen him sitting in the gutter shivering, taken him home, dressed him warmly, and fed him. Mark had stayed with him for four years, assisting him while absorbing the man's goodness, care and compassion. He was one of many boys who had found safety at the Reverend Phineas Breckenridge's house. Many were funnelled into the armed forces to give them a proper job off the streets. Mark had worked his way through the ranks and earned many promotions. His position as a captain was due to his dedication to duty.

Mark's stepfather died early last year, so after serving overseas for many years, Mark returned home to be near his mother. His stepfather's death prompted Mark's transfer to a new regiment that would be stationed in London. The move allowed him to see his mother and be near home. It was supposed to be a desk job for a while. He visited his mother shortly before reporting for duty in London. As a parting gift, his now twice-widowed mother had purchased the cologne for him at the market. He had no idea where she had obtained the money, but Mark finally registered that he knew the man she spoke of and realised he was one of the preachers' younger converts. Jimmy arrived at the preacher's home at the time he enlisted. It was only after they married that Mark realised the same preacher had helped both James and him. Cathy and Jenny had taken refuge at the same church after Josh was arrested. He had no idea that the boy he knew as Jimmy was named Callan, as he had never heard it. If Josh looked like the lad he knew as Jimmy, that would confirm it was the same lad he had met as a boy. After planning to remain in London, Mark's mother died suddenly. He transferred into the 73rd Highland Regiment because he had heard it was being deployed overseas, but not to a war zone. He was sick of death and dying. He had never had the lust for war or fighting, but it was all he knew. He didn't mind being enlisted, but wanted to be far from the killing. Lachlan Macquarie had taken him on good faith, so he thought. He had no idea that his background had been well vetted.

Mark and Cathy lay in bed chatting one afternoon shortly before leaving the port. Mark drew her into his arms and said, "God is full of surprises, my love. With our shared stories, I find it incredulous that James and I were taken in by the same preacher who gave us a chance at a new life. Reverend Phineas changed my life in more ways than I can count."

Cathy pulled the sheet up to cover her nakedness and said, "Mark, I have seen God's hand at work often. We knew we would be safe if we remained at the church after Josh was arrested. The old minister was dead, but we were welcomed anyway. I trusted Him, even to this." She traced her finger over the small scar on her cheek that remained from their initial meeting. "This brought us to each other's attention quicker than normal." She turned to cuddle up to her husband's side.

Mark leaned over and kissed her upturned lips. "I can never say I'm sorry enough, my sweet. I have spoiled your beautiful face."

Cathy chuckled. "I am not beautiful except to you and maybe my children. I care not for a pretty face, as it can attract the wrong sort of people."

Mark brushed her hair from her cheek. "You have no idea how lovely you are, my Cathy, but it's not just on the outside. It goes all the way, deep into your heart." He thanked God again for bringing her into his life.

The preacher had taught Mark a great deal during the time he had been with him, and it had set him on a path that made him stand out from his peers. He had accepted the 'King's shilling' as a cabin boy when aged thirteen. His promotions had come through hard work and due diligence. He had received many promotions due to heroic deeds he refused to discuss. Now, he had an instant family and was determined to be an exemplary role model for them all. Cathy was all he could desire in a wife, and in turn, she said more than once that he was the answer to her prayers.

After three weeks in port, the newlyweds settled into their married life.

As the *Dromedary* and *Hindostan* departed Cape Town, the *Ann* was already well on its way there. Only eight weeks now separated the three ships.

~

Sydney

Cathy and Jenny watched their entry into the magnificent harbour before them. The two vessels had skirted the coast in a wide arc and entered from the east. A solid wall of rock and greenery was before them.

It was only three days after Christmas, and the day had been celebrated by eating more of the bland rations. Cathy could hear Mark's voice bellowing orders from up on deck, where she stood.

Today, he was in full regimental dress uniform along with all the rest of the soldiers, and he was preparing his men to return to official duty. They often had drills during the voyage, but today their training would be put into action. Colonel Macquarie kept his men in tip-top condition with his twice-daily inspections. The sleeping quarters of the tightly packed soldiers had been kept immaculate, and therefore, the health of the men and their families had remained good. Of the three hundred and sixty men who travelled with them, only six men were in sickbay with minor injuries rather than illness.

Lachlan had met with Governor Bligh, whose ship, the *Porpoise*, was anchored in the mouth of the Derwent River. He relieved him of duty and assumed command. He had a feeling the previous governor would return to

Sydney before finally departing for London. The man had survived three mutinies to date, and Lachlan wondered if the Admiralty would side with him or Macarthur and Johnston. He huffed in resignation. He wished he knew more of what was ahead of him. Time would tell.

The soldiers had stored their dress uniforms, but now they were unpacked, brushed clean, and ready on the lower deck for the new governor's final inspection. Each man was issued new hats, and they had drilled for their duty over the last few days while wearing their old uniforms. All were waiting in formation for them to be piped into position onto the deck. Once dressed in their finery, the scarlet-coated soldiers would line the ship's railings as it entered the harbour. However, they would not take their places just yet. From out at sea, it looked like they were sailing for a solid rocky wall, but as they drew near, the headlands looked as though they magically parted.

The twin ships' billowing white sails looked magnificent, as did the splash of red of the soldiers, plus the higher-ranking officers in their brighter red jackets and the new governor's blue uniform. The sailors were all in their best white attire, befitting the viceregal passenger.

The men stood equally spaced along the yardarms and spars, right to the top of the crow's nest. Cathy had her arms around Jenny's shoulders, and the other ladies from the cabins were nearby, watching the spectacle.

Elizabeth Macquarie saw Cathy standing off to the side of the other women. She subtly made her way towards them. "Mrs Duffy, I wish to thank you for your companionship during our journey. As you have discovered, the soldiers' wives are not always those you would choose to have as friends. However, I am pleased that you will be close at hand when we both start new, and possibly dangerous lives on this foreign shore. Mrs Jones is a friend to us both, but she is employed, not someone I can freely chat with."

Their eyes fell on the gaggle of rowdy, slovenly-garbed women and children on the main deck below them. The nearly one hundred women and children who had travelled with the soldiers stood clustered near the longboats. They could see little from where they stood. Their cleanliness was wanting, and their body odour wafted to the upper deck.

Cathy didn't know how to reply, so she just said, "Thank you, ma'am."

Other than the governor's wife, the women on the elevated poop deck were Cathy, Mrs Prichard, Mrs Jones, and Mrs Bent. They stood looking at the grey-green foliage of the shrubs on the headlands that they were passing through. On this upper deck, the ladies could stay out of the way and yet enjoy the view of what was happening. It was also where the official welcome would take place.

As the ship sailed through Sydney Heads, the passengers could see that the cliff was made of three distinct promontories. Once their vessel passed between the north and south heads, they saw that a third middle headland was inset, permitting safe passage that opened into a magnificent and mighty bay.

The women gasped in unison at the sight before them.

With gusting light winds behind them, they heard the captain issue the order to drop to half sheets. The winds eased as they entered the harbour, and the remaining sails luffed with the now intermittent puffs. The two sluggish, loaded ships continued their path southwest towards the other anchored vessels further down the harbour.

The rank-and-file soldiers on both ships emerged from below to a fife and drum beat. They took up their positions and lined all the decks except the top one. On the *Dromedary*, the officers, led by Governor Macquarie, mounted the steps and took their places above the helm near the women. Behind him came the senior officers from the regiment. Once Governor Macquarie was in position, the ship's cannons fired a salute from the gun deck below. Jenny jumped.

Mark took his place as close as he could to Cathy and Jenny. He flicked his wife's hand lovingly as he moved behind her. She stepped back from where the viceregal couple stood, bringing her closer to her husband. This was a side of Mark that Cathy had not seen. He looked resplendent in his crisp red dress uniform. More cannons responded from onshore with echoing explosions. Jenny jumped each time and clung to her mother. The cannon fire acknowledged the arrival of its new commanding officer.

Jenny covered her ears with each bang. Mark had earlier explained that the explosions were only cloth-wadding blanks and no cannon balls would be fired, so there was no danger of being hit accidentally onshore by the volley. It was all noise and bluster as a sign of welcome to the new leader. Although Jenny knew this, she jumped at each blast from beneath her feet.

Elizabeth Macquarie expelled a long breath as the last cannon fired. When the cannons started, she had stepped back to permit Lachlan to accept the official welcome alone. Although still one step in front of Cathy, she said over her shoulder, "Now for the official welcomes and speeches. I detest these, and I dare say many more will follow." She sighed and added, "Prepare to remain standing for some time."

All the soldiers remained ramrod straight until the ships were anchored. A crowd was hastily gathering along the foreshore; more were running to every vantage point possible. A long boat was being loaded from shore and was already on its way to greet them. Lachlan turned to his wife and, with a wiggling finger, beckoned her to his side. "Mrs M, ready, dear?" The simple request spoke volumes. They knew that although the journey had taken seven long months, the following days and weeks ahead would be trying. Gone were the mornings spent together writing their journals. Gone was the intimacy of sharing a cabin and being together most days. Gone were the days of pleasant company, but thanks to the paperwork given to him in Rio de Janeiro and then more information gathered in Hobart Town, they knew they were walking into a hornet's nest.

The volley of cannon shots from on shore boded well. As the King's appointed leader, Lachlan Macquarie had yet to wrest power from the usurpers; however, with the knowledge that the two main perpetrators were no longer there, he knew he had some months before they could or would return. Hopefully, it would take some years before their case was heard.

From the moment Lachlan stepped ashore, he would assume power. He would brook no defiance from the militia and free settlers who overthrew Bligh. Governor John Hunter had given him some hints about how to do that, as had Governor Arthur Phillip. Lachlan could transfer any of the troublemaking soldiers to wherever he wished. He planned to send some of the rabble to India.

In the months since Rio, Lachlan spent much time in thought, prayer and discussion with his two captains, Mark and Henry. Neither had been privy to the letters handed to Lachlan in Brazil, but he had willingly sought their ideas on the journey south. In Hobart Town, Bligh had informed him that the locally produced rum was one of the significant issues, as, due to a lack of coinage, alcohol was now the legal currency; the situation would not right itself until enough cash was available. Corruption amongst the military was rife. Lachlan knew that from Admiral Hunter. The liquor was also imported in shipments of huge casks and then decanted into saleable bottles at a ridiculously cheap price. Lachlan had fallen silent for a while when issuing instructions to his captains. If he had known of this before departure from England's shores, he could have requested coins to be supplied. He could not wait nearly two years before finding a solution to that immediate problem. Hindsight was always twenty-twenty, but this was something he needed to get his head around. But how?

A few times on the journey, various foreign ships were seen. Captains Prichard and Pasco had managed to commandeer one enemy vessel and plunder their spoil. That single act gave Lachlan an idea, but as yet, he had no way of putting it into action, as stolen coins would not do for legal currency. He needed to keep everything above board. He would try to purchase some large coins and use those. Maybe he could source some in Batavia. The thought tickled his fancy, and he smiled at how the Sydney Corps would react when they found that their source of income would be outlawed. He knew from the reports that John Macarthur and his cronies would not welcome any idea that seized power from the free settlers. Thankfully, Macarthur was currently not here. Macarthur would get a big surprise when he returned, as things here would be dramatically changed from when he departed.

Paterson was the New South Wales Corps' senior ranking officer, and Lachlan expected him to be a puppet at their beck and call. Would he be?

Lachlan knew that his authority would not be welcomed. He was glad that Mesdames Jones, Duffy and Bent would be near his wife, Mrs M., as he affectionately called Elspeth in public, over this transition period. His affection for his cousin had grown over their confined time together. He still missed his beloved Jane, but Elspeth was dear to him. They had drawn closer over the loss of their tiny daughter, also named Jane, shortly before their departure. He had enjoyed sharing a cabin with his wife more than he would admit, and she had been willing to share his bed each night, where she was attentive to his needs and desires. His gaze rested on her as she now stood beside him. He smiled as their eyes met. He leaned towards her and whispered, "I shall miss the quiet times we had together on board, Elspeth. I fear the weeks and months ahead may well test our faith and patience."

Elizabeth was a little shaken by his admission. He rarely displayed emotion, let alone showed affection in public. His softened facial expression was followed by a slightly crooked smile that she had come to love dearly. He saw her shock. He said, "I mean it, my dear Elspeth. You are a wonderful travelling companion and helpmate."

Standing at his side, she whispered, "Thank you, Lachy," in reply.

He straightened, drew and released a long breath, then uttered, "Ready to face the music, Mrs M?"

"No, Mr M, but for you, I will do my best." Looking forward, she mentally prepared herself to take on a new role.

He chuckled. "You always do, my dear; you always do! And what's more, you do it well."

Cathy saw the new governor flick Elizabeth's hand affectionately, much as Mark had just done to her. She smiled, knowing the affection shared by both couples was genuine.

The vice regal couple could have no further conversation as the official party now climbed the steps towards them. For a moment, they hooked little fingers before the first of the welcoming committee topped the gunnels.

Elizabeth took a small half-step backwards and let Lachlan Macquarie assume the role he had been sent here for. He would make an outstanding governor. She wondered how she would fill her time and what her role would be. She was determined to find a position for herself. With no child to fill her arms and heart, Elizabeth needed to find something to throw herself into.

She stood and watched as her husband was officially welcomed, and then, at his call, she stepped forward to be introduced. A puff of wind blew her curls into her eyes, and the action of moving them looked like a salute.

The greeting officers were surprised but returned the action. That honour, given in innocence, sealed her position of respect.

The officers stepped aside to permit the Macquaries to leave the deck; a cheer sounded from above. As the masts and rigging were lined with the one-hundred-plus crew, without waiting for the captain's permission, they called for three cheers for the new governor of the colony. The soldiers around the decks of their ship and the *Hindostan*, which was anchored within earshot, joined in the joyful shouts and hurrahs.

The visiting officials looked at each other askance, wondering what this thin, middle-aged, greying Scottish soldier could do to bring the rabble on shore into line. Many of the 73rd regiment he had brought with him were from the highlands of his beloved Scotland. Their reputation preceded them, and the visiting military knew they had met their match. They all doubted anything could be done to resurrect the filthy town besides a good fire, but perhaps this Scotsman could do it after all.

~

Transitioning from the ship's cramped quarters to the rickety Government House in Sydney Cove took some adjustment. The bulk of the unpacking was left to Robert Fopp, Mrs Jones, Cathy and Jenny as Mark had to escort the new governor on his official duties.

Elizabeth accompanied her husband wherever and whenever possible.

The official swearing-in ceremony occurred two days after disembarking. On New Year's Day, 1810, Lachlan Macquarie officially assumed the position of Governor of New South Wales. It was about a month shy of two years since the *coup d'état* ousting Governor Bligh in what was being called the Rum Rebellion.

Cathy was permitted to watch the signing of the documentation.

Jenny remained at the house and was delighted to spend time in the kitchen with Mrs Ovens. Robert Fopp and Mrs Jones occupied their time unpacking and repairing the Macquaries' clothing that had been stored for so many months in the hold of the vessel. Many items had gone mouldy, and all needed washing, ironing and repair.

Cathy had offered her assistance, and it was readily accepted. Any mould spots on the first lady's gowns were quickly embroidered over and embellished with flowers. The revived gowns looked magnificent.

~

Cathy waited until Mark's position had consolidated before she told him her big news. It had been over three months since Mark and Cathy's wedding ceremony in Cape Town. On retiring to their room that night, Mark quietly closed the door, and Cathy knew what he wanted. She peeled off his uniform coat and hung it ready for use the next day, but did not attempt to remove her own clothing. "Mark, my darling husband, it's been a long day."

He looked down at the lovely, fully-clad woman in his arms. "Yes, darling wife, it has been, but now it is time for bed." He started to unbutton her gown, but he stopped when she pulled away slightly.

She gave him a coy glance. "Mark, there is one topic that we have not discussed. I fully meant to after we wed, but it soon became obvious that it would not be necessary for some time." She lifted her lips for a kiss.

After a few minutes, he asked, "And that is...?"

Cathy blushed. "...that is, a woman normally has a blood flow each month unless..." She hid her head on his shoulder.

Mark pushed her away a little. His face reflected the anguish that flooded over him. He knew she had been sick a few times over the last week. "Cathy, darling love, unless what? Are you unwell?"

When she lifted her face from his chest, the glowing look on her face belied his worry. She finished her previous sentence, "…Unless there is a reason for the flow not to come. Since our marriage in September, my monthly flow has been absent." Mark's face showed that he had no idea what she was talking about. Cathy lifted her hand to his cheek to pull him close. "Mark, I am trying to say I am carrying your child. You will have your own babe in arms in late June."

Mark was stunned. It took him a few seconds to register the impact of her words. "You're in the family way? Really? We are going to be parents ourselves?" Then his face fell, as he wondered if it meant they could not be intimately together. She noted his expression of mixed delight and disappointment. He pushed her away and reached for his shirt again.

She took it from him. "Mark, you darling man, it doesn't mean we can't enjoy ourselves. However, we must be more careful as I grow larger."

Mark finally found the words to express his delight. "Cathy, my darling love, I shall do nothing to endanger you both. Are you sure it is safe for our enjoyable activities to continue?"

She nodded, then grinned saucily. "Absolutely, husband mine. In fact, my desires will need to be sated more often until the babe is born, so you must be aware of that. After the birth, I will need to recover. We must abstain for six weeks. So be warned. We may need to make up for that time now."

His linen shirt was shed and dropped to the floor, and he was already unbuttoning her gown. The bulk of her attire quickly followed. He groaned with delight. "I am at your command, my love." With her clothing removed, he lifted her and gently placed her on their bed. He caressed her cheek before saying. "I thank God for you in my prayers daily, my darling Cathy. You have made my life complete." His finger traced over the small scar that remained on her cheek. He bent and gave her a long kiss. "I have a confession to make, my sweet. The day we met, I was distracted and wondered how the Lord could find me a wife when I would be on a ship for months, being sent to the ends of the earth. It's why I was not concentrating on what could be in front of me."

She drew him down for another kiss.

Not to be silenced, he said, "When I saw that my carelessness had drawn blood, oh my darling love, I was gutted. My heart nearly stopped when Jenny hugged me and told me about my cologne and that you had made it for your husband. Cathy, I had rarely seen my mother since I was nine. For her to purchase a gift for me was extraordinary. To choose this particular cologne, I feel that God was preparing the way for us even before James passed away. I will honour his name all my days."

Cathy nodded and pulled him down to her, murmuring her returned love for him. She added, "AS you like it, then I shall keep making it for you, my beloved."

Chapter 9   Life Lessons
The Ann

*R*everend Marsden sat and listened to the Maori chief's words. He wondered about this strange man whom he had met in London, and he was intrigued that he would take notice of two convict lads. After listening to them chat, he waited out of sight until the boys left and went to bed.

As Ruatara descended from the poop deck, Marsden challenged him. "Chief, why bother with the convict boys? Why them and not the sailors or the soldiers we are travelling with? Why not me?" The minister stood with his arms folded and a flush defused his cheeks.

Rather than be offended, the Maori chief laughed. "Reverend, you teach your flock from written stories of many years ago. These two boys were convicted of theft. In my land, possessions are shared by all, except the chieftain's robes of honour, so we have no such crime of theft. Therefore, for me, they have done no wrong. We have no written words, so we teach our young with stories, told around a fire. Our ancestors' stories are passed down to the young until they are well enough known to be taught to the next generation. We listen to them retelling and correcting them so the stories are unchanged. Your tales in the bible were once told in this way. It would have been many years before the storytellers could write and then record the written words."

Marsden nodded. "Go on."

Ruatara gave him an understanding smile, then continued. "As to the study of the night skies, the stars above are our friends and our guides. They are constant, although at different heights in the sky as we travel across the seas. They are as unchanging as your Bible stories. Even the wise men, whom you told me came to find the baby Jesus, used the stars at night to find their way. This knowledge could one day keep the lads alive."

Marsden understood that but asked, "Why the convict boys?"

Again, the big Maori laughed, and with a shrug, he said, "The young will listen and remember. The older men think they already know everything and are unprepared to learn more. You have your knowledge and I have mine."

Marsden huffed somewhat angrily, then said, "You are elevating those two above their status. Thankfully, they are young enough not to cause trouble."

Ruatara heard the hesitation in his rescuer's voice. He gave a respectful bow before saying, "Mr Marsden, you rescued me in a foreign land. I learned a great deal in my short time there, but learning never truly stops. In my culture, one is not considered wise until one's hair is grey. The greying hair indicates wisdom or age, but even then, learning does not stop. I will teach what I know to whoever will listen. Here, on this ship, only these two lads are willing to learn what I was taught when I was younger than they are. Young Joshua is also teaching me to read your language."

Marsden knew that and was still not impressed.

Ruatara gave a snort of laughter. "I have discovered that speaking English is much easier than reading it."

Marsden nodded.

The chief chuckled again.

Without waiting for Marsden to reply, he put a hand on the minister's shoulder and said, "Goodnight, friend. As you say, the stars are safe in the heavens, and it's time for me to sleep."

Marsden watched him walk away, but a seed was sewn. The minister remained on deck, looking heavenward and wondering about the wisdom of this tattooed man he had rescued.

The clinking of the ropes in the rigging and the drop in temperature eventually sent him back to his stuffy cabin. If the convict boys could teach the Maori chief to read, then so could missionaries. A slow smile settled on his lips.

~

Captain Clark decided not to journey so far south for the final leg of the voyage. Although the southern route was shorter, the seas and weather were atrocious.

Taking the direct passage east may take longer, but the convicts had little protection against the vicious cold and horrendous seas. He was going to make sure they arrived in good health.

The winds were right, and the seas were kind, so the *Ann* ploughed ever eastwards.

Every evening possible, Josh, Billy and Ruatara sat on deck after dark and learned the stars and how to navigate from them. Having realised what the boys were being taught about celestial navigation, many sailors sat within earshot and listened.

Ruatara taught them how to feel the current of the water with their fingers and how to read the night sky.

Albatrosses joined them occasionally. The Maori man refused to allow anyone to harm the majestic birds. The wisdom of the Maori chief was absorbed by many.

Reverend Marsden often stood out of sight on the lower quarterdeck, but he was avidly listening to the stories of the ages being taught to the young. It set him thinking that if he could capture the chief's interest in his thirst for farming knowledge, as well as the Bible, then perhaps he could also arrange for some farm-experienced missionaries to return with the man to his homeland. They could teach them not only to farm crops but also to share the Gospel with them.

Those on board were already showing some interest, and he hoped to nurture that. Another smile settled on the rotund preacher's lips. A fertile field was indeed before him. He had already spoken to the three men he was travelling with. He had been pleased that three missionaries had accepted his invitation to traverse the globe for God's work. Reverend Robert Cartwright and family, William Hall, a missionary and shipbuilder, and lastly, John King, a flax weaver.

They all expressed their interest in working with Ruatara in his homeland and initiating missionary work there, rather than in the colony of New South Wales. Now – the chief had to be persuaded to permit them to come. Would he have the authority to give such permission? Marsden didn't know.

The *Ann* reached Cape Town in December, where it stayed only to resupply. The *Ann* was on her way again as the *Dromedary* and *Hindostan* were leaving Hobart Town and making their way north.

~

By Christmas, the *Ann* had reached the western coast of the great southland. They traversed the southern ocean, staying well clear of the overpowering cliffs of the bight.

Then they turned south to a new settlement, Hobart Town, on the banks of the Derwent River in Van Diemen's Land. They arrived in the infant settlement in late January and again restocked with water and fresh produce.

There was a delay in leaving the island, first due to a storm and then because of a lack of wind.

In the Derwent River, they were becalmed for over a week.

The heat was again stifling below decks as the January sun bore down upon the ship.

A shade sail was again erected over a rope between the masts to give shade to those below decks. All the cabin passengers sought relief under the canvas's scant protection.

Sharks were seen attacking the effluent and rubbish tossed overboard, so no one was willing to swim.

In the heat of summer in Hobart Town, Josh and Billy were again sleeping on the floor of the mess room near the galley. Some nights, they were even permitted to sleep outdoors on the poop deck with Ruatara between them. This occurred because, on a particularly hot evening, the boys had fallen asleep during their lessons. They remained blissfully unaware that they were breaking a plethora of rules made by the Navy.

The two lads had shown themselves to be trustworthy, and after the experience in Rio de Janeiro, Captain Maclaine had soldiers check on them during their nightly rounds.

~

Eventually, the *Ann* made it out of the river and back into the ocean. The transport ship wended its way northward.

By mid-February, the vessel was only days away from reaching its destination.

Chapter 10 Sydney Cove
1810

$\mathcal{A}$s John Hunter had warned Lachlan, Government House in Sydney leaked like a stricken vessel. Governor Macquarie quickly relocated his entire household to Parramatta, settling into the relatively new two-storey house on the hill that John Hunter had built when governor. It was on the hill above the old military redoubt. Sadly, he had only lived in his new house for a short while before being recalled to England.

Lachlan intended to have the roof re-shingled in Sydney as soon as they moved, knowing they would need to spend time in town quite often. This double-storey building had been erected in the year the colony was founded. For it to still be standing twenty-two years later was amazing. Lachlan had read John's journals to learn about what he would find when he arrived. John had been the captain of the *Sirius* in 1788, but had returned as the second governor in 1795, three years after Arthur Phillip departed.. John knew the workings of the colony far better than even Admiralty House, as he had friends still living in the settlement. Crispin Milroy had been his personal security guard, much like Mark was for him. Crispin's father-in-law, Linus Rosedale, was one of the gardeners John brought to the colony to teach others how to till the land. Both men wrote with every returning ship and provided John with detailed information about the state of affairs. It was through reading these letters that Lachlan gained insight into what to expect on his arrival and how to approach some of the problems.

The Parramatta house was smaller, but as they had no children, they managed well indeed. They preferred this residence to the one in Sydney, and Elizabeth quickly managed to persuade Lachlan to make Parramatta his permanent headquarters. It had some staff quarters at the back, and this left the house to the official family, the Duffys, and Mrs Ovens.

Lachlan's office was just inside the front door, and the reception rooms were nearby. The viceregal couple occupied the master bedroom upstairs. It contained a lovely four-post bed that was surrounded by brocade drapes. The room was decorated in solid dark timber and had lime-washed white walls.

As a married couple, Mark and Cathy were given a small room on the lower floor at the opposite end of the building, and Jenny was in a small servant's alcove nearby. Mrs Jones and Mr Jarvis occupied small servants' rooms on the ground floor below their employers, and Mrs Ovens was in a small room off the kitchen. Robert Fopp had his own tiny butler's room. One of the maids and the convict housekeeper, Jemima Fisher, was outside near Henry Antill's rooms. Joseph Bigg, the coachman, had a small room in the coach house. The resident security guard, Sergeant Charles Whalan, and his wife, Elizabeth, were both former convicts whom Governor King had employed, and they were also located in the staff rooms outside.

Elizabeth Whalan worked as a maid at Government House while Sergeant Whalan was quickly appointed to the position of Sergeant of Lachlan's Bodyguard of Light Horse, on Governor King's recommendation. Even Governor Bligh spoke highly of this man.

Mark, Henry, and Charles were to rotate security duty for Lachlan.

On viewing the house, Elizabeth Macquarie claimed the front upstairs room for her retiring room. This room had a delightful aspect over the town and two fireplaces, making it snug in winter. However, as it was currently the height of summer, the temperature outside was woefully hot, and the English gowns they had arrived in were soon abandoned for the lighter fabrics that were much cooler.

Cathy had made new gowns for both herself and Elizabeth from some Indian muslin that they had purchased in Cape Town.

Now that Mark had been told about the baby, Cathy revealed her condition to Elizabeth soon after they moved to Parramatta.

A look of sadness flitted across Elizabeth's face before a somewhat forced smile replaced it.

Cathy was concerned. "Ma'am, are you not well?"

Mrs Jones was walking down the wide staircase. Elizabeth beckoned for Cathy to follow her, and she closed the door of her retiring room before answering. "I am delighted for you both. Don't mind me; I had already suspected your condition and had hoped to be able to tell you we were due together." Her face melted in grief. Tears overflowed as she hiccoughed, "I lost my baby this morning, Cathy. I should be abed, but I'm all too used to this."

Elisabeth all but collapsed into Cathy's arms.

Cathy was distraught on behalf of the governor's wife. She also knew the trauma of losing a child at a few months along.

After they had lost their second baby, Cathy miscarried again only months later. She wept and laughed and wept again in quick succession. Her emotional state was shot to pieces, and her concentration was zero. Josh had been her sanity and saving grace. He was such a loving child that he would hug her. Even as a toddler, he would do what he could to assist her around their small rooms. Cathy knew the benefit of such hugs and enfolded the weeping lady in her loving arms. Elizabeth had no child to cradle.

~

The Ann

Eight weeks after the arrival of the Macquaries, the *Ann* entered the majestic harbour.

No guns welcomed this ship, but a flag had been raised on the south headland as soon as she was sighted, even before she entered the heads. The flags she carried indicated that she was transporting male convicts. This simple system gave the governor and soldiers a few hours' warning.

As the *Ann* drew closer to shore, Ruatara stood on the quarterdeck with the boys on either side of him. Having sailed into this bay several times over the years, he knew the beauty of the harbour entrance. He wanted the boys to experience the sight as it was one they would never forget. They would probably never be on a ship to see this sight again.

Once through the majestic heads, Captains Clark and Maclaine told them to stay out of sight once they drew near to the town. After entering the majestic heads, they shinnied down the various ladders to the main deck. Here, they stood close to the hatch that led down to their cabin, but they could still see the town as it drew closer.

Captain Clark said, "As soon as you see the crew at the capstan, *vamoose*, boys."

The boys looked at each other and then at their captain.

Josh asked, "Sorry, sir, but what does that mean?"

The captain gave a croak of laughter. "It's a Spanish slang term for 'Run as fast as you can.' Savvy?"

"Will do, sir." Josh grinned. Since their illness in Rio de Janeiro, the boys had been treated as if they were free. "May I say thank you on behalf of us both?"

The captain smiled. "You have both proved your worth, lad. I shall add a note to your files and hope you get a good placement."

Josh's gaze met Ruatara's, and he saw them both grin.

The captain saw their action and said, "Speak up, lad; I'm guessing you have something planned?"

Josh took a deep breath and stood at attention. He replied, "I hope so, sir, but I am unsure. My mama and sister should be here already, and she said that she would try to get me assigned to her. So, sir, can you give Billy a recommendation? Chief Ruatara asked if Billy could stay with him for a while so they could continue their reading lessons. Reverend Marsden made that suggestion as the chief will live at the Parramatta Rectory with them. Billy would take over the chief's care."

Captain Maclaine chuckled. "You have it all worked out, don't you, chief?"

Ruatara smiled. "Having a friendly face in a foreign port would be nice. I had a bit of a rough time on my last visit, Captain, so I could use a companion if nothing else. Billy and I can stick together. I can show him around; what is more, he's too weedy for the chain gang."

The red-coated soldier flicked his eyes over both boys. They would soon change into their clean clothing and pack their belongings. "I'll see what I can do for you both, but I will promise nothing. Arrangements may have already been made. I'm not sure how they allocate young convict lads, but you may have to be locked up with the general population for a while."

An expression of melancholy flashed across all three faces.

A frown creased the captain's face. "Oh, blast you all; yes, I'll see what I can do." The captain turned his back on them so they didn't see him grin. He had already written glowing reports for both lads but didn't want them to know — yet.

As the last sail was lowered, the ship slowed, and the anchor was dropped. It pivoted around as the flukes on the anchor arms bit into the sea floor.

The *Ann* sat well out from the shore as they would need permission to land anyone. They also needed a doctor to come on board to ensure the vessel carried no diseases.

Both captains waved for the boys to vanish.

They did, as they realised they could continue to watch from their cabin porthole. They watched as a long boat was being loaded with a group of waiting men on the shore, and kept their eyes glued on it as it pulled alongside.

The heat below was building again, and Ruatara came to check on them. He brought jugs of water and told them to open the cabin door.

The hatches on deck were opened for the felons below.

The boys caught a glimpse of the rope ladder being thrown to the side of the boat. Although they could not see the ladder being climbed, they saw the soldiers in the all-but-empty boat as they sat waiting in the hot sun. The soldiers were obviously hot as they dipped their hands in the water and daubed their faces.

The February heat grew throughout the day, and the tiny cabin was like an oven again. The galley was cool compared to their cabin, but even after their last experience, the boys dared to leave their cabin only when instructed to do so. Captain Maclaine came in and sent the boys to help cook a meal for everyone. They followed his instructions willingly.

The convicts were served a spicy stew made from pickled pork and dried peas. This dish had become regular fare, and with the cook's assistance, they had sourced a range of herbs and spices at the stops, which varied the otherwise bland food.

Billy had watched, tasted, and learned. He had a light hand when it came to bread, and he had learned to capture and make wild sourdough yeast.

Therefore, his bread was delicious. For a boy who had never had enough food, he was a fast learner. No one had even realised that when the chef had fallen ill twice on the journey out, Billy had just taken over and produced a meal that was better than his mentor's fare. Even the two captains sent their compliments, only to discover that Billy had cooked their meal. Billy had taken delight in the presentation of his food. Not so much for the convict slop, although even that was tasty, but for the captain's meals. The food was always well-presented on their plates, unless they were in a storm. Then, everything he made was non-spillable and could be stuffed in pockets and eaten at their convenience. Billy's hardtack ginger biscuits were also delicious.

Ruatara had introduced ginger rhizomes to the galley, and he said this spice also helped settle an upset stomach.

The cook had shown Billy how to grate and dry the spice. No one complained about the tasty treats; they were eaten by choice more than necessity.

Ruatara's culinary tastes meant that more curry was added to the menu. Chilli dishes were a favourite.

Knowing that this would likely be one of the last meals the boys would help prepare, they dug out the last of the special rations they had set aside for a special occasion.

The stew they made for this final meal was a tuna stew, but it was cooked as a ginger curry and served with brown rice.

Billy had heard how Ruatara made soup from the skeletons of the giant fish, and he had made a large vat of tuna stock. They added chunks of pan-fried diced tuna, and the sauce was thickened with a product Ruatara had introduced to them. It was tapioca starch purchased in Rio, and they had eaten it in various forms, including as a filling for a coconut pie. Today, the curried tuna was thick and creamy.

They caught three monster tuna shortly before turning towards the shore. Again, Ruatara played a crucial role in their capture. The chief had purchased some shells and a few shark teeth in Cape Town and had shown the sailors and both boys how to make fish hooks that would attract fish without requiring bait. He had chipped and polished the inside spirals of the shells and added a shark's tooth as the barb. He made a strong thread using the long hair of various crew members and some soldiers.

This thread was far more robust but finer than the braid rope they had used for trolling. He had also made a thick rope-like line using the coconut husk fibres.

The shell hook was successful, and every other day, fish of some sort was added to the menu. The coconuts were long gone, but the limes had been eked out and were used to flavour the otherwise bland food. Billy assisted whenever he could. Even the lime skins were dried and powdered for added flavour.

Now they had arrived at their destination, the long boat the boys had seen had brought out the Chief Surgeon, D'Arcy Wentworth, Major Gilmore, who was in charge of convicts, and other officials.

The ship's doctor, George Martin, presented his log, and D'Arcy Wentworth pored over it, nodding approval. "So, no illness on board?"

George was pleased that his ship had remained in good health. "No, sir, none. No signs of scurvy either, thanks to one of our passengers." He didn't elaborate, but was sure he would be questioned further. The delicious smells wafting from below were not unpleasant, as was expected on a convict ship. George's mouth was watering as he knew what was for luncheon.

The brows of the Chief Surgeon from Sydney knitted together. "Ho, and how so, Martin? And what is that delicious smell? It smells suspiciously like curry."

George nodded and explained the presence of the Maori and his recipes, which included limes. Since the discovery of citrus juice to stop the sailor's curse of the bleeding disease, the difficulty had been getting the lower-class sailors and convicts to consume it. "I believe from that smell, we have tuna curry for luncheon today, sir."

He grinned and watched as the chief surgeon perused the log as he listened. George continued, saying, "As I said, we have an unusual passenger, a Maori chief. He made our journey far more pleasant, as you can smell."

D'Arcy paused when he heard that comment, but quickly returned to the paperwork. He finally gave the ship a clean bill of health. "You can disembark when the major gives the all clear." When he stood to leave the sick bay, he asked, "Who is this chief?" He had met one a few years before and liked him.

George said, "Chief Ruatara, sir. Reverend Marsden came across him in London and paid his fare to return here."

D'Arcy smiled, then chuckled. "He's a strange but fascinating fellow, that one. I met him some years ago when he lived here. I questioned him about his tattoos, and he mentioned that they sometimes use lime juice on the ones on the limbs and torso, but not on the facial markings. They are called the *Mataora;* only the men get the full-face ones. Women have their lower lips and chins marked in such a way. The lime juice is used on the face only if there are infections."

George nodded. He, too, had questioned the chief about the technique used. He found they were stained with ground-up charcoal and used a small shell chisel to cut the skin.

By the time they had finished chatting, they had reached the deck. D'Arcy's mouth was watering from the delicious aroma from below decks. He had never had that experience on a convict ship before.

Major Gilmore was waiting for their return. "Doctor, I believe that a lad named Callan is below. I'm to take him back with me. He's been assigned to Captain Duffy."

The captains, the doctor, and Ruatara, who had just joined them, looked in shock.

The major saw the exchange of glances. "Is there a problem? Has he been confined in chains or something due to bad behaviour?"

Captain Maclaine replied, "No, sir, just the opposite. Josh and a lad named Billy Green have been exemplary. They were assigned as cabin boys and served as attendants to the passengers in the cabins. Both have recommendations in their records. I believe they are the cause of the delicious smells from below."

The major frowned. "Then what's the problem?"

Ruatara stepped forward. "Major, Josh Callan is hoping to be assigned to his mother. He served as my cabin boy for the entire journey ard taught me to read a little. He's a good lad."

The major grinned. "Ahh, yes, well, I should explain that his mother has recently married. Her new name is Duffy. Her husband is a captain in our new governor's security detail." He saw the four faces relax, and all showed relief. "I gather from your collective reaction that he has behaved?"

The four heads showed various affirmative replies.

The major chuckled. "So, he'll fit into Government House then?"

Ruatara spoke up again. "He will, sir. He will pull his weight and do what is required." He would miss his student and friend, but he hoped to see him around town.

Reverend and Mrs Marsden arrived on deck and overheard the conversation. "As far as convicts go, the boy has caused no problems. I believe there was an incident in Rio de Janeiro, but that was not avoidable."

Major Gilmore turned to Captain Maclaine, his brows knitted in concern. "Explain, please, sir."

The military captain gave the minister a filthy look. "Josh and the other lad, Billy, were told to remain in their cabin while in port. They did, and both ended up with heatstroke due to no fault of their own. They did nothing wrong and obeyed the rules above and beyond their safety."

The various men glared at the minister.

The ship's captain continued, "It was my fault, sir, as I ordered them to remain in their cabin. They would probably both be dead if they had not opened the door."

D'Arcy Wentworth butted in. "Heat stroke? What happened? How did you revive them?" He was fully aware of the dangers associated with this condition.

Marsden grunted, and without waiting for his answer, he escorted his wife away and moved to the gunnels to await assistance to disembark.

They would descend in a chair rather than the indignity of climbing down a rope ladder.

A situation had undoubtedly occurred, but both lads had gained the trust of these four men. Five pairs of eyes watch the Marsdens depart.

Reverend Marsden seemed to oppose any person of low

socioeconomic status who had a criminal record. It did not matter how minor, but he drew a solid line between convict and free. The other clergy on board were not so petty.

The Cartwrights arrived on deck and waved their farewells. This family had decided to move to Ruatara's land if permitted.

Knowing the power this man wielded in the colony, they remained mute.

Once Marsden was far enough away, Captain Clark filled the surgeon and the major in on the whole situation.

Neither man was surprised at the minister's words, but both remained silent while he was within earshot.

However, the minister's omission of the entire story appeared as though a felony had occurred rather than an accident. Both captains had discussed rumours of Bligh's strict laws when he was at sea. Captain Clark mentioned Bligh's practice of writing "Not drunk today" next to one or other of the crew's names in his ship's log. However, Clark knew for a fact that one man who received such treatment was a teetotaller. His friend was never drunk. The innuendo stuck, and the sailor had not received a well-deserved promotion. He said, "Don't get me started on the injustices of half-truths."

Major Gilmore nodded in understanding. He knew Marsden's nickname was 'the Flogging Parson' as he disliked convicts in any way, shape, or form.

Ruatara left to get Josh.

As the visiting doctor saw the minister was now on the ship's far side, D'Arcy quietly said, "I understand, and let me assure you, he is known for his dislike of felons." D'Arcy Wentworth swallowed nervously. If only Marsden knew why he was in the colony. Thrice, he had been charged with highway robbery; twice, he was found not guilty, and the third time, the case was acquitted due to lack of evidence. He left the country, volunteering as a doctor for the colony before they could change their mind. He was the father of many illegitimate children to three women and quickly became the new governor's close friend. He sided with the emancipists rather than the free settlers, which was enough to get the reverend on the wrong side.

D'Arcy was close friends with Simeon Lord and Andrew Thompson and encouraged the new governor to give the freed convicts a chance to improve themselves. He was hoping that the knowledge of Marsden's appointment as one of three men chosen to oversee the roads trust would not be to his liking. If the reverend objected to Governor Macquarie's proposed idea, he would put his name forward to work with his friends. However, today, he chose to remain silent. He nodded his agreement. His blue eyes sparkled with unuttered mirth. He had been a rebel in his youth, and little had changed. His cousin, an earl, had spoken on his behalf in court and then advised him to behave. Now, his position of authority was consolidating under the new governor's auspices.

The pair had met numerous times to discuss the filthy town's future direction. As a medical man, he had sown the seed of a new hospital in Sydney. The small building in Parramatta was inadequate, but the main town needed a permanent, fully equipped facility. Two new buildings were already planned, but they needed a proper architect.

Ruatara brought Josh to the major. He sent Billy to wait in his own cabin, but had yet to tell either of them why. Ruatara had opened his porthole before he went on deck. Therefore, his room was much cooler than the boys' minute cabin.

At the chief's instruction, Josh hastily gathered his scant possessions and followed his tutor.

The small group of men parted as Josh arrived with the chief.

The major saw a gangly young man stand quietly by the chief's side. His breeches were too large, but he was clean and well-groomed. He certainly did not appear to be a convict.

The major spoke with a stern tone. "Into the boat with you, lad; you've been assigned."

Josh didn't quibble. He walked to the opening in the railing and was about to drop his bundle down into the boat when he returned to thank Ruatara. He offered his hand to shake, but was drawn into a warm embrace. Once released, he bowed to the other men he had served. He had voiced his thanks earlier and departed with no further comment.

Captain Clark watched his head disappear from view and said, "I'll miss that lad."

The major overheard and smiled before he followed the lad's exit.

~

Word had filtered through town that a ship had been sighted and was due to berth that day.

Knowing the *Ann* was expected, Captain Duffy brought Cathy and Jenny to Sydney a few days earlier, as the viceregal couple had various functions to attend while there.

When the notification came of a vessel's arrival, Cathy and Jenny wandered down to the waterfront and were informed by a military friend of Mark's that it was indeed Josh's ship.

The governor had ensured Josh was pre-assigned to Mark and would, therefore, live with them at the official residence. Hopefully, the boy had behaved himself and was not ill.

As Cathy was now five months gone with child, she tried to walk every day she could. A soldier hovered nearby for their security.

Her appearance on the waterfront with her daughter was not unusual. She did this whenever she was in town. However, today, she had another purpose. She knew this was the ship her son was supposed to be on.

Cathy and Jenny walked past the hive of activity at the cove and meandered to a seat a little further around the bay.

After some time, Jenny pointed out that the longboat had pulled away from the ship, and they stood to walk and meet it.

The distance was too far to recognise the faces, but no short lads were on board. They dawdled towards the approaching boat, and Cathy watched it draw close. She wondered how long it would take for Josh's paperwork to be processed.

Jenny was almost bouncing with excitement. "Mama, do you think I'll remember him? It's been so long since I've seen him."

Cathy heard the long boat scraping against the jetty and saw a rotund man and a woman being assisted from the longboat. Another female passenger was handed ashore, followed by another man. Then her breathing quickened. Had she caught a glimpse of Josh in the boat? Surely not! Why? Was he in trouble?

Although they were here in Sydney for this very moment, she found it difficult to believe. They were to be reunited.

The heat was sapping, and her nerves made her feel lightheaded.

Cathy and Jenny stopped walking and watched the remainder of the passengers alight from the rocking long boat.

Jenny gasped and was instantly gone from her mother's side.

Cathy didn't have time to stop her, but she watched her daughter run along the waterfront and catapult into the arms of a gangly youth.

The youth dropped a small bundle when he recognised his sister. His arms were out wide to receive her. He welcomed her with a laugh and held her close, telling her of his love.

It had been nearly a year since Cathy had seen her son, and Josh had shot up in that time. She would have run to him herself but for her baby.

She picked up her pace and soon had her son in her arms. He had grown so much that he was now taller than her.

As he gathered his mother into a group hug, Josh had time to say, "We did it, Mama; we made it!" before his tears choked him up.

All Cathy could do was nod.

The three wept with delight.

Chapter 11 Fresh New Start
New South Wales

$\mathcal{A}$ bright-red-uniformed soldier appeared beside them on the shoreline. It was the major who had been in the longboat with Josh. "Good morning, ma'am. I have to do the paperwork for this young man's assignment. I believe he is being sent to Captain Duffy?"

Cathy knew this man well. He was of a superior rank to her husband, but he had become a close friend of hers. "Good morning, Major Gilmore. Thank you for permitting my son to disembark first."

He bowed in acknowledgment of her words. He had meant to watch the boy's expression, but had forgotten to do so at his pronouncement. The lad still had no idea his mother had remarried. He ensured that the lad was not informed when on board. He didn't want to spill that information in public. He looked at the children beside her. "Please accompany me to my office. Children, please come." Proffering Cathy his arm, the major ushered them to his stuffy office. The two children had not released each other, and whispered their welcomes to each other.

An angry glance from the major silenced them.

Jenny had learned to be silent unless spoken to; however, that did not stop her from bouncing with joy at reuniting with her brother. His warm welcome was enough for the moment. She had seen his face fall when he heard of his assignment. Her mother and Mark had told her not to mention their marriage or her new family name, so she remained quiet, but she couldn't help grinning.

Major Gilmore ushered the beautiful, dark-haired woman to a chair and motioned for Josh to stand at his desk.

Jenny was beckoned to her mother's side.

The major walked to his desk and seated himself carefully, flicking the tails of his scarlet uniform coat out of the way. He tugged at a ribbon and carefully opened the enormous convict assignment ledger.

Josh stood watching and waiting. His stomach was turning somersaults, and he wondered who Captain Duffy was. Why had his mother smiled as though she was happy about his assignment? He noted that she looked well, even glowing, and had put on some much-needed weight. He tried to stand still, but he couldn't. He shifted weight from foot to foot.

The major cleared his throat. "Is your name Joshua James Callan?"

Josh had learned to reply rather than nod. "Yes, sir, it is."

The major wrote something and asked, "Are the following details correct? Age, fourteen; eyes, blue; hair, dark; skin…" He looked at the boy. His description when leaving England had been sallow, but he looked tanned and was glowing with health. A strange change for someone emerging from a convict vessel. He shrugged and kept writing. He crossed out sallow and wrote his new description. "…swarthy." He looked at Josh with a raised eyebrow. "Not many convicts improved their looks on the voyage out. I gather you were not confined with the masses?"

Josh smiled. "Yes, sir, you are correct, and no, I was working as a cabin boy for the passengers."

The major was impressed that the boy didn't blather. He said, "You have been assigned to Captain Duffy and his wife for the remaining years of your term. You are to live with them and obey their every wish. You will stay out of trouble and aim to learn everything you are expected to do. I might add that most convicts do not get a choice of placement. Do you agree with this?"

Josh wished he could see his mother's expression. She had so wanted to have him assigned to her. He was shattered but gave a reluctant nod, and his heart sank. "Yes, sir. I do." He sounded dejected.

The major found it hard not to smile. "Fine, then I shall complete your paperwork. Wait while I do," he wrote while Josh watched.

Josh glanced at the certificate he was filling in. The words, "Ticket of Leave," almost jumped off the page. He had no idea what that meant, but it implied some sort of pass or a level of freedom. He looked at Major Gilmore's smiling face.

The major stood. "Now, to introduce you to your placement." He walked from his seat, and Josh followed his movements, expecting him to leave the room. He stopped and stood beside his mother. "Joshua Callan, this is Mrs Duffy. Her husband, Captain Mark Duffy, will watch over you for your final years." The major watched his face as the realisation of his mother's new name dawned on the lad.

Cathy held out her arms to him again. "I've missed you, Joshy."

Major Gilmore bowed and walked to the door, saying, "I'll give you some privacy, Cathy, then I will arrange a carriage to take you home. Excuse me, won't you?"

Without releasing Josh, she said, "Thank you, Geoffrey."

Josh waited until the door closed, then fell into her arms.

Jenny threw herself into a group hug, and the three relished another hug of reunion in the privacy of the major's office.

Knowing that he would be attending to the governor until he could get away, Mark planned for his friend Geoff to give his family some privacy to reveal the changes that had occurred over the past year.

Eventually, Josh pulled away from the loving embrace, and the children pulled up chairs and sat with their mother. "You're married?"

Cathy revealed her change of status to her son, but only mentioned that she had met her husband on the way out.

Josh hardly spoke. He was overwhelmed by how things had turned out.

However, Cathy had yet to tell him where they were living. She took her son's hand and held it to her cheek. "Josh, I will tell you the entire story later, including my childhood in London as I promised, but son, Mark was on my ship, and we met in May last year while still in Portsmouth. Being stuck in close quarters, we saw each other daily. We married in Cape Town in September, only weeks after the anniversary of your father's passing."

Josh nodded. He was relieved that she had completed her year of mourning before remarrying. He glanced at his little sister and saw she was bubbling with excitement.

Jenny said, "You'll love him, Josh. He's nice."

Cathy continued. "Mark was offered a job on the way here, which means you have a unique position. You see, Joshy, Mark is part of the governor's private security detail, and as such, we live at Government House in Parramatta, as will you."

An abject apology followed Josh's very descriptive expletive. He slapped his hand over his mouth. "Oh, Mama, I'm so sorry!" He blushed before adding, "…but that is … well, it's incredible." He had gone from a boy all but living on the streets in London, existing as best as he could by picking pockets and scrounging food, to living at the most important house in this new town.

Jenny burst in, saying, "I wanted to tell you, but Mama and Mark said I had to let Mama do the talking. It's wonderful, Joshy; really wonderful. We have miles of lovely land around the house, and, oh, it's just so beautiful, and it smells fresh and clean. Josh, we see the stars every night."

He chuckled. "I love it, Mama! I did as you said and kept my nose clean. I met a man on board, and I dare say you will meet him later. He's a Maori chief, and his face has the most incredible tattoos, so you can't miss him." He was about to tell her all about the chief when she silenced him. He, too, had a lot to tell, but obviously, now was not the time. They had already been in the office for over half an hour. He realised that his mother had more to reveal to him. He fell silent.

Cathy took his hand, "Joshy, there is something else I need to tell you before you meet Mark. We are having a child. I am nearly five months along."

Jenny was still bouncing with delight. She had sat reasonably quietly until now, but could no longer hold her excitement. "Josh, our brother or sister, will be here in June. Oh, and you will love Mark. I do. He smells like Papa."

Josh had certainly not expected that news. He was wondering what to say when he saw someone enter. With a swift glance, he saw the silhouette of a red-coated officer at the door. Thinking it was Major Gilmore returning, he didn't take much notice of the man until he saw his mother's face light up. He turned again to see who had entered.

The tall, dark-haired officer was not the sandy-haired major, although this man was also in uniform. When his mother held out her hand to him, he realised this must be her husband. Still tongue-tied, he stood and gave the man a bow.

Mark proffered his hand for a shake. "Hello, Josh. I've heard a lot about you and feel like I already know you. I'm pleased to meet you."

Josh automatically took his outstretched hand, and it was instantly grasped in a vice-like grip. It was usual only to bow when two strangers met, but this man quickly pulled him into his arms.

"Hello, lad." With Josh's face pressed into the soldier's shoulder, he took a breath. The scent was familiar, but the man was not. Jenny was correct.

The strong arms that wrapped around the young man held him close. Josh was unable to pull away from the soldier's vice-like bear hug.

Josh had no choice but to draw another breath. He suddenly recognised his cologne. It was his father's orange and sandalwood one that his mother made. He struggled to be released. When he finally managed to break away, confusion and anger were etched on his face, and ignoring Mark, he turned on his mother. He was about to question why she had betrayed his father's memory when Jenny chipped in.

Jenny beamed with adoration. "Doesn't he smell like Papa, Joshy? It was the first thing I noticed about him on the ship." Jenny hugged Mark.

Mark lovingly flicked Jenny's cheek, ruffled Josh's tidy hair, and grinned. "Okay, let's do this properly." Mark gave a formal bow and said, "Hello, Joshua. I'm pleased to meet you. I'm Captain Mark Duffy, and I'm married to your mother. Therefore, I'm your stepfather. Rules here mean that you had to be assigned to me rather than your mama, as she's a new arrival."

Josh was about to say something when Mark interrupted. "Oh, and my mama purchased the cologne as a gift for me from a stall in Covent Garden, and she must have bought it from your papa in London. Jenny was the first to realise the link." Mark had not laughed at Josh, but his easy tone made Josh realise he was not hiding anything.

Josh saw that the man had an honest face, but he turned to his mother for confirmation.

Cathy nodded and then giggled. "Mark, give him a chance to adjust to everything, will you? He's only just discovered I've remarried."

Mark gave her a heart-melting smile.

Josh saw and gasped. He had seen that look on his parents' faces before. They were in love. His jaw fell open. He had presumed that it was a marriage of convenience. It was not.

Jenny giggled at Josh's very expressive face.

Mark leaned down and gave Cathy a lengthy, passionate kiss. "All right, my sweet. I've come to tell you that I've been given two days off to escort you all home. Henry Antill and Charles Whalan will oversee the escort back to Parramatta. We'll grab a bite to eat at the house in town first. Then, while you are resting and packing, Josh and I can get acquainted while I take him down and collect his clothing allocation from the Government Stores. I could do it while we're here, but I'd like to see you home first. You need to rest." He turned and examined his stepson's clothing. He motioned for the boy to turn around.

Josh did as requested, but with a happiness he had not experienced for many months. He couldn't stop grinning. He wore the cream breeches that Ruatara had given him, along with a clean linen shirt and an unbuttoned, oversized cutaway coat. His small bundle held another set of clothing Ruatara and the captains had purchased for him. He had outgrown the other clothes he had been given. However, although Josh wore no vest, he was far better dressed than any ordinary convict. The clothing had obviously belonged to a gentleman.

Mark approved of his attire. With a slight nod, he said, "Well, we won't be swapping those clothes as they are better than what you will be given. Keep them for your Sunday best. Your mama can put the hems up on the trousers. As we all worship with the governor and his lovely wife, we tog up as best we can. I'm guessing you grew out of what you had on when arrested?"

Josh nodded with a grin. The man's obvious affection for his mother and chatty banter were beginning to calm his frayed nerves.

Mark turned his gaze back to his wife. "While we're at stores, I'll grab some fabric for you, my love, so you can do your magic and make him more shirts and undergarments.

Cathy chuckled at her husband's almost lustful gaze. She had already made Josh six new garments.

They heard a carriage arrive, followed by a gentle tap on the door.

Mark assisted her in rising, and the family moved to leave the office.

Josh barely had time to adjust to his mother's marriage and the news that she was having a baby before the entrance and the bear hug from this man. He gave Mark a sidelong glance as they left the office. Mark obviously liked, if not outright loved, his mother. Rather than being annoyed, Josh was delighted that his mother had found someone to care for her. The alternate option at home was unthinkable.

Jenny took her brother's hand as they moved to the door. She was still hopping with delight.

The major was waiting for them outside. Major Gilmore greeted the captain. "The carriage is at your disposal, Mark. It's too hot for your family to walk anywhere, especially in Cathy's condition. Oh, and here's Josh's Ticket; I thought you'd like to give it to him yourself and explain the details and rules. Not many convicts get these on arrival, but even fewer get assigned to Government House."

Mark pocketed the official document that Geoffrey handed to him.

The family climbed aboard the carriage and headed up the hill to where they had stayed for the past few nights.

Mark interlaced his fingers with Cathy's on the short journey and sat grinning contentedly.

Josh put his arm around Jenny and drew her close. "I missed you, sis."

Mark saw the boy's loving action and did the same to his wife. "We did it, Cathy. We are now a complete family." He dropped a kiss on her hair.

Josh was more than overwhelmed. He remembered that his mother had mentioned looking for a husband, but he was surprised to learn that she already had one. Their life would be far better than what they had left behind in London.

The carriage took them the short distance to Government House on Bridge Street. This lovely residence overlooked the quay looking westward. It was surrounded by extensive green space, some of which was set out as farm gardens. The building was stark white amongst the deep olive greens of the surrounding trees. The entire area was enclosed by a paling fence and crisscrossed by gravel paths. Josh leaned forward to see as much as he could of the official residence and its setting.

Mark noticed his interest and said, "Josh, this is not where we are living. Our rooms here are nice, but the official residence is located half a day's drive west. You will notice that once inside, this house requires extensive weatherproofing. However, it's a vast improvement from where we were all born."

Josh's head swivelled to Mark. "Huh?"

Mark smiled. "I was born in London and grew up in the Rookery too. I know what you all went through, and because of that, we have much in common." Josh nodded, but didn't reply, and turned his attention to what they were passing. The carriage took them to the stables at the rear of the building and paused near the back entrance so Mark could assist his family to alight.

Cathy was tired after the morning's excitement. The carriage would need to take Mark and Josh to the store, and while they were away, Cathy would have a nap after packing.

Jenny had gone directly to the kitchen to help prepare luncheon, and she was content there, working with Mrs Ovens.

Mark escorted Cathy to their room and showed Josh where to leave his belongings. It was a small alcove off their room where Jenny was sleeping.

Mark said, "When in town, you'll be sleeping in the staff quarters near the stables, but I'll take you there later." After another long kiss for Cathy, Mark reluctantly left her to escort Josh to the Government Stores.

Cathy suggested, "Mark, take him for a drive around town, as Josh may not be back for some time." She stroked Josh's cheek and said, "It's a good life here, son. Give it time, but you will love it. I certainly do." Mark slid his arm around his lovely wife's growing waist. He bent to kiss her again.

She said with a gentle chuckle, "Go, Mark, and do not distract me further." Jenny returned and handed them a packed lunch basket. It contained bread, eggs, and slices of cold meat.

The disappointment on Mark's face made Josh laugh. "Sheesh, you two! You're embarrassing me, and after the past twelve months, that's a hard thing to do."

It was astounding to see his mother chastising a tall, red-coated soldier, but the fact that this man was his stepfather was still hard to swallow. Mark gave her a final long kiss on her already reddened lips, and reluctantly, they left the small room. Both children chuckled. The tour around town started with a loop around the headland and past some of the convict gardens at Farm Cove. Mark pointed out the dilapidated hospital building and the location of the men's convict barracks. Both were shoddy timber structures that were barely weatherproof. There were patched holes in the shingle roofs.

The carriage traversed various roads and eventually arrived back at the quay. Mark pointed to a large building on the foreshore. The carriage drove on as Mark continued his description of what they passed. Finally, it stopped close to where they had caught it earlier. "That is the Commissariat's Store, which we call the Government Store. All convicts receive an allocation upon arrival. Your allocation will be required, as there is no other source of clothing. You will be given a jacket, shirt, waistcoat, and breeches, although not as good as what you are wearing. You will also get woollen drawers, worsted stockings, a hat of sorts and what they call shoes. In terms of shoes, they are not what you would see in London, but they are sort of leather slippers with no left or right foot. I have heard that you need to soak them in hot water and wear them until they dry. They then take the shape of your foot. They are darned uncomfortable, but as you have no other footwear, take them. I can buy you some better footwear later from the cobbler. You will also be issued with bedding; take that too. Government House is also given food rations from stores so that you won't need your allocation of food, but until productivity picks up, food here is quite basic."

Josh was now relaxed in his stepfather's presence. "Mark, whatever I'm given, it will be more than we had at home."

Mark nodded. He wondered how much his mother had told him about her life. Mark saw his uncertainty. "Josh, you and I have had little time to talk, so I will just let you know that the Governor and Mrs Macquarie know exactly what life was like for you and your family in London. He knows my history, for he made detailed enquiries about me before we met." He saw Josh frown and explained. "I was rescued by the same minister, Reverend Phineas Brackenridge, who took in your papa. It's where Cathy and Jenny stayed before departing. He permitted many children to live in an abandoned crypt in the cemetery. He was wonderful. I transferred into the governor's regiment shortly before we sailed. I had served elsewhere, and it was only after my transfer was finalised that I saw my mother for the first time in years. She gave me the gift of the cologne. Weeks later, she was dead. I had time to bury her decently at St Augustine's cemetery in Hackney, although it's called St John's now. I believe you know it?" Josh nodded. He knew George McGillicuddy was training for the ministry and that Reverend Phineas had left money to his father's friend to pay for the fees. Another man, Reverend Josiah Winchester, was assigned as rector until George was ordained.

Mark smiled. "Anyway, only a week later, I had to report for duty. When your mother swapped ships in Portsmouth, the governor already knew all about her past, and I mean all, before she was transferred on board. I had no idea until I requested permission to court her. He revealed that he knew everything about her, and you, too, by the way." He watched Josh to see how he digested the information. Cathy had told him Josh knew little of her horrific two years on the streets.

Josh swallowed his pride and said, "Mark, I trust Mama and Jenny when they say you are a good man. Jenny has always been a good judge of character. I will accept you and all you have done for my family with a grateful heart and say, 'Thank you.' But it will take a bit of time to get my head around everything."

Mark nodded his acceptance of the utterance. He watched Josh's face as the lad continued watching as they drove past the windmills and Dawes Point Battery. Having done the circuit of the industrial point, they eventually pulled to a halt outside the major's office on the docks. He had not realised how nervous he had been about meeting his stepson. He was now relaxed, happy that their meeting had gone so well.

They entered the vast store, and Mark soon had Josh carrying an armload of supplies. Mark purchased some fabric for Cathy, but it was different from the expected serviceable linen shirting. He placed an order for the linen to be delivered upon the next consignment's arrival. He bought an embroidered Indian silk sari. It was a mauve-blue colour, the exact shade of Cathy's eyes. He also purchased a flat bolt of cheesecloth and another bolt of flannel for napkins. As they returned to the carriage, Mark said, "Your mother told me she has already made you some shirts, so this is just to tell her I care. I try to get her a gift every time I come here. The other two lengths of flannel and cheesecloth are for our child." Mark cradled the exotic fabric as they were driven back. He released a sigh of contentment. God had indeed answered his plea for a good wife, only she had come with two children. He already liked what he saw in the budding man before him.

Chapter 12 New Plans

Over that first summer, on days when the governor was stuck in his office, Josh spent his time with Ruatara and Billy. Lachlan's big broom had seen many of the trouble-making 102nd Regiment of Foot leave on the *Hindostan* and return to London for reassignment. Unfortunately, not all could be so banished. With the 73rd regiment replacing them, as they arrived, more of the 102nd would go. The *Ann* had brought another battalion of Lachlan's regiment, but more were on the way.

~

Two years later, when Chief Ruatara returned to his homeland, Billy went to live at Government House in Sydney as the cook.

Joseph Bigg oversaw Josh's work while in town. Up until then, Ruatara took the boys to a swimming hole half an hour's ride away. Ruatara had shown Josh a hidden treasure the week they arrived.

As planned, the chief had moved in with Reverend Marsden, and from there, he explored the area. Farming was particularly interesting to him, and he devoted time to learning about soils, tilling and fertilising the land.

He sought out farmers, especially John Hunter's friend, the farmer, Linus Rosedale, and questioned them for details. Linus and his family provided him with the necessary information to prepare the ground for a crop and also taught him how to keep the soil fertile. Many weeks were spent on the Rosedale farms learning what was required for growing a healthy crop, and then how to harvest it and store the grain. Ruatara absorbed everything he could. He had first met Linus during his first visit to the settlement, some years earlier. He was now a welcome visitor at his house.

When he was in the colony years before, Ruatara wandered up the creek from Linus's house and found some of the local Baramattagal tribe catching eels in the waterholes. Having not eaten these since he left home, he invited himself to join their feast. He was quickly accepted and welcomed as a member of their tribe. The men investigated his markings, and he willingly permitted them to feel his face. Both had dark skin, and he was welcomed as often as he wished to come.

Mark's jaw dropped when he first met the Maori chief, but they quickly became good friends. Cathy was busy with their infant son and already expecting their second child.

Mark knew how important it was to spend time with Josh, and therefore, that meant spending time with Ruatara and Billy as well. Mark had grown fond of his stepson's unusual companions.

Being a Londoner, Josh had not spent any time on a horse, but that changed on arrival. Josh then taught his companions to ride.

The chief laughed and asked when he would ever need such a skill. Josh shrugged and taught him anyway. "It beats walking in the heat, Chief." The chief agreed.

Billy and Ruatara loved the gentle beasts they were permitted to ride, and the trio was often seen together on another exploratory jaunt.

Joseph taught Josh the basics the week he had arrived, and now the lanky young man could ride any horse bareback or saddled, broken or unbroken. Joseph also showed the lad how to shoe his steed. He had been sent to the young blacksmith, Thomas Tindale, for a fortnight to work as a striker, and he had learned how to reshape a horseshoe to fit various breeds of horse.

Over those long months, Josh endeared himself to one other man: the governor. Governor Lachlan Macquarie loved to ride, and Josh could have their steeds saddled and ready to go at a moment's notice. When Lachlan discovered that Josh could now ride, the lad accompanied him, acting as a groom should he need something.

Lachlan had been thrown into a situation where he had to rely on his friends, but there were few he could claim as such. Thankfully, he had brought some family members with him. With few trustworthy locals, this initially meant Mark, Henry, and Josh were his companions.

The lad was brought into the meetings after the discussions they had while riding. On those trips, Josh had come up with some ideas that Lachlan wished the others to hear. Three other men attended when possible.

On ex-Governor John Hunter's recommendation, Simeon Lord and Andrew Thompson were chosen as Lachlan's two magistrates. These two were controversial at best, as they were emancipated convicts. However, ex-governor Phillip Gidley King trusted his military so little that he had five emancipated convicts as his bodyguards. Charles Whalen was quickly drawn into the protective group.

A third magistrate, the Reverend Samuel Marsden, had been elected to the bench, but he refused to attend meetings if Andrew or Simeon were present. Lachlan was not only upset but disgusted as he voiced his ire at Marsden's un-Christian attitude.

Marsden was a thorn in Lachlan's flesh; rather than putting his weight behind reforming the convicts, he became a roadblock.

Lachlan shrugged and replaced him with someone more congenial.

The last man invited to attend the meetings was D'Arcy Wentworth.

He was a surgeon in the colony with Thomas Jamison and, therefore, saw the seamy side of the town in a way no other did. Both doctors had been set aside by Bligh, but were quickly reinstated on Lachlan's arrival. D'Arcy pinpointed many issues that would have likely escaped the governor's notice.

These meetings took place in the drawing room of Government House in Parramatta.

Josh sat on the floor as unobtrusively as possible. He felt like a fish out of water, but was interested in the frank and lively discussions of his elders.

Andrew Thompson and Simeon Lord made many suggestions, but D'Arcy seemed to know how to deal with the rabble causing trouble in town.

The upshot was that, in addition to being a surgeon, D'Arcy was elected as Chief Superintendent of Police. This new role needed to be integrated with his other duties, but included a pay rise.

Thomas Jamison was reinstated as chief surgeon. Simeon returned to his magistrate duties and was expected to commit some time to medical duties as well.

Andrew often stayed and had further discussions with Mark, Henry and Josh. In 1802, Andrew had constructed a floating bridge over the Hawkesbury River at South Creek, Windsor. He charged a small toll to cross this, and for this reason, his expertise was needed. The older men were of a similar age and had much in common. Mark had been horrified to hear that Andrew had become ill after the floods earlier that year. He had not fully recovered and felt his chest had bands of steel tightening daily.

Each visit, D'Arcy checked Andrew over before the meeting, but the hero of the flood hardly complained; however, his health did not improve. Some days, he could scarcely remain upright.

Josh noted that the hero's complexion became paler at each session. He was saddened to hear that Andrew Thompson had died near the end of their first year. Andrew was only thirty-seven when he succumbed to the infection in his lungs. He died a hero, as all knew of his impressive two-day feat of rescuing so many to the detriment of his own health. He had never fully recovered.

When Lachlan returned from his funeral, he locked himself in his office for hours. With his trusted friend gone, he knew he must continue his plans to improve the colony.

Young Josh was one of the few he would permit to accompany him when he was in such a dour mood. The lad knew when to keep quiet and when to chat. Now, he just wished for silence; Josh gave him the required space. After a good gallop on the domain at the back of his house in Parramatta, Lachlan would shake off his melancholy and return to work.

~

The earlier meetings raised various ideas for the colony's improvement. Initially, the Tank Stream in Sydney was filthy again, as Lachlan was told it was when John Hunter had arrived. Effluent was flowing into it, contaminating the water. Therefore, two of Lachlan's first decisions concerned health and hygiene. The hovels in town would need to be replaced with permanent dwellings, and the wattle-and-daub buildings would be removed. The streets were already laid out, but the town grew faster than Lachlan could arrange supplies to replace the old dwellings. Stone was not fast enough, so he started sourcing clay for brick making. He needed to open up new areas for development, and that entailed exploration.

They needed more roads and more money. Funding the projects was a big issue. With virtually no cash in the town, many vendors had made their own coins or tokens to purchase items from their stores. While effective, they were very localised; however, many had found their way into circulation as regular currency. This was another issue that needed to be addressed quickly, but how?

After Josh was assigned to work in the stables at Government House in Parramatta, he was horrified to discover that Joseph Bigg, the governor's coachman, liked to tickle the sides of the rum bottle. Josh often needed to cover for him. He had learned to keep quiet about the coachman's drinking habits, but he was always ready to step in when needed. Joseph now handed him the reins.

~

At nearly sixteen, Josh was now at eye level with Mark. His initial term of confinement would have finished had he kept quiet. He still had four more years to serve. The two had grown close and spent hours together every chance they could.

Mark had never meant to step into James's shoes, but Josh and he had bonded quickly. Josh often called him "Father" when they were in a deep discussion.

After a random comment by one of Mark's friends, Captain Rudi Greenwood, a couple of years after they arrived, Lachlan set about sourcing coins, which came in the form of silver Spanish doubloons called Reales. After the torrential deluges of five years earlier, the roads had been all but washed away. New coinage was now in production, but few knew what was happening. Mark's muscles were often needed, and Josh had to cover for his absence. Neither could discuss the secret project. This would change the colony, and all involved expected trouble. Currently, Alcohol could purchase almost anything, as few coins existed. English small coins circulated, but the only larger coins were foreign; many coins were taken by sailors on visiting ships, as they were worth more overseas.

~

Simeon suggested that he instigate a road toll system to help pay for the road upkeep, and then D'Arcy chipped in with an idea about taxing spiritous imports. Both men were given oversight of these projects.

Eighteen months after Rudi's initial comment, Lachlan sourced 40,000 Spanish coins to use as currency. Rudi suggested a place to convert them to legal tender by using the basement of the government printer—the success of Spanish coins as the colony's unique currency was outstanding. The outer circle became the five shilling Holey Dollar; the middle, small coin was the Dump, and it was valued at fifteen pence. Mark's muscles were needed to help press out the centre.

Rudi was given the authority over the coin project and was busy with a small team of helpers punching the holes in the Spanish coins and converting them to a local currency.

Mark helped when he could or when his bulk was needed for some heavy work. It would take over a year before there were enough finished new coins to release into circulation. In the meantime, it needed to remain a secret.

The 'Rum Tax,' as it was called, was directed to pay for a new hospital in Sydney, one D'Arcy dearly wished to build and run himself. Henry, Charles, and Mark knew their positions as security guards were vital, as Lachlan was already upsetting the free settlers. The only place Lachlan felt safe was while riding with Josh on the domain at the back of his Parramatta house. The pair would gallop across the grassy field, and Lachlan delighted in the lad's company. When walking along on horseback, Josh was encouraged to talk freely. He saw things others missed.

One morning, Josh said, "Sir, you have started a new police force, but most of the problem comes from the pubs. Drinking and debauchery are rife, and every other building seems to be a drinking hole. Most serve illicit grog, and whoring is almost done in public view. And... and..."

Lachlan had looked at the lad's embarrassed face. "And what, laddie?"

Josh swallowed nervously before saying, "Sir, Jenny is asking me about things she should know nothing about. Life in London was tough and rough, but here, things are done in public that would have gone on behind closed doors back home. It needs to be cleaned up." He was horrified that he had just discussed prostitution with the governor.

Lachlan paused and looked at the lad before saying, "Josh, you are so right. It is so glaringly obvious that I should have thought of that myself. I shall draft an edict about the restitution of moral behaviour and make church attendance part of the new revision of my Ticket of Leave system. I shall revise all the venues and instigate a licensing system to clean up the industry. Governor John Hunter issued only ten liquor licenses, but now I shall expand on that and shut some of the seedier ones."

Within weeks of that conversation, more than fifty public houses were closed, immoral acts in public were outlawed, and church attendance was once again required as part of holding a Ticket of Leave. Stills making illicit grog were confiscated and publicly destroyed. However, Lachlan's mind had not stopped there. He established schools, including one specifically for indigenous children.

Before he left England, his discussions with Governor Phillip outlined what he ideally envisioned for Sydney. Arthur Phillip's dream was of the rows of stately white buildings along the straight streets in a town that he had hoped to call New Albion.

Lachlan discovered upon his arrival that what he found was vastly different from Phillip's dream town. John Hunter had warned him, but he had not realised how bad things had become again. The excrement-filled streets, fetid buildings and filthy creek were a disaster waiting to happen. John Hunter mentioned it was bad when he arrived, just two years after Phillip departed. Lachlan took a broom to the town and cleaned it up. Clean water was another thing Lachlan attended to. He believed that clean sources of water stopped illness.

The Colonial Office in London had given him a brief to restore confidence in the colony, which included improving morals, encouraging marriage, enhancing education, prohibiting the sale of alcohol, and improving agricultural practices. However, Lord Castlereagh's instructions were difficult to achieve in a penal colony on the other side of the world. His ideas just did not work.

~

It took until the following year before D'Arcy Wentworth arranged an adequate police force, but by then, Andrew Thompson was dead. His death didn't help matters, as his estate was left in such a way that his family in England had only a year to claim it, or the property reverted to Lachlan. As Andrew had been very wealthy, many were angry. Simeon was left a good inheritance, and although it was not written in his will, but a codicil, Simeon had to care for Andrew's common-law wife. They had discussed this issue during one of the meetings at Government House.

Lachlan had asked why Andrew did not just marry the woman, and he muttered something about her being a Roman Catholic and her not wanting to marry a Protestant. Lachlan had nearly choked on his tea. "But she will live in sin with you? Really?"

Andrew was embarrassed but nodded. "It's not for want of asking her, sir." He shrugged. "I'm not getting any better, so I have asked Simeon to ensure she can access ample funds. If I left it to her, she would become a target for unscrupulous, greedy men. This way, I know he will care for her for her entire life." Simeon did as his friend requested.

~

With time somewhat heavy on his hands, D'Arcy threw himself into his magistrate duties. He could not do much until the new toll gates were constructed. The first of these was at the end of George Street in Sydney. All vehicles, including stock, carriages, and transports, leaving town were required to pay a toll, unless they were government vehicles or those on road repair duty. Residents within a one-mile radius of the gate were also exempt, and a maximum toll was charged only once per twenty-four-hour period. People were aware that there were hundreds of toll bars in England, so few were surprised by their installation. D'Arcy's new hospital had its foundations laid, and although the building materials were beginning to accumulate, it remained only a building site. Someone needed to redesign the edifice. They had got that far on faith, plus a wing and a prayer. It had an outline of what would be erected, but little else. Would it even be large enough?

~

Shortly before Mark received his promotion to major, Lachlan had mentioned to Mark that soon half of the 73rd regiment would be sent to India to serve under Brigadier General Miles Nightingall when suitable transport could be arranged. This was the very same man who had refused the post of governor due to ill health.

Mark knew that it was time to vacate their rooms and move on with their lives. He had already broached the idea to the governor but had yet to tell Josh. Mark was stunned that Lachlan had already made plans for them.

The governor had made so many changes that the extensive security detail, with the plethora of soldiers, were no longer required.

News arrived that the 46th regiment was being sent out to replace the tired soldiers of his regiment.

Mark had no wish to leave the colony and decided to sell his commission. He knew his soldiering days would soon be over. Mark had never sought promotion, but those had come through due diligence. He never spoke of his fighting days to anyone. His promotion to major had just come through, and he felt a little guilty resigning so soon after this had been achieved. However, his sell-out fee would be more than ample for their future needs. Mark had no idea that he could sell his commission until the governor suggested it.

After years of working at Government House, Josh's conviction time was half over. Knowing he could be called to harness up a government carriage at a moment's notice, Josh always had a cloth handy for his hands. When he was summoned by the governor that morning, he was covered in neatsfoot oil from polishing the tack. The housekeeper, Betty Eccles, came out to the stables and asked that Josh attend the governor in his office immediately.

Five minutes after receiving the summons, Josh stood at the governor's door. He entered the delightfully light office and saw the greying head bent over some paperwork. He noted that Mark and Henry Antill, who had also been recently promoted to major, stood at attention just inside. Both were ignoring his presence. Josh waited silently.

The only sound in the office was the scratching of the quill nib on the parchment. Outside, the mahogany grandfather clock ticked loudly. It chimed a quarter past the hour. Josh watched as the familiar elongated scrawl of the governor's name was scratched across the bottom of the document.

Lachlan Macquarie sanded and shook the parchment. He stood and pushed back his chair, his eyes still on his desk. "Joshua James Callan, your time is complete, as I am wiping your last years of your conviction due to your good behaviour." He held out the signed document to Josh and broke into a beaming smile. The man's yellowed teeth showed the volume of strong black tea that he consumed in this hot land.

Josh accepted the sheet of parchment in a somewhat dazed state. This was not what he was expecting. 'Certificate of Freedom' was printed across the top. "Thank you, Your Excellency." He was stunned.

Lachlan came around the desk and said, "Josh, I was wondering, as now you are free, would you be interested in staying on and going on the paid staff? Joseph needs assistance in the stables, and as you are of sober mind, I would like you to oversee Mrs Macquarie's saddlery and carriage tack to keep it in good order. It would mean you could also stay reasonably close to your family. However, since the instigation of the tolls and turnpikes, I have plans for you all, if you are interested."

Lachlan's eyes flicked towards Henry, and he dismissed him with a quick salute and a tip of his head.

Henry returned the salute, swivelled, marched from the room, and gently closed the door.

When he had gone, Lachlan motioned for Mark to take a seat next to Josh.

The governor seated himself and pulled out a map of the town from under his chair. He unfurled it on the small table that sat between them. "Josh, Mark has said he and your mama are thinking of doing something other than soldiering."

Josh's gaze turned to his stepfather. "Mark, do you really wish to sell out?" He knew Mark had done nothing else.

Mark put his hand on the young man's shoulder. "I already have, son. Cathy and I waited for your freedom papers to tell you about our next move. Listen to the governor, Josh, for he has plans that concern you."

Josh was flabbergasted. "But Mark, you have just been promoted."

Mark put his finger to his lips. "Listen, son; the governor will explain."

Lachlan listened to the interchange and said, "Yes, he has, laddie. And now he can retire on a substantial sum, regardless of whether the tollgate generates income or not. That was part of my plan; I just didn't tell him. I hoped he would stay, so I worded my comments to infer that he would need to transfer to India should he wish to remain in the regiment." His smiling face met Mark's grin.

Mark nodded a "Thank you."

Josh knew that the Parramatta tollgate residence had just been completed. A third one was under construction on the Windsor Road to the north of town.

The governor continued. "Josh, although I wish you to remain here with me, your family will move to the toll house on our southern road to the west. It's walking distance from your rooms at the stable."

Mark knew that having so many children around was hurtful for the childless viceregal couple. The First Lady had lost two more babies, only a few months along. Mark and Cathy realised that their presence at Government House with the second child on the way was causing Elizabeth some anguish. Cathy carried her babies easily. She worked sewing for Elizabeth up until the day before the births. Not only that, but the two ladies had become good friends.

Josh knew all about the miscarriages as he had needed to call Doctor Wentworth, or whoever was on duty, in the middle of the night. Mark's son, Gideon, had been born on the 11th of June, six months after they arrived. Gideon was now eighteen months old, and he was an adorable child. Their second baby was due in a month. The family had outgrown their tiny room, and the new child would cramp them. Jenny, at thirteen, was reaching maturity, and she shared a room with Mrs Ovens rather than Mrs Jones, who snored so loudly that Jenny found it difficult to sleep. She had been found curled up under the kitchen table more than once. The family needed a fresh start, and the new two-storey toll gate building gave them that opportunity.

Mark knew nothing about farming, but he and Cathy could run the new toll gate until it was established for the governor. It had been built on Pitt Row, just down the road from the cemetery gate. Josh would be close, but he would be earning his own money. If things got busy, there would always be room for the lad.

On hearing Mark's plan, Josh was struck dumb. His head pivoted from one man to the other, unsure what to say.

Lachlan saw his uncertainty and said, "Josh, I wish to tell you a little of my background. It may help you understand why I care about you, Mark, and your mama. Mark told you his story, but a person is far more than just a rank or status. I, too, had a poor upbringing, but it was on the small island of Mull in the Western Isles of Scotland. My father died when I was about the same age you were when you lost yours. I had many older brothers, and we knew cold, poverty, and hunger far too well. I was sent to school by a benefactor and received my education. When I was your age, I enlisted as an ensign in the second battalion of the 84th Regiment. It was known as the Royal Highland Emigrants."

Lachlan's glance flicked to Mark before he continued. "Very few know my background, and if anyone asks, you know nothing, okay?"

Both assured him of their silence.

Trusting them as he did, he continued, "Josh, I was not born with a silver spoon in my mouth. Like Mark, I worked hard to get where I am today. I was not even supposed to be here as governor, as Brigadier General Miles Nightingall was supposed to take on the role, but he declined due to illness. I had recently been promoted to Lieutenant Colonel and bravely put my name forward lest the Brigadier General not recover. I think that the powers would have refused my offer, but at a friend's instigation, I attended a Royal Levée where I met the King. I must have won his favour, as I was offered the position the following morning. I have served in various places in America and fought against the rebels there, as well as in the West Indies, India, Asia, Egypt, and again in India, with only brief spells in England. During my years of service, I learned everything I could and have transitioned from periods of great wealth to being heavily in debt. I only mentioned all this so you will realise I know what I'm talking about."

"Oh! Yes, sir." Josh had no idea where this was leading. He knew that Mark had also travelled widely during his military service, but wealth had not been his goal. Security had been foremost in Mark's mind when he enlisted.

Lachlan reclined and frowned. "I'm trying to say that no one is too poor to be given a chance. In Scotland, poverty is not a crime. As you are aware, I have already amended certain rules to provide emancipated convicts with a better future. Charles Whalan is a case in point. Josh, you and Mark are part of my plan. Charles, Simeon Lord and Andrew Thompson are a few success stories, but many more will follow."

Josh now gave him his full attention. "How do our family fit in, though, sir?"

The governor shifted in his seat, and he pulled out a second map from under the other. "Ahh, well, as you know, I plan new roads in this new colony, but I have no money to build or maintain them. The storm in 1805, before my arrival, eroded many roads to such a point that they were almost impassable. There is no money to repair them. We do have convicts, but we lack the funds to purchase supplies. As you are aware, the year we all arrived, we did an extensive tour of the lands on this side of the Blue Mountains. Our colony is still desperately short of both funds and food. You two are instrumental in this, as this can only develop with good roads to transport said produce quickly. Mark, I want you working with D'Arcy Wentworth and Simeon Lord, who are trustees for the board of roads, and they are overseeing the maintenance of our vital transportation system."

Mark gasped, "Sir, really? We can be part of your plan?"

Lachlan's gaze bore into Mark's. "Not just 'part-of', Mark, but you, in particular, will be 'instrumental to' the project. You see, D'Arcy Wentworth and Simeon Lord have offices in Sydney and other positions that now fully utilise their time." He gazed at the soldier and said, "I need you to be the eyes and ears of my road project, second in command, if you will. I need you to be the point of contact for people who come to report problems out this way. Mark, I want you to work under Wentworth as his assistant for the toll gates. Also, your friendship with Simeon Lord will give you some authority. Mark, I trust you. I do not need to explain how much I value that. Most of the free settlers here have come to feather their own nests rather than assist our long-term project of building a new way of living."

Lachlan knew the place would never achieve the status of Governor Phillip's dream of creating a New Albion, but he would do what he could to make it a pleasant and fairer place to live. "I need people whom I trust to give me the honest truth. Not a buttered-up fiction of life. Josh, you're involved, as when Mark travels, which he will need to do occasionally, you will be relieved of duty here and run the turnpike and tollgate with your mother's assistance." Mark duplicated Josh's gasp. He had not realised his new job would take him away from his family.

Lachlan gave them one of his slightly lopsided smiles. "Oh, and Mark, the new toll house building here has a room for accommodation. It will be fully furnished, all of which will become your possessions as I realise you have none. Call it a bonus. I believe there are six bedrooms in the two-storey building, with four located upstairs and two downstairs, though one is designated as a servant's room. If you keep the upstairs rooms for the family, there will be adequate space for public use downstairs, or you can use it as a guest room, a sitting room, or a dining room, and there is a bedroom off the kitchen. The large room downstairs can be exclusively used for overnight female accommodation. I made sure there are locks on the door. You will retain the income from this. It's my way of saying thank you for keeping me safe. It means Henry can move into your room here." He grinned. "Oh, and before you leave, your final duty will be to arrange a community concert. Ask young George Ellis to play his fiddle. Make sure he's the last to play."

Lachlan could hardly contain his grin. The look that Josh gave Mark was one of absolute astonishment.

Mark could not agree more. He knew of George's skill but had remained quiet about the man's talents. "A concert, sir?" They were being given a house with everything in it. In England, they would have been thrilled with a single room. But neither of them had any idea how to arrange a community concert.

"Yes, to be held here, on the front hill," Lachlan said with a smile. "Oh, and by the way, you will MC it." Mark could do nothing more than nod.

~

The concert was a raging success. The governor was thrilled with the finale, and George's skill astounded the community. His ability was better than Mark had ever heard at Covent Garden, and he had heard many. The crowd of hundreds listened in silence as George serenaded his beloved Charlotte Rosedale. It was as though he played just for her.

The following day, the Duffy family bid farewell to the viceregal family. The Duffys had to head to Sydney so Mark could help with minting the final batch of coins, as Rudi needed his help to meet their deadline. Mark also needed to meet with D'Arcy Wentworth about the toll money. These few weeks would be a short holiday before they moved into the tollgate residence.

Once they returned from Sydney, Jenny, Mark, Cathy, and their son settled into their first home. Being city folk, neither had ever had to make their own food or even milk a cow.

Cathy, leaving Government House, learned to skim the cream off the milk and to churn butter. Jenny's time with Mrs Ovens meant she became their teacher. In her years in the kitchen, she had been overseen by a competent cook. Jenny could now make butter, bake bread, and feed the family. She had also acquired numerous other household skills, including candle-making.

Cathy had spent her days sewing gowns for Elizabeth Macquarie and only ventured into the kitchen when required to assist with candle making, as she didn't like Jenny working with hot wax and tallow. Because beeswax was scarce, rush-wick tallow candles were commonly used for the staff. Unless clarified properly, these candles emitted a strong odour.

The tollgate staff rooms had a double bunk added, and more young girls were assigned to assist.

Many male convicts were sent to clear and work new farmlands and grow food for the still-hungry settlement. Others were trained to garden at Linus Rosedale's family farms. The Farm at Emu Ford was reopened, and the crops grown there were sent to Government Stores. This effort did not completely stave off hunger, but it did help.

With the promise of convict labour, Lachlan revised the Ticket of Leave system and placed more convicts in the community rather than the Government Barracks.

Western Toll-bar

MARK DUFFY, Toll Keeper.

This Gate Clears the Toll Gate at Pitt Row

20th. April 1813

Paid. 16 shillings 4 d

For. 775 sheep & 1 horse

Chapter 13 Parramatta Turnpike

Weeks turned into months. With the arrival of Mark and Cathy's daughter, Rosemary, another new face came to assist at the toll gate. Alice Murray now helped Cathy with their baby girl and little boy. This lass was a fourteen-year-old convict who had been caught stealing a length of fabric in the southern farmlands of West Sussex, but Cathy soon realised there was much more to her conviction. Alice knew her way around a kitchen and a farm, although the tollhouse had little land attached. However, she was also a capable cook. Jenny loved having someone her own age to work with and chat, but Alice shied away from all men except Mark and Josh.

For Cathy, that was indeed telling.

Since the Duffys moved in, a stable had been completed at the back, along with a holding yard for the horses, if required. This was becoming increasingly frequent. The new building had a large loft with hooks for hammocks, in case farmers needed overnight accommodation. A large stockyard had also been constructed on the other side of the tollgate. The stables-cum-barn building had two stalls for Mark's workhorses, a small tack room and a large storeroom for stockfeed.

After some months, Mark purchased the lease on the tollgate with the money from selling his commission. He also bought a small carriage for use on his inspection trips. He set it up so he could sleep in it if required. He also purchased a gig for Cathy and the children's use.

Josh taught her to harness it and how to drive. With the money Josh earned as a paid groom, he bought a roan stallion, which was regularly seen in the holding yard at the tollgate. Josh was always on hand when Mark was away, so Mark was content that his family was safe. Thankfully, his overnight trips away were rare.

~

By the time Rosemary was walking, nineteen-year-old Josh had realised he was needed more often at the increasingly busy tollgate than at Government House.

Charles Whalan had become a friend of the governor and now frequently accompanied him on his morning rides.

The turnpike and tollgate on the road west were becoming full-time jobs. On moonlit nights, it was a twenty-four-hour shift.

~

1813 passed with the exciting news that another child was on the way. This time, it was for the Macquaries.

Cathy was one of the first to know. She happened to be at the house when Elizabeth called for assistance from someone. Cathy found her friend retching into a bowl.

Elizabeth admitted that she was ten weeks along and had not dared to say anything due to the number of miscarriages she had already had. Elizabeth found that carrying a child was no easy business. Morning sickness overwhelmed her.

On this day, Cathy came to her assistance, and with Mrs Jones's help, the two ladies were able to clean Elizabeth up and get her a cup of hot black tea. The two ladies pandered to her for the next two weeks. Hopefully, Elizabeth would not lose this one if she could carry it past the three-month date. Elizabeth stayed in bed for many of those early days.

Lachlan's new currency was circulating throughout the colony, and drunkenness was less prevalent.

D'Arcy took over the toll money collection, so Mark could now concentrate on his tollgate.

The people of New South Wales had six months' grace to use their old currency, and most of these coins went through as tolls. Both old and new coins flowed regularly through the takings, and Mark was able to inform both Lachlan and D'Arcy about the success of the new currency. The release of the new money had gone without a hitch, and the settlement was beginning to respond to Lachlan's tight rein. That year, nearly £100 was collected at Mark's gate alone.

Thankfully, many small English coins were circulating, but the new Dump coins were the most frequently seen. The Holey Dollar was a larger coin, and not usually used as a toll coin. Its value was five shillings, and few were used as tolls, which were usually only a penny or two.

~

Elizabeth's confinement drew closer.

Government House was preparing for the arrival of the most important person the colony could imagine.

The viceregal couple travelled to Sydney to see the doctor. While there, another ship arrived.

This ship brought an unexpected passenger. A man with a half-melted face introduced himself as the Earl of Collingsford, but called himself Perry White. He knocked on the viceregal door with his two small daughters in tow. He came looking for his wife, who had arrived on the *Wanstead* as a convict, and he was seeking assistance and information about her.

Compassion for the severely scarred man saw Perry and his daughters move into the official residence for the few days before the household returned to Parramatta.

Lachlan was drawn to Perry because of his burns. Perry had been caught in a raging fire and came off second-best. Lachlan had been praying for a friend who could infiltrate the masses and report back to him. Lachlan realised that Perry's horrific injury gave him the ability to be reasonably inconspicuous while wandering the streets. He could listen to the gripes and grievances of the convicts and the ordinary men.

Perry quickly befriended both Mark and Lachlan.

On their arrival in Parramatta, Perry and Lachlan had seconded Henry and other trusted soldiers to follow them to one of the debauched inns near the gates of the official residence. There, Perry found his wife and, much to his surprise, a son he didn't know existed. The child's presence explained the mystery of her actions.

Henry accompanied them back to the residence and saw them safely accommodated before returning to the inn and dismissing the security detail.

With nowhere else to go, the White family remained with the Macquaries while Perry had a home built for his family.

~

1814

Lachlan wrote off the month of March, having booked only one function. It was an official dinner that he had been unable to change. Of course, it was during dinner that their baby arrived.

Elizabeth finally managed to carry another baby to term, and he was born alive. She dared not get excited as she had already lost their darling daughter Jane at only eight weeks old. She had been healthy at birth, then had sickened and died quickly in the cold of England.

However, Elizabeth and Lachlan were finally parents again, this time of a little boy named after his father. As the baby boy, Lachlan Junior, grew, Cathy and her younger children were invited for playtime with the lad and Perry and Katy's little boy. Young Lachie was everything the viceregal couple desired. He was fit and healthy and the apple of their eye. As a groom-cum-footman, Josh accompanied his mentor on his early morning rides. Most mornings, he was chatty and good company. Occasionally, he fell silent.

When in Parramatta, the governor would conduct twice-daily inspections of his troops. Josh stood holding his horse. Once the morning inspections were completed and the daily orders issued, they would watch as the various road crews and work details were dispatched on their way. The governor and Josh would set off on a vigorous morning gallop through the domain behind Government House. Today, they were to try out new saddles made by Ben Parker and George Ellis for the two stallions.

Lachlan often challenged Josh to a race, and after always letting the governor win, Josh was reprimanded for his chivalry. From then on, all the races were neck and neck. Both enjoyed the freedom of the exhilarating rides and often rode back via Salter's old dairy.

Josh would have loved to stop and see what they were doing, but the blushing and somewhat fawning girls made being around them embarrassing.

Two girls from the gaol milked the cows at what was now known as the Government Dairy. They then separated the cream to make some into butter, but for some reason, it tasted off. No one else seemed to know what to do with so much milk or how to turn it into a reasonably edible cheese. It was an industry Lachlan wished to see developed, but he trusted that the good Lord would one day provide the right person for that job. To date, only basic goat's cheese was being made on Rosedale's farm. The new dairy could only produce soft cottage cheeses as there was no cool room. An attempt at making hard cheese was not as successful as desired. The product was added to convict rations rather than being served on the governor's table. It was almost unpalatable. It tasted mouldy.

The tollgate was now used twenty-four hours a day, and Josh didn't mind the few night calls that came through on a moonlit evening. He put in the nights at the tollgate and returned to Government House for his stable work, but Mark was struggling to cope with the combination of late hours from the tollgate and the demands of his young family. He was barely pulling himself through some days.

Josh remembered that the judge had said he was not worth tuppence, and that comment still rankled. It was the value of a cow to pass through the tollgate. For each head of cattle was tuppence, every ten sheep or pigs was threepence. A carriage with four horses was the most expensive toll at three shillings.

Cathy found she could take most of the daytime tolls as there was little traffic, but an unruly customer occasionally required Mark's overpowering presence. He was usually tinkering in the shed. One particular driver of an expensive vehicle caused Cathy the most upset. The man was a known troublemaker and belittled the small cost of the toll that the governor required.

When Mark or Josh was on duty at the gate, he paid his toll with little hesitation, but his behaviour was obnoxious when Cathy was on duty.

Mr Ardeth took pleasure in harassing her. He was a weasel-like man, and she knew he also beat his female servants and worse. Two of his convict maids were in the family way, and he had returned them to the female gaol, asking for two more young girls.

Mark had told Lachlan, but Ardeth broke no law. The convict girls were no better than slaves.

Cathy heard a carriage pull up, and, not recognising it, she went to greet it and take its toll. She checked the cost before she went to collect the money. The new four-wheel carriage drawn by four horses cost three shillings to pass. Mark heard her say, "Three shillings, thank you, sir."

Rather than hand over the coinage, the driver jumped down and quickly grabbed Cathy around the waist. "Give us a kiss, love, and waive the toll."

Cathy knew their room was directly above them, and their window was open. "Mr Ardeth, unhand me this instant!"

The sneer on the man's face made Cathy's blood run cold.

He said, "Not on your nelly, my little dove. I have been dreaming of kissing your pretty lips. You can tell your man that I was only going to water my horses, but I'm not paying your ridiculous toll." He tried to pull Cathy closer, and she screamed as she struggled against him. She lifted her knee to stop his advances, but he was wise to her action and twisted her sideways.

Having done the night shift, Mark had been dozing upstairs when the foul-mouthed man decided to accost Cathy. He heard her scream and was downstairs in an instant. He released his wife from the arms of the brute, and Mr Ardeth found himself grabbed by the scruff of his neck and pushed back into his carriage, where he fell onto his hands and knees.

Mark was seething. "You touch my wife again, and I'll have you arrested. As it is, you will receive a fine from Doctor Wentworth of at least forty shillings for refusing to pay the toll. However, depending on his mood, he may raise it to ten pounds. I only have to report you accosting my wife, and he will pour the weight of the law upon you using his magistrate's hat." Mark had felt like thumping him for harassing his wife, but refrained as Jenny and his children had drawn close.

The man still did not offer to pay the toll. He turned his vehicle around. Mr Ardeth knew he had met his match in Mark and would need to travel via the rough back road in future. He gave them a sneer as he retraced his path.

Cathy was still shaking and was taken inside by Mark. "Are you all right, love?"

Cathy nodded. "I am unharmed, but I cannot abide that man."

Mark waited until the door was closed before he drew her into his arms. "I do not think he will travel this way for some time."

Her head was pressed into his shoulder, and he could tell she was weeping. He could feel her shivering. His hands caressed her back lovingly, and she soon relaxed.

He once again asked, "Are you okay, sweet cakes?"

She nodded, but she was far from that. She hated men like that, as it brought back horrible memories of her youth. "Memories, Mark, that is all."

Mark understood her fears. He said, "Come along. Let's get some tea." Without releasing her, he kept his arm around her shoulders, and they walked through their home to the kitchen.

Mr Ardeth's behaviour was reported to D'Arcy by the afternoon mail. The man was issued an official warning, and his name was recorded for refusing to pay the three shillings.

D'Arcy also sent him an official notification regarding the incident involving government staff, along with a fine of fifty shillings.

D'Arcy and Simeon informed Mark about the outcome and that they had strongly advised Mr Ardeth not to use that route again.

Aside from an occasional incident like this, Cathy and Mark's lives were generally good. Their family was healthy, and their life was wonderful compared to their upbringing. Mark was making good money at the toll gate from the growing accommodation areas. He had enclosed the upper loft in the barn and added more hammocks for men wishing to stay. Rather than accessing this area with a ladder, they now had proper steps with a railing. There was now a hob stove up there for the cold winter nights and windows for the hot summers. Money from the rented accommodation went into their pockets. Few women stayed, but when they did, they occupied the inside room.

Mr Ardeth only returned when his wife travelled with him, and he paid the toll without argument.

Bushrangers, who were escaped convicts, were another problem. Some had taken to raiding outlying houses for food and money. Most of these didn't come close to town, but a few knew there was money at the tollgate.

Mark had arranged to pay Josh for his percentage of the work. Then he asked Josh if he would like to become a partner in the business. With this option, Josh could think of nothing better. He knew that his years working for the governor were over. Now he had to tell the governor.

An unusual friendship had sprung up between them in their four years in the colony. Although Josh saw Mark as a wonderful father figure, Josh turned to Lachlan when he had concerns about something. He had not sought him out often, but the governor read the lad like a book.

~

When Perry arrived in March 1814, on the convict ship *General Hewitt*, it brought three forgers, two of whom were architects.

One felon, Francis Greenway, was a skilled stonemason and architect, and he was tasked with designing and building a new lighthouse. Although simple, his skill with the sandstone medium was evident, so he was asked to oversee the hospital's construction.

The other felons were Henry Kitchen and Joseph Lycett. They were set to work under Lachlan's Ticket of Leave program and under the ever-watchful eye of supervising soldier John Watts. He was a military officer who had accompanied the convicts. Watts, a draughtsman himself, was set to work enlarging Parramatta's Government House. Two new wings were added to the main building, and new staff outbuildings were constructed at the rear.

Henry Kitchen was commissioned to design a new weir in Parramatta, and Joseph Lycett, a master forger and artist, was tasked with recording as much as he could in paintings and drawings. He was frequently seen sitting on a hillside, drawing or painting. Other artists were also asked to record the growth of the infant settlements.

In mid-1814, the Macquaries and Josh returned from another long tour that took them out to Bathurst, one of the developing areas. On the morning ride, Josh was silent. He had spent much time thinking about what he would do with his life.

Lachlan enjoyed the gallop through the domain at the back of his house and noticed his companion's contemplative mood. "Spit it out, lad. Something is eating at you."

Josh started. He had been so deep in thought that he had not realised his inattention to the governor. "Sorry, sir. I was wondering if I could make an appointment to discuss something with you?"

Lachlan frowned. It was not like Josh to be as quiet. He had barely said a word all morning. "How about right now, lad?"

Josh nodded. He loved his job working with the governor's horses and even came to think of the older man as an uncle or grandfather, enjoying his life at the official residence. However, his mind kept turning to his mother's new maid, Alice Murray.

Lachlan saw that he was still distracted. "Fine, then let's sit on the log and have a natter?"

Josh nodded but didn't reply. He wondered how the governor would take his request.

They cantered back to the enormous log on the cliff's top that overlooked the water. This tree had been cut years before, and after the dead crown had been used as firewood, the long trunk was left where it fell. It was a perfect vantage point to look over the town.

When Lachlan had time, he would wander to this seat and watch over the town's growth and activity. He also used this area for quiet time alone to pray. The place was peaceful and yet close to home. He loved stretching his legs if he had been at his desk for hours. Josh, Charles, or Henry normally shadowed him for safety. However, they usually stayed out of sight.

Today, Josh and Lachlan sat together and talked. Josh knew the horses would not wander far and tied the reins to the saddles so they could crop the lush grass while the men talked.

Lachlan seated himself comfortably and said, "Okay, spit it out, laddie."

Josh chuckled at the governor's informality. He doubted he would say that to anyone else but Mark. "Yes, sir."

Lachlan waited while the young man collected his thoughts.

Now somewhat more relaxed, he revealed his concerns. Josh took a deep breath and said, "It's Mama, sir. There have been a few times where she has been accosted, and as Mark has travellers staying more often, I was wondering about leaving your employment and moving to the tollhouse. Jenny and Alice are not enough protection for her."

Lachlan realised that this could have been the problem. "Josh, Mark is what, forty-two now?"

Josh nodded. "Yes, sir. Mark is not coping with the nights and the babies, and well, he has asked me if I would be interested in going into partnership with him full-time, with a plan to take over the night work myself." Josh glanced at his boss and wondered what his reaction would be. It meant he would live in the same house as Alice, and he liked that idea.

Lachlan's slightly lopsided smile met his eyes. "Josh lad, Mark spoke to me some weeks ago, just before we left on our trip. He said much the same, only that he wanted to make sure you had a future doing something you liked. He does not wish to force you to follow in his footsteps." He glanced at the young lad, who was now a confident young man. He had come a long way from the callow youth who had arrived. "Josh, I used Mark's muscles and strength to produce our new currency with Rudi and his friends. The timing of the tollgate opening was somewhat inconvenient for several reasons. I know that he felt he was burning his candle at both ends. However, he didn't want to let me down. He was close to burnout when he left."

Josh gave a small gasp but didn't interrupt.

Lachlan chuckled. "Mark has it all thought out. He may not be your father, but he loves you as though he were. The money he is earning through the accommodation side of the tollgate has brought in enough to enable them to live quite comfortably, as I had hoped it would. He intended to look around to buy or build a house in town and eventually move there, but I have other options. I hope he might open a small shop, but it wouldn't be in town. Then you can run the tollgate yourself. However, that won't be for some time. I have said that until you come of age, I will not let you run it alone, and Mark will be the lease owner until I say otherwise. That is still two years away. I hope that you may find a life partner to assist you and start your own family. Mark and your mama are determined to set you up as your father intended to do before he died."

Josh found himself tearing up. The mere mention of his father still hurt. For Mark to want him to be set for life in his own business meant so much to him. Josh found he was unable to speak. "Mark said that?"

Lachlan nodded and continued. "Mark loves you, lad, as does your mama. Jenny is growing up and will soon find her own husband, but the little ones are years away from independence. I hope you realise that."

Josh nodded and said a soft "Yes." The lump in his throat precluded any further conversation. Yes, there was far more reason than Alice's presence to move there.

Lachlan looked across at the man-boy who had grown so fast. He hoped his own son would be like this lad. "I will voice what Mark and your Mama never will. Josh, if something happens to Mark, you will be the man of the family and must care for all your siblings until they are independent, as well as your mother. It is the least you can do for all that Mark has done for you." The horrified look on Josh's face almost made Lachlan laugh.

"Laddie, he's not sick, so don't look at me like that. I'm just saying in case it ever becomes necessary. In a place like this, death is one's constant enemy. We all must be prepared for that eventuality when it occurs."

Josh released a long sigh, "Oh, sir, you had me so worried there for a bit. Mark is a tower of strength. I remember him telling me about grabbing that rat Ardeth by the scruff of his neck and dumping him in his carriage. That terrible man is the one who made a pass at Mama, and no one is permitted to do that. Mark is so protective of her, and with good reason."

It had taken nearly two years, but Cathy had eventually opened up about her past to her son.

Josh had digested the information and then hugged his mother. He knew what conditions were like in London, and although furious with his grandfather for his despicable action, he adored his mother. It also made him appreciate his father even more. Oh yes, he would protect his family. He would do anything for them, and that included Mark.

Lachlan saw he was deep in thought and sat, letting him mull over his words.

Josh repeated that thought by saying, "Yes, sir, I would do anything for them, and yes, sir, that includes Mark. I will make you a promise, I will do as you suggest if it should ever become necessary."

Lachlan placed a caring hand on his groom's arm. "I never doubted that you would, young Joshua. However, that brings us full circle. I would suggest that you see out the week and collect your pay. I will provide you with a reference, even though you will probably never need it; however, please store it safely, as I do not write these often. I want you to know that I may occasionally need your services. You would be paid, of course. There are few in this place I trust with my own family; you are one of those. Charles, Mark, and Henry are more, as is Perry White. If I need you and you're free, would you be willing to return for a short while? To look after Mrs Macquarie and Lachie?"

Without hesitation, Josh replied, "Of course, sir. Anytime! My only proviso is if my family needs me at the same time."

Lachlan laughed. "Fair enough, lad. I would have thought less of you if you had not put them first." He fell silent for a few moments before adding, "If I had done that, I may not have..." He fingered the pockmarks on his face. He shook his head. "No, forget I said that; there is no use crying over spilled milk. The past is the past. Just do not ever make the error I made, Josh."

Rather than ride back, the two men decided to take a leisurely stroll downhill to the house, leading their horses to the stable.

They walked down the grassy embankment towards Government House.

Josh wondered if he should mention his growing attraction to their maid Alice, but as he had not said anything to her yet, he decided to see how things developed. A word from his mother made him take things slowly.

~

The Whites occupied the only two spare guest rooms at the official residence. Their house completion was still some months away.

With the new coins in circulation, Rudi Greenwood and Lance Upcroft were heading back to England due to family deaths. Duty called for them.

Through them, Lachlan found another coachman, who gave the official family a little more freedom, as there were now two drivers. Joseph was based in Parramatta, and Brenton Wright was in Sydney. Brenton had come to the governor's notice through their involvement with the production of the new currency. Brenton was working with Rudi, Lance, Mark, and William Henshall to do the physical work of minting.

Lachlan had Brenton Wright's conviction quashed when a new witness came forward to corroborate his story. Brent was to remain in Sydney and work from there as the coachman. Brenton would be in charge of the new government stables currently being built in Sydney.

~

After months living at Government House, Perry and Katy White moved into their accommodation in one of the cottages on Phillip Street in Parramatta. Two more cottages were under construction, and Perry had taken the option on all three. Perry was busy with Lachlan planning what to do next in the colony. The viceregal couple was aware of Perry's illustrious status as an earl, but he refused to use the title in the colony.

Mark had been on duty at Government House in Sydney when Perry arrived, so he knew the secret and promised his titled friend that he would keep silent. He had overheard the gentleman with the melted face's introduction and had been drawn into friendship. They were three very unusual men. Perry was from the top end of society, Mark from the very lowest, and Lachlan was thrust into leadership, but they formed a firm friendship because of their shared faith. They had regular prayer sessions, which helped create a strong bond of friendship.

When Perry was at a loose end, he would wander up to the tollgate and sit chatting with Mark. He needed to talk to someone, and he chose Mark. They fell into a deep conversation about their backgrounds.

Perry groaned. "Mark, I lived as Perry White for a decade because of my melted face. I hid from everyone except my minister. It was only because of Katy that I re-entered life. If she had not misunderstood a platonic embrace I gave her friend, Mary, she would not have stolen something, been arrested and sent here. That is all beside the point. Mark, I value your friendship for the same reason Lachlan does, and Henry too. We know we can trust you both. The fact that you have remained silent about my true status proves my point."

Mark smiled. He was amazed at who God had brought into his life. "Perry, Cathy and I were born in the worst slums in London, and we lived at the Rookery. As you've been to London, I'm sure you will have heard of the evil place if you have not visited it out of curiosity."

Perry admitted that he had. He had been horrified at what he had seen and vowed to do something about it on his return home. However, the fire occurred only weeks later. He nearly died, but Katy's father did die. He still felt guilty that he lived. Perry told Mark of the saga and the long recuperation. "I never returned to London until this trip here, Mark."

Mark understood. He nodded and told his story. "We had nothing. Our parents all but cast us out. Cathy's father sold her when she was thirteen, and I was nine when my mother remarried. I was banished to live on the streets; a minister found me and took me in. But Cathy was rescued by James, her first husband. Both he and I had been taken in by a minister some years apart. That wonderful man paid for my enlistment in the Navy, and I ended up here as part of the governor's security detail. We'll never go back. For you to count me as a friend is more than I can believe. I value your trust and your friendship, and I will keep your secret, but know that I am always here to listen."

The hand Perry placed on his friend's shoulder gently squeezed it. "Mark, I learned that those born with silver spoons in their mouths are often not worth the time spent in conversation, let alone friendship. We were not always rich. My father inherited the dukedom from an absolute scoundrel. The old duke was one of the vilest men I know. Admittedly, I only met him once, but I knew of his filthy acts and degraded life long before that. He hunted for underage victims." He shuddered. "He paid for my education when he realised he would have no legitimate male heirs. Mind you, he has many illegitimate ones, mostly born to servants in his house. There were so many that Father needed to start a school for them."

Mark gasped. "How...? No, don't answer that." He swallowed. He knew about the debauched peers who haunted the poorer areas in London. There was one group in particular that liked to deflower little girls. One of them had been reported to be an elderly duke, and he wondered if it was the same man. "Perry, I met one such duke in London. I think his name was Julian, Duke of Cheatham. Would that be him? He was often in the company of Lord Wiskhamford and Lord Edgar Oxenborough-Thorpe. All were partial to very young children."

Perry just nodded. His face fell. "That's him! I didn't know he hunted there, but I shouldn't be surprised; hunted being the operative word. It will take many years before Father gets it all sorted. As to the friendship between those three, it would not surprise me. He was best friends with Francis Dashwood, who was also a member of the same club. I believe it was known as the Hellfire Club, but he also belonged to Boodles in London. The fact that it was next to Almacks, where all the debutantes attended, was a temptation for them. I think it all started with the same person. When Dashwood died in 1781, the Hellfire Club changed its name, but it didn't die out." Perry sat shaking his head.

Mark knew of the club but wished he didn't. Rumours of Black Masses, virgin de-flowerings, and sacrifices were associated with that group. He had heard whispers that they even liked little boys. His stomach roiled when he heard about their sordid lusts. His minister had told him about it, but he had never realised that peers were part of that debauched group.

Chapter 14 Future Plans

fter Joshua's departure, Lachlan missed his shadow. Josh had been gone for over six months, and he was lonely. Even though he saw him every few days, it had been nearly a year since the lad voiced his wish to join his family. Lachlan had selfishly delayed his departure. He sat at his desk and thought back to the projects that were underway. In the five years since he arrived, Sydney Cove had now become known as simply Sydney. The derelict wattle and daub buildings were gone, the Tank Stream was reasonably clean again, and new wells had been sunk in various places. On the voyage here, Lachlan had pondered for months on how he would achieve the commission he had been given. Thanks to John Hunter, he knew he had to clean up the colony and restore order.

The hospital's stone edifice was well underway. The rum tariffs that D'Arcy Wentworth and his team received to build the hospital had tapered off, but there were enough funds in the kitty to complete it. He chuckled when he realised that everyone was now calling the building the Rum Hospital because of the source of the money. This was because, as part of the contract, the governor agreed to grant Wentworth, Riley, and Blaxcell permission to import an initial 45,000 gallons of rum and, later, a further 65,000 gallons of spiritous liquid. As the masses were still consuming alcohol, the sale of this grog filled the government coffers. The final costs of the hospital construction and later the road repairs were from the tariffs on other imported spiritous liquids. Yes, the name of the Rum Hospital was apt.

All distilled liquors attracted such a tariff, but sweet rum was still the favourite tipple, so it sold well. The fermented molasses was a potent brew. Once the hospital was completed, Lachlan intended to use the funds for other purposes. The new barracks at Hyde Park were more than half built, as were many other projects. He had a list of buildings he wanted constructed, and with Perry's assistance, he added more. Thanks to Perry's involvement, a bank was now being built. Ex-convict Mary Reiby's waterfront store currently handled the town's banking, and Parramatta needed such a facility.

D'Arcy found it challenging to guarantee the safety of the tolls now being collected. He needed somewhere safe to deposit the funds. This year's takings were expected to exceed £500, which would go a long way to repairing the roads and funding other projects he had in mind. The money would then be used to pay workers, and the currency would be kept in circulation to be collected in tolls. The obsolete tokens and foreign coinage could be melted and removed from circulation.

Lachlan relaxed in his office chair and thought back to the construction and preparation of the first market, which had only been months after his arrival. A massive fair followed that in Parramatta. Only a few months later, his friend, Andrew Thompson, had died. That in itself caused more problems. He had been left as a sultanate beneficiary if Andrew's family refused to claim his estate, which is what occurred. Lachlan sighed in resignation at the constant demands on him. He also had a mental hospital being constructed at Parramatta. It had gone up quickly as its need had been great.

Reopening the Emu Ford prison farm had been one of his few failures. Having said that, it had served the purpose for the short term. It had supplied food at a time that was in short supply.

He wished that the Home Office had a way to notify him of the number of convicts they were sending. Did they not realise that housing and feeding them when they arrived by one unexpected shipload after another made it virtually impossible to cope with them all? It was not like they had a spare three-hundred-bed building sitting just waiting for them. He leaned forward and jotted a note on his to-do list. "Enquire about the construction of convict barracks and start with a female facility." Perry's wife Katy had been pushing him to do this. Governor King had first mentioned it, but it only remained a dream.

He reclined in his chair again, deep in thought. With a supply of currency circulating since last year, the situation of illicit rum was not as valuable. Rum was still used as an unofficial legal tender, but despite fines for its use, he was determined to stamp it out. However, for the moment, he had it under control. He was fully aware that there were still dribbles of spiritous liquids making their way into the town from other ports and even outlying farms, where no duty was paid. However, Lachlan was slowly stamping this out of circulation by decreasing its value. It would always be consumed, but alcohol was no longer permitted to purchase things. Wages needed to be paid in cash only. He had instigated an enormous import duty of three shillings per gallon on all spiritous liquids, and the funds were directed to be used in the colony. As the Rum Hospital and other buildings took shape, hundreds of convicts were put to work in the brick pits, stone quarries, and construction sites.

With Elspeth's assistance, they had more than two hundred projects either underway or planned. Francis Greenway had been a fantastic find by Perry, but he had an ego bigger than Lord Castlereagh, who thankfully, was in

London. Henry Kitchen and John Watts were good, but Greenway knew his material. He was a stonemason's son and knew precisely what the stresses and strains the sandstone could take. His talents of workmanship were as immense as his ego. Once, when Lachlan asked for a simple job to be constructed and drawn up, he received a curt note from Greenway saying he would do it, but was not impressed that such a menial task was being asked of him. Lachlan had laughed at the time, but it also made him angry. He had set Greenway's compatriot forger, Joseph Lycett, to record the colony in paintings and drawings. His work to date had been exceptional. Yet, that man, too, had caused problems. He had been caught forging five-shilling bills while working at the police office. He had just been sentenced to two years in Newcastle. Somehow, the man had either sourced or made a small copper plate printing press and was literally making his own money. He wondered if it was made from the smelted coin tokens. Forged £1 notes began appearing everywhere. Lachlan huffed at the audacity of the man who betrayed his trust.

Lachlan's arduous trips had also taken a toll on his health. He had not been well before he came, but the rough conditions were detrimental to his precarious health. He did reconnaissance along the foothills of the Blue Mountains, but his recent trip to Bathurst was eye-opening.

D'Arcy's son, William, had said that the governor needed to see the vast plains for himself. So he went. The potential for grazing out there was immense. The vast, wide-open plains could feed thousands upon thousands of beasts. He was determined to open this area as soon as he could. He had already gazetted the town and signed the approvals for the subdivision of a new settlement that hopefully would become the hub of a new area of development. With the revision of the Ticket of Leave system, convicts could be assigned much faster and would be off-stores much sooner. The more he could get placed, the less drain they would be on the government coffers. However, expansion would mean encroaching on more of the Aboriginal lands. He had no wish to do this, but he had little choice. He needed to feed his people.

He had come to relish a quiet day in his office. However, today, he was bored. Lachlan shook his head as if to scare away the thoughts and memories. The paperwork was piling up on his desk, and he knew he needed to concentrate. He felt overwhelmed. He dipped his quill in the ink and set to work clearing his desk. He could hear his wife and little Lachie laughing on the front lawn. It was the last straw. He dumped his quill down roughly and walked out to join them. He did not realise how much he would miss Josh when the young man left. At least he had his little Lachie and his Elspeth; he would have the afternoon off and spend it with them.

~

At the toll house, Josh shared a small room with his little brother on the top floor of the residence. Although Mark and Cathy had been married for four years, Josh had not had to share a house with them as a family before moving in here. At the governor's residence, he had lived in the stables with the coachman. It took some adjusting to get back into the new family structure. Most of the gate work was done during the daytime, and due to the inclement weather, Josh and Mark constructed a small booth that they could shelter under and be protected from the elements.

Thomas Tindale, the blacksmith, made a small, lockable metal box that they bolted to the back wall of the small booth. When the traffic was queuing up, they could drop in the coins rather than keep them in pouches around their waist. A chalkboard kept a tally of what passed by. In the house, a larger locked chest contained the bulk of the takings. This was kept under Mark and Cathy's bed. Only Mark and Josh knew where the key was hidden, but a slot in the top meant that the metal safe did not need to be opened to put in coins.

Alice and Jenny often took the tolls if the men were busy outside in the stables. They dropped the coins in the tin outside and returned to their duty. Josh assisted Alice as often as he could without being too obvious. A mere brush against her was enough to flush his face.

~

Over the weeks, life settled into a routine at the tollgate.

Josh had been with them for over six months when one morning, he was supposed to be overseeing the toll gate while also doing the books. Perry White had come to visit Mark, and they were out in the stables with their tea. A carriage with four horses was seen rumbling towards the tollbooth. Josh stood from his desk to collect the toll when Alice called that she would take the three shillings. Josh was upstairs counting the takings to give to D'Arcy Wentworth later that afternoon. He had undertaken to keep the bookkeeping up to date and ensure the figures were tallied correctly. He had heard Alice's call that she would get this toll and knew that his mother, Jenny, and the children were within call should she need them. His concentration returned to the job at hand.

Outside, the carriage slowed, and the toll was collected and clinked into the box. He heard the gate open. As it did, Josh heard Alice shout, "No, unhand me! Leave me alone," then came a muffled cry.

Josh had not bothered to look whose carriage it was, but now he flew to the bedroom window. Mr Ardeth's fancy vehicle was speeding through the gate, and Alice was nowhere in sight. Forgetting the large pile of coins on the desk, Josh flew downstairs to see if Alice was unharmed.

His running feet on the wooden steps drew his mother and sister from the kitchen. His mother asked, "Josh, whatever is wrong?"

He called as he ran, "It's Alice. I heard her cry, and then it sounded like a muffled call. She may be hurt."

Josh burst out of the door, calling her name, to see just an empty courtyard. "Alice, Allie, where are you?" Alice was nowhere in sight, and the carriage was a puff of dust quickly fading into the distance. Josh released a long, strangled cry. "Nooo! She's gone. He's taken her."

The toll gate stood open, and Josh felt his heart skip a beat. Where was she? Why had Ardeth taken Alice? Josh walked to the small shelter and found her duster in the dirt. She had obviously been taken against her will.

Jenny realised what had occurred to her friend and went to tell Mark.

Within minutes, Mark and Perry saddled their horses, mounted, and set out to follow the carriage.

Mark ordered, "Josh, you must stay here. If something occurs, fisticuffs or worse, your convict background will see you imprisoned. Perry and I can handle him."

Cathy had come to Josh's side. Josh wanted to flatten Mark and chase after Alice himself. He said, "No, Mark, she's my girl; I want to... no, I need to come."

His mother's caring hands were restraining him.

Mark had been blind to the growing rapport between the two. He said, "Josh, that is all the more reason for you not to come. Currently, you have no claim on her, but I do, as she is assigned to me. However, I need you to go to the governor and tell him what has occurred. Tell Henry Antill to get some of the 73rd regiment to mount up and follow us, and we will scour the countryside if necessary. We'll bring her back safely for all of us."

Leaving Josh no time to argue, the two men rode off hard. Their dust ball followed the carriage westward.

Josh watched them until they were out of sight. Then he closed the tollgate behind them and took off on foot to the governor's residence. He didn't like leaving his mother unguarded, but this was an emergency.

Henry was on duty and saw Josh running up the hill. He followed him and noted that the young man walked straight to the office.

Josh hardly waited for a call to enter after his knock. While still puffing, he said, "Sir, Mr Ardeth has stolen my girl, sir. He's taken, my sweet Allie."

Henry had followed him in and overheard the statement.

Lachlan had been hard at work, attending to his bookwork, and he was thoroughly bored again. He relished the interruption. He saw Henry hard on Josh's heels. Lachlan carefully placed his quill down and closed the ink well. "Josh, my boy, what do you mean he's taken her? Who has taken whom?"

Josh explained what he had heard and how he had recognised the carriage. Only when Alice had gone did he realise the depth of his feelings for her. "Mr Ardeth, sir, he took my girl, Alice, sir. I heard her outside and... and she was gone." Josh sank into a chair, and his head fell into his hands. He muttered, "I haven't even told her how I feel." He was still puffing and took some time to regain his breath.

Lachlan was not surprised at Josh's affection for the very capable lass. He dug a little deeper for some information. "Josh, has Mark followed? Is that why you are here?"

Josh nodded. "Perry White is with him. Mark asked me to request that Major Antill accompany them with some of the 73rd. He and Mr White are hard on the carriage's path, leaving only minutes after it did, but they will need backup. They are headed west, sir, but I don't know where they are going." He angrily brushed aside a tear.

Lachlan nodded, then looked at Henry, waving his hand and said, "Tell Mrs White where her husband is, Henry. Take a detachment of the 73rd and follow them."

Henry departed with a grin. He felt like cheering as he was permitted to follow the kidnapper. On his way to the barracks, he told Katy White what was happening, then continued to the riverside stables behind the rickety barracks. Soon, fifty of the finest riders of the 73rd regiment were hard on the abductor's heels. Henry grinned and said to his friend, "This outing certainly beats doing drills."

Lachlan offered Josh tea, but with the message delivered and the posse's departure, Josh wanted to head back home to await news. He also didn't like leaving his mother and sister unguarded. He wished to be there when Alice returned, as he was determined to declare himself and officially ask to court her. Lachlan asked, "I'm guessing she is partly why you wished to move home? You should have told me, lad."

Josh nodded bashfully, then left before he embarrassed himself further.

From his front door, Lachlan watched a dejected Josh meander back down the hill towards his home. Lachlan understood all too well how the heart reacts when you lose someone you love. However, in Josh's case, hopefully, Alice would return fit and well. He wondered what the reason for her abduction was. With his security detail all but gone, Lachlan returned indoors and suggested that they lock up and stay inside. Charles Whalen was called from a nap. He was off duty, but Lachlan needed him to be on guard. His two front guards were still there, and he instructed them to stay alert and keep a lookout for trouble. He knew that some free settlers still had it out for him, and this could well be a diversion to harm him and his family. Thankfully, John Macarthur had not yet returned from England, but he had friends who had remained. Yes, he would keep his family safe. He pulled out his pistol and musket, loaded them and placed them at hand.

By the time Josh returned to the toll house, an hour had passed since the carriage left the tollgate. The small table clock on the mantelpiece chimed as he entered; it was ten o'clock. Josh knew the money was still on the desk upstairs, and he had yet to finish the books. D'Arcy Wentworth was due to arrive in two hours to collect the takings. He still had to have them ready. His mother greeted him with a hug, knowing that if she said much, they would both weep. She bustled around, handed him a mug of tea and sent him back to work. She and Jenny would deal with the tollgate, and he needed to finish the books. Josh gave a reluctant nod and moved towards the stairs. "Mama, has Alice ever said anything to you about how... no... if she feels anything towards me?"

Cathy shook her head, but her eyes turned to Jenny, who was standing at the kitchen door. Josh saw her subtle nod. "Jen, do you know?"

His little sister answered with a grin. "She cares too, Josh, but she's a convict and can't wed without permission."

Josh's face lit up. "She said that? Really? Is that her only concern?" Jenny nodded. He ignored the rest of the comment, knowing the governor would give his permission willingly. With a spring in his step, he returned to finish the work upstairs. He wished he could have followed her, but knew Mark was right. If he had caught Ardeth, he would have fought him and punched his lights out, but if the regiment arrested the evil man, Mr Ardeth would face justice and hopefully never cause his family harm again. His timid wife obviously lived in fear of him.

Josh had just packed the coins into their respective bags and placed them in the chest when another carriage was heard outside. Taking a quick glance, Josh saw D'Arcy Wentworth and his large security entourage coming to collect the tolls. He had just tied the last bag, ensuring it all tallied. It had been a busy week. There was over £100 in coins, which weighed a lot. His books balanced, but he had tuppence over in his tally. He huffed, damned tuppence again! The judge's comment still haunted him. He shoved it in the slot. He needed to ask Doctor Wentworth what to do with that. He was sure it was only that someone had forgotten to write down a horse and rider as they passed, but they had taken their toll. A rider now only cost tuppence to pass.

It was ten minutes to noon, and there was still no sign of Mark or the posse who had followed Mr Ardeth. Josh had missed the posse passing, but Cathy said about fifty riders had joined the hunt. Josh was locking the metal chest when he heard a knock on the front door.

As Cathy welcomed their illustrious guest, she said, "Doctor Wentworth, we have a situation in progress." She filled him in about the morning's kidnapping and Mark's absence when Josh appeared carrying the metal chest. With so many coins inside, it was heavy.

D'Arcy acknowledged the money's arrival with Josh and turned back to Cathy for a full explanation of the morning incident. When she had filled him in, he said, "And you say Mark has followed him?"

Josh replied, "Yes, sir, with Henry and the bulk of the off-duty 73rd regiment on their heels. Mark and Perry White were following the carriage before the dust had settled. I thought they should have returned by now, and I'm worried."

D'Arcy blanched. "If the 73rd is with them, who is with the governor? I presume the Henry is Major Henry Antill, who has gone to Mark's assistance?" D'Arcy could see the anxiety on the young man's face.

Josh nodded. "Yes, sir." He had not thought about the governor's safety. He felt gutted that he had not been concerned about them, rather than Alice. "Sir, Charles Whalen is at the house, but he's off duty today."

D'Arcy turned and walked to the door. After giving hurried instructions, more than half his men rode off towards Government House. They, too, were part of the 73rd regiment but were stationed in Sydney. The value of the toll takings was far less important than the governor's well-being. The greying Scotsman had all but turned the colony around. It had gone from being filled with filthy hovels and disease-ridden water to being on the way to becoming a nice place to live. D'Arcy didn't mind that his own pockets were reaping the benefits from both their friendship and the extra work. He did not need to fiddle the books, as his various roles, including senior surgeon, head of the police, and administrator of roads and bridges, brought in ample funds for his comfortable lifestyle. His children were being educated, and his abodes were improved dramatically. He wasn't keen that the governor often had a dig at him to marry one or other of the three women who had birthed his ten children, but so far, he had resisted the pressure. One of them already had a husband. The governor's safety was worth the forfeiture of most of his own security detail. He had already collected the takings from the northern tollgate and planned to return to Sydney after collecting this money. However, D'Arcy returned his attention to the family inside. He decided to stay until he knew the outcome of the chase.

Rather than leave the chest from the Broken Back Western Toll gate in the carriage, he instructed the security detail to move the chest indoors. He had his men move his carriage to the stable yard, and they released the horses into the yard. He set the youngest of his men to collect the tolls. Andrew Baum was only eighteen and known to all as Drew, and he was new to the regiment. He was a locally born lad and enlisted to see if he could make a difference in the town. D'Arcy knew that he always volunteered for this boring guard duty, wondering if Miss Jenny was the real attraction. Cathy, Jenny and Josh would at least be relieved of that onerous duty for the time being.

Carriages, herds, flocks and riders came and went all afternoon. From inside, the prices were announced to each person passing by. Each time, the soldier on duty was asked why they were there. Then, at two o'clock, one rider from the west brought information. He was riding eastward and had met up with Mark and Perry, then, a little later, the posse. He had given Mark and the group directions to where the carriage had turned off.

D'Arcy came out and pumped him for information.

The rider explained. "They went to Castlereagh, Mr Wentworth. The horses on the carriage were nearly blown, but they were still moving along at a pace. Mark and Mr White had stopped in Penrith as they had lost them. Mark stopped me and asked for information. I saw the fancy carriage turn onto the northern road along the river, and I put them on their tail again"

Cathy, Jenny, and Josh heard his words, and all gasped.

Josh moved forward and said, "So they have nearly caught them?"

The man said, "They should have by now, lad. They were not far behind them when I passed."

D'Arcy noticed the acute anxiety on the young man's brow. It occurred to him that there was more than just concern for a missing convict girl. "She'll be fine, lad. I'm sure Mark and Perry will return soon enough." The haunted look that Josh gave him confirmed his suspicion. The boy was in love with the abducted girl. D'Arcy placed a comforting hand on the lad's shoulder.

Josh waited until the traveller departed, asking his mother, "Can I ride out and meet them now, Mama? Please? They should be on their way back by now and in no danger. Drew is here. He'll be on guard."

D'Arcy's eyes met Cathy's. She was nodding. With the soldiers outside, he decided to let the lad go. He said, "Go, Josh; bring her home for us all."

Josh was out the back door within moments. He was saddling his roan stallion, Cloud, when Cathy arrived with his oilskin coat, some padding for Alice to sit on, a warm cloak and a blanket for her. "Joshy, Alice was only in her day dress and apron when she left. By the time you return, she will be cold. She will also be in shock, so be gentle with her son." After tying Alice's things on the back of his saddle, Josh hoisted himself up, turned Cloud's head, and headed out to follow the road west. "Thanks, Mama; I'll look after her."

Cathy knew he would. "Go find her, son." She watched as he went through the toll gate, hunched over Cloud's back, and took off like a jockey in a race.

Alice was only sixteen, and although she had been through a lot in her young life, she had not let it taint her. Alice absorbed the faith she had found in their house. She listened to Mark, Cathy, and Jenny as they discussed their beliefs. She slowly relaxed, realising she was safe. After a few months, Alice had opened up to Cathy about her past. Cathy didn't worry about her revelation; she had lived through much the same herself. What had occurred to Alice was similar to what James had rescued her from.

By late afternoon, Josh had found the group. They were halfway back from Penrith and nearing Toongabbie Creek when they met. Alice was in front of Mark on his stallion. He had his arms wrapped around her, and Josh felt a stab of jealousy. The posse of the 73rd regiment followed them, surrounding a shiny black carriage. Josh rode to Mark's side. "Is she all right, Mark? Is she unharmed?"

Alice had been asleep against Mark and woke when she heard his voice. She struggled to sit up. Mark eased his grip on the young girl. "She's okay, Josh, just cold and tired."

Alice was now awake. She reached out a hand to him. "Joshy, you came!"

He took her hand and said, "I brought you a coat and blanket, Allie."

The group stopped while Josh hopped down and untied Alice's warm things. He left the padding on his saddle for her.

Mark let her slide down and don her warm attire. Rather than return to Mark's tired horse, Josh lifted Alice onto Cloud's back and hoisted himself behind her. Once mounted, he wrapped the blanket around her. She wanted to snuggle against him, so he softly said, "Make yourself as comfortable as possible, love." He flicked her cheek affectionately. "I'm so glad you are safe."

Alice's gaze lifted to him in shock. She was sitting upright, somewhat uncomfortably, on the front of his horse. She wished to lean against him as she had done with Mark, but she was nervous. Her gaze met his smiling face before flicking over to see Mark grinning at her.

Josh kissed her head, pulled her against him, and said softly, "I nearly died when I discovered you had gone, my sweet Allie. I wanted to come after you, but Mark would not let me ride with them. My heart did a flip, my sweet girl."

Alice sighed and relaxed, then snuggled into his embrace. "Mark told me that Josh. He said you nearly landed a punch on him." He could hear the amazement in her voice.

He pulled her a little closer. He dropped his voice again and whispered, "I would fight the devil himself to keep you safe, my love."

Alice lifted her face from his chest. "And I will do anything to help you in any way I can, Joshy."

He dropped a kiss on her upturned lips. "I'll never let anyone else hurt you again, Allie." With so many people close, he had to keep his voice low. "I want to court you properly, Allie, but we already share a house. I will ask if you will be my girl, though."

Alice sighed with delight. "I'd love that, Joshy." Her head hurt where she had been hit, and she wanted to go back to sleep.

Josh was equally delighted. "So would I, sweet Alice." He wished to sweep her into his arms and carry her away. However, she was already in his arms, and he had to ensure they arrived home safely. He knew that as night fell, the bushrangers preyed on lone travellers. She had had enough trauma for a long while. They needed to stick together as a group. Knowing she had now agreed to be his girl, he was again concerned for her comfort. "Are you warm enough, sweetheart? Snuggle closer if you are cold." He tucked the blanket around her again and adjusted his position to make her more comfortable. Thankfully, his saddle did not have a pommel, as it was an English saddle with a slight rise at the front. The padding Cathy had insisted on was a blessing.

Chapter 15 My Beloved, My Love

*A*lice wiggled and now rested fully against him. Once settled, she said, "I am warm and comfortable, Josh. I have everything I want, including you." Her last words were almost a murmur. The tiredness was nearly overwhelming her.

Josh's heart sang. "Sleep, love. I will keep you safe." He pulled open his coat, and under it, she wrapped her arms around his waist. None could see her action as he made sure she was encased in the blanket. She could hear his heart beating as she rested against him.

Not long afterwards, her regular breathing told him she was asleep again. Her arms relaxed, as did she. He felt her weight on his chest, but she trusted him to keep her safe, and he would. He wanted to keep her like this forever.

Mark looked across at the young couple. He remembered standing on the ship's deck with Cathy wrapped in his arms like that. He knew the emotional joy that such love brought. For Josh to have found his lady love at his age was wonderful for his stepson. When he noticed Alice had returned to sleep, he moved closer to Josh. "Son, as she's asleep, let me tell you what occurred."

Josh's beaming face met Mark's glance. "Thank you, Mark; I'm ready to hear it all now."

Mark told him about the chase and the meeting with the farmer, who set them on the right path towards Castlereagh. They had taken two wrong turns following the false dust clouds of other vehicles, and finally realised that they had let Ardeth's carriage get clear of them.

The first wrong turn had taken them to Rooty Hill Government Farm, and the second had been at the Mulgoa turn-off, where they followed a farm gig.

On their return to the main road at Penrith, they were finally given directions to Ardeth's grazing land.

The posse had met them in Penrith, and they travelled *en masse* to the farm. They discovered that Ardeth had recently built a small wattle and daub cabin on the farmland and had just turned in through the farm gate when the posse caught up.

A fracas ensued that left Alice knocked out by Ardeth and the coachman injured by a stray bullet from a soldier.

Mark took a swing at Ardeth and sent him flying backward. He had hit the ground hard, and quickly his prostrated, unresponsive body was loaded unceremoniously into the carriage.

The coachman's bullet wound was bandaged, and he was placed in the carriage on the floor beside his employer.

The poor horses were given a drink and a chance to graze before they were turned around, and the entourage headed back to Parramatta at a steady pace.

Soldiers rode on either side of the vehicle's doors, and two were now in the driver's seat.

On arrival back at the tollgate, Cathy was waiting to greet the weary travellers.

Alice was still asleep in Josh's arms, and Mark carefully lifted her from Josh's saddle and waited for him to dismount.

Josh took his sleeping beauty from his stepfather and carried her inside. She hardly stirred as he cradled her against him, still enfolded in the blanket.

Perry waved farewell to Mark, and then he and the remainder of the 73rd regiment continued into town with the carriage.

D'Arcy joined them by hopping into the carriage and said he would return for both chests tomorrow. Some of his soldiers would stay in the tollgate stables for the night.

For once, Josh did not take his steed to the barn, leaving Cloud for Mark to brush down and tend to.

Mark lifted a hand of thanks to D'Arcy, knowing they would catch up tomorrow when the entire saga was reported. For now, Alice needed attention, and though she had all of Josh's, Cathy hovered.

Cathy and Jenny opened the doors, and Josh carefully placed Alice on her bed. Rather than leave her, he bent and kissed her brow.

Cathy shooed him away while she tended to Alice, and he reluctantly left Alice to his mother's ministrations.

Jenny joined her mother to undress her friend and put her to bed.

Josh would not leave the area as he wanted to know she was comfortable.

Jenny remained with her friend until she settled.

Alice tossed and twisted for a while, murmuring in her sleep.

Jenny tucked the blankets around Alice again, but left her arms free as she kept fighting to get them from under the blankets.

Josh leaned against the wall until his mother emerged. His wait was short.

Cathy said, "We have changed her into her night attire, and she is asleep again. She has no other visible injuries but a bruise on her temple, rope burns on her wrists, and a bump on her head."

She saw Josh nod. Cathy continued, "She said to say thank you to Mark and good night to you, son." Cathy said that he could not see Alice, but she was well. She waved Josh away.

Josh sighed in frustration. Recollecting his steed, he went to check on his horse.

Mark was outside in the stables and called for Josh to join him. He needed to reveal details of the chase to Josh with no ears around.

Josh's movements were somewhat sluggish. He passed four soldiers heading into the kitchen for a meal and thanked them for staying. Josh obviously did not wish to leave his watch on Alice's door, but he knew he would not be permitted to see her again that night.

Mark patted the top of a barrel of grain. "Josh, I need to let you know all. I said little on the journey as I was unsure if Alice was asleep."

Josh took a seat on the upturned barrel.

Mark said, "First, I need to say that she was not violated by either Ardeth or his man. She said that herself. However, she has been physically abused and held against her will. She has bruises you will not see, as he punched her up quite a bit when she tried to escape. Josh, all she wanted was to get back home, and by home, I mean to you. She was somewhat upset you had not come to her rescue, but she understood when I told her why I had not permitted you to ride with us."

Josh groaned. "She will hurt tomorrow, Mark, but I am relieved she was not defiled. However, I love her no matter what occurred. She's been through enough as it is. Being on a convict ship is enough punishment, and I know her journey out was unpleasant. I am guessing her life at home was as bad as Mama's."

Mark knew exactly what he meant. He married Cathy, knowing she had once been a streetwalker. He was also aware that it had not been her choice. He knew that Cathy had told Josh of her background, so with the horses now in their stalls and the soldiers inside being fed, they sat in the barn alone, and Mark revealed Alice's background. "Josh, normally I would never speak of your mother's history, but she told me she revealed everything to you, so you know what your mama went through before she met your father. You will understand why Alice must be treated carefully. Few women in this hellhole escape such violations. Lachlan and Perry have placed Perry's cousin,

Janey Brien, in the position of identifying girls at risk and placing them in safe homes. Hence, Alice is with us, and more are scattered in other homes. More safe places will follow as he finds them."

Josh had been horrified when he discovered what his mother had endured. He sat staring at Mark and nodded. This town was full of the most undesirable people on earth, and many of them were the military guards, not the convicts. He had heard of women being violated in their sleep by the guards while in prison. Yet amongst them were a smattering of those, like him, who had been caught up in the sticky web of lies and injustice. Josh knew Janey Brien and had heard from Lachlan that she, Perry, and Katy were tackling the problem of keeping some of the youngest convict girls safe. He wanted to know more, so he said, "Go on, Mark."

Mark continued, "Son, like your mama, Alice was sold by her parents to save her family from an outstanding debt. However, she was not put onto the street, but kept under lock and key and abused at the man's every whim."

Mark was livid when he heard the girl's story from Cathy. "We all knew she grew up on a farm, but the rest of the story was that the farm failed when her father became ill, and Alice was sold to a merchant to pay off their outstanding debt. She was kept indoors for months and was cruelly violated. Then, one morning, the man forgot to tie her to the bed and lock her in. She escaped and headed to the marketplace, where she intentionally stole some fabric while standing next to the market manager. She knew she would be arrested, but that was far better than how she had lived for the past months. She realised that the only way to escape the man was to be in prison."

Josh felt like he had been punched in his guts. He was winded and felt ill. The fact that Mark was telling him now meant that he had known her background before this incident. "Why didn't you tell me? Why didn't I realise?"

Mark knew his turmoil and could see his anger growing. He said, "Josh, you did not need to know about her background before. Now you have declared your intent to court her. I felt you should know before it was too late." He saw the lad shaking his head. "Alice was sent here because we could keep her safe."

His stepson gave him a half-hearted smile.

Josh added, "We almost failed." He wiped away the moisture that had seeped from his eyes. As it was moonlit outside, he was thankful Mark could not see him properly. He was so angry with men who abused women and girls. His mother had not spared the details of the two years she spent on the street before his father rescued her. For Alice to experience something similar riled him. He also realised Mark had watered down her story.

Josh wasn't sure he wanted to know all the details, as that was for Allie to share with him should she choose to. He replied to Mark, "I don't care what she went through, Mark. That makes no difference to me. Papa loved Mama just as you do. What they endured has shaped them into who they are today. I love Allie. None of it was her fault, and I want to protect her in any way I can. No, I *will* protect her."

Mark smiled. He knew the young man would do that.

After some profound moments of thought, Josh asked, "Mark, why did Mr Ardeth take her? Did he say?"

Mark had been waiting for him to ask this. "He did, son. He said it was to get back at your mama for rejecting him. The man thinks he's God's gift to women and that none dare to rebuff his advances. He is an abusive dog."

Josh nodded in understanding.

Mark chuckled before adding, "He didn't have a chance to say more as I knocked him out. Perry had to restrain me as it was, or I may have killed him. I felt like kicking him to kingdom come. His, um, wiffles will certainly hurt tomorrow. I doubt he will be able to violate another woman for some time. It was after my well-aimed kicks to his private parts that the soldiers stepped in as the coachman went to the aid of his master. One fired his musket, and the coachman caught the bullet in his arm."

"Oh, I wondered where the blood came from." Josh had seen blood on Mark's cuff. It was not from either Alice or him. Perry didn't look like he was bleeding, either. "If I'd landed him a facer, he could have had me arrested, so thank you!"

Mark then admitted to Josh that he had lost his temper, and the man had still not roused by the time they arrived in Parramatta. "Josh, I struck him so hard that Perry, Henry and the contingent of the 73rd regiment have taken him to the hospital with his employee. He fell like a rock after my well-aimed kick as it lifted him off the ground." Mark had the decency to look embarrassed.

Josh grinned.

Mark said, "When D'Arcy entered the carriage out the front, he checked he was still breathing, which he was, but he had not stirred. The employee did not appear to be overly concerned about his master. Both will be kept under guard and manacled to their beds. Henry said he would let me know what would happen to him tomorrow. The driver was merely following orders, but he will still be charged with assisting a kidnapping."

They heard the back door bang and watched as Cathy entered the stables. She said, "Your dinner is hot if you're hungry. I have shooed the soldiers away to stretch their legs, although Drew Baum remains on the gate watch. Alice is still asleep, and Jenny is setting the table." She tousled her son's hair. "Come and eat, son. You both must be famished."

Josh nodded and headed indoors.

As they returned to the house, Mark slung his arm around Cathy's shoulders. After letting Josh enter, he pulled her back and said, "Have I told you how much I love you? Today brought it all back tenfold." He quickly told her what Mr Ardeth had said and why he had hit him. Mark knuckled up her chin and kissed her.

Cathy willingly accepted her caress. "I love you, too, Mark. And thank you for bringing her back."

He gave her another kiss before saying, "Sweetheart, I told Josh of her background. He wishes to court her and needed to know, just like you did with me. I would never have asked you about what occurred to you, my love, but I'm glad you did tell me, because as you know, the governor already knew and questioned me deeply about my knowledge of your background."

Cathy wrapped her arms around his neck, pulling him down to her again. It took some time before she answered. "I saw what Josh was like after you had left, Mark. Jenny let him know that Alice had admitted to liking him. After D'Arcy arrived with men here to protect me, Josh set off after you like a man possessed. I think we will need to rearrange the sleeping quarters in the house quite soon."

Mark slid his arm around her shoulder, and they walked inside to join their family. "Not until they are legally married, my love. D'Arcy can't marry Ann as she already has a violent husband she ran away from. I'm not sure D'Arcy would wed her anyway. He seems to shy away from such a binding union."

The little ones were already in bed, asleep; it was just the four of them who sat around the table discussing the happenings of the day.

Jenny served the stew and sliced another fresh loaf of crispy, crusted bread. She thickly buttered it and handed it to her brother.

Josh had not realised he was hungry. He had half an ear on Alice's room, which was just off the kitchen. As her door was ajar, he heard her murmur in her sleep. He was on his feet in a moment and stood watching her door lest she appear.

Jenny knew her brother's anxiety and said, "Josh, she won't wake for ages. Come and get some food into you." She had just returned from taking some stew out to Drew. She rarely had time to see him alone, and tonight, they had managed a few moments together with no one around. He had meant to kiss her on the cheek, but she had turned her face as he bent down. Their lips had connected, and they had their first innocent kiss. Her heart was beating twenty to the dozen.

Drew was as surprised as she was, but he recovered enough to ask, "Jenny, I would like to speak to your stepfather. Should I see him while I'm here?"

She nodded and murmured, "Yes, please, Drew," and fled inside as they heard the soldiers returning. She moved to the table and sat with her chin on her hands in dreamland, hardly hearing what the others were discussing.

Josh reluctantly seated himself and remained silent as he ate. His emotions were in turmoil. He didn't mind that Allie was a convict; he had been one too, or that she had an unsavoury history. He was a convicted thief. Didn't they all have something they regretted in their past? He had begged

God's forgiveness and lived a clean life since his conviction. No, his quandary was, what did he have to offer her? Yes, he loved her, but the tollgate was Mark's business. He had few skills and no training for anything. He sat deep in his own thoughts until his mother touched his arm.

Cathy saw he was preoccupied. "Josh, Mark asked you a question."

Josh shook his head and rubbed his eyes as though to brush away sleep. "Sorry, Mark, I was miles away." He had not even noticed that he'd finished his stew.

Jenny had been woolgathering, but she stood and cleared the table and took the now-empty pan from what had been a giant peach cobbler that she had served with whipped cream. It had fed everyone.

Mark smiled while watching Josh. He loved this young man as though he were his real son. Cathy was correct; he was a good lad. Mark had thought long and hard about his own future in the colony and did not want to spend his life as a tollgate keeper. He, too, had put some thought into their future, and now seemed a good time to bring it up. "Jenny, come and sit, as this is about you, too." He waited until Jenny rejoined them.

The two young ones listened intently. Mark started, "Josh, I had hoped to delay this conversation for some time. But I can see your mind ticking over, and I thought that while we are here alone, the four of us can discuss our plans for the future so that we won't be interrupted."

Josh blinked. He was now fully focused on Mark's words. What was he going to say?

Mark continued, "Josh, I'm a soldier with little training for work on the land, so farming is not a possibility for us, even if I went and did one of the Rosedales farming courses, I don't have the passion for the land. I took this position as the governor needed someone trustworthy to man the new tollgate. But even then, he had you in mind to take over running this when you are ready. He trusts you and wishes to keep you close at hand."

Josh attempted to say something, but Mark silenced him.

Mark glanced at Cathy, who gave him a subtle nod. "Son, Governor Macquarie always planned that you would take over here. However, you will need to have some years under your belt before we move on. He and I have discussed this. D'Arcy Wentworth made a suggestion that I think may suit us all." He noticed Josh's rapt attention, and Jenny sat grinning. He realised Cathy must have said something to her. He continued, "Josh, as I said, one day you will take over here, but that leaves us with a need to find something else to do in a couple of years."

Again, Josh tried to interrupt. He now understood Lachlan's odd comment.

Mark silenced him again. "Hear me out, lad."

Josh nodded and kept quiet. He zipped his lips with a smile.

Mark continued, "The area down near Cowpastures will go ahead soon, and the governor wishes trustworthy eyes and ears to be at hand near a certain farm. He is sure that Macarthur is due back soon, and the governor is concerned about this stirrer. He has asked me if we would be interested in running a government store there, and we have agreed. We won't be leaving for a few years, but that is the long-term plan. You will take over then, and hopefully, if you marry Alice, you may even have a couple of children to fill the upstairs rooms."

Ignoring that bit of his comment, Josh knew there was more. "Cowpastures, eh? Is that because it's where Macarthur's main farm is?"

Mark nodded. "Yes. As I said, John Macarthur is not yet back from England, but the governor expects news of his return at any time. He wishes someone he trusts to be on site down there. He already has plans for a new town nearby, which he plans to name Campbell Town, as it is good pastureland. He is planting new centres of growth in various places. He needs places to stock produce and become a hub for distribution and resale, like a small Government Stores outlet. However, he also needs it to become his eyes and ears, allowing information to filter through. Shops are a great place to talk."

Mark paused before adding, "As you know, the governor's wife and Mrs Macarthur are well known to each other and have an unofficial friendship. So, he wants to get started while things are peaceful. However, it will take time."

Josh nodded. He was aware of the clandestine meetings between the two lady friends and how, when Mrs Macquarie lost a child, Mrs Macarthur came to comfort her. The two Elizabeths enjoyed tea together whenever they could. They knew each other from England and had secretly maintained their relationship. They shared a deep faith and genuine friendship that could not be shown publicly. Both ladies were aware that it would be curtailed when John Macarthur returned, so they made the most of the time they had.

Mark could see that Josh understood what he meant without needing to say the words aloud. He said, "So, Governor Macquarie wants us *in situ* near Macarthur's farm but not on top of it. That means you will be needed here. As I said, that will not be for a couple of years, but that is the plan. However, if you don't wish to take over here, especially after today, then I fully understand that, and you can come with us if you wish."

Josh's mind was awash with the prospect of running the tollgate by himself, with just Alice to help. Mark had found it hard enough before he came, and there were three women to assist him. "I might need some more help, Mark. I presume Jenny would go with you?" He looked at his little sister, who had stayed quiet until now. Josh saw her smile in return. She had a glazed look about her.

Mark reached for Cathy's hand and said, "Unless the lovely Jennifer finds someone to marry before then, she will always have a home with us if she wishes. However, that will be up to her to decide when the time comes, that is, if she has not met someone already. It will be her choice who she marries. Her dreamy look makes me wonder." He gave her a loving smile.

Jenny gasped. She presumed that she would be given little say in who she married. Few girls had that choice. Drew had indeed caught her attention, and he even mentioned that he would speak to Mark, but he had no time to do that yet. As he had just asked to court her officially, she hoped he would talk to Mark before he left the next day. Her heart leapt with excitement. She blushed delightfully. Since enlisting, Drew was nearly always part of Mr Wentworth's detachment of security guards when collecting the tolls. If she could choose her husband herself, this young soldier would be top of her list. A slow grin spread across her lips. She felt sure Drew was serious about his question tonight.

Her mother noticed her absentmindedness. She had already noticed that her daughter had blushed shyly a few times during the day. She had not associated it with any particular man but decided to question her daughter later.

Mark, oblivious to the side issue, had noticed her blush but had not connected it to his comment. He continued, "Josh, I do not doubt that you will be able to employ someone or even assign a convict or two. With Ardeth off the streets, I do not imagine there will be much more trouble."

Josh released a long breath. "May I think about it, Mark?"

Mark relaxed. "Of course, lad. There is no need to make any decisions for months, possibly even a couple of years, but I wanted you to have some security about your future. The governor has a lot on his plate, and our new shop is low on the list of building projects. But it will get done. I presume you will ask to court Alice tomorrow?"

Josh flushed a deep shade of red, "I already did, Mark."

His mother turned swiftly towards him. She had been concentrating on her daughter and had missed this growing interest in the other pair. Cathy was stunned. "When, Joshy? You have not had a moment to chat with her since she arrived back."

Josh bit his lip before saying, "As soon as she came up before me, I asked her while she was getting settled. When she snuggled under my coat and rested against me, I could feel her heart beating against mine; I knew I wanted her to stay there forever. Sorry, Mama, Mark, but she is the real reason I wanted to live here." He blushed again.

Jenny giggled. "I told you they liked each other." She sat with her arms folded, smiling. The next couple of years looked rosy for her, too. Her mother married at fifteen, and she was about to turn sixteen.

Mark was about to throw his head back and release a deep laugh when Cathy quickly clapped her hand over his mouth. "Shh, you will wake her, Mark."

Mark kissed her palm and chuckled softly instead. "You win, wife of mine. I suggest we all go to bed. It's too dark for any carriages to go through tonight, but Josh, can you sleep down here anyway? Drew is on gate duty, so he can nap on the settee."

Josh had no intention of going up to the room he shared with his little half-brother. There was a truckle bed in an alcove where he slept on moonlit nights.

Mark had heard the soldiers retire for the night in the stables, so he went out to the tollgate and showed Drew where he could nap if he needed to attend to the gate.

Jenny measured out the cracked barley and put it on to soak overnight for the porridge the following morning.

The house soon fell silent after a round of "goodnights" from everyone.

Josh knew he wasn't on night duty, but he remained dressed anyway. He lay on his bed, having just removed his boots.

His friend, Drew, settled on the settee on the other side of the room. With only a year between them, they had spent time together when he came on security duty. Drew had an even worse life than Billy's until D'Arcy Wentworth found him in the hospital at death's door and took him under his wing.

Chapter 16 An Unexpected Future

$\mathcal{K}$ookaburras and cockatoos started the day with their raucous dawn cries, and a myriad of other birds joined the carolling magpies.

Josh stretched languidly and was about to get up when he heard the crunch of carriage wheels on the gravel outside. Rather than wake Drew or Mark, Josh padded out in stockinged feet to see the smiling face of the governor. Drew was dead to the world. So much for night duty! He chuckled. He opened the door to see the governor looking worried.

Lachlan greeted Josh and said, "Hello, lad. Henry and Perry have informed me of what occurred. I'm checking on the lassie before seeing Simeon Lord about the two prisoners."

Josh ushered the governor past the sleeping soldier and into the kitchen, pulling Alice's door closed as he passed by. He then stoked the fire and put some hot water on to boil.

Although their voices were hushed, Mark soon arrived downstairs to join their illustrious visitor over a mug of hot black tea at the kitchen table.

Lachlan loved visiting this home, where he was welcomed as a friend rather than kowtowed to as the governor. He was also entertained in the kitchen at Rosedale's farm, but Linus was currently ill. They had closed their house to any visitors. It was past dawn now, and the household would soon stir. The three men reviewed yesterday's activities.

Lachlan intermittently frowned and nodded as he heard the story from Josh, then from Mark and his pursuit. He listened intently, then said, "I called in at the hospital on the way here. You will be pleased to know that Ardeth is awake and cursing your name loudly, Mark. He has a black eye and a broken nose. His visage is no longer as attractive. His coachman is holding his tongue, but I imagine he will sing like a bird when separated from his master. I shall call upon Simeon to hear this case personally, as neither of the accused is a convict. I feel that Marsden would have given them a light sentence because they only took a convict girl, but I want such men gone from the towns. You know Marsden's ideas about felons and his bias against my plans to reinstate said convicts into society. However, thankfully, he is not here to hear the case as he has not returned from New Zealand. Simeon will do it."

Both listeners nodded their agreement.

Mark said, "The reverend's nickname says it all, sir."

Lachlan chuckled. "It's true and apt. The Flogging Parson is not a name I would like as a minister. He should not even be a magistrate. I feel it conflicts with his church work." He shrugged. "I disapprove of his methods, and as you know, I try to treat all men and women equally, be they black, white, convict, or free. We are all made in our good Lord's image. Few others believe that, but it's why I have a school for native children. Assimilation is our only way forward, but I'm not even sure that is the correct approach. All children need education to make that possible. It is why I attempt to learn some of their languages. I do not feel Marsden is a good example of our faith. He tends to take delight in arguing with me on every point. Especially if it concerns the emancipation of convicts and their reinstatement into positions of authority, he abhors Simeon Lord and was the same with Andrew Thompson. I am currently in a battle with him over the orphans." He released a long sigh. Mark agreed.

After a moment or two, Lachlan continued. "It's a pity the missionaries left following your friend Ruatara, Josh. They could have been useful here, but they came out to minister to the heathen and are certainly doing that in setting up a mission over there. Thankfully, Marsden left soon after his friends and went on an extended trip to help set up the mission. When his friends departed, I sent some goods with them. Ruatara admitted that he did not believe what Marsden so forcefully tried to teach him, but he was willing to sit and listen to gain insight into the ways of our culture. Anyway, Marsden followed suit and took grain and a hand mill, amongst other tools and things. As you taught him to ride, I also sent a mare, a cow, and a uniform for Ruatara." Lachlan chuckled. "It may give your friend a little more authority amongst his people. I gave him a new red uniform coat."

Josh grinned. Ruatara would like that. He nodded and said, "Yes, sir, he would."

Mark could imagine the dark, tattooed skin and the red uniform as an impressive sight. "Sir, I learned to respect all he taught Josh, but he has been gone from his homeland for some years, and I believe that although he was a chief, he was only a minor one. He told Josh that the head man was Te Pahi."

Lachlan nodded. "It's what he told me, too. I pumped him for information on how we could assist him and pave the way for his return home. He mentioned that they do not eat grain crops at all, only root crops. It was the grain crops that took his fancy in England as he became partial to our bread."

Mark agreed. "Yes, he may have only been there for a few weeks, but I gather he saw a lot in that short time. The sweeping green fields were not something we saw in our part of London, so he must have visited some farms."

Josh butted in. "He was upset he was there for so little time, but he did get to see what he wanted. He had to take the offer of a free passage home as he had no money. It was only two weeks after arriving that the reverend found him, but they did not leave England immediately."

"I presumed he had done that, Josh," Lachlan said. "He mentioned the various crops and met with farmers to learn about them. I know that Thomas Kendall also took bags of assorted seed grain with him. He also took some fruit tree seedlings and some poultry. I have not told you, Josh, that your friend has taken a third wife. Rahu was the wife of one of the previous chiefs."

Josh knew this as Ruatara had written to him with the news.

Lachlan drew a deep breath and then told the young man what he had recently learned. "Whalers massacred the head chieftain and many others in his tribe. There has been much trouble between these two groups. As you know, when poor Ruatara left here in 1811, he was abandoned on Norfolk Island by the whaling crew, and it took time for him to find a passage back to his homeland. When he eventually arrived in 1812, he found his people had been decimated shortly before. The head chieftain was dead, and his heirs were either missing or unfit for the job. Ruatara was elevated to the head chief, but his position still needed to be solidified. Hence, Marsden and I have taken steps to see that he will succeed."

Mark said, "I figured this third wife must have been Te Pahi's wife. Ruatara mentioned her a few times. I don't think I could handle more than one wife." He chuckled. "I have three women in my home as it is, but thankfully, only one is mine. I hope Josh takes one of them off my hands soon." His cheeky grin made his listeners smile.

Lachlan grinned. "I have a house full of women, too, Mark. Henry, Lachie, and I are outnumbered, but they all get along quite well. Charles, Robert Fopp, and my coachman don't count as they live in the staff quarters." He chuckled again before adding, "About your comment re Josh's beloved, lad, have you had time to think this over?"

A nod followed the lad's red flush. "I asked Alice yesterday if I could court her. But, sir, she would need permission to wed as she's still serving time."

Lachlan leaned back in his chair. He looked at the young man and then at Mark. "What do you think, Mark? Should I throw my weight around, and withhold my permission, or put the lad out of his misery?"

Josh looked distraught but knew they were teasing him. His beseeching eyes made Mark laugh. "Oh, Josh, never fear; we support your choice." He turned to the governor and said solemnly, "Yes, sir. I think he is deserving of such a punishment." Lachlan roared with laughter and quickly clapped his hand over his mouth.

Josh's eyes flew to Alice's door; however, it remained closed.

Moments later, Cathy appeared at the kitchen door with Rosemary in her arms. Gideon and Jenny followed in her wake. When Cathy heard Lachlan's voice, she dressed quickly and fed the baby. She greeted him with a smile and breezily said, "Good morning, sir."

The three men stood as she entered.

Lachlan said, "Morning, Cathy! I'm here to report on yesterday's events. Can you please see if Alice is awake?"

Cathy nodded, and she handed Rosemary to her husband. Cathy knocked on the door and entered the room as the men retook their seats. She closed the door behind her. Minutes later, the two ladies joined the group at the kitchen table. Josh jumped to his feet on their entry. Alice blushed when she saw Josh, but took the seat he pulled out for her next to him.

Now that everyone was seated, Lachlan repeated his plans to prosecute Mr Ardeth and his coachman.

Alice gasped, and Josh reached for her hand under the table. He caressed it with his thumb. He saw her shy glance and smile.

Lachlan had seen Josh's subtle action. He decided to see the couple privately before he left. He realised that although it was very early in their relationship, they needed to move quickly. He had always had a soft spot for this lad, so he would fast-track their approval if they wished. They were already sharing a house, so he would rather see them wed. "Alice, I will ensure that you and the family here are safe. I shall either incarcerate the man or send him and his family out of the colony. The coal mines in Newcastle need workers, and I think it would be fitting to send the immaculately dressed popinjay there for a time of service."

Alice nodded. "His wife is nice, sir. I would not like to see her harmed by such an evil man. I feel that she will bloom in his absence."

Cathy noted her glance at Josh before she continued. She said, "I think Mr Ardeth's over-frilled, immaculate attire could do with a bit of coal dust, sir." She bit her lip, trying hard not to laugh.

Lachlan agreed. "The final decision will be up to Simeon Lord. Plus, he owns a ship that does the coastal trading to Newcastle, so I know Ardeth would arrive alive and be required to serve hard time in irons, with no other means of escape."

Alice nodded, but with a sly grin. She whispered, "Good."

Gideon was hungry, so Lachlan asked Josh to accompany him into the sitting room. Once there, he asked, "Josh, are you serious about courting Alice?"

Josh had lain awake the previous night, thinking about Mark's words. Their conversation this morning reinforced that decision. He cared for Alice deeply. He had not known how much until she was abducted. He was in seventh heaven when she lay cradled against him last night. He took some time to answer, but turned to the governor and said firmly, "I am, sir. I had a lot of time to think about it when she was taken yesterday. We have grown ever so close over the months since I have been here, and yesterday, we declared our feelings for each other. I would like to marry sooner rather than later, as we already share a house, but I have not asked her yet. It may be a bit soon to talk about marriage, sir. However, it's certainly in my near future if she will have me."

Lachlan nodded his understanding of the situation. "Go fetch her, lad. I'll give you a moment of privacy and see what she says."

Josh exited the room and asked Alice to join them. He had not even been able to say a private good morning to her, let alone discuss marriage. Their feelings had only just been declared. He felt he knew her well, but he suddenly became shy and fell silent.

Lachlan realised Josh's embarrassment. He felt he was pushing them a little, but he turned as they entered and quizzed them about their feelings for each other. Alice's head dropped in acute embarrassment.

Josh went to her side and said, "Sir, can we have a moment?"

Lachlan nodded and walked to the far side of the room.

Josh took possession of her hands. "Sweet Alice, I know things have been rushed. But I realised when you had gone how much you mean to me. Yet, I had no claim on you to chase you. I know I only asked to court you yesterday, and we've not had time to talk at all, but I know I already wish to marry you. You don't need to answer, but just be assured I am not tinkering with your affections. There is much to discuss before that is required. Alice, I want you as part of my life forever."

Alice glanced at the governor before replying. "When I was taken yesterday, Joshy, all I wanted was you, but when Mark came and saved me. I was sad. When I heard your voice later, my heart sang. I realised you cared for me as I always hoped you would. Rather than say yes right now, can we have an understanding? Can we discuss it afterwards?"

Her head tilted to the waiting man. She lowered her voice even more and added softly, "Soon afterwards."

Josh was delighted. "That would be perfect. Yes, we could have an understanding." That was one step further than a courtship but not quite an engagement. "I think that's great, Allie." He wished to kiss her, but knew that would not be appropriate. He lifted his voice and said, "Sir, we've had a chat."

Lachlan turned and walked back to the couple. "I don't wish to push you, but as you are already living in the same abode, your situation should be resolved sooner rather than later. If Marsden were here, he would be having a fit. He would see you married today without Banns being read."

Josh nodded. "Sir, we have barely had time to talk, but we have agreed to an understanding for the moment. Can I make an appointment to see you next week? By then, we should have discussed many things."

Lachlan nodded. "Tuesday would do fine. I'm in the office all day. Alice, can you come as well, please?"

Alice nodded, followed by a servant's bob. She could not believe the governor knew her name, let alone wished to see her. "Yes, Your Excellency."

Lachlan chuckled, "Sir, will do fine, dear. You can amuse little Lachie while we chat. Then you and Mrs M. can join us for tea."

Her gasp of "Oh!" made him smile again.

Lachlan said, "Alice, this is a new life out here. Take the opportunities to better your position while you can. I know your background, or I would not have assigned you here."

Alice took a deep breath and bravely replied, "Thank you, sir. I hope to be of use wherever I can. My life here is so much better than at home. My new family care for my well-being, and I care for them. They have taught me much about their faith and being washed clean of our pasts."

Lachlan smiled. He saw Josh nod. "Alice, all of us will one day stand before our Lord in judgement. Many who think they are good people will be turned away because they have no faith in Christ. Our Lord asks that we treat all equally and follow His teachings. If you can learn what they are, then you have won the race that we are all on. Mark, Cathy, and Josh now all have a strong faith. However, here, many are in denial of God's power and His willingness to forgive our sins."

Alice smiled. She looked at Josh and said, "So I have discovered, sir. When Janey Brien singled me out for this placement, I thought I was being punished again. I was so very wrong. Regardless of my shackles, I'm free. Freer than I have ever been in my life. Learning about what Jesus did for all of us was life-changing." She released a happy sigh and smiled.

Satisfied with her reply, Lachlan nodded. He honoured her with a nod-bow, then turned to the lad. "Until next week, then, young Joshua. Talk over our earlier discussion about your future here. It's what is behind my haste." He bowed to the young couple and quickly moved to let himself out.

~

Later that morning, D'Arcy returned to collect the money, and he reported to them with a contented huff. "That overdressed popinjay has been tried and convicted to ten years at Newcastle digging coal. He is to travel on my ship under the command of my captain. He will not have a chance to escape. His coachman was forced under duress of the now said felon, Ardeth, threatening to violate the coachman's wife, so he was let off with a year working on the roads."

Everyone released a sigh of relief.

They were loading the chests of toll takings into the carriage and harnessing the horses in the back stabling area when one horse reared, then bucked. Its back hoof connected with Drew's shoulder. He was sent flying, and he was thrown some distance from the rearing beast. He was knocked out cold.

Jenny had been watching from the kitchen window. Seeing Drew lying on the ground, she came running out of the door, letting it bang.

That unexpected sound, made the unruly beast rear again. The other soldiers managed to get it under control and away from the injured lad as Jenny attended to his wounds. She drew the unconscious soldier into her lap and waited for assistance. She saw that Drew was bleeding and realised the horse's hoof had torn his shirt and broken the skin on his shoulder. She pressed her clean handkerchief on his skin to cover the wound and stem the bleeding. The departure was delayed while Drew was carried inside to the truckle bed in the sitting room. His injury turned out to be more than a simple bruised shoulder. The muscles in his arm were severely weakened. When he roused, he could hardly lift his arm. His head hurt, but his shoulder was worse. He woke to find D'Arcy Wentworth standing over him and probing his injury.

The man ministered to his injury and instructed him to stay at the tollgate until well. Drew was put on extended leave.

Jenny was left tending the prostrated soldier as the others returned to the kitchen. The hoof of the rearing horse had hit hard, but hopefully, the flesh wound would not become infected.

Cathy and Jenny would need to douse the wound daily with eucalyptus oil or raw spirits and keep the bandages clean.

Although in pain, Drew could not wipe the smile from his lips.

~

While Josh and Alice were at the interview with the governor, Mark walked in to find Jenny wrapped in Drew's good arm and being thoroughly kissed. As she was not struggling and she was leaning over him, she was, in essence, doing the kissing. He realised that his wife's supposition was correct. Rather than rouse on them, he merely cleared his throat.

They flew apart instantly, and Drew struggled to raise himself from his sickbed. Still kneeling beside the narrow bed, Jenny was not embarrassed at all at being caught in such a compromising position. "Yes, Mark, do you want something?"

Mark tried hard not to smile at her audacity. An unmarried miss being caught kissing a man in bed would automatically require an engagement, but he knew that this was what Jenny wished. He tried hard to sound severe. "Yes, I do. A request for her hand would be a good start, Drew."

Drew blushed. "Oh, sir, I intended to. Indeed, I did. Before this... but well... things have not turned out as we had hoped. But I had no intention of being injured either, sir." He was blustering and tongue-tied. He had just been thoroughly kissed by his lady love, and his emotions were shot. He was pleased that a blanket covered his lower limbs. Permission was not what had just been on his mind. Wishing he were not incapacitated flashed through it so that he could drag her into his bed.

Mark chuckled. "Relax, lad. Her mother has already told me that there was more to Jenny's happiness than Ardeth's arrest. I presume that your, um, friendship is of some standing?"

The young couple before him nodded guiltily.

Mark took in their faces. Jenny was almost defiant, and Drew's face showed guilt. "Jenny, scoot, and I will talk to Drew."

Jenny wanted to object. "But Mark, you said I could choose who I wished to marry."

Mark saw Drew's look of horror. Her stepfather took her hand and said lovingly, "I did, but has he asked you yet, my dear girl?"

Jenny shook her head. Her face dropped. No longer did it show her happiness.

With his arm secured in a sling, Drew had managed to sit up. "And I won't, Jenny, until I get permission. Go to your mama while we have an overdue discussion, love."

Mark watched while smiling at how Drew handled Jenny.

She was about to object when Drew stopped her, "Jenny, I can't ask him while you are here, so just leave, will you? I'm not up to an argument."

Jenny nodded and left her beloved to Mark's care.

~

By the time Josh and Alice returned from the interview, Jenny and Drew were officially engaged. He had no ring, no house, no family, and little future if his arm didn't heal, but Mark and Cathy didn't care. He loved Jenny, and she returned his affections. On top of that, the lad was a boy of strong faith.

Mark knew his background. D'Arcy first took him under his wing when he found him ill in the hospital. He was what was termed a street rat, with no one to care for him. It was because of D'Arcy's endorsement that Drew had been accepted for enlistment. Mark frowned. This injury may now preclude him from fulfilling that career path. Only time would tell.

A new idea occurred to him. Mark smiled as he knew Josh liked him, and Drew could easily still work at the tollgate.

Josh and Alice had the governor's approval to marry even before they were officially engaged. Josh's interview with his previous boss had fast-tracked their application. When they arrived back at the tollhouse, Jenny was sitting beside Drew under his good arm and gazing adoringly into his face.

Josh's jaw dropped at the sight, exacerbated by the fact that his mother and Mark were in the room with them. Josh stopped on the threshold of the room and looked at the faces of the four occupants.

Alice's gaze flicked from Drew to Jenny and asked, "Are you engaged or something, Jen?"

Jenny nodded and snuggled up to her fiancé. "Yep. It's been an eventful morning. How did things go with you?" She reluctantly moved slightly away from Drew as she saw him wince. "Sorry, Drew, I must be more careful." She began padding the cushions around him to make him more comfortable.

Drew was not accustomed to anyone being concerned about him or his well-being, and he felt embarrassed. "Quit fussing, Jen; I'm fine."

Usually, she would have been somewhat insulted by the gentle chastisement, but Josh watched as she disentangled herself from under his arm again. Josh shook his head. He had not expected his sister to become engaged before him. His feelings for Alice were still new. They had decided to properly get to know each other before making the step to become engaged.

~

Sydney

Eventually, the Colonial Secretary, John Campbell, sent through the signed paperwork and a letter he had received that he knew Josh would wish to read. Having been on the receiving end of many complaints from Reverend Marsden, John recognised the reverend's distinctive writing. The letter had arrived on a whaling vessel that had come from *Aotearoa*.

John knew the minister had followed the Maori chief and the others to his homeland. John devoured the long screed and knew that Josh and Lachlan needed to know its contents sooner rather than later. He was about to despatch Alice's marriage permission and included the minister's epistle with a note.

~

Parramatta

The paperwork for the marriage approval was sent by a rider, and Alice was in the yard as the man passed through. He handed her the letter and left her to watch as he rode towards the town.

It had been three weeks since the abduction, and Josh and Alice had settled enough to feel comfortable with each other. Until then, both were very shy around each other. They had spent time discussing both their pasts and futures. They worked the tollgate together.

Josh was on gate duty and was surprised the rider did not require a pass. As he approached, he asked, "What did he want, love?"

Alice had not heard his approach. She swung around. "Sorry, Joshy, but he gave me this." She passed over the fat letter.

Josh flipped it over and broke the official seal, but did not open it. "It could be our permission, love."

Alice's face lit up. "But we are not even engaged yet, Josh."

His eyes flicked around the area and saw it devoid of people. He tucked the unopened missive in his pocket and dropped to one knee in the middle of the yard. "Will you marry me, dear one? I wish to be with you regardless of what this contains."

Alice giggled. "Yes, Josh, I will, but get up; someone will see you."

He stood, but then he swept her into his arms and soundly kissed her.

Jenny giggled from inside as Drew slid his good arm around his girl. As Mark suggested, Drew recuperated at the tollgate residence. His limb ached badly, but each day he woke with a grin. Jenny was here, and that was enough.

Cathy tapped Drew's arm. "Even though you are engaged, this is inappropriate in public, lad."

Drew dropped his arm and turned and apologised to the lady, whom he hoped would soon become his mother-in-law. "Sorry, Mrs Duffy!"

The redness that diffused up his neck made Cathy chuckle. "Drew, it's not that I mind, but you two are in full view of the window. You are only engaged to Jenny, so you must protect her reputation."

The contrite couple both nodded.

Jenny said, "Mama, did you see what Josh just did?"

Cathy had not seen the public display of affection between her son and their convict maid, but she had chastised them occasionally over the previous weeks. The sooner they all married, the happier she would be. She and Mark had already mentally sorted their rooms. As Jenny and Rosemary shared the room upstairs, the two small children would move in together, and Jenny and Drew could move into Josh's room. But that would leave Josh on the truckle-bed downstairs until they wed.

Josh and Alice walked indoors, hand in hand. He had forgotten all about the letter in his back pocket. It could wait. He wished to share their joyous news.

With a second engagement to celebrate, the afternoon passed before Josh remembered the letter.

Mark had just dropped the tollgate after a mixed flock of Marsden's Southdown and Teeswater sheep had been ushered through the gate by his shepherd. The toll on those was ten pence per score of animals. The healthy flock passed through every few weeks, and Mark willingly took the minister's coin. Marsden's few Spanish Merino sheep were kept close to his mill. They rarely were on the road, but then again, other than the Macarthurs, no one else had them. Barbary and English coarse wool sheep were the other breeds common in this land. Elizabeth Macarthur was often seen on the road riding to and from her Camden estate.

Mark knew that she and Crispin Milroy, Linus's son-in-law, were experimenting with some of his flock. This had been going on for some years while Mrs Macarthur's husband was absent. Every now and then, a flock of what looked to be pure merino lambs would be added to her sheep from Cris's farm. Mark knew that some crossbreeding experimentation was occurring. Her husband had sent written instructions about keeping the Spanish Merino ewes pure, but said nothing about putting the rams over the very fertile Barbary sheep. Elizabeth Macarthur's flock increased fourfold as her new sheep dropped up to four lambs each compared to the Spanish Merino's single lamb. She called them Australian Merinos.

Mark ensured they were on friendly terms with her, as they would be the closest shop to purchase supplies.

Elizabeth's husband was still not back from England, but she had told

Elspeth Macquarie that he had written to say he hoped to be permitted back the following year. He was to face a court-martial upon his return home. Who knew what would happen then? He had left in October 1808, and he had been gone eight years already.

Marsden's purebred merinos often lost their single lambs, but Elizabeth Macarthur's lambs carried the best traits of both parents.

Mark knew that her flock now consisted of nearly five thousand animals, most of which were cutting a good quality fleece. The lambs that favoured the ewes were turned into tasty mutton. These were the crossbreed failures. He stood in the side gate to stop any of the flock from straying into their vegetable garden. Josh was standing at the toll bar, ready to drop it into place.

As the last of Marsden's sheep filed through the tollgate, Josh sat down on a nearby log and heard the crunch of the letter in his pocket. He reefed it out and opened the envelope.

It contained not only the permission to marry Alice but also an opened letter from Samuel Marsden addressed to John Campbell.

The Colonial Secretary's note read...

Josh,

I felt you needed to read this for yourself. When you have finished, please deliver it to the governor on my behalf.

Thank you and congratulations.

John Campbell

Josh unfolded the legal document. After perusing it, he read the accompanying letter.

The screed was from the reverend, who was still in Ruatara's homeland. He sighed. At least his neat writing was easy to read.

Josh skimmed over the greetings to John Campbell and read the news about their European-style new town that Chief Ruatara had arranged for them. His eyes devoured the information about their work over there, but he noticed an absence of his friend's name until he was halfway down the first page. Sitting bolt upright, his cry of "Oh, no!" brought his mother to his side.

Cathy appeared outside and saw her son's slumped shoulders. She sat beside him and asked, "Joshy, what is wrong?"

Josh reread the paragraph. Surely, he had misread it. He had not. Ruatara was dead. His face blanched.

Cathy asked again, "Josh, who is it from and what does it say?"

Josh lifted his gaze to his mother's face. "He's dead. Ruatara is dead. He died last year, and he's gone. His wife, Rahu, killed herself the following day, heartbroken."

He fell silent. He blinked to clear his glassy eyes and held out the letter. The following paragraphs outlined how Ruatara had fallen ill.

Josh read the story aloud.

Marsden wrote, "*Only months after my arrival, Chief Ruatara fell ill. He battled valiantly for weeks but succumbed to a bad chest complaint at Easter.*

Although he died without committing to our faith, he paved the way for our work to continue. We have much to thank him for. Can you let the two lads know, as I'm sure they will feel his loss intensely?"

Josh looked at the date of the letter: Easter 1815. That was over a year ago. It had taken that long to travel around the world and reach Sydney. He read the remainder of the information and sat in stunned silence.

His mother had left, and he hadn't even noticed.

She returned with a mug of hot, sweet tea. Cathy drew him to her and rubbed his back comfortingly as she had done when he was a small boy. He felt like sobbing as he had when he was little.

He wiped the tears away on his sleeve and sniffed. He turned to her and said, "I have to give this to the governor and then let Billy know." He was shocked. Ruatara had written to him twice since his return. His English writing was poor, but he described his welcome home and subsequent marriages.

The devastation of his people at the hands of the whalers' greed shocked him. Then he wrote after he married for the third time. He had told Josh in that letter that he was now the head chief and would get to wear the ceremonial Kiwi feather cape.

With the news digested, Josh knew he needed to speak to the governor sooner rather than later.

After Ruatara had left in 1811, Billy, now a skilled cook, took over the kitchens at the Sydney military and convict barracks. He was filling out like his old teacher, Clive. He was no longer the skinny boy Josh had befriended in gaol. Billy was still at the Sydney barracks, and they kept in touch with the occasional letter or when Josh had to go to town.

Billy's time had been up before Ruatara left, so he was settled doing something he loved and was thrilled he was being paid to eat.

Josh finished his tea and silently left for the official residence.

Cathy watched him go, and Alice came and slipped her hand into Cathy's. "What did it say? Are we not permitted to marry after all?"

Cathy turned and faced her. "No, sweet girl, that is all fine. He has just received news that his friend Ruatara is dead. He has gone to tell the governor, and I must tell Mark."

Cathy drew her maid into her arms for a big hug. "I'm so glad you were sent to us, Alice. You are so right for my Josh." She kissed her future daughter-in-law's forehead.

Alice hugged her back. Cathy was the mother she had always wanted.

Cathy had a feeling a double wedding was on the cards.

Chapter 17 Death at the Tollgate

*T*he two couples had been married for six months when another incident occurred. Two months after the abduction, Cathy was correct; her children decided on a double wedding. They waited until Drew was well enough to attend his own wedding and for Banns to be read for both couples.

Drew wondered if his time as a soldier was over, as his shoulder could no longer support a gun resting against it. However, D'Arcy said that he would be welcomed if he wished to rejoin in the future. Although his healing took a long time, the young man greeted each day with a smile.

After eight months, Drew thought he would be able to cope with the pain of a musket recoil if required. He had asked to speak to D'Arcy on his weekly round to collect the tolls. He broached the subject of returning to duty to Jenny earlier that morning. She reluctantly agreed. D'Arcy gave him a thorough check-over and cleared the way for his return to active duty. Although tender, his injury was well on its way to being fully healed. The muscles were still weak, but he could ride and shoot a pistol rather than a musket. Therefore, this would be his weapon of choice.

After the double wedding, Drew and Jenny had taken over the upstairs room, and Gideon moved into Jenny's old bedroom with Rosemary. Josh moved into Alice's small room off the kitchen. They had removed the bunks and built a wide bed that reused both mattresses from the bunks. Weeks after the wedding, Alice realised she was expecting a baby. She was not sleeping well as she was frequently ill. Her morning sickness continued for much longer than his mother's had. Shortly after Alice announced her condition to Josh, Cathy announced she was also carrying another child; the toll gate residence would soon be filled with screaming babies.

A few weeks later, although Jenny had said nothing, Josh suspected that she, too, was with child.

Alice had just returned to bed after using the chamber pot when Josh heard the tinkle of the tollgate bell. With a soft groan, he pulled himself out of their bed. He hated this part of the job. He was content to stay snuggled up in bed with his loving wife beside him. He struggled into his oilskin coat and pulled a knitted cap over his cold ears. He shoved his feet into his new slippers rather than his boots, knowing this should not take long. He muttered as he walked to the front door. "Who the heck would want to be using the tollgate at two in the morning in the middle of winter?" He was so tired he could hardly think. He looked outside to see what sort of vehicle it was and checked the price list for a two-horse, four-wheeled wagon. It was ten shillings. He should know it off by heart now, but he had so little sleep lately that he was crying tired. He tried to keep as quiet as he could, as the guest room had two travelling females in there, and the barn accommodation had half a dozen soldiers of Mark's military friends in hammocks. Drew was out with them, as this was the first night he had been back on duty.

Jenny had grumbled that it was unfair that he stayed with them, but he explained that if he was on duty, he had to be with the regiment. They had been late in retiring as the soldiers had arrived after the family had already gone to bed. Josh and Mark stayed up talking to them until midnight. Josh yawned and rubbed his eyes. He was still muttering to himself when he opened the front door. Rather than find an impatient driver waiting for him, he found a musket barrel shoved up his nose. Josh was instantly awake. He now wished he had taken the time to dress properly. His hands flew up in instant surrender.

Unbeknownst to Josh, Mark had been woken by muffled voices outside. He peered out the window and saw that the three men on the wagon were all holding guns. With a hand over her mouth, he shook Cathy awake and told her to take the children into Jenny's room, lock the door, and hide under the bed with her. Sensing danger, Cathy nodded and did as he instructed. She wrapped herself in her blue woollen dressing gown and moved silently.

Mark pulled on some clothing and grabbed the loaded musket from on top of their wardrobe. After ensuring his family was safe, he descended the stairs. Josh's voice kept them calm for the moment, but he knew these men would be after the money under his bed upstairs. If they got that far, hopefully, they would leave the other rooms alone.

Josh's mind was racing. After the abduction of Alice, Mark kept two loaded pistols in the house. One was on a high shelf just inside the door, but Josh could not reach it without the crook noticing. The other was in their bedroom. Mark had a loaded musket in his room. Josh had not even bothered to grab the pistol as he rose to collect the toll. He was cursing himself under his breath when he caught sight of Mark's head peeking around the wall that hid the steps from view. There was very little light inside, but he was sure Mark would have his musket with him. He heaved a silent sigh of relief.

The ticking clock kept pace with Josh's heartbeats. Everything seemed to happen so fast, yet at the same time, slowly; for it was as though everything was happening in slow motion. Suddenly, he could see. Josh realised that the moon had been behind a cloud, and now the light was framing the burglar as he stood in the doorway of the sitting room. With the muzzle of the gun tapping on his chest, Josh was forced back into the sitting room by the invader. He was motioning for Josh to move away from the door.

Josh wondered why. Then he saw two other men come inside. Not a word had been spoken. Josh would have cried out to alert the family had he not seen Mark appear. Also, he could have sworn that he heard the back door close and hoped Alice had gone to wake the soldiers in the stables. He now just had to stall for as long as he could and hope they would get things under control. He was not alone. He prayed that no one would get hurt except the burglars. "Dear God, keep us all safe tonight."

With the entry of the other two raiders, the leader kept his gun trained on Josh's chest. He waited until he was joined by the two other beefy and unkempt men. Both had muskets, but they were not trying to keep quiet as they entered the building. Their heavy boots were loud enough to wake everyone in the house.

All Josh could do was pray, so he did. He prayed that Mark would have a clear shot and not miss the attacker. He prayed that the two women would stay asleep in their room. He prayed that Alice could get the soldiers in time and that he would survive to meet his unborn child. Oh, how he prayed. Josh moved beside the settee so he could see the kitchen door and also the steps to the bedrooms from his vantage point. The moonlight now fully lit the guest room door and also the foot of the steps. From his chosen spot, he watched as Mark twisted the key in the door of the occupied guest room, then pocketed it. He smiled to himself. At least the two women in there should be safe as long as they stay silent. His eyes flicked back to the men.

The three intruders had their backs towards Mark and did not see him creeping up behind them. Josh watched Mark as he flipped his musket around and lifted it high. The closest one went down with a grunt as Mark hit him with the side of his rifle stock. The second was struck with the sharp butt end of Mark's gun. At the sound of the first grunt, the initial intruder turned from watching Josh.

Mark's single order of "Drop" made Josh dive behind the settee.

At that moment, all hell broke loose.

The first man lifted his gun to fire at Josh when a flash from the kitchen door made him aware that Alice stood there with his pistol. Moments later, the two intruders whose Mark's gunstock had hit roused and, although groggy, aimed at Alice and Josh. Three flashes occurred simultaneously: one from Mark, one from one of the intruders and a third from behind Alice by one of the soldiers who had appeared in the gloom.

As Josh had hoped, Alice had indeed gone and woken the soldiers in the stables, and they had arrived seconds after the first shot was fired. The first man was groaning and making a large pool of blood in the middle of the sitting room doorway. His arm hung uselessly. He tried to stop the bleeding with his other hand.

Alice had thankfully not killed him, but he was unlikely to have use of that arm again if, indeed, it didn't need to be amputated.

Mark's shot had killed the man closest to him, as he got the musket shot almost point-blank. The other two shots were between the other burglar and one of the soldiers. The taller soldier's shot had been accurate, and his target lay dying with a hole in his stomach, but the shorter soldier received a ball in his shoulder. Hence, he had not fired. His gun fell to the floor.

In the dim light, Josh could not tell who had been hurt. The burglar who had been aiming for Alice fell at Mark's feet.

Alice saw Josh crawl out from his hiding spot.

Seeing the carnage around her, Alice flew into Josh's arms. "I thought he would kill you."

"Are you okay?" Josh cradled her to him. She nodded. He held her close and felt their child move as her stomach pressed against him. He nearly lost them both, as well as his own life.

Mark hated killing. He had seen enough death and dying and had no wish to take a life, but these men invaded his home and threatened his family. He was shaken by what had occurred, but was stirred from his stupor by the door behind him being pounded upon. The fracas had woken the guests. He groaned as the situation was not yet over. Rather than unlock it immediately, he said in a hushed voice, "Stay quiet until we know if it is safe."

The knocking stopped. After a few seconds, Mark fitted the key into the lock and quietly twisted it. He grabbed the tieback cord from a curtain and wound it tightly around the man's injured arm to stop the bleeding.

Alice realised she needed to attend to the wounded and ran to grab some rum and bandages she kept on hand for minor injuries. Ignoring the wounded crook, she went straight to the side of the injured soldier. She was horrified to see that it was Drew. He was now leaning against the doorframe and groaning. Alice knew she needed to stem the bleeding before anything else was attended to. She saw that the other soldier had gone to the crook's side. She didn't care if that man died, as he had tried to kill her belovéd.

The first raider objected to Mark's rough treatment of his injury. He moaned in agony and said, "Murderer, blooming murderer! You shot me. I'll see you hang for this."

Mark towered over the man. His rage was barely controlled. "Shut it, you stupid idiot. You and your cronies broke into my house. You are lucky you are not dead like your stupid mate there. You may soon be if you don't let me stop the bleeding."

The crook was about to say something else when Mark said, "Do you want me to gag you, too?" The thief fell silent, having seen his fallen friend.

A shaft of moonlight fell on his arm, and he could see it was mangled. Mark still had to confirm that only three men were on the wagon and that no more were waiting outside. As he had fired, his gun was empty, and he collected the musket from the injured soldier. Because of the dim light in that area, he still did not realise Drew had been shot.

Mark stealthily moved towards the front door. As he opened it, he saw someone at the head of the horses. Seconds later, he saw two of his friends appear behind the lad. Soon, the two soldiers had the youth apprehended, and he was quickly trussed like a chicken. He was thrown on the back of the wagon and tethered well. Mark smiled, but he wondered where the last two soldiers were. They appeared moments later, accompanied by a fifth member of the group. He joined his compatriot on the wagon after being tied up securely as well.

A voice from behind Mark said, "That's it, Mark. We got them all. We have two here, one dead inside, one dying, and the third with his arm hanging off, and he may or may not make it. Your daughter-in-law is a pretty good shot. If she had not fired when she did, Josh would be dead. However, Drew has another injury to his bad shoulder."

"Damn!" Mark turned to see his friend, Captain Guy Manning, standing behind him. "Thanks so much for being here tonight, Guy. I had no idea what the note meant, but I knew I wouldn't leave my family without backup. Can you send one of the chaps to get a doctor?"

Guy nodded. He called one of the soldiers, and he was sent to get the doctor from the hospital.

Mark had found a note in the outside money box earlier in the week. It had been poorly written on a filthy scrap of paper. There was no specific information, just a warning, and he had no idea who had put it there, but it had enough of a threat to call in some help from his friends. It was enough for him to tell Josh last week, "Ensure your pistols are loaded and handy, son. Call it a creepy feeling, but stay alert." He said nothing about the note, and he now realised he should have done so. Josh had done as suggested, and he had also shown Alice how to fire a pistol. He had no idea that she would ever need to use it. He had heard a woman would do anything to protect her children and family. Alice certainly had.

On D'Arcy's last visit two days earlier, Mark had told him of the potential threat. Guy and his friends were ordered to stay out of sight in the stables. This stakeout was to be Drew's return to duty assignment, so he was with them rather than inside. Now he lay injured again. Hopefully, he would live. Mark was gutted. He left the crooks to the soldiers and returned to his family. He first checked that Josh and Alice were uninjured. They were on their knees beside Drew and tending to him. As all was now clear, Mark took the steps two at a time and went into Jenny's room to give Cathy the okay.

Cathy had heard the silence, crept out from under the bed, and watched from the window. She saw the two men being arrested outside and the soldiers now standing guard over them. Knowing all was well, she unlocked the door and waited. When Mark came in, she flew into his arms. "I heard shots, Mark. Are the children downstairs safe?"

Mark drew his wife to him. He said, "Yes, sweetheart. They are safe. Alice shot one of the crooks, but one of them got Drew. He has a bullet in his bad shoulder, but it looks like a through-and-through. The young ones are with him now." He brushed back Cathy's hair and kissed her forehead. He still held her with one arm and said, "Sweetie, get Jenny to settle the little ones, and can you come and assist?"

Jenny appeared at his side. "Did you say Drew got shot?"

Mark had forgotten she was there. "Yes, Jen, but he's going to be fine. Alice said the bullet passed..." He realised he was talking to thin air.

Jenny had run out of the room and was almost tumbling down the steps. "Drew, Drew, are you injured?"

Someone had lit the lamps, and she saw her target sitting between her brother and sister-in-law. He was wan and woozy, and his shirt was covered in blood. Jenny skidded to a stop at his feet. "Drew, what happened?" She grabbed the cloth Alice held out to her and dipped it into the water basin. She tried to mop his perspiring brow.

"Jen, I'm pretty sure I'm okay. The ball went straight through." His breathing was even, but he was obviously in great pain. He moaned every time one or other of his attendants moved the pads on either side of his shoulder.

Josh moved so Jenny could take his place at her husband's side. He thought he had better see to the other injured men. "Let him lean on you, Jen. He may pass out."

Jenny moved in beside Drew and carefully slid her arm around him. Josh checked the two immobile men. One was already dead, and the other was only seconds away from the same fate. He had blood oozing from his lips, and his breath was rasping, which bubbled as he breathed. There was nothing he could do for him. One of the soldiers remained next to him.

Alice left them together while she changed the water and brought clean rags. When she returned, she bandaged Drew so tightly that the bandages all but cut in under his arm, but they held the pads in place. With this added pressure, the bleeding had all but stopped.

Drew tried to struggle upright. "Jen, help me up?"

Jenny held tight and refused to let go. "Drew, sit still. You will start the bleeding again."

He gave a subtle nod. "It hurts, Jen. It hurts like hell." He rested his head against hers. "Sorry, love!"

It was how Cathy and Mark found them after they had put their two little children to bed again.

Time seemed to crawl by slowly. The sound of hoof beats made Mark check who had arrived. Hopefully, it was the doctor. The next half-hour was taken up with the tramping of many footsteps through the house. The mantle clock chimed three.

Only an hour had passed since the bell had woken Josh.

Jenny watched her man being carried out. Mark lifted Drew and carefully placed him in the wagon, surrounded by pillows. Drew was taken to the hospital on the wagon that carried the body of the intruder and the still-cussing third man, although his complaints were getting weaker. The other uninjured men had already been escorted to the lock-up and would be incarcerated until they could be dealt with. The remaining injured man was likely to expire before dawn due to blood loss. Alice's shot had hit his arm bone, and it had shattered.

Mark had to stop Jenny from climbing up beside her husband as she was dressed only in her lawn nightrail.

Cathy threw a blanket around her shoulders.

Mark promised that Drew would be fine. He prayed that his words were true.

As the wagon vanished, the two visiting women finally appeared from their room.

Cathy saw them and shooed them back inside. "We'll tell you all about it over breakfast. For now, we are safe, and we all need to sleep."

They returned to their beds without a word spoken.

By half past three, the house was once again quiet. The babies had slept through it all.

Jenny cried herself to sleep. Angry with herself for not having even told her husband that she was expecting their child. She was determined to be up at dawn and run to the hospital to tell him at first light.

Josh did not return to bed. He mopped the floor and removed as much of the blood as he could. Knowing they had yet to deal with the two visiting women, he attempted to right the house and remove evidence of the carnage. There was little he could do about the shattered doorpost behind where Drew had been standing, but he managed to clean up the disorder as much as possible. He would sleep later.

Jenny finally slept and didn't even hear the sounds below.

The dawn chorus of birds began outside. Josh put the kettle on the hotplate and heard a carriage draw up.

The pre-dawn light brought a knock at the door. Josh answered it; Alice was up and ready to defend her family. Her hand shook as she held the pistol this time.

Relieved to see who it was, Alice and Josh invited the two weary soldiers in. The wagon was taken to the stables by the other soldiers. Guy and Josh assisted Drew up the narrow stairs and helped him undress.

The first thing Jenny knew was someone creeping into her bed and drawing her to him. Drew had insisted on coming home to recover. He learned that a gunshot wound hurt far more than the horse kick, but the rats in the hospital were enough to make him want to leave the fetid place. He knew he would get better nursing at home. Once treated and sewn up, Drew demanded that Guy take him home. Both realised that Drew's soldiering days were now permanently over. His place was beside Jenny.

Jenny stirred as he pulled her close and realised someone was cradling her. "Drew, you're back?" She pushed herself up on her elbow, and in the dim light, she saw him grin at her words.

Drew chuckled weakly. "My nurse up there had a beard, and he didn't smell too good. So knowing what my nurse here was like, I thought I'd come home and crawl into bed with her."

Jenny gave a sleepy chuckle. "I hope he didn't try to get into your bed."

"No, but the rats did. Jen, that place is filthy." He went to pull her down to him again. "Now come here, love. I'm tired and hurt like hell, but I wanted to be with you."

Jenny thought now was as good a time as any to tell him of their impending parenthood. "I'll lie down in a moment, but I must tell you that soon we will have to share our room."

Drew had no idea what she meant. "Huh?"

She lay down beside him and snuggled up to his good side. "You must get well so you can cradle our child," she said.

Drew had been tired until she uttered those words. "A child! You're going to have a baby?"

Jen nodded and replied, "No, sweetheart, *we* are going to have a child. It takes two to make a baby, and it was a lot of fun."

Drew was delighted. "Cor, Jen. I'm going to be a dad!"

She sighed contentedly. "Yep, your own blood family, my love; now go to sleep." With that thought, he pulled Jenny to him and closed his eyes.

Once Guy and Josh had seen Drew upstairs, Josh banished the tired soldier to his hammock in the stables. Guy envied the injured young man who had been absorbed into this wonderful family. With a resigned sigh, he knew his hours of sleep would be short, but that was soldiering for you.

The sound of another carriage woke Jenny. She remembered their brief conversation, which seemed like hours ago, and sighed with relief. She noticed the sun was well up. She turned to look at her husband. Drew's big brown eyes were gazing lovingly at her. "Did I hear correctly? Are we going to be parents?"

Jenny nodded. "Yes, I think it will be early next year sometime, Drew. I haven't told Mama, but Josh guessed yesterday, although I didn't confirm his question. I was not going to say anything until I was sure, but after last night, you needed to know."

Drew tried to reach out to her, forgetting his new injury. He groaned in agony. Jen had also forgotten and commiserated with him. He said, "I suppose the good thing is that I write with my left hand as I can't do much with this stupid injured arm anyway. At least I will have an excuse to use my left hand now without ridicule."

Jenny had fallen silent; she had blanched and then sat up quickly. Moments later, she was heaving into their chamberpot. She groaned. "Ohh, this confirms that I am expecting. Mama has this every time. I suppose we will have to let her know today as well. That's all three of us with babies on the way." With a groan, she fell back on the bed.

Drew winced in agony as the bed bounced. Since he had gone to sleep last night, his entire life had changed. He had not wanted to return to duty, but he tried to pull his weight and support his wife financially. Now, it would be his wife and child that Mark would need to continue to support. That was not what he wanted.

His life had flashed before him when he had been shot, and he realised how little he had achieved. He turned his head. Jenny was already asleep, and he relaxed, thinking about what he could do now to earn an income; sleep overwhelmed him.

By the time they awoke again, it was nearly noon.

When they finally surfaced, they found that the female visitors had left as soon as possible.

Josh, Alice, Mark, and Guy had been interviewed by the magistrate, who arrived late in the morning. They gave their side of the evening's events. However, the man was still in the sitting room.

Mark filled in the earlier incident about the note and said he was still none the wiser about who had sent it. All that was needed was for Drew and Jenny to be told about the background of the incident.

Drew needed to give his side of the proceedings to ensure they correlated with the recorded details.

Only when everyone was assembled did the magistrate supply the final missing bit of the puzzle. "Mark, you mentioned that you found a note."

Mark nodded. He was about to say more, but the man stopped him.

The magistrate continued, "Before I arrived, I individually interviewed the men who were arrested. As the leader died overnight, Tommy finally felt free to tell me all. His mother had been assigned to the felon, and their life was, excuse the term, ladies, but sheer hell. Tommy, the lad holding the horses, is only fifteen, and he's been used to doing that job numerous times over the past years. The difference this time was that he overheard the man say he had no intention of leaving anyone alive to 'dob him in', which were the exact words he said. The lad refused to have anything to do with killings and so left you the note."

Mark gasped.

The magistrate motioned for him to remain silent. "The boy's tongue was loosened as his mother was now free of her owner's vile attentions. She will be looking for a new assignment."

Astonished murmurs emanated from around the room.

The magistrate continued with hardly a pause. "Apparently, this crook has been responsible for numerous thefts in and around both Sydney and Parramatta. He has even been known to take beasts, and you know how valuable they are."

Deep in thought, he paused for a moment, thinking of the pending cases about other burglaries. All were unsolved. "Regarding this case, I have a proposition for you, but all must be in agreement."

Jenny clutched Drew's hand and they waited.

The magistrate looked around the room and noticed everyone hanging on his words. "I am prepared to be lenient with Tommy, as he will give me a list of the other crimes he knows this evil ne'er-do-well was involved in. I believe I have approximately sixty unsolved break-ins and thefts. I'm sure that the dead man was responsible for many, if not most of them."

There were nods and replies of "Yes" from around the room.

The magistrate was happy. "Thank you all for your approval. Drew, I hope your wound heals quickly." With that, he took his leave.

As the magistrate left, they were making Drew comfortable when the doctor came to check his injury. He told him that he needed to sit quietly but did not need to stay in bed. As long as he felt up to it, he could walk with assistance and sit where he wished. The wound required daily dressing, and his wife could wash him.

Jenny looked at Drew's shocked face and giggled. "Well, you did say I was to nurse you."

Drew had never had anyone wash his private parts but him. Flushing, he said moodily, "You can do the bits I can't reach."

Jenny chuckled. "We'll see about that later, husband mine. It might be fun."

Drew shot her a filthy look, and her response was to poke out her tongue. He chuckled in reply. Being married was not so bad after all. For the first time, he knew he belonged to this family. Having been abandoned as a small boy, he had never known the warmth of acceptance.

Drew's adoration of his young wife was a joy to her mother. Cathy had found two wonderful husbands; now both her children were in love matches.

Josh saw their jovial interaction and laughed. He then swallowed, thinking about Alice washing him. A glance at his expectant wife made his thoughts of everyone else flee. It was certainly worth the wait. He knew in theory what went where, but Mark took him and Drew aside the night before the wedding and explained how to pleasure a woman.

Mark did not say much to the boys about how he, too, was an innocent when he wed, but what he did say made them admire him even more. Cathy had been an excellent instructor, and they enjoyed each and every encounter.

Josh smiled. In their short marriage, Alice had him twisted around her very capable little finger, and he loved it. She only had to lick her lips and tilt her head towards their room, and he would be by her side instantly. Oh, yes, it had been worth waiting for.

Guy and his four friends retired to their hammocks after lunch and said they would return to Sydney the next day. Like Josh, they had been up at two o'clock.

Mark took over the afternoon shift while Josh slept, as he would be on duty again overnight.

Drew was left alone to stew, and stew he did.

Dinner that night was kangaroo tail casserole, followed by apple dumplings.

After eating, Drew could no longer keep their joyous news to himself. However, Mark noticed that he was not as happy as expected, and after their meal, he helped his stepson-in-law into the sitting room. "Spill, lad. Something is eating you."

Drew nodded and motioned for them to walk deeper into the room.

Once alone, Drew said, "It was bad enough when I had just hurt my shoulder, but a ball in the shoulder means no more soldiering, ever. I need to support my wife and child, and now I can't. I'm damaged goods, Mark. I don't know what to do."

Mark blew his lips out, knowing that this conversation was long overdue. He said, "Ahh, I wondered if that was it. You returned to duty too early anyway, lad, but that is neither here nor there. As to your future, Josh has already spoken to me about that. Although he didn't specifically have you in mind, this may work out for the better."

Drew had no idea what he was talking about, as Mark and Josh had not yet told him about the possibility of the Camden store or that Josh would one day run the tollgate alone.

Mark filled him in on their future move to the shop, which was nearly complete, and then Josh and Drew could partner in running the tollgate together. This would suit both parties, allowing them to share the workload. Having the use of only one arm would not be a hindrance in this position. The profits from the accommodation were sufficiently lucrative to support both families easily. The girls were already best friends, and Drew had fitted into the family like a hand in a glove.

Josh stuck his head in to say Alice was heading to bed, and he would take over duty in an hour.

Mark called to him and filled him in about their conversation.

Josh was ecstatic. "You'll stay on, really? That's fabulous! I wondered how I would cope when they leave next year, but if you are here too, we'll split the business. Oh, this is marvellous." He had not even let Drew reply.

Drew was somewhat overwhelmed that his future was not as dim as he had thought. His arm hurt, and his brain was fogged with pain, but he understood that he could have a secure future with the family. "You really want me, Josh?"

Josh chuckled, then sarcastically said, "Oh, let me see. I'll kick my sister and her family out on the street. Of course, I blooming well want you. I could not be happier!"

Josh stretched and yawned. "This actually takes a load off my mind. I trust you already, Drew, and that's huge because it's not our money we're dealing with, but the government's. And your shoulder proves that many want to take those funds for nefarious purposes. No, this is perfect."

He yawned again and said, "Do you mind if I go and say goodnight to Alice? I'm doing the night duty tonight. I'll catch a nap again while you are still up. Wake me when you go to bed."

Drew waved him away while still grinning. If his arm didn't hurt so much, he would have danced a jig.

Chapter 18 Babies Galore

The months following the invasion brought about significant changes for the residents of the tollgate.

Alice presented Josh with a healthy son. James Joshua Callan was a lusty lad who tried his parents' patience. Jimmy's regular demands for food were followed by only an hour or two of sleep for his parents.

Josh would rise and change him, then bring him to his mother to feed at her breast. He adored watching the babe place his hand on his mother's breast and stroke it, but his body was crying out for sleep. Knowing how he felt, he realised that Alice would be even more drained.

Alice certainly was exhausted, and Josh felt like tearing his hair out with the constant calls for the gate during the night. He wished it would rain as they rarely had night calls in the wet weather.

Thankfully, Josh's night duty had been relieved by Drew, who, realising his brother-in-laws frazzled state, took over every second night. The fact that the governor had also recently changed all the toll charges didn't help. This was because they now had sufficient funds for the already repaired roads. Most toll costs were about half the previous price, and everyone had to relearn all of the charges.

Drew's arm was still troubling him, and it would never be as strong, but it had healed remarkably well. He settled into his new position in the family. The puckered scar was unsightly, but Cathy and Jenny made up a solution from flowers and rosehips. The oil was soothing, and soon, the puckered appearance healed to a smooth scar. He had full use of his fingers, but no strength in his arm. He certainly could not hold a musket steady. Drew loved this family time, and he could hardly wipe the smile from his lips. He had fallen on his feet with Jenny and her family.

Josh and Alice felt they were just getting Jimmy into a good routine when he started teething. His reddened cheeks were accompanied by grizzling and dribbling. This became an even more miserable time for his parents.

Cathy commiserated with him. "Son, I've done this four times already and know what it's like. Your father was wonderful when you two were little. He would do what you are doing and assist me when he could. As you grew, he would take you for an hour before meals and entertain you. Not only did it give me a complete break, but it meant I could get meals cooked uninterrupted and that they were on time."

Josh gasped. "I remember him doing that, Mama. I had no idea that's why he played with us then."

Cathy chuckled. "It wasn't just that; your papa also adored you so much. I was only sixteen when you were born, and I knew very little about anything. I was battling with how to feed us all with little food, and I needed some space to think."

Josh reached out for her hand but remained quiet. He had vague memories of the scant meals they had. Food was never plentiful, but there was always something to eat. The family had prayers around the table after their evening meal. This was a time to ask questions, pray, and give thanks.

At Jimmy's Baptism, Lachlan and Elizabeth gave him an ivory teething ring that little Lachie had used. The cool, smooth, bonelike chew eased the pain, giving the fretful child some relief. It was not long before the problematic tooth cut through. Once again, the healthy babe settled into long nights of sleep. Finally, his parents could rest.

~

For some time, nights were interruption-free unless the moon was out. Even then, the boys needed to see to the gate only once or twice a night.

Mark and Cathy were due to have their third child any day, and when the momentous occasion arrived, everyone expected this birth to be as easy as her previous confinements. Cathy had been sick for almost eight months, and she was larger than she had ever been.

When the time came for her lying-in, the midwife called in Jenny and Alice to assist. It was mid-afternoon, and Mark was banished from the room. He was pacing the corridor outside their room like a hunting lion.

After twenty hours, Cathy laboured in agony; finally, Mark could not stand it any longer and knocked on the door. Mark said to the midwife, "I need to be with her as I have been before." He pushed the door open and went to his wife's side. "I'm here, love. I refuse to be shut out any longer." He went to Cathy and took over, mopping her brow.

Alice saw the anguish painted on his face and said, "She's not even halfway ready yet, Mark."

The midwife even looked worried. "Can you support her if we can get her up to walk?"

Jenny was close to tears. She had no idea this was what birthing was like. Her own condition meant this was ahead of her in the following months.

Mark had done this for the last two deliveries. He saw his stepdaughter's pale face. "Jen, please go and rest. You don't need to be here for a while, and I can take care of your mama. Go and sleep and see if Josh is coping with Jimmy." Both girls had been up with Cathy most of the night before. Alice had only just left to feed Jimmy.

Jenny nodded. At over seven months along, she was exhausted and was pleased to be sent from the birthing room. Although this was before her, she was becoming stressed at seeing her mother in such pain with nothing to show for it.

The midwife and Mark stayed with Cathy while Alice fed Jimmy. Cathy was still not ready to push the baby out.

Half an hour later, Alice returned with tea, toast and honey for Cathy and a tray of tea and pickled pork sandwiches for Mark and the midwife. It was an hour from sunset and twenty-four hours since the pains had started. Delivery was still hours away.

By this time, the entire family were on edge. It was taking far too long. Cathy was trying to nap between contractions. Mark was bleary-eyed, and the midwife was currently asleep in the chair on the far side of their room.

Before she had gone for a nap herself, the midwife said she could still hear the baby's heartbeat with her strange cone-shaped instrument, so all was well with the child. The fifteen-minute naps between contractions seemed to refresh Cathy.

Josh could not stand the tension inside. At least he and Drew had slept last night. One vehicle had passed, and with only two wheels and just one horse, the shilling toll was dropped in the tin outside, and the gate quickly closed behind the gig. He flopped onto their bed. Josh tried putting his fingers in his ears to dull the cries of agony from his mother. It didn't help.

Finally, tiredness overwhelmed him for a few hours before Jimmy's wailing woke him. He took his son in his arms and realised the boy was wet. He laid him on the bed to change him and prepared a clean flannel napkin, a wipe cloth, and a wet handkerchief. Alice had taught him to lay a wet cloth on his son's stomach just before he removed the napkin. He had caught a golden shower in the face a few times. This cold-cloth trick meant the already-wet flannel could catch the stream. Josh changed him, and he was ready to hand him to Alice. Jimmy was not yet on solid food, so Alice was the only means of feeding him. She settled down to satisfy his hunger, and Josh stood leaning against the door frame of their small room.

Jimmy's hands cupped her swollen breasts as he drank. His eyes were fixed on his mother, and occasionally, he would stop and grin at her. Milk would dribble down his cheeks, but then he would latch back on and take his fill of his delicious meal.

Josh relished his new family. He wished to be as loving a parent as his own papa had been. As he exited their room, another cry of anguish was heard from upstairs. Josh froze. His mother still travailed in childbirth. He presumed she would have given birth by now. With little to do, Josh set about peeling the vegetables for the family meal.

Alice still did most of the cooking, but Jenny and he assisted by peeling the vegetables. Yesterday, little had been done. Their chickens got the scraps and repaid them with delicious golden eggs.

The hours passed slowly. Cathy travailed in pain for most of the day. The vegetables sat under the cloth, untouched, and a massive pot of soup and slices of bread were eaten by those who were hungry.

Josh waited and paced. He realised that the one thing he had yet to do was to pray. His prayers had been in short supply for some time. Life had become busy, and he had forgotten to make time for prayer. He and Alice had always had a brief prayer time before they slept, but of late, she had been asleep before he made it to bed. The dinner table prayers were all the family had managed.

With nothing to do inside, Josh took a mug of tea outside into the afternoon sun. He loved catching the sunset over the Blue Mountains. It looked as though it sizzled as it hit the trees. From this spot, he could not hear his mother's cries of agony very well. His heart was breaking.

Sometime after the burglary, a large elevated plank was placed on two stumps along the road's edge for public seating. It doubled as a hitching rail, but today, Josh sat in a patch of late afternoon sunshine and prayed.

Having finished his tea, his head was in his hands, and his heart was heavy with worry about his mother. He didn't hear anyone approach, but when he looked up, Lachlan Macquarie was seated beside him.

"Troubled lad?" Lachlan enquired.

Josh nodded. "It's Mama. She has been travailing in labour pains for two days, and nothing is happening. The babe should be here by now. I've been sitting here, praying for her."

Lachlan's face fell. He knew all too well the anguish of waiting for the birth of a child. He was half-pleased that his beloved Elspeth had given birth while he was entertaining guests downstairs during an official function. However, even with the doors closed, he could hear her screaming in pain. He had gone to be with her right at the end of the birth. When Jane was born in Scotland, he had been able to escape outdoors, but when he went to check on his wife, he was required to hold her during the actual delivery. He was in awe at what she went through merely to have a baby. He thought of his bonny son, and he almost agreed. He said, "Josh, there are times when our faith keeps us strong. Women crave to hold a child in their arms. My Elspeth has lost eight wee bairns at various stages. You know that your mama is strong and healthy and that she has gone through this many times before." He was unsure if he knew about the sister who had died at birth, so he refrained from mentioning her. So many children died early, if they even made it that far along. He knew that from experience. "I shall pray for her, Josh. How about now?"

Josh nodded his thanks. They offered Cathy up to the Lord in prayer and asked for the safe delivery of the child.

Lachlan had come to tell them the new shop building was complete. It had a three-bedroom flat above it. He planned to stock it like a smaller version of the Government Store in Parramatta, giving them a head start. He was about to tell Josh when the cry of a tiny child was heard.

The look that both men gave each other showed relief.

"It sounds like your prayers have been answered already, young Joshua." Lachlan stood and brushed down the seat of his trousers. "How about we go and find out what they have?"

Josh nodded, grinning. He wondered if he had a new brother or sister. "Thanks, sir." Josh paused and turned to the governor. "Sir, may I speak freely?"

Lachlan nodded. "You always have, lad."

Josh grinned. "I just wish to say thanks for taking me on. I was a young convict with no skills except to pick pockets. Yes, I could read and write, but I knew nothing of life. Your sponsorship has given me and my whole family a future we would never have had in London. I told you that when I was convicted, the Judge threw at me that I wasn't even worth tuppence. That hurt. It really hurt. But, sir, you never made me feel that way. You have paved the way for us all and eased our path in such a way that we can never thank you enough. I just wanted you to know that I really appreciate that."

Lachlan chuckled. "It works both ways, lad. I was aware of your mother's history before she joined the ship in Portsmouth. Her losses were great, and her life was tough. I felt that she needed a break. I also investigated Mark when he transferred into my regiment. I was impressed that both were honest with each other and with my good wife. Little was held back by either of them, and I admired that honesty." He saw that Josh understood that and continued. "In my position, it's hard to make friends. Percy White is one, and Henry Antill and Charles Whalan are others. Mark, I came to both like and trust like a young brother. Living in cramped quarters for months on end, you get to know a person quite well. I was honoured to stand with them for their marriage in Cape Town. Since then, they have only confirmed that I was correct in placing my trust in both them, and you laddie. I have come today to tell them about the shop, but it may not be a good time. However, let us go and find out the good news about your newest sibling."

They turned again to go indoors and paused at the sound of something new. The cries of the new babe were now echoed.

Josh was the first to realise what he was hearing. "Two! She had twins? No wonder it was taking so long." Josh threw his head back and laughed. His relief was profound; however, he still did not know if she was safe.

Lachlan chuckled. "As I said, let's go and see what she has had, laddie." Lachlan pushed the door open of the tollgate residence, and they saw a grinning new father as he had just come downstairs.

Mark saw who Josh was talking to. "Hello, sir. Cathy is feeding our latest arrivals. We have two, sir." He looked overwhelmed. "Two!"

Josh wished to know how his mother was. "Mark, is Mama well?"

Mark nodded. "She is now, son, as are your new brother and sister."

Josh's eyes were as big as saucers. He knew full well how much trouble one small baby could be. "Do they have names yet?"

Mark grinned. "They certainly do. We had two names picked, but never expected to use them both. Elizabeth is the elder by five minutes, and Jonah Lachlan is the boy. His name is in line with our Old Testament boys: Joshua, Gideon, and now Jonah. Elizabeth is, of course, after our first lady, but our little girl will be known as Eliza, and Jonah will be Joe."

Lachlan congratulated them. He could now return home and let Elspeth know that Cathy had survived the double birth. "Mark, I'll return tomorrow to discuss the store. There is no hurry, but the building is already finished."

~

At ten the following day, Lachlan rode back to the tollgate. He did not arrive alone, as one of his security detail had come to guard the tollgate while he spoke to the family. He did not wish to be disturbed, and the best way to achieve that was to cover the gate. He presumed that Cathy would still be in bed, but was shocked to find her in the sitting room with both tiny babies. Alice sat next to her with Jimmy, and Jenny waddled in, looking almost ready to produce another child any moment. Lachlan shook his head in awe at this amazing family. He pushed a moment of jealousy away. He wondered again if it was his disease that made bearing children difficult. He touched his pockmarked face and sighed. Could his one night of pleasure in Egypt have caused the loss of all his children bar one?

Mark arrived with Gideon and Rosemary in tow, and Josh and Drew appeared from the stables. Drew's arm was still in a sling, but more because it ached than needing to wear it. The bullet seemed to have gouged out a chunk of the muscle, and his arm had virtually no power any more. Drew knew he would never regain full use, but he made no complaints, as he was alive and about to become a father. As he was on duty when it occurred, he retired on half pay.

Lachlan greeted them all. He drew a deep breath before slowly releasing it. "Well, dear friends, I have come to tell you that the shop and residence above it are ready. However, the family is growing so fast that I feel it would be a good idea to have the crew construct a decent-sized house for you all while they are down there. There is room behind the shop for a sizeable residence."

Mark was flabbergasted. "Sir, you have already done so much for us. You do not need to do that."

Lachlan reclined in his chair and relaxed. "No, I don't, do I?" He grinned mischievously. "Call it payment for services rendered. You have all gone beyond the pale for the government's sake, and in this case, I need to keep the building gang occupied. This particular building crew needs to be kept out of town for some more months, and I don't have any other projects lined up for them to work on. They lack the skills to work on the main stone buildings currently under construction in Sydney. The shop is mainly of double brick with a sandstone base and corners. It looks a bit like a box, but it's functional."

Cathy said, "But, sir, there will only be Mark and me for some time."

Lachlan chuckled. "…and four children, plus you will need at least one maid and another man to assist you. I'm working on that, but we'll see who the good Lord supplies. We all know that He will send the right people at the right time. Although I was thinking about suggesting Tommy and his mama to start with."

Cathy tried to protest. "But, sir, I feel so guilty. We do not need servants." Her eyes glanced at Alice.

Lachlan knew her anguish about the assigned people. "Cathy, I will address my comments directly to you, but what I say, I need you all to listen to as well."

She nodded, but remained quiet.

He inhaled then released a long sigh. "You all know my attitude towards the greed of many of the free settlers. I abhor the wanton behaviour of some of the women and the excesses of drink and the foul abuse by the men of their so-called free status of the ex-militia. In England, their activities would likely result in them being behind bars, but here, they seem to get away with it. Many of them are far worse than the convicts they degrade and reject. Josh, you and Alice are perfect examples of what I mean. In reality, neither of you did much wrong. Many of the soldiers in the militia were taken from prisons in England, and they are worse criminals than the convicts they guard. They are put in positions of authority over the Irish, in particular. The original trained soldiers who arrived with Governor Phillip and those who followed them were sent home to fight in another pointless war with another greedy man." He sighed again. "I can say that, as I fought in it too, as did Mark."

Mark nodded. He, too, had served and seen things that still woke him at night. He had long ago discussed the horrors of war with Henry and Lachlan. Now, Mark knew what he meant and agreed wholeheartedly.

Lachlan saw his nod and said, "Fine, to continue my saga. Perry and Katy White have been my eyes and ears in town as you have been here. Katy appealed to me to have Janey Brien assigned to them, and it was not long before Janey brought something to my attention that needed addressing. You see, in her position with the Whites, she has been able to come and go from the Female Prison at will." He looked across at the young convict girl. "Alice, dear, Janey singled you out and sent you here. However, there are others she has found; many have been placed with some of the Rosedale families and other similar homes." His eyes scanned the faces around him. "We have placed them in what I like to term safe houses. Cathy, with your permission, you will be one such house. As such, I would like to ask if you will continue to help me with this. I am unable to be directly involved, but to know that someone is looking out for the very young. For those to be caught up in the system makes my blood boil.

Cathy released a long, drawn-out "Ohhh" and nodded with a smile.

Lachlan looked at her and asked, "So, will you assist me in taking some of the vulnerable ones? I will send no men that I don't trust, and they will all be hand-picked, lads like Josh."

Mark glanced at Cathy and cocked an eyebrow. Another subtle nod answered the unvoiced question.

Mark replied, "Sir, we are honoured, and if this is what you wish us to do, then we are willing to help in any way we can. Josh and Drew, are you in, too? After we leave, I'm sure you could use some more help here. Move upstairs and install some maids. You could immediately use a couple of girls to help in the kitchen and laundry, and a couple of young lads to do the yard work and even take the tolls if required, including night duty."

Both young men were delighted.

Drew gave his brother-in-law a not-so-subtle nod. His face read like a book. He would agree to whatever the others wanted as long as he could remain with them.

Lachlan chuckled. He was pleased Drew had finally found a loving home.

Josh said, "Yes, sir, we're in too. We could house four, and it doesn't matter if the girls have skills, as teaching them is something we can do for them. We can train them and then secure a better placement for them, allowing us to take in more. However, some babysitting skills would be good."

Lachlan slapped his hands on his knees. "Excellent! I was worried for a while. Fine, then I shall get some house plans sorted and put the team on constructing a separate residence at the back. I will ensure it has a guest room or two for us when we visit."

With his plans now sorted, he again offered his and Elizabeth's congratulations. "My Elspeth would love to see the new young ones, so you may receive a visit from her and young Lachie quite soon."

Cathy was about to stand and curtsy when he forbade her to move.

Lachlan said, "Cathy, you and your family are friends. Honour me by treating me as one of them. Good friends are few and far between. Trusted ones are even more precious." With that, he stood, bowed his farewells and departed.

Mark followed him to the door. "Sir, about moving to the store, I know Cathy would skin me alive if we left before Jenny's baby arrives, but if all goes well there, we should be able to leave soon after that. Can I say in about eight to ten weeks?"

Lachlan nodded. "That timeframe works perfectly, Mark, as I should be able to have the new house underway by then. We'll keep Jenny in our prayers, too." He clasped Mark's hand in his bony ones. "Have you got a moment or two? Come, we can chat now."

Mark nodded and followed him out the door.

Lachlan and Mark settled themselves on the log outside.

Lachlan gave Mark one of his twisted smiles. "I meant what I said, Mark. It's nice to know I can knock on your door at any time and know I will be welcomed with a mug of tea at the kitchen table and not kowtowed to with dainty china in the sitting room."

Mark knew he meant every word he said. "Sir, I'm a street waif from London who joined up to have a life and see the world. I did all that, and still did not find contentment within myself. When I heard the 73rd regiment was coming here, I knew I had to come. I now know that it was God speaking to me. I had heard you were a stern commander, but that suited me just fine. My last tie in England was gone as my mother had just died, and I wondered how God could find a wife for me confined on a ship bound for the Antipodes. He did, and a mighty one at that. I wish to express my gratitude for the honour of being called your friend. I am unworthy of such, but accept it anyway."

Lachlan grinned. "Mark, I was a penniless Scottish lad who joined up for much the same reason as you. I saw myself reflected in you and thanked the good Lord for the opportunities I was given. I have twice found a wonderful woman to be by my side, but sometimes I still wish I had my Jane with me. Don't get me wrong, I have a great love for Elspeth, and that affection has grown over the years. Jane was the light of my life and my reason for living. When I lost her, I lost direction for a long time. I fell into a mired pit of self-destruction, and, well, these pock marks are the evidence of that indiscretion. My wee Mr Mac still needs to take the occasional bath in quicksilver, and I wonder if there is something in that that causes my Elspeth to lose so many children. I only have myself to blame for that, but only a man from the services will understand the temptations of such wanton women in India, Egypt and beyond. You and Henry understand me like no other. Neither of you pander to my whims, and both of you keep me from being maudlin. Yet I know I can seek either of you or Perry out and know my words will stay between us."

Mark gave a nod of acknowledgement. "Thank you, sir. I will miss Perry when we go. He has not had an easy path in life because of his burns. Katy does not even seem to see his horrifically melted face. She is also a queen amongst women."

Lachlan knew that Mark was aware of Perry's title. "When they eventually go home, they will make a great change over there. Perry has another friend who was out here for what, in reality, was no crime at all. He was charged with a crime before he committed it. That friend, Sam Corbett, is now an earl. I'm not supposed to know. Perry and Katy plan to join

Elizabeth Fry in her work in London with the female convicts and incarcerated women."

Mark knew of his friend's plans. "I do wish I were there to see the astonished looks on the faces of toffs and nobs in London when they begin their work. Perry and his papa, Lord Percy, Duke of Cheatham, will stir up a hornet's nest."

Lachlan chuckled. "I know, and I intend to keep in contact with them for as long as I can."

They turned and faced the residence, so Lachlan's identity was a little obscured from the public. A carriage came by, and Josh exited to take their three-shilling toll. Lachlan watched in silence as his new groom lifted the toll bar for Josh.

Lachlan gave his groom the sign to ready his horse.

As the passing carriage moved through the tollgate, his man appeared with the two horses.

As Lachlan stood, he said, "Mark, keep a guest room for us, as we will come and visit just to relax a little and have a break from the maddening crowd." He gave a sideways glance at his friend. "When we're alone, will you call me Lachlan? Few do, and I would like you to."

Mark shook his head. "I'm honoured to be a friend, sir, but that is one step I am unable to take. As my former commanding officer, I must always treat you with the utmost respect. To me, that would be irreverent and disrespectful."

Lachlan gave a shrug and another sigh. "Know the request will remain. Maybe one day you will feel able to." Perry was the only one willing to call him by name.

Mark watched as the governor mounted his steed. As Lachlan turned to wave, Mark said, "Thank you, sir; maybe one day."

~

Drew and Jenny's baby, Matilda, arrived in mid-June. She was as beautiful as Jenny had been. The twins were thriving, and Jimmy was oozing love to anyone who would pick him up. The ooze usually ended up on the shirt of whoever held him.

The family knew that the overcrowded residence would soon be bursting at the seams. Four screaming babies and two small children were enough to frazzle the nerves of the bravest soldier.

The three new fathers commiserated and were often found occupying themselves in the stables or on the log seat at the front of the residence, holding mugs of hot black tea and trying to remain awake. The large house was overcrowded.

~

Lachlan appeared at the toll gate again at the end of July. On this visit, he did not even dismount from his cantankerous steed.

Mark came and held the reins as they spoke. "Mark, do you mind not taking any female visitors for a few weeks? I have three young girls who we need to move out of the gaol as soon as possible. All have been vilely abused, and they need somewhere safe to heal and live. With all the babies in your house, I'm sure you could use the assistance. I also have a lad who reminds me of Josh. He looks about fourteen or thereabout and needs a gentle guiding hand. You can take all or some of them with you when you leave next week."

Mark was thrilled. He knew that the more hands they had helping the women, the quieter the house would be. "Sure, sir, send them along. We had not planned to have anyone stay until we left, as we were packing our boxes into that room. All I ask is that they come with a standard issue of convict clothing rations. We're running short on bedding as it is."

"Wonderful!" Lachlan's horse was fresh and needed to gallop. The stallion was champing at his bit and impatient to get going. "I'll run off some of this beast's friskiness, then I'll tell Janey to send them over. Perry can bring them in my carriage. I don't want them seen walking here until they recover."

Mark had to move quickly as the horse was almost bouncing in circles. "Anytime is fine, sir."

Lachlan held on as the horse propped. "Thanks, Mark. Let him go, and I'll give him a good, long gallop."

Lachlan braced himself in the saddle. The stallion was fresh and itching to unseat his rider. Lachlan bravely lifted his arm in farewell, and the horse took off.

Mark watched him brace himself as his steed lay his ears back and left the yard at full gallop.

The sentry at the side gate saw his boss charging towards them and had the gate open for his passing.

Lachlan eased his steed through the opening and then let him take off up the grassy hill at hell for leather pace. His groom-cum-security soldier was hard on his heels. The pair sent sods and the occasional sparks flying. The horses all but flew over the grassy hillside towards the gallop in the domain at the back of Government House.

They headed past the Government Dairy, down the dusty track beyond the farm and towards Elizabeth's gardens. A dust cloud followed their wake.

~

The very young-looking, seventeen-year-old Philip Longford, known as Pip, along with Maisie Morecroft, Hester Jones, and Julieanna Peterson, arrived that afternoon. The three girls were between fourteen and fifteen years old.

Perry drove to the rear of the building and brought the four young people in via the kitchen door.

Cathy welcomed them with a babe in each arm. While Perry took Pip out the back to the stables, the girls stayed with Cathy. She was obviously struggling to hold two wiggling infants at a time, and Hester and Maisie came to her aid.

Jenny opened the door while holding Tilda, and then the three girls saw Alice feeding Jimmy.

Hester said, "You have four babies? Really? At least we all know how to help you with that. We all have lots of younger siblings."

Cathy was relieved.

They saw that Cathy's need was so apparent that they had forgotten to be scared or nervous about their first placement as convicts.

Cathy said, "Mark and I are about to leave for our new life at a store in the south, but in the meantime, we could do with all the assistance possible."

Julieanna carried the girls' meagre possessions through into the house.

Cathy walked towards a door near the staircase. "Girls, you will be in here until we get things sorted. We have been using this room to store items we will be taking with us. Over the next week, you can decide whether to join us or stay here. Either is fine, as you will be kept safe in either home."

Julieanna followed Cathy into the ladies' guest room. There was a pile of filled wooden boxes, a stack of baskets and numerous piles of wrapped bundles. The room was light and airy with floral chintz curtains and matching bedspreads. "Oh, ma'am, this is lovely." She had never been in such a beautiful room. Like Cathy and Mark, she had been brought up in the backstreets of London. The other two girls were from Birmingham and Liverpool.

Maisie and Hester were frozen in the doorway. They were both weeping as they had never seen such a beautiful room.

For the three girls to be permitted to share such a lovely area without fear of abuse was overwhelming for them all.

Chapter 19 The Camden Store

$\mathcal{H}$ester was two years younger than the newest mother, Jenny.

Only days after Hester's arrival, she realised she could be carrying a child herself. Weeks earlier, she had been asleep in the gaol, and one of the guards had violated her. The following morning, Janey Brien found her bloodied and partially naked in her pallet bed. She was unresponsive as the evil man smashed his fist into her face, silencing her after she had awoken, struggled, and then tried to cry out.

Her bruises had faded over the weeks, but she was emotionally fragile. She had bled the following day after his forceful violation; she had torn and been badly hurt. She had not had her monthly flow in the weeks since the abuse. The attack was eight weeks ago.

Maisie realised Hester's problem and told Cathy of her suspicions. The fear was compounded because Hester knew that being in the family way meant she should be returned to where the attack had occurred; therefore, she remained silent about her suspicions.

Hester was standing in her room, looking out the window with her arms held over her stomach.

When Cathy silently entered and drew her into her loving embrace. Cathy said, "Hester, dear girl, you will get no condemnation from me or my family. If you are with child, then here at the tollgate with Jenny and Alice is the best and safest spot for you. I can't take all of you with me, plus Alice and Jenny will need a friend and helper. Stay here and stay safe."

Hester turned her teary face to Cathy. "I don't even know which guard it was. I don't know who the child's father is, Cathy. Why do men do this to us? I had no say. It was dark, and I was asleep. I struggled, and he had his hand over my mouth. He forced himself into me, and it hurt so much. He kissed me. It was then that I bit him and screamed. He hit me and knocked me out and... and..." She broke down.

Cathy cradled her in loving arms.

Hester sobbed for a while, then stuttered. "I suppose... I'm glad I don't know what else he did to me... but I was covered in blood when I was found. I ached all over, and my bottom, back, and front hurt something bad. I was wondering if more than one of them had at me."

Her soft sobbing broke Cathy's heart. She whispered, "Hester, trust that God will get the glory from this. He knows what has occurred and will not condemn you."

Hester gasped and tried to pull away. "He won't?"

Cathy's head shook. She spoke quietly and lovingly. "No, He won't. You did no wrong. None of this is your fault. God knows that. We live in a sinful world, but that's not how God made it. He made it perfect, and there was no sickness and no sin at all. Mankind was tempted by Satan and sinned. But, dear girl, God loves us. He sent His son, Jesus, to die for our sins when He had done no wrong Himself. We have only one choice in life. We either choose to follow God's way or our own way."

Hester gave a nod and a shy smile.

Cathy continued. "Dear girl, the life that grows within you now is innocent of the crime. Give the child the wonderful life that none of us had, but we all wished for. Here, things are different from what we were used to at home. In this land, we all get to start afresh. If you tell God you are sorry for any sins you have committed, then you have already been forgiven. Like us, we are starting new lives."

While enfolded in Cathy's loving arms, Hester said, "I had not been with a man before, and it hurt so bad. He was so rough that I bled all day afterwards. Mama had told me that men did things to girls, but I had no idea what she meant. I felt him push something into me before he knocked me out."

Her gut-wrenching sobs hurt Cathy like it was done to her all over again. She, too, remembered that first time and how traumatic it had been. She had no idea how an older man's body could get so big and hurt a young girl so much. At least the man who had stolen her childhood had not been abusive. But he had been much older and bigger, and she had torn as well. Cathy hugged the girl, letting her weep. Although she didn't need to tell her about her background, Hester needed to know that she was amongst friends who understood. Alice had already mentioned to Hester that she had been treated in a similar way by her captor.

As Cathy's own history was revealed, Hester's weeping eased. Thanks to Janey, Cathy discovered that many women in this colony had been violated in some way. Much to her horror, Hester's situation was almost normal for the convict women in this penal colony, especially if held at the prison. One or more of the guards needed to be replaced. Cathy brushed the hair from Hester's face. She had her at arm's length and said, "Dear girl, the governor knows of your attack. It's why you are here with us. Janey Brien is his eyes and ears in that horrible gaol. They are doing what they can to save the most needy, of whom you three are some, but I wish we had known before you were hurt. Hester, stay here in town, and you will be as safe with Alice and Jenny as if you were with us."

The distraught girl nodded. She was fearful enough to have a child at fourteen, but to be alone and far from help would be worse. Cathy left her alone to wash her face and clean herself up. Jenny and Alice came in and consoled her. Their loving care endorsed her decision to stay.

~

Rather than the Duffys leaving in July as hoped, it took three months longer than expected to finalise the stock needed for the shop. The barn at the back of the house was slowly filling with what needed to be transported with them.

Lachlan explained in detail that the shop was officially an extension of the Government Bond Stores from Sydney and Parramatta, serving all the Government Farms in the area, but in reality, it was built for their use.

~

At the end of October, a convoy of wagons and carriages left for the new store.

A rider from Government House met them as they were about to depart, and he handed Mark a letter from Lachlan. The governor's elegant script that was scrawled across the front read,

"Do not open until you are settled in. LM."

Cathy saw him take the note, then pocket it. "What's that, Mark?"

He shrugged lackadaisically. "I dare say we'll find out in a few days. We can't open it until we have settled in. Come on, love, say your farewells."

Mark, Cathy and the four small children were in a travelling carriage.

Lachlan had sent his unmarked carriage for the family to use as he was not planning any long trips for a short while. It would take at least two days to traverse the distance, and as there were bushrangers around, the carriage would wait for the wagons to be unloaded before returning.

A caravan of wagons carried the new shop stock and the three young convicts who had chosen to come. The various wagons carried an assortment of armed soldiers and strong convict men who were to unload the new stock.

Hester chose to remain in Parramatta, and the other three had said they would move with Cathy and Mark. Hester saw that Jenny was going to miss her mother dreadfully. She knew that feeling well, as she missed her mama.

Josh and Jenny stood arm in arm, watching their mother move on to a new life without them. No sooner had the gate closed than a driver with a single horse arrived to pass through.

Josh greeted him, "Hello, Mr Anderson. The tolls were reduced in May for some vehicles, as the main road repair has been completed. It's no longer fourpence but tuppence."

The man held out his hand with the two bent coins. "Ho, Josh, this is nice to hear. I have been unwell for some time, so I have missed this bit of good news." Mr Anderson doffed his hat at Josh and proceeded on his journey.

Josh was still getting his head around the new charges. The fares had halved on many of the vehicles, as the main roads were now in good order. Even after four months, some toll amounts needed checking.

The afternoon the caravan of vehicles left the tollgate, Henry Antill arranged a small group of better-quality convicts, under the watch of some of his soldier friends, to move the furniture around the tollgate residence.

The men who arrived were keen to work, but they discovered that the large bed downstairs would not fit up the steps.

Mark and Josh constructed a solid double bed in Alice's room when they married, but it never occurred to them that it was too big to move out of the room.

Alice and Josh's clothing was moved upstairs to Cathy and Mark's old room. It sat in piles on the floor of the room that was now devoid of furniture. Mark and Cathy had taken their bed and luxurious feather mattress. It had been packed onto the wagons and was now headed to Camden.

Josh pulled a face and said, "We're just going to have to sleep on the floor, love. I'll hunt around and see if I can buy us a bed frame. We can bring up the mattress from our bed downstairs."

Alice shook her head. "You can't, Josh. Hester will need the mattress. She'll need to sleep comfortably before her baby arrives. We'll cope as we're used to sleeping rough."

Hester was moved out of the visitor's room and into the maid's room. She was six months gone with child and was uncomfortable. Her youth was on her side. As her condition progressed, Alice insisted on Hester having an afternoon rest each day. However, today, things were too unsettled for everyone.

Pip and an older man, George, had gone to assist Mark. Tommy and his mama had been assigned elsewhere, so George Blake, who had been injured recently and now only had one eye, took their place. He was unable to work on a chain gang. His crime was petty theft, and he was halfway through his seven-year term. Perry had found him cowering in the hospital. His injury had been caused by another convict when he had attempted to protect a young lad named Adam. Both were sent along to the tollgate.

Adam was also fourteen, and he was thrilled to be assigned to somewhere clean. He had been caught picking pockets in London.

When Josh first met him, Adam reminded him of Billy; he was all skin and bone. When Adam met Josh's horse, Cloud, he immediately took to the magnificent stallion. Josh decided that if he could learn to be a good groom, he could have a good life.

Adam was shown his sleeping quarters above the stable. "Oh, Mr Josh, is this really for me?"

Josh gently put his hand on the boy's shoulder. "It is, Adam, and we will give you the same opportunity that I was given. I didn't know one end of a horse from the other when I arrived. I had held the reins for gentlemen in London, but had never ridden one. I was assigned to the governor's house, and their coachman, Joseph, taught me much about the care of a horse and all its tack. If you are willing, I will teach you. You can make a home with us for as long as you wish, even after your term is up. Would you like that?"

Adam grinned. "Would I ever, sir! I used to make friends with the cabbies in London just so I could pat the horses." He released a sigh of absolute delight.

~

Toward Camden

As the carriage trundled down the road, Cathy managed to hold her tears until the tollgate was out of sight. Mark cradled her to him as she wept. They had the two babies top to toe in the one cane basket at his feet, and even though the road was bumpy, they slept. The two older imps were gazing out the carriage windows.

Mark said, "Love, it's time Josh and Jenny stood on their own feet."

Cathy had no idea the parting would hurt so much. "I know, Mark, but I will miss so many of their children's milestones. I've never been apart from Jenny before, and she's still only a child herself, even though she is now a mother."

Mark was floundering; he had no idea what to do or say. The first thing that came to mind was, "Cathy, we can go back. We can turn around and cancel everything." He expected her to grasp at the straw, and he was already trying to figure out what to say to the governor.

She pulled from his arms. "No, Mark! Absolutely not!" She was adamant. "No, they must cope as best they can, but it does not make the parting any easier. They need to have the apron strings cut. My life is with you and these four imps. They need us now."

Mark still was not sure she understood that he was happy to turn back. "Cathy, I am serious. I'm sure the governor will understand."

Cathy shook her head. "No, Mark! We are going to do this. We have a new life ahead of us, and we have four other children to make a life for. If nothing else, we owe it to the governor to at least get this store started for him." With her decision made, Cathy blew her nose and took a deep breath. "Mark, I have had my cry. We are now to face a new future, and I will freely admit I'm scared stiff."

"I am, too, love." He had travelled down to the building site a few times and knew what was ahead of them. They were to move into the residence above the shop and settle into their new life until the house was completed.

The two convict girls would sleep in with the babies, and Pip would be in the servant's room near the back door. Mark was still wondering why they needed a shopfront in an area with very few residents nearby. To his knowledge, there were only a few farms in the Cowpasture vicinity that had more than just a convict overseer. Even Elizabeth Macarthur did not live there full-time. Admittedly, her staff did, but after the recent drought, there had been a few incidents where the indigenous people were involved in some clashes with the locals. He presumed it was why the governor had not been in a hurry for them to move down there.

Lachlan had briefly said something about one day proclaiming a town nearby. Mark had not realised it was imminent.

Gideon and Rosemary were fully occupied, gazing out the windows and watching the kangaroos and emus scampering out of the way of the caravan of vehicles. The children had not been in a big carriage before, and for the first hour, they were interested in all they saw. Many wallabies and emus fled at the approach of the bouncing carriage. Then came the regular cries of, "Are we there yet?"

When the babies awoke, hungry and smelly, Cathy called for the two girls to join them. Occupying four children in a bouncing confined vehicle was beyond Cathy today. She had to feed both babies, and she couldn't occupy the other children while she concentrated on the job at hand.

Mark took Gideon and sat up with the driver, leaving the females and children to occupy the well-sprung carriage.

They stopped at the Government Farm at Rooty Hill for the night. The children slept in the carriage, and everyone else slept around the campfire. The road ahead turned off at Prospect and headed south along the Cowpastures road.

The lumbering luggage wagons were gone before the children awoke.

On arrival at the new home, Cathy saw a two-storey building constructed much like the tollgate residence they had in Parramatta. The new building had been whitewashed and had two smaller box-like structures on either side. "What are those, Mark?"

Mark had seen no evidence of these on his previous visit. "I have no idea. Store rooms, I hope. They were not here when I came down last time."

Cathy, followed by a trail of children and maids, went indoors to look around their new residence.

Mark and Pip wandered around the back of the building. One of the boxlike buildings was being filled with bulky stock items from one of the wagons, while the other building, set further back, was larger. It was a small stable for one horse, complete with a sleeping area in the loft above. It was large enough for a few men.

Mark realised that Pip could sleep in here with George rather than indoors if he wished.

A short distance behind the shop, Mark saw the foundations of a much larger building. He wandered over to have a closer look. He knew that the residence had been planned, but he was not aware that the house had been started or that it was to be immense. Cathy would surely object to that, but they were only to live in it, not own it. The house foundations were at least ten times the size of the shop, which was not a small structure. No rooms were yet defined.

Mark stood watching the hive of activity around him. There were soldiers with muskets on guard duty, watching the convict builders work. Another group had travelled with them, and they were busy unloading other wagons that had arrived before them.

Travelling with children necessitated many stops, but he did not realise the governor had sent so much stock and produce. There were more soldiers on guard at the front near the wagons as the convict workmen unloaded the stores from the wagons into the store room. He stood watching all the work, feeling decidedly uncomfortable. He watched as some items were carried into the shop at the front of the existing residence.

Mark had no idea how he was going to arrange things for sale. He had never run a shop before and was seriously concerned about his ability to do so. In this venture, Cathy had the upper hand. He knew that she and James had the market stall in Covent Garden, and she was looking forward to making items and things to sell. She had already made another batch of the orange peel and sandalwood cologne that he loved so much. He was also aware that she had brought supplies in Parramatta to make more cologne. He had found it challenging to source almond oil and orange peels for her, but the vanilla essence was readily available. Her ability to 'make do' was incredible.

In the years they had lived at Government House, Mrs Ovens and later Betty Eccles taught her many things, but would that be enough?

Cathy had also brought a small box of pine resin and beeswax and planned to make some waxed cloths for sale. He was not even sure if that sort of thing was what they would sell. In London, they did not need to keep flies out of food. Here, in New South Wales, it was not just desired to keep food covered, but it was very necessary. Creatures of all sorts found their way into nooks and crevices of any kind.

He smiled. The sweeping salute to brush the flies from your eyes, nose or mouth was seen by everyone. They jokingly referred to it as the Great Australian Salute. Many times, he had seen soldiers on duty wave away the pesky blighters. He had done it himself more than once. The recent drought multiplied the annoying critters.

For the ants, anything sweet was an attraction, although some adored meat. He knew that spiders crept into shoes, bedding, and any clothes left on the ground. He had discovered that the wisdom of keeping one's shoes off the ground was good advice. He found a dead straight branch, augured holes in it, inserted short offcuts, and made a shoe rack. This was mounted on the back wall of the tollgate residence. He would need to make another one for this house.

He had requested some bolts of inexpensive cheesecloth to be included in this consignment and planned to use it to cover the windows once it was dyed a darker colour. He hated the flies that crawled in his mouth and up his nose. He had seen a flat bolt of cheesecloth in the Government Dairy behind Government House and realised that they used it for both window coverings and draining cheese. It was brilliant. It was held in place by thin wooden beading. The official residence had already utilised this product, but until Mark saw the bolts, he had not realised the netting was cheesecloth.

Mark had no idea what was in the rest of the barrels and boxes. He shook his head and realised he had been standing in the backyard for some time. He returned indoors to see how he could be of assistance. Releasing an exasperated sigh, he was about to climb the stairs, but needed to move out of the way quickly. It reminded him of the day he met Cathy. He could hear her giving directions upstairs and went to see what she needed.

He had completely forgotten about the letter that still sat in his pocket.

Mark returned to the kitchen, where he found somewhere to sit. He knew that a table and chairs had been the first things to be unloaded.

He was surprised to see a black billy on the hook over the fireplace. He lit the set fire and pushed the billy over the flames. He looked around and noticed a line of mugs, a container of lemon myrtle leaves and a gum branch twig. Releasing a sigh, Mark knew his black Chinese tea leaves had not been unpacked yet. The thought of him being picky about the sort of tea he drank made him grin. He'd come a long way from the street urchin taken in by Reverend Phineas.

Chapter 20 A Rosy Future

$\mathcal{B}$ack in Parramatta, the remaining furniture was distributed throughout the residence. Josh wondered what they would do without a wardrobe and a bed when he heard a wagon arrive. Ducking downstairs to attend to the gate, he discovered that the vehicle was stopping at the tollgate residence rather than wishing to pass through it.

On the back of this vehicle was a carved bed frame and a giant feather mattress. It was only then that he saw Perry White walking around the back of the wagon.

Perry said, "Hello, Josh. I knew Mark had taken their bed, and you know I like perusing the for-sale advertisements. Well, I saw this for sale for a few shillings. I hope you don't mind, but I bought it for you. I asked the man about a wardrobe, but he didn't have one; he only had a hall stand with hooks, so I got that too. You will have to find a wardrobe for yourself."

Josh had long since discovered Perry was an earl and was unsure how to address him. He knew not to call him My Lord, as his identity was still to be kept secret. "Mr White, I mean Perry, no, I mean, sir, you did not need to do that for us."

Perry gave Josh his lopsided smile. "Perry is fine, lad. No, I didn't, but I have. When the man saw my face, he threw in some feather pillows in sympathy. My burns have never benefited me much, so I am going to make the most of them."

Josh chuckled; he was delighted. "Alice will love this. Thank you so much. I accept with great delight. We were discussing what we would use upstairs and were thinking of taking two of the guest room mattresses for us tonight."

Perry said, "What is even better is, as you can see, this bed is in three sections: head, foot and base. It will easily fit up your narrow staircase."

As the crew that Henry had sent had not yet left, Josh asked the head guard to arrange the unloading of their magnificent gift. He stood back and waited beside Perry.

Perry asked, "Did Lachlan's letter reach Mark in time?"

Josh nodded. "I saw him tuck it in his pocket. I presume he's read it by now."

"Good! The instructions were not to open it until he was settled. I wonder if he waited?" Perry smiled at the young man. "In case you are wondering what it contains, well, Lachlan has them there not so much to run a shop but to be a hub for the new government farms he has just released. The letter outlines the salary Mark will receive and that he will serve as a test venue to determine if smaller Government Stores can be established around the colony, facilitating easier access for government-run farms to obtain supplies. Lachlan has found that when something breaks on a farm or they need a new tool, they have to arrange for a soldier to be dispatched to obtain said implement from either Sydney or Parramatta. It's inconvenient, to say the least. So, he decided to establish a test facility there to meet their needs. Once more people move into the area, their building will become a proper store, but in the meantime, they will basically be retired on a regular salary."

"Oh, sir, Mark will not like that." Josh knew Mark hated sitting idle.

Perry gave another half grin. "We know, but Lachlan and I are currently wording a proclamation about the theft of stock in the area. Plans to develop the Government Farms in that district are currently underway, and he requires a depot for new residents to source building materials and other necessities. Everyone blames the Aboriginal people, but we are fully aware that much of the damage and theft is done by illegal farmers and bushrangers. Admittedly, there have been some clashes with the local tribes, but it's the absconders and bushrangers who are causing most of the problems. You know that the tanner, George Ellis, was attacked by three of them and left for dead."

Josh knew and was thankful that his friend survived.

Perry continued. "The public notification is still a few months away, but Lachlan has already got boundary fencers working in the area. He knows it's inevitable that the area will eventually be used for private farming. Macarthur's farm is a case in point. They are just one of many who are keen to make money from the fertile plains in future years. In the meantime, make yourselves comfortable here. I will add that Lachlan has more plans for you in the future, but they can wait. Mark is pivotal to what he plans for the area because Lachlan trusts him implicitly. He wants the supply chain *in situ* before things are needed."

While they were talking, Josh heard Alice squeal with delight. He chuckled. "I think she likes the bed, sir."

Perry noted they were alone in the yard. He laughed, "I do not doubt that lad. Enjoy it, Josh, and dare I say, you should christen it as soon as you can." With another throaty laugh, Perry jumped into the driver's seat and missed seeing Josh blush. He turned the wagon and headed off before Josh could think of a witty reply.

Josh managed to wave and shout "Thank you" as Perry drove off.

By the time they were settled into their new room, more vehicles had come and gone.

A flock of Marsden's sheep was herded through, followed an hour later by a mob of horned cows.

Each time, Josh or Drew greeted the drovers, drivers or owners by name.

For Josh, the excitement of running the tollgate without Mark to oversee everything was dulled by the weight of knowing he was now fully responsible for anything that went wrong. Up until now, that pressure had been borne by Mark.

~

Three weeks after the family's departure, Jenny and Josh received word from Cathy that they had arrived safely and that Mark had read the governor's letter. They were settled into their new life, and being once again on a government salary brought them the security of a regular income.

Josh read the screed to their family over dinner.

"*Dear ones,*

Mark had been worried about running a shop, and he presumed that it would be selling frivolous things like my colognes. For him to be integral in supplying the needs of the Government Farms is a delight. I had no idea he was worried about our regular income, but the governor's idea of paying us a salary is wonderful. Surprisingly, many local farmers have already purchased goods from our store and replaced many of their tools. Mark only has to list what needs replacing once sold. Then, a soldier is dispatched weekly with the order. Our delivery is made from the Sydney Store; hence, the wagons passing through your tollgate for us.

We have received one delivery of bricks and lumber, which is already in need of replacement. Even the Macarthur's farmhands come and purchase things like nails and saws. There is also a cash flow. We have no say or knowledge of what stock was sent for us to sell. To find that much of it is building supplies or farm needs is wonderful.

Mark was concerned about his ability to sell fabric or dainty items. However, there is no town here but a selection of outlying wattle and daub dwellings inhabited by Ticket of Leave holders and ex-soldiers. There are few, if any, women.

With no meeting place or structure, Mark is working with Pip and George to build some outdoor tables and bench seating under the shade of a large tree. We already have one, but it's too small. Men who come to collect goods willingly pay a penny or two for a mug of tea, some cake and a chat. I think I will expand this facility and offer them the option to purchase soup, pies, and bread.

Groups of men sit outside and catch up on the happenings of the colony. So even though the store is not the shop Mark supposed it would be, it's becoming a meeting hub for many of the residents (and much nicer than a public bar). He loves spending his time in such a way. He often shares his faith with visitors, and a few have changed their way of living as a result of these conversations.

I have been making waxed wraps for food, and we also have some personal grooming items for sale, such as Papa's cologne. I have even been doing some haircuts for those wishing to return to town on business. I am no barber, but I can cut hair and shave with a cut-throat razor, as can Mark.

Some men who arrive for personal grooming have not seen a brush or even a bath for many a month, if not a year. Their smell is abhorrent, so a large, hollowed-out log has been set up outdoors as a bath for ablutions.

Pip suggested a picket screen around it for some privacy, so George and he are currently working on that project, made from straight branches, rather than pickets.

The governor has had a hand pump installed for our well, and it supplies all the water we could possibly use. It took us a while to realise we had to prime it before water would come out of it. This is also a source of patronage, as the water is sweet and does not contain leeches. The water pump is at the front of the shop and is free for anyone to use. Many come to fill barrels for their homes.

Life here is vastly different to our life in the slums of London. There is so much space around us. I find it quite lonely as there are no other women nearby. This is a man's world out here, and I am learning to stay close to home. I must admit, though, that it would be perfect, but for the fact that you are not here.

I miss you all so very much, and especially, I find myself thinking about what your munchkins are now doing.

I must also tell you about the incredible house that is being constructed behind the store. When we heard the governor mention it, I objected even then. The building is huge!

Darling ones, there are eight main bedrooms and four smaller ones, but it also has an entire servant's wing with sleeping quarters for eight more staff members in a side wing at the back. The building crew will also construct a large stable and barn with additional accommodation.

When the various workmen from outlying farms arrive to purchase items or place orders, some come with herds of animals. So, holding yards for these beasts need to be erected quickly. The house building is currently on hold as everyone is splitting logs for fences. I expect that the building crew will have this done in a matter of days.

The field next to the storeroom is now ringed by large posts for the railing fence that will hold over a hundred beasts.

My dear ones, there will be room for you all should you ever wish to make the move and live with us again."

The letter continued with more news, but Josh was called away to the gate. He planned to finish reading it later.

Jenny read on.

"Soon after we arrived at the store, George was delighted when a lactating cow and three expectant nanny goats were brought from Sydney for the family to use. He has taken over the milking and care of the growing mixed herd."

When Josh finally sat down to read the last page of the long screed, a smile settled on his lips. He missed her. His mother wrote about their children's growth and homely matters, but a seed had been planted deep down in Josh. He glanced at Jenny and saw she too was smiling.

~

Months later

There was still much confusion over tolls. Josh and Drew set about erecting a large sign that stated the various costs of new fees.

This occurred because Judge Bent nearly came to blows with Josh over the requirement that he pay the toll, just like everyone else.

	£	s	d
For each and every Head of Horned Cattle, the Sum	0	0	1
For each and every Score of Sheep or Swine	0	0	5
For every single horse	0	0	12
For every Cart drawn by a single Horse or Bullock	0	0	2
For every Cart drawn by two Horses or Bullocks	0	0	3
For every Cart drawn by three Horses or Bullocks	0	0	4
For every Cart drawn by four Horses or Bullocks	0	0	5
For every Wagon drawn by two horses or Bullocks	0	0	5
For every Wagon drawn by three horses or Bullocks	0	0	6
For every Wagon drawn by four horses or Bullocks	0	0	7
For every single Horse Chaise	0	0	6
For every Curricle, with two Horses	0	0	9
For every four-wheeled carriage drawn by two Horses	0	1	0
For the same drawn by three Horses	0	1	3
For the same drawn by four Horses	0	1	6
No one is exempt.			

The sign was mounted over the turnpike, easily visible from the gate. It also noted that all had to pay.

Only government vehicles on duty were exempt from paying a toll. The bad-tempered judge was no exception unless he was on official court duty. As the court was in town, as was his house, these trips were rare.

The judge's ninepence fee was a mere pittance compared to what he earned. Josh found it hard to hold his tongue. He politely told the irate gentleman to take it up with the governor or Doctor Wentworth.

Thankfully, that is just what the egotistical man did. He believed he should be exempt due to his position of authority.

Josh explained that only government vehicles were exempt. If he were on government duty, he could avoid the toll; however, he was not. Taking your wife on a private picnic was not considered work. Therefore, this was a pleasure trip as there were no courthouses out west.

After being on the receiving end of a verbal diatribe, Josh knew that the fine for not paying the toll could be as much as forty shillings or even a public flogging. He pointed this out to the irate judge.

Judge Bent turned his curricle and pair around and stormed off towards Government House. He may have arrived on the same ship as the governor six years earlier, but they had more than one disagreement even before landing. Things had not improved in the intervening years.

As the dust of the carriage settled, Drew appeared beside Josh. "He still won't pay, eh?"

Josh shook his head. "Nope! If the governor is at home, it may well blow up today. I think I would like to see the judge publicly whipped. I wonder if anyone would dare to hold the cat-o'-nine-tails for that spectacle?" Josh sniggered at the thought. "D'Arcy Wentworth would be the only one game enough." He chuckled at the thought of that display. Josh turned to Drew and said, "Justice Ellis Bent and his brother Jeffrey have already argued with the governor about permitting convicts to practice law once they have served their time. By that, I presume he means Simeon Lord. Sir's friendship with Andrew Thompson and Mr Lord still causes brows to be raised, but Governor Hunter vouched for both men, and that was enough for our governor."

Drew was in awe that Josh knew so much about these men and the arguments that occurred behind closed doors.

The judge would probably head through the bumpy road past the Government Dairy and across the governor's private domain, therefore bypassing the tollgate.

They were still outside when a well-known vehicle drew up.

D'Arcy was due to arrive to collect the tolls that afternoon.

The boys greeted Doctor Wentworth and the soldiers who accompanied him, then Josh explained the recent incident.

D'Arcy knew the issue of old. He had been battling with the judge since his arrival. He said, "It's a measly ninepence. The man is a miser, and he should not take it out on you two lads. You are only doing your job."

With the carriage taken around the back of the residence, D'Arcy and his security guards came in for luncheon. It was a habit that started after Alice had been attacked.

D'Arcy waited until the strongbox from the carriage had been brought into the sitting room. The collection from upstairs would be added to this reinforced steel case. Once the soldiers departed to find food, D'Arcy motioned for Drew and Josh to stay for a while.

D'Arcy settled himself comfortably and said, "I have a bit of news for you. You may already be aware, but the new bank is set to open soon. We held our first official meeting last month, and John Harris, Robert Jenkins, Thomas Wylde, Alexander Riley, Doctor William Redfern, John Campbell, who serves as the Colonial Secretary, and I were elected to the board. Campbell was elected the bank's first president, and Edward Smith Hall, from a charity group, was appointed as its first cashier and secretary. I don't know if you're familiar with Hall, but he founded the Benevolent Society of New South Wales to assist the poor and unfortunate people in Sydney. He's a merchant who has become close friends with Simeon Lord. He's a good sort and should do his job well."

Drew had little to do with any money but knew this man's good works well. "Sir, I have had personal experience with Mr Smith Hall's benevolence, as you know yourself. It was he who took me to the hospital where you found me. I owe my life to both of you."

Josh kept forgetting that Drew knew this debonair man very well. His eyes flicked from one to the other, resting on D'Arcy and asking, "Sir, what will that mean for the collection of tolls?"

D'Arcy smiled. "Very little, as there are no plans yet for a branch out here. I will still call in to collect the cash, but as the edict of some years ago, no tokens will be accepted for tolls; only legal coinage will be accepted. That in itself will set the cat amongst the pigeons. All bartering will soon be replaced by currency, and over time, the colony will crack down on payments of any sort made with anything other than coin or cash, which will be the only legal currency, as inn tokens will no longer be accepted."

Knowing how many paid the toll with tokens issued by various other establishments, including public bars, this was a joy for Josh. These metal disks were imprinted with a value, but they were supposedly not usable outside the said establishment. He had already refused to take them as a toll fee, but he had been caught a few times taking a penny-sized token and a real one, instead of tuppence. The dodgy coins were nearly always passed on with a genuine penny sitting on top. Some of the inns supplying them had since closed, so they were worthless. Alice had taken a couple of the larger ones to use in the kitchen. One of the Liverpool Arms tokens was currently under the screw of the meat mincer to stop it from marking the kitchen table. He had replaced it with a genuine penny for the toll collection.

~

1817

A year had passed since Mark and Cathy moved away. Letters arrived weekly, and the returning wagons carried replies.

Hester had a little boy, and life at the tollgate settled into a routine that suited everyone. Jenny knew Hester was interested in someone, but was unaware who that was.

The Government Store in the Camden Valley was now supplying a trickle of private farmers who had discovered how well-stocked it was.

Alice was expecting their second child when they received their now weekly mail from Cathy via the supply wagon.

Bushrangers had raided the shop for supplies, and Mark had been wounded in the kerfuffle. George had been tied up, and Pip had been locked in the store room. The two girls, Cathy, and the children were unharmed. As the building was finished, all the soldiers and convicts had gone.

October 1817
Government Supply Store
Camden Government Farm

My very dearest ones,

My letter this week carries some disturbing news. My heart has still not quieted. A group of savage bushrangers raided us. My darling Mark has been shot much as Drew was. His arm is all but useless, and although the bullet passed right through, he has an infection and is unable to cope with the shop. His fever is raging, and I am worried about him. I do not know how we will manage, but we must do so. The governor has been informed and will hopefully assist in some way. My only means of medical assistance is through one of the lovely Aboriginal women I have met. She came in one day a few months ago, and she was fingering some of the cheesecloth on the windows. We made friends, and now she is making some ointment to put on Mark's wound after she had puffed some yellow powder from a mushroom-like thing onto the wound. It seems to be working, as the wound is no longer yellow with pus. She covered whatever she put on him with paperbark.

Oh, my dear children, I miss you so much. All things considered, I am managing well.

We are praying for you through the birth next month, Alice. I wish we could be with you for this event.

Maisie, Julianna, and Pip are God's gifts to us. They have taken over everything while I nurse Mark. George is keeping everything outside neat as a pin, and I have no idea how I would cope without any of them. However, I fear I must. The girls' terms expire in two years, and both have been offered paid positions on a dairy farm near Macarthur's place. Plus, Maisie and Pip may well marry.

Elizabeth Macarthur came for tea after she heard of the bushranger's attack. She has had cause to fear them as they have stolen numerous animals from their farm. Her husband is now back, and her freedom to visit has been severely clipped. She has once again lost that joy of life that she showed for the past nine years. She mentioned that he has been forbidden from participating in any political activities. However, I doubt that rule will stop him from interfering. The governor knows, as he wrote a warning to us.

Dear ones, know that we are, for the most part, safe. The bushrangers only came for food supplies. Mark tried to stop them, but he paid the price for his bravery. Thankfully, the children were all asleep.

Keep safe, my dear loves.

I shall let you know how Mark is in my following letter.

All my love

Mama.

Josh and Jenny gazed at each other. Both were shocked and wondered what to do.

Alice said, "If it were my mama, I would up stakes and move down to her. Josh, I'm happy if you wish us to go there with them."

Drew slid his arm around Jenny. He kissed her forehead. "Sweet cakes, I'm happy to go too. If Mark's injury is similar to mine, then he won't be able to do much for many months. I don't care where we live as long as you and Tilda are there."

Jenny had not broken eye contact with her brother. "Josh, can we leave here? Will the governor mind?"

Josh was still winded by what he had read. "I really have no idea, Jen. But if we are all in agreement, then I suggest we ask him."

Alice snuggled up to Josh's side. "I love your mama so much, Joshy. She reminds me of my own mama."

All four were deep in thought when they heard the wheels of a carriage approaching. Josh kissed Alice quickly and went to collect the toll. The four-wheeled carriage and pair of horses were one shilling. He was closing the gate when another familiar carriage pulled up. Perry had come for a visit. Josh led the horse into the backyard.

Perry was hardly off the driver's seat before asking, "Josh, I've come to ask if you have received a letter from Mark?"

"We have, sir. Did you get one, too?" Josh was not surprised that either Mark or his mother had written to Perry to ensure they were supported after hearing the news.

Perry smiled. "I am relieved, as I did not wish to break the news to you." He blew out his cheeks and said, "I gather Mark's fighting an infection." They walked his steed and small gig to the shade and tied it to the feed trough.

Josh nodded. "We were just talking about what to do when you came. We think we may follow them, but we don't know what the governor would like us to do." Josh led the way inside through the back kitchen door. The others were still in the sitting room.

Hester had brought in a tea tray, so Josh ushered Perry to Mark's usual seat and poured him a mug of sweet black tea.

Perry took a long swig of the steamy brew, staring into the swirling liquid. Without lifting his eyes from his tea, he said, "Josh, do you remember when they left? I said the governor had plans for you, as well."

"Yes, sir, I do." Josh glanced at Drew and shrugged. He still had no idea of what those plans were.

Perry finally lifted his gaze and scanned the four faces waiting expectantly. "I called into Lachlan's office before coming here. He said I could tell you what he meant."

Josh twigged as to what Perry was talking about. "He has someone already lined up to take over here, doesn't he?"

Perry nodded. "He has indeed. Thomas Quinn is one of Mark and Henry's regiment, and he is keen to take over. If you all wish to go, Lachlan has given his blessing. Why do you think he had such a large house built down there? Josh, Drew, ladies, this was his plan for you all along."

Josh drew Alice to him. "Sweets, it looks like we have some packing to do. Do you mind travelling in such an advanced condition?"

Alice's response was to kiss her husband silly. When she drew away, she said, "I'm delighted."

Jenny ran across the room and skidded to her knees in front of her brother. "You mean we can go, Joshy?"

Josh flicked his sister's cheek lovingly. "Mark and Mama need us, Jen. I think we will go as soon as we can arrange it."

Lachlan came at dawn the following morning and shared a mug of tea with Josh as he often did. "I can't stay long, Josh, but I wish to say that you have my blessing. Mark will need you down there more than I need you here. I can replace a tollgate keeper, but not a son or a family member. Go to your mother with my blessing, lad."

Lachlan would miss his impromptu visits as he missed Mark, but life must move on. Thankfully, Perry would remain at hand. This young man had come to him as a convict and had become a friend; more than that, he was a trusted confidante. Yes, he would miss him. He said, "I'll come to see you off, lad, but when we are in the area, we will come and stay for a night or two, so keep a room free for us."

Thomas Quinn and nineteen-year-old Mitchell Roberts, one of the young recruits in the 73rd regiment, came to learn the ropes of running a tollgate.

Tom needed a crash course in running the business, so Perry and Drew set to work planning the trip to Camden.

Lachlan again supplied the Government Wagons, along with a detachment of Ticket of Leave convicts and some obligatory armed guards. While the girls packed, Drew manned the gate.

Josh drilled the new men and checked that Thomas had all the instructions down pat. He spent hours teaching him how to do the bookwork and ensuring he knew how to prepare the cash for D'Arcy to pick up later that week. They planned their departure for the day after the collection.

Tom and Mitchell needed to memorise the toll charges and learn how to fill out each of the required toll tickets. These were vital as they had to be produced if a person intended to pass through more than once a day. The new rules meant that they only needed to pay the toll once every twenty-four hours.

Perry was overseeing the packing on the wagons as he was currently at a loose end. Josh was inside, working out what to pack first. Perry was still there when D'Arcy arrived.

D'Arcy came to pick up the final collection from the tollgate with Josh in charge. The tall, dark-haired gentleman with piercing blue eyes tousled Josh's head like a child. Josh was drawn into a giant bear hug from the doctor-cum-head of police. "Josh, I'm glad you waited for my arrival. I hate goodbyes, but I would not have missed this hug for anything. Not just to say farewell to you and Alice, but Drew and Jenny too."

Josh pulled away, unsure of what to say. "Sir, it's been an honour working with you as well. I'm a poor lad from the streets of London. I fell on my feet here and have a life I never would, or could have dreamed about at home. To call men of your stature, the governor, and Perry White, my friends, is beyond my comprehension. Sir, my life here is beyond my wildest dreams. In London, I may have been flicked a penny to hold your horses, but otherwise not even acknowledged."

D'Arcy smiled. "Life here is what you make it, lad. So make it a good life. I certainly did. My past was nearly as unsavoury, but I won't go into that, but know that I do understand totally."

Josh was shoved out of the way as their carved bed was carted out the door. He said wistfully, "I wonder what we will sleep on tonight?"

D'Arcy chuckled. "Probably one of the new horsehair mattresses that are currently being brought in through the front door."

Perry pointed out the cartload of replacement furniture that had just pulled up. The feather mattresses were to travel with them to Camden.

D'Arcy went indoors and met Tom, Mitchell, and Drew, leaving the unloading of the wagon to Perry and Josh. This session took a little longer than usual, but soon, the money was on its way back to Sydney with its guard.

Josh's life at the tollgate was over. He released a long sigh and returned to the nearly empty house. He had hardly entered when Hester beckoned him to the kitchen. Hester had settled in well, but with his mother's departure and then the birth of her child, he'd not taken the time he intended to get to know her.

She said, "Mr Josh, sir, would it matter so much if I did not go with you? You see, Mitchell and I, well, we have a… well, relationship of sorts. You see, he wants to marry me."

Josh's face brightened. "Really? That's wonderful, Hester. Although we will miss you, I do hope you will have a wonderful life."

Alice sidled up to him and slipped her arm around his waist. She said to Hester, "I told you he had not noticed anything, Hester." She chuckled as she pulled Josh's head down for a long, loving kiss.

Hester giggled when she saw the longing look on Josh's face. She beckoned Mitchell to her side, and he whispered something to her. She nodded and grinned.

Mitchell nervously asked, "Sir, no, Josh, I know Hester is assigned to you, but as she is not going with you, can her papers be transferred to me? We'll marry as soon as we can get permission."

Josh was delighted. "Of course, Mitch. Leave it with me."

The afternoon was spent packing while Tom and Mitchell were on toll duty for the first time unsupervised.

Josh had one more duty to perform in town, and that was to visit the governor and transfer Hester's assignment to Mitchell. He wondered if he should also ask for permission to fast-track their union. She already had one fatherless child, and as she would be the lone female in the house with two men, it would be better for her to be married. As she was now fifteen, she had reached the legal age to wed. Mitchell was a kind lad and would care for her. It would give her the security she craved. Mitch was underage to wed without special permission.

Josh excused himself from the frenzy of activity and went to see the governor.

Lachlan and Elizabeth welcomed him, and the governor escorted him into the office.

Before Josh had a chance to say anything, Lachlan said, "This is both a sad day for me and a new beginning for you, laddie. You have come a long way in the years we have known each other."

Josh tipped his head as a bow. "And, good sir, much of that, if not all, I owe to you. You paved the way for us all in our new lives, and to honour you, we will do everything we can to grasp the opportunities offered to us. I shall miss you too, sir and ma'am." He gave them a reverent bow.

Lachlan chuckled. "Well, I said we would come to say our farewells tomorrow, so to what do we owe this unexpected visit?"

Josh smiled and then proceeded to submit his requests for Hester.

Lachlan grinned. "Ever watching out for another person's happiness, young Joshua. I would be delighted to arrange this immediately." He duly wrote and signed the document and then handed it over to Josh.

With the permissions in hand, the viceregal couple walked with Josh to the front door. As his usual entry was via the kitchen, this was an honour as only official visitors used the main entrance.

Knowing he had two days' drive ahead of him, Josh had walked up from the tollgate to stretch his legs. Before departing, he turned to the governor and said, "It's truly been an honour, sir. I have learned much at your feet and will strive to live my life as a good witness to what you have taught me. You taught me not to be ashamed of my faith and to turn to God in all things. My father said the same, but it wasn't until you duplicated his words that it truly sank in. You stepped in when I no longer had my father to guide me, and I will never forget that." He had teared up but knew this may well be the last opportunity for some time. He now turned to Elizabeth. "Ma'am, you, too, have been an inspiration, first to my mother and sister, but also for encouraging Mark to court and then marry her. You were so right about him. He is a good man. I thank you from the bottom of my heart."

Although acknowledging Josh's bow was the correct form of farewell, Lachlan had put his hand out to shake.

Josh took it in both of his hands, shook it and abruptly turned before they saw that tears threatened to overwhelm him.

The vice regal couple followed him outside.

He was a convict boy who was told he was not worth the tuppence he had charged for a horse and cart to pass by his tollgate. However, he had befriended the governor and had become a confidant and friend to him. He would miss him dearly. He presumed the early morning visits would have ceased when Mark left, but they hadn't. They often shared a mug of hot, black tea in the tollhouse kitchen at dawn.

At the gate of the viceregal residence, Josh turned for a last look.

The viceregal pair continued to watch him. They stood with Mrs Macquarie's arm hooked through the governor's elbow.

Josh lifted his arm in a final wave, then turned and walked away. The next phase of his life was about to start. He released a long sigh, thinking of how his life could have turned out vastly different had it not been for this man. The judge's words once again floated through his mind. He grunted. "Tuppence indeed! So much for that."

~

The dawn came all too soon.

Sleeping on horsehair mattresses after lovely soft feather ones was not conducive to a good night's sleep for any of them.

Hester had risen before them and was cooking breakfast. She had also packed a large picnic hamper. The large basket contained enough for the two-day journey.

As promised, Lachlan came for his mug of steaming hot sweet tea just after dawn. He tried to chat nonchalantly. "Perry White is heading home when Katy's term ends, so I am using him elsewhere. Because of his scars, he can intermingle with the toughest convicts, and the felons do not realise he is my ears on the ground. Their tongues are loosened when he sidles up to them to listen to such controversial conversations. He has informed me of a few situations in which I have been able to nip in the bud."

Josh nodded. Was Perry replacing him as a close friend? He could only say, "That's nice. I hope he continues to be a help."

Lachlan nodded. "He is, but, Josh, he's not you." Parting with this lad was hard. "You, my boy, are like a son. Perry is merely a friend." A lump stuck in his throat when it came to say his farewell.

Josh was finding the same thing. His eyes welled with unshed tears. This wonderful, compassionate man meant a great deal to him. Before he realised what the governor intended, Josh was pulled into a bear hug.

The governor said, "Take care, young Joshua Callan."

Lachlan didn't wait for a reply but was gone before Josh recovered from the surprise hug.

Josh watched him leave. He wondered how many hugs the great man had given to ex-convicts, and he doubted that any other would have received such care. He watched the governor's cantankerous stallion gallop away, then, after a sniff and a surreptitious wipe of his eyes, he turned to complete the morning tasks. A new future awaited them.

~

The first of the furniture wagons had left the afternoon before. The last of their possessions were loaded, and the governor's borrowed carriage was piled with children, Alice, and Jenny.

The governor's drivers pulled the carriage and wagons into the front yard and waited for them to board.

Drew was to follow, driving their new cart. The gentle beast in the shafts he could manage with one arm. Josh would follow on Cloud, who was champing on his bit. His steed was used to pulling their small vehicle, but that had already been left with another new horse and another government driver.

Today, Josh would be in the saddle. Cloud was not a patient beast at the best of times, and tugging a vehicle for two days was beyond his endurance. This morning, the stallion wanted to be off and going.

Rather than leave with the family vehicles, Josh waited. When the dust of their carriages was far enough down the road, Josh mounted his fresh steed.

Josh was determined to pay the toll for the very first time. He had worked out how much two wagons, each with four horses pulling them, and then there was the governor's carriage with a pair in front and another horse pulling the small cart.

The wagons were five pence each; the carriage was one shilling, and the roan and Drew's cart was tuppence.

As Josh mounted to move off, Tom opened the gate.

Josh called for him to repeat the toll costs as they passed.

Tom hesitated when he got to Josh. "Josh, shouldn't Drew have to pay fourpence?"

Josh groaned and handed him a handful of coins. As he drove off, he said, "It's tuppence, Tom. Only tuppence to pass for a horse and cart!"

He click-clicked Cloud and left the tollgate's front yard for the final time. The next amazing phase of his life was about to start. As he rode away from the closing gate, he thanked God for the governor's friendship. He thanked God for reuniting his family. He thanked God for Mark and his new siblings, and he thanked God for Alice, Jimmy, and their soon-to-arrive baby.

Cloud's hoofs thundered down the road at full pace. Josh sat low in the saddle and held on for grim death. He had never had a ride like this, even when racing the governor.

After a mile, Cloud settled into a canter.

Josh's face held a grin that filled his face.

They were to spend the first night at the Government Farm at Rooty Hill, where they were to sleep in hammocks in the barn.

Chapter 21 The Value of Tuppence
1819 and beyond

Within weeks, the family had settled into the well-established store and residences. Catherine Alice Callan, to be known as Kitty, arrived a fortnight after they arrived.

Drew and Jenny decided to live above the shop and were on call if required. The rooms were large and well-situated. This left Josh, Alice, and their two infants in the large house at the back, much to their delight. There was so much space, and they loved the high-ceilinged, airy rooms.

~

The family grew, and the Macquaries came for regular visits as the farmland opened up.

The governor informed the extended Duffy family that, within a few years, the land in the valleys surrounding them would be opened up for private farming, and the stock would need regular replenishment.

Lachlan wasn't wrong. Some farmers even tried growing grapes and other exotic crops. John Macarthur's farm at Camden had Burgundy-style grapes growing and producing a half-decent wine.

Farms were being cleared quickly, and they were sent many supplies for when the building started.

When Lachlan and Elizabeth visited, they would stay with their entourage for a few days. The viceregal couple occupied their main guest room whenever possible. Little Lachie shared with Gideon, and the pair often required a bath to remove whatever mire they had found. Mud was a particular delight for both young lads. Mud fights were commonplace, as this delightful gloop surrounded the water pump. The joyous giggles of the lads brought joy to the hearts of the gloating parents. It was a perfect way to cool off on a hot day. For the rest of the entourage, the guarding soldiers, a small tent city was erected in the main courtyard.

On this trip, Lachlan proclaimed that a new town would be situated nearby, and it would be called Campbell Town in honour of his beloved wife.

The Duffy's store was in the perfect location for the development of the new town. Once the residences in the newly proclaimed area started, their stock of building supplies was replenished almost daily.

Maisie and Pip married and moved on to greener pastures near Macarthur's farm. George stayed with the family. Julieanna married one of the farmers and also moved away. More needy girls arrived along with a few younger lads. Perry, Katy, Janey Brien, and Lachlan sent more girls to them who needed a safe place to serve out their terms.

Lachlan instructed them to keep them safe until they wished to leave or marry, and they did just that. Most left them to wed.

After a year or so, each moved on when they received their Tickets of Leave.

Martha Alexander was one of the unfortunate girls who had arrived in 1819. She arrived at their house two years after Josh and Jenny joined their mother and Mark in the Camden Valley.

Martha needed their safe haven badly. Like Hester, she had been savagely abused while in prison, but it was from the crew of the ship she had travelled on. These vile men had done the same thing to her and some other girls *en route*; one of the girls later died while giving birth.

The crew involved were convicted, incarcerated and locked up in Parramatta Gaol. They were later hanged.

Martha was only supposed to remain in the prison for one night, but it was a night too long. They got to her, and she was found unresponsive on the pallet bed in her room.

Thankfully, she did not conceive after her violation. She had been so horribly assaulted that she had spent six months recuperating at Hetty and Joel Walker's farm on the Hawkesbury River before she was well enough to travel. Martha had needed those months of respite before being sent to Cathy and Mark for her long-term assignment. During those months, she discovered that forgiveness was a cleansing experience.

Hector Macdougal, Walker's overseer, was an assigned life convict at the riverside farm, and he was a man with a strong faith. Martha's physical healing occurred much faster than her emotional well-being. Hector guided her on that eternal journey.

When she arrived at Camden, Cathy welcomed her with loving arms. Her wholehearted acceptance of Martha gave the poor girl the security she craved. Martha didn't mind George, as he spent most of his time with the few animals they had, so he was no threat, and everyone else was happily married. When the deliveries of stock came with convicts and soldiers, Martha stayed well out of sight. As she was literate,, she took over the education of the growing number of children in the family.

They had set up a small classroom next to the shop, and she loved this work. Her father had been a gentleman merchant and sea captain. Her mother was the only child of a wealthy merchant who travelled extensively. Martha travelled widely with her parents on their ship. Her stories kept the children entertained for hours, but she also used them to teach the children geography, history, culture, and, of course, literature.

~

An increasing number of farmers were slowly settling the area, and the new permanent residents cleared the land.

The Government Store was now becoming the shop that Mark had initially been so worried about. However, with the ladies in the family running the sales, Mark was content.

They now sold the pointless fribbles and furbelows that he abhorred, but with Alice and Jenny behind the counter, he left them to it. All he needed to do was direct what needed to go where when a new load of stock arrived. He ensured replacement stock was ordered before the last items sold out.

Now forty-eight, Mark stifled a groan when he awoke each morning. His knees hurt, his back ached, and his wounded arm had never fully recovered. However, he didn't wish to worry Cathy. Like Drew, there was a hollow in the muscles where the bullet had gone through, and the years of fighting in wars around the world had aged him. He still occasionally had nightmares, but they were not as often these days. He was not too proud to ask the boys for assistance, and they willingly acquiesced.

Drew and Mark had two good arms between them, and although they could do most things, Josh did most of the heavy lifting around the store. When a new load of supplies arrived, a crew of convicts would come with them, accompanied by the obligatory guards.

More often than not, these soldiers were friends of Mark's. They would be found sitting under the large tree around the various tables, scoffing their mugs of tea and fresh scones while watching the convicts unload the stores. The felons were well-known to the soldiers, and all were well-behaved.

When new stores arrived, the convict men rolled the barrels of produce into the immense storeroom that Lachlan had built last year. It was like a small version of the warehouses on the dockland.

Mark watched as huge sacks were carried on other men's shoulders. Another rat-proof room had been added to the storeroom just for bulk food supplies. However, once unloaded there, only Josh could move them out again.

Mark decided that they needed another able-bodied man to assist George and Josh, but they did not want just anyone.

Martha was still vulnerable and fearful of strange men. No other girls had been sent, and that in itself was unusual, until Martha explained they were now all being sent to Hetty and Joel Walker's farm, on her recommendation.

~

Six months after Martha's arrival, Mark wrote to Perry and asked him to find a suitable young man who was both trustworthy and capable of doing some heavy work.

After the New Year in January 1820, the wagons took the mail back to Parramatta.

Two letters arrived on the same wagon. A lad named Jack was to arrive the following day.

The day after the letters were delivered, Jack Turner came. He was a newly arrived convict, and he became the latest resident of the staff quarters with George. He had been granted a Ticket of Leave on arrival, as he and his friend, Charles Lockley, reported a planned mutiny on their ship out.

Perry's letter carried news that a friend of his, Major Ned Grace, had arrived on the same ship and recommended Jack. Perry had taken Jack's friend, Charles Lockley, to work at his house as his groom-cum-gardener, while Ned delivered Jack to Mark.

Perry heard about the men's bravery from Lachlan, who had spoken to the captain of their vessel when it had docked. Major Ned had been the person they sought out to inform about the mutiny. As their overseeing military officer, Major Ned Grace had come to know both men well. On the journey out, they had met in his cabin, and Jack taught them about his faith. As Ned knew Perry, he endorsed their story. The two convict men were rewarded with immediate release from their convict shackles. They both needed to serve their terms, but now they could do so while earning some money.

Mark, however, received a letter from Lachlan. Lachlan's missive to him said that this young man was a special case and was totally trustworthy. He didn't reveal more, except to say that he and Martha had met before. Mark was to say nothing, but Jack was far more than any ordinary convict.

Jack's arrival had been preceded by two letters of recommendation to Lachlan. Mark was to tell no one, but he was to treat Jack well.

All Mark was permitted to say was that Jack, like Mark and Josh, had been London-born and bred. Jack and Josh were much the same age.

This new way of living for Jack was an eye-opener. With Mark as his teacher, he learned fast.

Mark was astounded when Jack suggested regular prayer times before they ate. The men often found him on his knees, praying. They realised Jack was another man of faith. His prayers were not for show, but deeply rooted.

It did not take long before George excused himself from the group conversations. The three wives and Martha voiced their wish to join in.

Unbeknownst to most of the family, Martha and Jack had met nearly two years ago in London. Their reunion had been a total surprise for both of them. However, Lachlan's initial note had forewarned Mark.

Both wished for an extension of their friendship in London, but Martha had been arrested before they could meet again.

Cathy witnessed a conversation on the day of Jack's arrival, during which the pair held hands. For a girl so vilely abused, Cathy had been astounded that Martha let the new stranger so close to her. She turned to Mark, who was watching with a silly grin plastered on his lips. "Lachlan may have mentioned they knew each other from London. I was told to say nothing."

On return indoors, the pair confessed that they had previously met. Both had cultured voices, unlike the Cockney accents of the family.

They treated each other with great respect, and Mark saw that Jack would not press himself on the poor, abused girl.

~

An incident similar to the one that caused Mark's injury hastened Jack's confession of affection.

Within a month of his arrival, Jack proposed to Martha. After they were engaged, Jack would sneak a quick kiss on her rosy cheeks, often flushing them. He never manhandled her or sought her out for a private rendezvous, but he made sure she knew that he respected her.

Martha was surprised that she felt both safe and comfortable around him.

For Jack, no job was too insignificant to assist her with, be that carrying the heavy cane basket load of wet washing or helping with the nightly dishes.

~

Rather than leave after their marriage, the newlywed Turners stayed on until their first child, Marcus, was born. He was named in honour of Mark, and the happy babe joined the ever-growing number of children in the extended household.

Jenny and Alice had healthy, if somewhat noisy, children, and with Cathy and Mark's four, the house rang with the sounds of laughing children.

Until Martha's arrival, Mark taught them as best he could, but he knew his sons should have a better education than he had. His four children were now of an age to attend school, and he was determined that his daughters would receive an education as well as his sons.

Ten-year-old Gideon was already well advanced in his studies. Martha had stopped teaching when she had the baby, so Mark wrote to Perry for advice. Perry arranged for Gideon to have a tutor.

Colum Strachan joined the household and soon turned one of the upstairs rooms into a larger classroom. He lived in the men's accommodation with George.

New girls came and went, and life at the store became busier.

~

Midway through 1821, Perry wrote to Mark to inform them that they were leaving the colony with Lachlan and Elizabeth early the following year.

Perry's friend, Major Ned Grace, would oversee them from now on.

To Mark's immense surprise, Lachlan transferred the ownership of the store into Mark's name, with a condition attached.

Perry's letter contained the deed document and a lengthy screed of thanks from Lachlan, along with instructions for the store's future.

Mark had never thought of becoming a landowner. In England, it never would have occurred. The condition was that Josh would inherit it on Mark's demise, not Gideon. Mark didn't mind in the least. If Josh had not befriended the governor, none of this would have occurred. Well, mayhap it would have, but God had it all planned, and they were merely pawns on the giant chessboard of life.

Mark still had his military pension, and with George, Drew, and Josh's assistance, the vegetable garden and the sale of the cows' and goats' progeny provided a very comfortable income. Their store was selling far more than just the government stock. Funds were building nicely in the bank in Sydney.

~

In January 1822, Lachlan came for a final visit.

Elizabeth did not accompany him, but the new Governor, Sir Thomas Brisbane, did, along with an entourage of officials, including Mark's friend, newly married Captain Guy Manning, on his second tour of duty.

The entourage stayed with the family for two days, exploring the locality and inspecting the government farms. The surrounding area was to be subdivided into town lots, but that would not occur for many years yet.

Lachlan sought out Mark after dinner, and they sat outside for hours mulling over the past years. He admitted he had been recalled home because of the John Bigge report to Admiralty House, but he was also far from well. Lachlan had done what was needed to feed the people, and the baton had now been passed to the new leader. Mark would miss his friend.

At dawn on the day of departure from Camden, Josh was up and stoking the kitchen fire as he usually did. A voice behind him made him smile.

"Is your tea here as good as it used to be in Parramatta, laddie?" Lachlan had come for a farewell cuppa.

Josh replied with a chuckle. "It is indeed, sir, only here I believe it's supposed to be stirred with a green gum twig and drunk unsweetened. I still prefer honey in mine. The bushmen here call it 'billy tea.' They consume this tipple by the boiling billy full, and it is followed by a thick slice of camp bread with lashings of treacle." Josh placed a tin mug of the hot, sweet brew in front of the governor emeritus. Sir Thomas Brisbane assumed the role of leader on December 1st, so Lachlan was now officially retired.

Lachlan accepted the mug with a nod and sat staring intensely into the hot liquid. "I missed this more than I realised, Josh. If Henry, Mark, and you had not been by my side in those early years, I'm not sure I would have coped. Charles Whalan filled a gap, but he drew closer as our sons became best friends. Perry arrived about the time you left, but it was never the same." He sipped the hot tea and licked his lips. "Ahh! Perfect!"

Still without looking up, Lachlan said, "Did you know I must return home to face a fight for my reputation, and it's a battle I'm not sure I will win? I have poured my heart and soul into this colony, as has Elspeth."

Josh nodded. Mark had mentioned the situation last night.

Lachlan continued. "There are nearly three hundred building projects either completed or underway, and the town has now become a decent place to live. However, there was so much more I wished to have completed. I must consider myself blessed to have achieved this much. I had the powerful wisdom of the previous governors, Arthur Phillip and John Hunter, to guide me, and I have passed on as much knowledge as I can to your incoming leader. I have left Sir Thomas Brisbane a list of whom I trust, and your names are on it, of course."

Josh had never spent much time in Sydney before it had been cleaned up, but he distinctly remembered the stench of the squalid town when Mark showed him around on that first day. He had visited many times since and noticed the many new buildings under construction. "Thank you, sir. We will all help if necessary. As to Sydney Cove, I remember the smell of that place far too well, sir."

Lachlan nodded. "Don't we all? It's a wonder anyone was alive at all when we arrived. The water was so contaminated that illness was a way of life for everyone. Few privy facilities were in good enough repair to use, and with only one public cesspit operating, the town was disgusting. Men would urinate or defecate where they wished. It all washed into the Tank Stream when it rained. It was no wonder everyone was sick. Other than a few private wells, that creek was their only drinking water." He shuddered at the memory. "I remember on my arrival, D'Arcy's muttered words of a big fire being needed. He was almost correct, but those dilapidated wattle and daub buildings are now gone." He smiled to himself. "Governor Phillip's dream of 'New Albion' will never be built, but Sydney is far better than it was on my arrival. I am sad to be leaving under a cloud, but the wilds of Scotland are calling me home. Lachie will not like the cold, the isolation or the lack of prestige of being the governor's son, but Elspeth and I will love it, for it is home." He took a long draw of his tea. "I hope to retire there and live on my farm in peace. My soldiering days are over, as are my days of leadership, but they were good days, Josh, and I have done my best."

Josh nodded.

He took another long draw of his tea and added, "Elspeth and Lachie need a break too, and I think I will see if we can afford a trip somewhere. Italy sounds nice, and it's warm there too. I will miss this warmth in Scotland. It will probably be snowing there today. Admittedly, that is one thing I'm not looking forward to." He shivered in the summer heat.

Josh listened to his mentor's reminiscences. Yes, this man was his friend. He spoke softly, saying, "I have said this many times before, but I can never say thank you enough for all you have done for us. Mark is stunned to know that he is now a landowner. We all came from poverty and squalor, and we all had nothing in London and no future either. For us to own this magnificent property is wonderful."

Lachlan locked his brown eyes on Josh's. He said, "You may not be his blood son, Josh, but you are his heart one, just as we are all God's heart children. I wanted you to have something, but I couldn't give it to you directly. You know, your convict status and all, because this area is still exclusively for government use. However, Mark was now a free settler and government employee, including ex-soldiers. He may leave it to his family upon his passing. As Mark was one of my security detail, no one raised an eyebrow when it was processed under his name. He knows my wishes; it's something mentioned in the letter I sent last year. I'm sure he will honour them. What he does not know is that after I leave, he is to receive the title to the large allotment next door to this one. He will have something for his children."

Martha knocked on the door and entered, followed by Jack, who was carrying baby Marcus. The little boy had his father's honey-gold eyes and a crop of unruly, light-brown hair. His toothy grin took in the governor, but he reached out to Josh. Jack passed him over.

Lachlan looked at Josh and smiled. "Jack, a word, please."

Josh got the hint, nodded and took the child for a walk.

Lachlan greeted the convict couple, then addressed Jack, patting the seat next to him. "Jack, sit for a while. I have news for you."

Lachlan proceeded to fill them in about what plans he had for them. "When you arrived, young man, I heard of your bravery in standing up against the rabble on board. As I am leaving, I have been righting a few last-minute wrongs. Mark and Josh now own this store. Your friend Charles Lockley is to run Government Stores in Parramatta as well as manage a new inn next door to the King's Wharf. He is to gain ownership when such a thing is permitted, and that is just a matter of time. So, that leaves the need for a reward of equal value for you. If you and Martha are willing, I would like you to move to Emu Ford and open an inn there. I have been out to Bathurst, and it will open thousands of acres of new farmland there. However, staging houses and inns will be required."

He pulled a bulky envelope from his coat and handed it to Jack. "This is the title document for some land in Emu Ford, and the foundations of the inn have already been started. It should be ready for you to move into before Easter. You will need to construct the stables and outbuildings, but you have plenty of time before the road traffic picks up. This includes £10 in government reward money to tide you over until it's a paying concern. In case you are wondering, Charles Lockley received the same for reporting the mutiny. I also have a letter for you from England. I am guessing the contents, but read it when you are not disturbed."

Jack was lost for words. He took the unsealed documents and gave the esteemed gentleman a nod of thanks. He opened the envelope and pulled out the deed.

Martha leaned over and took the document from his hand, but left him the letter and money. She was fearful he would hand it back. "On behalf of us both and our sons, sir, I will accept willingly. We will do as you ask and help whomever we can, as we have both been assisted. Mr Perry's cousin, Janey Brien, saved my life, and if this is how we can repay both you and them, then we are thrilled to do so. Major Ned is now doing the same for other girls." She slid the document into her pocket.

Jack chuckled, and Lachlan grinned, but they remained silent.

Jack was being given a livelihood, but more than that, his friends had not forgotten him. He recognised the writing on the envelope. Mr Wilberforce had told him to help people, and this was one way he could do that. Yes, they could and would run an inn. Mark had already found another teacher, so Martha was at a loose end.

Martha stood and began preparing for the morning meal.

Jack recognised the writing on another letter that the governor handed him once her back was turned.

Lachlan said, "Open it now, lad. I had one from the same person."

With a cocked eyebrow, he glanced at the governor. He flicked open the red seal. The letter contained information that the Prince Regent had sent funds from the Earl of Templestowe Meade's estate that had now reverted to the crown. Jack was astounded, and he handed the missive to the governor.

Lachlan grinned. "Good, that will help with your future."

Lachlan had long ago revealed to Jack that the prince had written to him before his arrival. He realised that Jack had not told Martha that.

Lachlan said animatedly, "Oh, and Janey asked me to let you know that she will be returning to England with Perry and his family. As she is their cousin, I have assigned her to them for her life. I didn't record where her term was to be served."

Martha heard the comment and turned.

Lachlan grinned knowingly. "Like your husband, she deserves her reward, so she is returning home to England. She will have a good life with them. At last count, I believe there are nearly eighty girls who have been saved from further vile abuse by her and placed in some of the safe houses we have scattered around the colony. Jack, as I said, I have your new place under construction. It should be completed by Easter. I suggest you are ready to leave when the new building is habitable."

Duffy's store was changing personnel again.

A crying child broke the morning silence.

Josh returned with Marcus, and the rest of the household was stirring. Any private conversation was over.

Lachlan returned to his room and prepared for departure.

Jack collected his son from Josh's arms and left to occupy his child.

Martha was busy at the stove.

Lachlan was pleased to have had time alone with his protege before the others had arrived. He hoped his son would turn out to be such a man as Josh. He shrugged himself into the tight-fitting military coat and turned to leave his room. He wondered whether the new governor would befriend convict emancipists as he had. With a shake of his head, Lachlan realised that it was no longer his problem. Thomas Brisbane would now have to deal with the greedy landowners and do his best to cope. John Macarthur, Ellis Bent, and his brother, along with Samuel Marsden, were now all problems willingly passed to the new leader.

~

After a hearty breakfast, the entourage exited the home.

Following their meal, a flurry of farewells, hugs, and handshakes ensued, and the various staff members seated themselves in the accompanying vehicles. Lachlan slipped a bulky letter into Martha's hands. "I believe these are yours, dear." He turned and left them to say his last farewell to Josh.

As Lachlan arrived at his carriage, he handed Josh an envelope. "Open it after we've gone, lad."

Lachlan hopped up into the vehicle, and they were moving off before Josh had a chance to see what he had been handed.

Alice and Cathy came to his side.

His mother asked, "What did he give you, Josh?"

Josh flicked open the familiar red wax seal. He saw a folded note on paper he knew well. He pulled it out and saw the familiar flowing script of his mentor. He gasped as he found a twenty-pound note wrapped in the letter. Then he read the note. He immediately teared up as he read the words.

Parramatta

January 1822

Josh,

When you first came to me, you told me the judge said you were not worth tuppence. You mentioned this again shortly before leaving for Camden, but each time you held a penny, I noticed the grim expression on your face. I know the words cut deep.

However, know this — he was so very wrong!

To me and to your family, you are worth so much more. Regarding the judge's words that you will never amount to anything, he was wrong about that as well.

I call only a few on this earth, friends, Laddie, you are one of them. You are also one of my closest confidantes, and I shall miss you greatly.

Upon my return, I plan to speak to that judge to boast about your many successes in the colony and to say that one day, you, too, will be a great landowner.

This money is a mere fraction of your true worth, which cannot be measured in monetary terms. Use it as you wish; it has no strings attached, as it is from my pocket, not government coffers.

Thank you for being my friend; for me, that was beyond price. Laddie, keep your faith strong and true.

Pray for me, as I will for you.

Your friend,

Lachlan Macquarie

Alice came to stand beside her husband.

Josh had forgotten that he had told the governor about the judge's cruel words when he was convicted. He knew that each time he took a tuppence toll, it hit home again. The judge's words had cut deep. Even years later, they still hurt. From that day forward, he had been careful about his words lest he hurt someone's feelings. That one comment was burned deep within him and scarred his soul.

Alice smiled. "He knows, my love. And he understands how deep it cut."

Josh nodded. He looked down at his beloved wife. "He does, Ali. I just never realised how much."

Cathy saw his face and noticed the tears in his eyes, but he was smiling. With a caring hand on his arm, she asked, "Josh, what is it? What did he say?"

While tears flowed unchecked down his cheeks, Josh gave his mother a beaming smile. He replied, "He said I'm worth more than mere tuppence, Mama." He knew she had heard the vile comment.

Alice gasped and clung to his arm. "But you are everything to me, Joshy."

He released a long sigh of contentment and slid his arm around his wife's shoulder. He dropped a kiss on her lips.

Josh had not realised the governor had known how much the judge's words had hurt him. He said with a huff, "Tuppence indeed!"

He drew Alice into his arms and looked down at her lovely, smiling face. "I love you, my dearest sweet. I hope I remember to tell you every day."

Lachlan Macquarie
31 January 1762 – 1 July 1824

Major General Lachlan Macquarie, the 5th governor, left the colony a much better place than he found it. He returned home to face the false accusations listed in the John Bigge report.

Unfortunately, he died before the verdict was given. He was exonerated of all charges and is affectionately called the "Father of Australia." *He is buried on the Isle of Mull in his beloved Scotland, and this epitaph is written on his tomb.*

If you wish to read more of the Duffys and others mentioned,
there are more in this collection,
A Lady In Irons *(Perry and Katy White's story)*
When Upon Life's Billows *(Governor Hunter and the Milroy/Rosedale story)*
The Saddler's Song *(George Ellis's story)*
His Majesty's Pageboy *(Jack and Martha's story)*
A Fist Full of Holey Dollars *(Rudi's story)*
More are coming.

Ned Grace's story is **Unshackled Lives,** and is free when you sign up to my
occasional newsletter. This is a prequel to the **Lockleys of Parramatta** series.

Chief Ruatara. - d 1815

Characters

James Callan -b 1775 manager of Covent Garden markets, d 2nd Sept 1808
m Catherine (**Cathy**) Parks *grew up in St Giles, London, in the Rookeries*
b 1780
Children 2 living (1 dead daughter after Josh)
  1 **Joshua** Callan b 1795 Red Lyon Street, Whitechapel, in England
  (nr Covent Gardens) d 1855, aged 61
  m **Alice** Murray mid-1815 double wedding
    1 James (**Jimmy**) Joshua Callan, b February 1816
    2 Catherine Alice (**Kitty**) b November 1817, Camden
  2 **Jenny** Callan b 1799 Red Lyon Street, Whitechapel (nr Covent Garden)
  m Andrew (**Drew**) Baum, Mid-1815 double wedding
    b Matilda (**Tilda**) June 1816
m2 Sept 1809 Captain **Mark Duffy** 73rd regiment
b 1772 *mother d August 1808 in London, grew up in St Giles, London, in the Rookeries*
Children 4
  1 **Gideon** Mark Duffy June 1810
  2 **Rosemary** Catherine Duffy 1813
  3 Elizabeth (**Eliza**) Duffy April 1816 (twin)
  4 Jonah (**Joe**) Lachlan Duffy April 1816 (twin)
Reverend Phineas Brackenridge, the old minister at Hackney. d 1799.
Reverend **Josiah** Winchester, Illegitimate son of the *Earl of Coldenhurst.*
Reverend George McGillicuddy - b 1780. *Cared for the Rev.Phineas when Wil left in 1797*
Perry White m **Katy** White (a cousin)- children
Janey Brian - Perry and Katy's cousin and maid
Lord Wiskhamford - hit and killed James Callan, and Josh pickpocketed him.
Billy Green - cabin boy/cook's apprentice on board. Hyde Park barracks cook
Clive - ships cook on *Ann*
Major **Geoffrey Gilmore**, Assignment Major at Sydney
Captain **Guy** Manning, Mark's friend, 73rd reg't.(His story is in *Jam or Marmalade for Tea*)
Linus Rosedale and family
Pip Longford, a convict servant
Maisie Morecroft, convict servant
Hester Jones, convict servant, with child to a night guard. Marries Mitchell Roberts
Julieanna Peterson, convict servant
George Blake, Camden convict servant
Adam (no name) Parramatta convict servant
Mitchell Roberts m Hester Jones
Colum Strachan - convict tutor
*For **Ned, Jack** and **Charles's story**, see **The Lockleys of Parramatta***
Charles Lockley and **Major Ned Grace**
Jack Turner (in *His Majesty's Pageboy*)
m Feb 1820 **Martha Alexander** arrived in 1819.

Real people:-

Ann *Aug 1809- convict ship 27th Feb 1810 (Rio Nov 1809, Sydney 27/2/1810)*
Captain Charles Clark
Reverend and Mrs Samuel Marsden
Chief Ruatara d 1815
Captain Archibald John Maclaine,
Lieutenant John Purcell and family,
Lieutenant Robert Drurie and family,
Assistant Surgeon George Martin and family,
Rev. Robert Cartwright and family,
William Hall, missionary & shipbuilder
John King, flax weaver and missionary
Governor Macquarie's staff, the governess Mary Rouse, Lachlan Macquarie Jr's tutor
NB **Thomas Quinn** *was the first Tollgate Keeper in Parramatta.*
He was a soldier from the 73rd Regiment.

Hindostan, May 1809, Troop ship - 73rd Regiment *arrived 28th Dec 1810*
Captain John Pasco
Surgeon Joseph Arnold
Lt Col Co'Connell
Soldiers Robert Young, Thomas Kelly, James Frazier were three members of the
73rd Regiment who later served as convicts in Newcastle.
Soldiers from the 73rd Robert Young, Thomas Kelly, and James Frazier were later reprimanded,
convicted and served time as convicts once in NSW.

Dromedary *May 1809 -* ***governor's transport*** *arrived 25th Dec 1810*
Captain Samuel **Prichard** (Master)
his wife and two-year-old son
Servant, 'Black Tom'
Lachlan and **Elizabeth (Elspeth)** Macquarie (in 1814 - son Lachlan junior)
S*ervants* George Jarvis (Indian-born manservant),
Robert Fopp (butler)
Joseph Bigg (coachman)
Mrs Ovens (cook)
Mrs **Jones** (waiting woman for Elizabeth Macquarie)
Deputy Judge-Advocate Ellis **Bent** (and his wife and son) & brother.
Captain Henry **Antill** (promoted to Major in 1811)
Ensign Alexander Huey
Ensign John Maclaine (Elizabeth Macquarie's nephew)
officers and rank and file of the 73rd. Regiment
and 136 wives and children of the soldiers, plus a crew of 102 sailors
Jemima Fisher, Government House housekeeper.
Sergeant Charles Whalan, his wife, Elisabeth and son.

Historical Notes

In 1809, Samuel Marsden travelled to England to recruit additional clergy to serve in the colony. There, he befriended the New Zealand Maori chief, Ruatara. He had gone to Britain in the whaling ship *Santa Anna* and been stranded there.

Marsden and Ruatara returned together on the convict transport *Ann* (or Anne), which was under the command of Captain Charles Clarke and which carried some 198 male convicts. They arrived in Sydney on 17 or 27 February 1810.

Ruatara stayed with Marsden at Parramatta for some time until 1811, after a failed attempt to reach New Zealand. Ruatara eventually reached home, where he did more to facilitate Marsden's mission to the Maori than any other native.

The story of his tattoos, marriage, and death is accurate.

TOLLS AND TOLL GATES - More followed the initial three toll gates.
1802 May 25 the first tollway.
To be levied on a floating bridge over South Creek (Reel 6039; SZ756 pp. 201-2) (a water toll) (Windsor) and built by Andrew Thompson.
NB replaced in 1814 by Howes Bridge

c. 1810 First Road Till Gates decreed
Toll bars to be erected on Sydney-Parramatta Road (Reel 6039; SZ756 p.203) (*Nr Central Station*)
1810 Mar 24
Proclamation re erection of toll bars on public roads (Reel 6039; SZ756 p.204)
1810 Dec 11
To Commissioner of Roads re tolls & leases of on Parramatta-Sydney Road (Reel 6002; 4/3490D p.40)
1811
Rate of tolls on public road between Sydney and Parramatta (Reel 6043; 4/1726 p.181)
1811 Mar 30
Proclamation of turnpike road between Sydney and Parramatta, regulations and schedules of tariffs (Reel 6045, 4/1733 p. 46; Reel 6038,
SZ1044 pp.188-92; Reel 6039, SZ756 pp.205-9)
1811 Apr 6
Francis Williams appointed Trustee and Commissioner of the Turnpike Road being constructed between Sydney and the River Hawkesbury: instructions for guidance of toll keepers (Reel 6039, SZ756 pp.209-10; Reel 6038, SZ758 pp. 188-9)
1811 Apr 10 1812 Apr 25 1812 Nov 2
1813 Mar 13 1813 Apr 24 1813 Nov 27 1813 Dec 11 1813 Dec 11 1814 Oct 29
Inquiry as to whether the Provost Marshal was exempted from paying tolls when on public duty (Reel 6043; 4/1726 p. 114)
To be levied on the ferry across the Hawkesbury between Wilberforce and Pitt Town (Reel 6039; SZ756 p.211)
Copy of voucher for stores issued to Toll House, South Head Road (Reel 6042; 9/2736 p.9a)
Regulations re toll dues on road from Sydney to South Head (Reel 6039, SZ756 pp.215-6; Reel 6038, SZ758 pp. 359-60)
David Bevan paid commission from the Police Fund for selling duties arising on Sydney and Parramatta toll gates (Reel 6038; SZ758 p.366)
Toll gate erected on new road between Parramatta and Windsor at Parramatta Bridge and Rouse Hill (Reel 6038; SZ758 pp.438-9)
To Wentworth re rates to be charged on Windsor-Parramatta Turnpike (Reel 6002; 4/3491 p.631)
Schedule of tolls to be charged at Turnpike Gates (Reel 6039, SZ756 pp.216-7; Reel 6038, SZ758 pp.440-1)
Re tolls to be charged for the ferry across the Hawkesbury from Windsor & at the bridge over the Chain of Ponds near Windsor (Reel 6039; SZ756 pp.212-3; Reel 6038, SZ758 p. 550-1; Reel 6044, 4/1730 pp.

Bibliography

Trove instigations of Tolls 1811
https://trove.nla.gov.au/newspaper/article/628283?searchTerm=toll%20gate
Toll cost revision
https://trove.nla.gov.au/newspaper/article/2176658?searchTerm=toll%20gate
UK Turnpikes & Tolls
https://www.parliament.uk/about/living-heritage/transformingsociety/transportcomms/
roadsrail/overview/turnpikestolls/
History of Turnpikes in the UK
https://www.campop.geog.cam.ac.uk/research/projects/transport/onlineatlas/
britishturnpiketrusts.pdf
The first toll road opened on 10 April 1811
https://www.facebook.com/rememberingthepastaustralia/photos/-today-in-australian-
history-10th-april-1811-australias-first-toll-road-opens%EF%B8%8F-t/3211977482159425/
London's Gaols
https://www.londonlives.org/static/Prisons.jsp#Giltspur
Convict Ship Ann 1809
https://www.freesettlerorfelon.com/convict_ship_ann_1810.htm
Holey Dollar and Dump
https://www.nma.gov.au/explore/collection/highlights/holey-dollar
Elizabeth Macquarie's Diary - Journeys in Time - Macquarie Uni
https://www.mq.edu.au/macquarie-archive/journeys/1809/1809.html
Lachlan Macquarie Administration
https://adb.anu.edu.au/biography/macquarie-lachlan-2419
Lachlan's building projects
https://www.visitsydneyaustralia.com.au/history-7-macquarie.html
First Government House Sydney
https://en.wikipedia.org/wiki/First_Government_House,_Sydney#, _ Sydney #
Old Government House, Parramatta
https://en.wikipedia.org/wiki/Old_Government_House,_Parramatta
Sydney map 1807
https://nla.gov.au/nla.obj-150430826/view
Murder at the Tollgate
https://canadabayheritage.asn.au/murder-at-the-parramatta-toll-gate-28-may-1814/
D'Arcy Wentworth
https://www.wikitree.com/wiki/
Wentworth-881#:~:text=After%20Catherine's%20death%20the%20children's,that%20they%2
0did%20not%20marry.
Macquarie's household.
https://issuu.com/nationaltrustsaustralia/docs/nt186_magazine_e14_issuu/s/21767216
Pennant Flags - Pr Jackson shipping
https://fiav.org/wp-content/uploads/2021/06/ICV2503-Ralph-Kelly-Colonial-Signals-of-
Port-Jackson.pdf

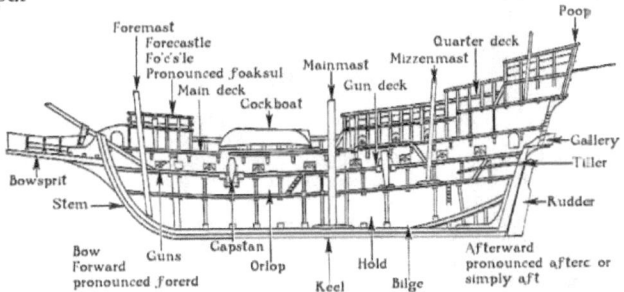

Australian Historical Fiction
(All are stand-alone stories)

First Fleet Convict Era Trilogy 1788-1800

Gentle Annie Soames

Her dreams lead to unexpected outcomes. An Australian First Fleet story.
A First Fleet story with the descriptions taken directly from the Journal of Doctor Arthur Bowes Smith was the doctor on board the Lady Penrhyn.

Annie Soames is a girl beloved by the community but not afraid to voice her desires. That leads to trouble, illicit love, and a world turned upside down.
Oliver Quilpie, the newly married Marquess, finds his arranged marriage unsatisfactory; he is irresistibly drawn to his wife's companion. Unfortunately, he can't keep his hands off her. In retaliation, Annie copies his every move while riding, dressed as a highwayman. However, she has now fallen in love with him. This ultimately leads to her arrest and banishment to a distant land. After some years, Oliver's wife dies, and his thoughts turn to Annie. He seeks to find her, but she has vanished. He is horrified to discover she was transported to New South Wales as a convict on the *Lady Penrhyn*. Will Annie want to see him?
ISBN 9780645441574   ISBN ebook 9781923097063   LP ISBN 978-1923097346
HC 9798244028607   Draft To Digital 9798233855122
Long-listed in the Historical Fiction Company Competition 2024

The Emancipated Potter

Sydney Cove 1788 to Parramatta 1795
Not all felons are convicts, and not all convicts are felons.
Colin Osborne's serene life as a talented potter is crushed by a self-important peer. A single punch sends Colin across to the other side of the globe. **Aggie Gibbs** is a young convict girl being hunted by a wayward soldier. The two find themselves in a town of criminals and lecherous men. Captain John Hunter is Colin's mentor, and he paves the way for a new life for his young friends. Then disaster strikes, and he must leave.
Can Colin keep Aggie safe? Will they fulfil Captain Hunter's wishes to build a decent life for the convicts destined to live out their lives in the penal town? Will John ever return to New South Wales?   Paperback ISBN 9781923097476   ISBN ebook 9781923097483
Large Print 9781923097506   HC 9798251872569   D2D ebook 9798233212536

Paternity Unknown

Sydney 1788 - 1800 The Aftermath of the First Fleet landing.
Can forgiveness be that easy?
Connie Waterson is traumatised after she became one of the victims of the attack when the convict women were landed on February 6th, 1788. She finds herself expecting an unwanted child. Along with her friends, she must learn to cope with the challenges of their new environment while protecting the life growing within her.
Nigel Bray is a young convict who almost instantly regrets his carnal actions on the day the prisoners from the *Lady Penrhyn* landed. Knowing that Connie is the unwilling recipient of his base desires, Nigel does what he can to ease her path. He is racked with questions: is the child his? Will she ever forgive him? What must Nigel do to win Connie's trust?
ISBN 9781923097438   ISBN ebook 9781923097445   LP ISBN 978-1923097452
HC 9798251874877   D2D 9798232509286

The Hunter to Macquarie Collection 1795-1822

When Upon Life's Billows

Sydney 1795-1821 - Governor John Hunter
Keep your friends close, and your enemies closer.
John Hunter loved his life at sea. The wind blows where no man knows, and John is caught in a storm. His ship, the *HMS Sirius*, was wrecked in 1790. Five years later, he became the second governor of the rough and filthy penal settlement of New South Wales. From a place he once loved, he now seems to be in the wrong place at the wrong time, trusting the wrong people.
Helena Rosedale is not your typical female convict. She fiercely battles to prevent the men from abusing her, earning her the nickname *"Helena the Hellcat"*.
Crispin Milroy, alone in the world, serves on the new governor's security detail. Can he win the fair lady's heart? Life in 1795 in Sydney Cove was harsh at best. Food is scarce, and disease often ravages the settlement. Life throws everything at these three, yet somehow, they manage to survive. Why does John trust this young couple when others betray him? What trials must Helena and Crispin endure to make their new lives in this unforgiving town bearable? How can John ease their path?
Paperback ISBN: 9780645783339   ebook ISBN: 9780645783346 Large Print 9781923097513
HC 9798251492620   D2D ebook 9798233358807

The Saddler's Song

London 1790s to Parramatta 1840s

The Strains of Starting Again.

George Ellis is the son of a tanner, living on the outskirts of London. Alone and hurting after a disease takes his family, he seeks a new life, setting up a business in New South Wales. His beloved violin is his most treasured possession, and his talent for making music is hidden from all but a select few.

Ben Parker, a saddler, is also heading to the colony. Combining their skills to start afresh in a new world, the young men find accommodation with a family. Two of the daughters steal their hearts — but how will the business survive in a stock-starved land where access to leather is limited? What is the saddler's song, and why is it so special?

Paperback ISBN: 9780645783353   eISBN: 9780645783360   Large Print 9780645783377
HC 979825105238   D2D ebook 9798233262449

Tuppence to Pass

London 1800s to Parramatta 1820s

An Unlikely Partnership

Josh Callan never expected much from life—just enough to get by in the gritty backstreets of London. But when he's caught stealing from the very man who murdered his father, Josh finds himself branded worthless by a sneering judge and sentenced to a distant, brutal world: the penal colony of Sydney.

Arriving just as **Governor Lachlan Macquarie** takes charge, Josh steps into a colony on the cusp of change—and into opportunities he never dreamed possible. As he earns the respect of the powerful governor and becomes a trusted confidante, Josh begins to forge a new path not just for himself, but also for his family and his beloved.

Can a boy dismissed as nothing rise to become something more? And what will his unexpected friendship with the governor cost or gain him in the end?

paperback ISBN : 9781923097070   eISBN: 9781923097087   LP 9781923097544
HC 979825188088   D2D ebook 9798233190605

His Majesty's Pageboy

London to Emu Plains, Australia, in the 1800s

Jack Turner, raised in privilege and known as Lord John. However, at age nine, his true identity is revealed. He struggles with society's immorality and shallowness. He finally meets a pure young woman he feels he could love, but because of his chequered background, he is unable to pursue her. Then, his life takes another turn.

Martha Alexander, daughter of a wealthy shipping merchant, met Lord John while at a society ball in London. She is expected to marry well, and she has feelings for John. But her father's drunkenness led to the loss of everything he owned, including Martha, dooming her to a forced marriage. How do these two young people end up as convicts in Australia?

Paperback ISBN 9781923097308   ebook ISBN 9781923097292   LP 9781923097568
HC 9798251886504   D2D ebook 9798233639654

A Fist Full of Holey Dollars

Sydney Cove 1810+

The Holey Dollar and Dump Story

Captain Rudi Greenwood is a solitary man trapped in a job without purpose, in a land where alcohol is the currency and rules are frequently ignored in pursuit of wealth. Rudi's life spins out of control. Will he listen to the minister and turn his life around?

Bethany Edwards is a grieving widow expecting her late husband's child. Rudi's attraction to the lovely widow compels him to reassess his views and contemplate someone new. She seeks Rudi's help and support, but is that all she truly feels? Will he take Reverend Cowper's advice? When **Governor Lachlan Macquarie** asks Rudi for help improving the roads, a casual remark alters Rudi's life and affects the entire colony. To tackle the alcohol issue, he proposes creating a new currency. With Bethany by his side, will he rise to the governor's challenges? What actions led to him being despised by the exclusives and free settlers in the colony?

Paperback ISBN 9781923097407   eISBN 9781923097414   Large Print 9781923097537
HC 9798251884937D2D ebook 9798233057052

Far From the Whispering Sheoaks
Set in Australia in 1817+

Fanny Little was in the wrong place doing something she thought was legal. Her actions led to her arrest, trial, and banishment. She was assigned from the female prison to ex-soldier **Gordon McKenzie** and soon found herself in the despicable and humiliating situation of being sold in the public marketplace. **Phil Bentley** is a man running from his jealous uncle. He is seeking safety on a secluded farm half a world away. With the community backing them, can Phil save Fanny from Gordon's vile abuse? Why is their relationship destined to spark controversy? And who is Jas? Why does Gordon wish to harm the child? Will they ever escape the shadows pursuing them? Paperback ISBN 9781923097315 eISBN9781923097322 Large Print 9781923097575 HC 9798251893915

Quest for Survival
Sydney 1798-1810 - Between the Governors

Nell Bywater intentionally gets herself arrested after hearing that convicts receive free food and clothing. As a twelve-year-old foundling, life is hard. Her options are few, and most of them are distasteful. She is assigned to Governor Hunter's nephew as a nursemaid for his small children. Then the Kents leave, and she is left alone in an almost empty house.
Aubrey Grey is a young convict assigned to convert the Kents' old house into a new girls' orphanage. There, he meets Nell. Governor and Mrs King oversee the new girls' orphanage, as well as Nell. Mrs King ensures Nell is kept safe, with Aubrey assigned as her caretaker.
As houseparents to more than thirty young girls, both find the security they have sought. However, there is more to life than a roof over your head and food in your belly. What begins as a simple assignment becomes life-changing for both of them when love intervenes.
Coming 2026/7

Bound Down in Iron Chains
An Australian Historical Tale, set in the Boys' Orphanage in Sydney in 1818+
Smuggling, Rum and Ructions
A gripping tale of betrayal, courage, and survival in colonial Australia.

When honest London bookkeeper **Howard Marlow** is wrongly convicted and sent to New South Wales, he's assigned to the Sydney Boys' Orphanage, where corruption runs deep and the accounts don't add up. There he meets **Naomi Buckingham**, a convict girl hoping for safety—but facing danger instead. As the two uncover coded ledgers and a smuggling ring tied to the colony's elite, they must risk everything to expose the truth. In a brutal world built on power and fear, can two convicts bring justice to those who have none?
Paperback ISBN 9781923097353 eISBN9781923097360 LP 9781923097551 HC 9798251894677
Coming 2026/7

Buddy's Promise
From the Shadows of London to the shade of the gumtrees

Raised on the streets of London, **Obadiah "Buddy" Jensen** hides a fierce loyalty behind a tough facade. When a dying boy begs him to protect his little sister, **Emily Bolt**, Buddy vows to keep her safe—never expecting she'll become the love he can't have.
Exiled to Australia as a convict, Buddy builds a new life, but when Emily reappears years later, everything has changed. He is married with a child.
She was six when he found her. She was lost when he left. Torn between past promises and present choices, can they find their way back to each other—or will fate keep them apart forever? An emotional historical romance of love, loss, and redemption across the seas.
ISBN 9780645783384 eISBN 9780645783391
Coming 2027

Linen Shirts Aplenty
The first female factory, Parramatta, in the early 1800s.

Biddy Murphy is an Irish girl who caught the eye of an upstart English peer. Convicted and transported as a wanton, she must face the shame of her fallen status.
Major Geoffrey Gilmore is the convict assignment officer in Sydney. His heart goes out to this beautiful but very skilled girl. Can Geoff ease her lot in life, or will their positions in the colony keep them apart? Will the hatred of the Irish mean that Geoff's attraction to this lovely girl be doomed before he can rescue her? Why do the wide plains of Bathurst draw them?
Coming 2027

Unlikely Convict Ladies Trilogy 1792-1840s
Dancing to Her Own Tune
Co-authored by Sheila Hunter and Sara Powter
Sydney 1790s to England 1830s

Annie White is released after serving seven years as a convict in Sydney. She has a visitor who helps her start a baking business. Annie is then asked to assist another ailing man, **Sam Corbett**. She nurses him back to health, and a relationship blossoms between them. They settle into a life together, barely making ends meet, when she realises she's expecting a child. Sam's past is laid bare, and he must come to terms with the revelations. They both must confront their accusers and discover that the answers to their questions are not what they anticipated. Their life experiences seem to cling to them, and, unable to shake them off, they end up back in England. They must face their ghosts and recognise they are not who they think they are. How can they transform their anger and spite into love and forgiveness? The Dance of Life goes on.   Paperback ISBN 9780645110715   ISBN9780645110722

Large Print 9781923097209 HC 9798763014136 D2D ebook 9798233565748
Long-listed for the Historical Fiction Company Competition 2022

Amelia's Tears
Parramatta 1828 – England 1840s
From Tears of Sadness to Tears of Joy.

Amelia Westaweller awaits her assignment in the Parramatta Female Prison. Forced to leave the relative safety of gaol, she is assigned and now faces her worst nightmare. A foul man claims her and makes her life a living hell. Then, her world goes black. A glimmer of hope arises when she hears from her brother, Jim, who has enlisted a friend to help her. She writes to Jim, pouring out her heart and telling him of the horrors of her new life. He encourages her to stay firm in her faith. All she can do is pray. When **Major Ned Grace,** her brother's friend, enters her life in Parramatta, he starts to ease her path. Things have changed, as now she has a child in tow. How can Amelia forge a new life for herself? What man could want her with her background and a child at her side? Who is the gentleman who turns her tears of sadness into tears of great joy?

Paperback ISBN: 9780645110739   eISBN: 9780645110746 HC ISBN 9798420617953
Large Print 9781923097216 D2D 9798232247898

A Lady in Irons
England 1800s - Parramatta 1808+

Katy Harrington is mourning the death of her husband after he died in a shooting accident. Barely coping, she awaits the birth of their child. If it's a girl, she must hand the family home to her husband's brother. The day after giving birth to a daughter, she and her daughter are left on the side of a road. She collapses and is found by someone she thought had died in a fire ten years before. **Perry White** badly scarred himself, nurses her back to health. They marry and move in with her widowed friend, Mary.
After some years, she discovers her husband and friend in each other's arms. Now living in a love triangle, she flees. Grasping the only straw available, she intentionally gets arrested and is sent to a colony far away. By doing this, her marriage can be annulled.
What happens in the Colony is different from what she expects. Governor Macquarie comes to her rescue, but what of Perry and her children?

Paperback ISBN: 9780645110784   eISBN:9780645441505
Large Print 9781923097223   HC 9798358108141   D2D ebook 9798233855122

The Convict Birthstain Collection 1820-1840s
No More, My Love
Hunter Valley, NSW, 1820s

Jess Elkin is distraught when tragedy ravages her family. Now widowed, she becomes the victim of a carriage accident and is nursed back to health by the driver.
Marcus Ryan, a hard-headed woollen mill owner, was not expecting to fall in love. Yet, when Jess's fortunes suddenly turn for the worse, Marcus must decide how far he will go to pursue her. Years after following her to Newcastle, Australia, Marcus vanishes. Jess is left wondering if he will keep his promise to return to her… Will she ever see him again?

Paperback ISBN: 9780645441536   eISBN 9780645441581
Large Print 9781923097230 D2D ebook 9798233092381
Long-listed in the Historical Fiction Company Competition 2023

The Vine Weaver

Hawkesbury River area 1820s+
New Beginnings and Old Threats

In the 1820s, **Joel and Hetty Walker** lived on a secluded farm on the Hawkesbury River, which became a haven for the protection of young convict women. A series of events brings **Fran Rea** to Hetty's attention, and she is taken to the farm. Fran and Hetty develop a cottage industry under the compassionate eye of farmhand **Hector Macdougal**; Hector's loving words change lives. It is to him that Fran turns when threatened.

The vines now must draw them close to survive the future revelations, and of those, there are many. Paperback ISBN: 9780645441512   eISBN: 9780645441529

Large Print 9781923097247   D2D ebook 9798233189494
Long-listed in the Historical Fiction Company Competition 2023
The story continues in "Scotch at The Rocks"...

Scotch at The Rocks

Glasgow, Scotland, early 1800s to The Rocks, Sydney 1830s

Orphaned children **Brodie Stewart and Heather Anderson** live on Glasgow's streets. Although hungry, they somehow manage to survive and stay out of trouble. Heather finds a job and looks to be settled; things go pear-shaped for them both. Eventually, they marry by declaration, but even that gets complicated, and they are both arrested soon after exchanging their vows. In 1838, they were transported to Sydney as convicts. Heather arrives within weeks of Brodie, and they are assigned close to each other. They are now living in the docklands of Sydney, known as The Rocks. They now have to forge a new life halfway across the world from their homeland.

Adventures abound, and Brodie gets press-ganged. While he's away, Heather's life changes and soon, she's officially selling Scotch Whisky at a shop in The Rocks.

You can take a Scot out of Scotland, but where did the Scotch come from?

Paperback ISBN 9780645441550 ebook 9781923097001 Large Print 9781923097254
Large Print 97810645783377   D2D ebook 9798232122638

Waiting at the Sliprails

The Bathurst Road 1830s
A Convict's Tale

Bea Dawes's term of conviction nears an end, and she has few options other than marriage to a stranger or going on the street.

Jack Barnes, the hired drover, wants a wife. Bea accepts his offer; then, she discovers that he could be gone for months, leaving her alone with Billy and Netty, part of the tribe of an Aboriginal tribe who live on his secluded farm. Bea learns to love her husband and also this wonderful Aboriginal couple. Drought ravages the farm, and Jack must hit the long paddock with the flock. In his absence, a visitor arrives, threatening to destroy everything she has worked so hard for. Can Bea touch her heart? Can she cope? Will the drought ever end? And when will Jack return?

Paperback ISBN: 9780645441543   eISBN: 9781923097032
Large Print 9781923097261   D2D ebook 9798233711145
PenCraft Award Winner for Literary Excellence, Christian Historical Fiction 2024

Convict Shadows of the Past

Two Jennifers, two hundred years apart
The colonial history of cheese in Australia

When she discovers her convict family history, eight-year-old **Jenny Kellow** learns that she was named after a convict from nearly two hundred years ago. Inspired by her grandfather's stories, she delves into her ancestors' convict past. From him, she hears tales of bushrangers, convicts, and life in the early colony of Parramatta. She embarks on a journey to retrace the footsteps of her convict great-great-great-grandmother to honour her. Jenny's quest begins with microfiche in the 1960s, when she discovers a small tin-mining town in Cornwall and the production of a cheese that set London alight. She uncovers that her ancestor, **Jennifer Kellow,** brought her cheese-making skills to Parramatta, where she taught others the craft. Echoes of the past can still be heard if you know where to listen. Who was the first Jennifer, and what does she have to do with cheese? Why is she so elusive? Did Jenny's ancestor, Jennifer, ever see those two small crosses carved into the bricks of the Female Factory? Would Jenny ever uncover her ancestor's story?   Paperback ISBN: 9780645783315

ISBN ebook 9780645783322   Large Print 9781923097278   D2D ebook 9798233906411

In Defence of Her Honour

London 1800s to Parramatta 1819
Will the real man of quality please stand up?

Bill Miller was raised and educated alongside the family's sons. The youngest, Bert Edison-Browne, had been his best friend. However, jealousy intervenes when Bill's excellent schoolwork begins to curtail their friendship. He wins a scholarship and enters Oxford University. When Bill's father dies unexpectedly, Bert insists that Bill take over as butler, but it's more to oppress him. Bert's jealousy grows and festers. He is now looking for a way to rid themselves of their new butler. A ruckus ensues, and Bill is arrested for assaulting Bert.

Molly Ross, the housekeeper's daughter, will vouch for him. It's too late; Bill has been arrested and is soon to be sentenced and transported. With Bill gone, Molly now fights to defend herself from Bert. After hitting him with a pan, she, too, is arrested and sent to Sydney. Bill and Molly arrive with letters of introduction and compensation from Bert's father. Soon, they will be running the best inn in Parramatta with an endorsement from the governor.

Paperback ISBN 9780645441567   ISBN ebook 9781923097049
Large Print 9781923097339   D2D ebook 9798233129810
Long-listed in the Historical Fiction Company Competition 2024

J Can't Stop Tomorrow

Irish Famine 1840s to Avoca Beach, Australia

Escaping bigotry and prejudice in Ireland, the O'Shane family lives on a secluded farm on the west coast of Ireland. The potato blight soon decimated their farm. It's always darkest before dawn, and the two remaining girls cling to the hope of a new life. With the kindness of strangers, the eldest girls, **Clare and Kerry O'Shane,** head to their cousin, Sal Lockley, in Parramatta, Australia.   A new, wonderful life awaits them both. **Shéamus Connor** is the annoying teenage boy who reluctantly draws Clare's affection. However, living in a convict town means ruffians abound. **John Moore** is a bad-tempered and troubled Irishman who is content to live alone on another secluded farm until he discovers Clare and two other lads need rescuing. Can John protect her from the pain inflicted by an evil world? Can Shéamus find his lost love, who has fled?   Paperback ISBN: 9780645441598   ISBN ebook 9781923097056   Large Print 9781923097421   D2D ebook 9798233594632

Madeline's Boy

England 1830s to New South Wales 1840
The race to protect an Orphaned Boy
All is not straightforward when money and titles are involved.

Orphaned, afraid and on the run, Chip must flee. **Madeline Brougham** was his mother's best friend. Maddie now needs to keep her charge safe and alive. She must give up her life to protect the boy she has loved since birth. Months after Chip's parents' demise, Maddie sets out to deliver Chip to his Uncle Humphrey, who lives in Sydney. Through him, she meets Chip's uncle's friend, **Tim,** who falls for Maddie. But will they find happiness? The menacing presence soon finds Chip, and Maddie needs to hide him again. They are relocated from hidden farms to secret valleys, ultimately ending up in an Aboriginal encampment. Can Tim find a way to be with Maddie? And if so… Will Chip ever be safe?   Paperback ISBN: 9780645783308   ISBN ebook 9781923097094   Large Print 9781923097469   D2D ebook 9798233351396   *Long-listed in the Historical Fiction Company Competition 2024*

Jam or Marmalade for Tea

England 1820s to New South Wales 1825 (Governor Brisbane Era)

Martha Hamilton is the eldest of four orphans struggling to survive on their own. She is caught stealing, tried, convicted, and transported to New South Wales. With her family gone, she becomes despondent. Life holds no meaning for her, and the ocean waves look inviting. **Captain Guy Manning** is a frustrated and injured redcoat soldier returning to Sydney for a new assignment. He notices Martha trying to jump overboard and rescues her. How do two cats bring them together? A convict ship is no place for romance, and she's far too young anyway, isn't she? Can Guy save her and forge a life together for them? What connections does she have to try to save her siblings? Why is marmalade important for their future?

Paperback ISBN 9781923097933   eISBN9781923097285
Large Print 9781923097490   D2D ebook 9798224495825
A NaNoWriMo 2023 book winner

A prequel to 'The Lockleys Parramatta' series

Unshackled Lives

Set in England & Australia in the 1800s
Australian historical fiction of early colonial days

Ned Lockley's childhood was a dream, but his adulthood is becoming a nightmare. Following a whirlwind romance that ends in bitter treachery, Ned finds himself adrift in a society collapsing under its own immorality. With his family ties fraying, Ned flees England to preserve his soul and his faith. The colony of New South Wales is no paradise. Now known as Ned Grace, he is tasked with the gruelling work of placing female convicts. Ned is thrust into a world of grit and shadows. As he struggles to find his footing, he must unravel a dangerous mystery: Who is Charles, and what does he mean for Ned's future?
Print ISBN 9781923097377   eISBN 9781923097384 LP ISBN: 9781923097391
D2D ebook 9798232096021

A 100-year, six-part Australian Colonial series
The Lockleys of Parramatta 1800-1900

Hands upon the Anvil

A blacksmith's life and love are more than work
Parramatta 1830s

Eddie Lockley's parents were transported for their crimes. Can a steadfast lad rise above his origins and guide others to succeed in a land of opportunity?
Ten-year-old Eddie longs to help his mum and dad. Living in a convict town with his family, the keen youngster has been working with the local blacksmith since his sixth birthday. But when a lieutenant doesn't stop abusing his older brother, the young boy yearns for the day when he can stand up and end the torment. Though he's thrilled when his mentor offers to send him off to learn his letters, Eddie fears he won't be around to watch his siblings' backs. But as he takes on the biggest adventure of his life, the brave believer soon discovers that God is looking out for everyone he loves. Does this young man in the making have what it takes to change everything for the better?
paperback ISBN 9780994578235 Ebook ISBN 978-0-9945782-5-9 HC 9798496177368
Large Print 9781923097148   D2D ebook 9798232476335

Out Where The Brolgas Dance

Gold is found, and so is love
Parramatta 1840s
How can a question change so many people?

It's the 1840s, and discoveries across the Blue Mountains continue. Major Mitchell's new road is complete, and towns are planned and being built. Abundant land is available for those who want it. Eighteen-year-old **William "Wills" Lockley** has laid a solid foundation for a respectable career as a blacksmith, but the Lockley lust for adventure flows deeply within his veins. He dreads the monotony of work at the blacksmith's forge and yearns for adventure in a new frontier. Wills meets six Englishmen (*Coping with what is now known as PTSD*) who have the means to make his dreams come true. What they discover changes the Colony and their lives forever. Gold fever ensues. While in the West, Wills must deal with an uncertain romance. Does **Cathy** even want him?
ISBN 9780994578242 Ebook ISBN 978-0-9945782-6-6 HC ISBN 9798755445504
LP ISBN 9781923097155   D2D ebook 9798233188794

Diamonds in the Dirt

Diamonds, love and money… but there is much more to life.
Parramatta 1850s

The youngest Lockley son, **Luke Lockley,** has completed his university education, and his life lacks direction. No job, no money, and no love. Desperately alone, he prays for guidance. How can Luke trust that God has a plan for him if he can't even find a job? He does the only thing he can … he prays. Within a week, life has changed … oh, how it has changed as his brother Wills turns up with a suggestion. Would Luke be interested in joining the expedition with John Evans? **Reverend William Clarke** needs assistance with a government mineral survey. The challenges, adventures and finds are life-changing for many. However, it gives Luke meaning, purpose and direction. The condition of his heart problems also takes a turn. Can he walk away? Will **Ellen** wait for him?
Paperback ISBN: 9780994578273 Ebook ISBN: 978-0-9945782-8-0
HC ISBN 979-8788011141 LP 9781923097162 D2D ebook 9798233366239

The Earl's Shadow
Who or what is the 'shadow'? How does it affect so many?
Parramatta 1860s

Charles Lockley, the Earl of Coxheath, spent his youth as a convict in Parramatta, unaware of his noble birth, with limited education and few social skills. Now, after a near-death experience, Charles must decide how to live the rest of his life. He is thrust out of his comfort zone in London. There, Charles discovers his purpose. He delivers a speech in parliament—an action that will reshape the empire. His eldest son, **Charlie**, shares many of his father's shortcomings. However, the past continues to haunt Charlie.

But how does Jim Leslie, the Cobb and Co. coach driver, fit into their story? And what exactly is 'The Earl's Shadow' that he mentions?

Paperback ISBN: 9780645110708 Ebook <u>ISBN</u> 978-0-9945782-9-7

Large Print 9781923097179 HC 9798836057053 D2D ebook 9798233679209

Once a Jolly Swagman
An old black Billy Can contains the secrets of an incredible life
An Australian Historical Novel Inspired by the songs of The Seekers
Set in 1870s Parramatta and Kent, UK

Rick Lockley, struggling to escape his family's expectations, runs away to find himself. Jack, a jolly swagman, takes him under his care. Even after years together, Rick knows little about the old man. On his death, **Jack** leaves Rick his precious billy can; the contents reveal Jack's identity. Stunned, Rick must travel to England to finalise Jack's wishes. There, he uncovers Jack's life of love, betrayal and a link to his own family. Rick also discovers there is much more to learn about this enigmatic man.

Paperback ISBN 9780645110753 Ebook ISBN 978-0-6451107-6-0

Large Print 9781923097186 HC 9798353687290 D2D ebook 9798233188794

Jonty's Journey
Gems, Love, Artists and a Golden Lion
Australia and South Africa 1880-1902

Sydney Jeweller **Jonty Evans's** passion for gems takes him to Africa at a volatile time. There, he finds the diamonds he wants and is given a lion cub. However, Jonty is all but kidnapped. His experiences in the Transvaal plunge him into questioning everything he knows about life. Soon, nightmares haunt him. (This is now known as PTSD.)

Upon returning home, he nearly ruins his chance with **Lottie Lockley** before it even begins, and he finds adjusting hard. Lottie's father, Luke Lockley from Parramatta, takes him under his wing and directs him to someone who can assist.

Jonty is then called back to Africa as a liaison and reunites with his lion, Chimbu, after saving the life of his security detail. His life journey introduces him to remarkable artists, politicians, poets, rebels, and the scapegoat soldier, Harry Breaker Morant. Can Jonty lay the past to rest and find his lost peace?

Paperback ISBN 9780645110777 Ebook ISBN: 978-0-6451107-9-1

HC ISBN 9781923097124 LP 9781923097193 D2D ebook 9798233808821

Fools Gold Trilogy 1840s- 1850s
The Breeze Gently Shifts (2028)
The Silver Thimble (2028)
Knots Behind the Tapestry (2028)

Mattie

The Story of an Australian Convict Child
An Australian Historical Story inspired by real Life.

An orphaned child, **Mattie Paul,** is convicted of petty theft, sentenced to seven years, and sent to Australia. She meets another convict woman who, at her death, gives Mattie a chance for a new life. She makes the most of everything that comes her way, earning her freedom, falling in love, marrying, and becoming a mother. But life is not kind to her.

She meets bushrangers, moves to Bathurst's gold fields, and opens a store. Yet, she is the kind of woman who made Australia what it is today. Can she survive alone in a man's world? She is a remarkable woman who breaks down all her barriers.

(Mattie's story continues in The Lockleys of Parramatta - bk 4 & 6)
Woodslane Press Edition 9781925403404 (Brown cover)
Paperback ISBN 9781503252370   ebook ISBN 97819023097018
Large Print 978099458204 D2D ebook 9798233382642
(The story continues in The Earl's Shadow & Once a Jolly Swagman) Released 2015

Ricky

A boy in Colonial Australia

Ricky English and his mother immigrated from England to join his father in the new Colony of Sydney. Upon arrival, there was no sign of his father. Ricky's mum uses the tiny amount of money they brought to get lodgings in a run-down building. Things go from bad to worse when his mother dies; he is thrown out of the hired rooms, and the caretakers confiscate all their possessions.

Ricky lives on the streets of Sydney Town as a street waif. Ricky finds safe places to sleep and befriends freed convicts who can help him survive. One day, he encounters a lost child and helps reunite her with her family. These people try to help him, but he insists on doing things his way because of his stubbornness. However, he has found a mentor and confidante. The story follows him through his life. He survives and turns his life around, helping others along the way. *(Will's story continues in Jonty's Journey)*

Pacific Wanderland Publications by Woodslane Press 9780994578211 *(Brown cover)*
Amazon Paperback ISBN 9781500770570   Ebook: 9781923097100
Large Print 9781533472748   D2D ebook 9798233505317

The Heather to The Hawkesbury

Four Scottish families brave a new life in a strange land.

Torn from their homeland by starvation, four Scottish families are forced to leave the Isle of Skye and seek a new life in Australia. **Mary Macdonald,** her husband Murd, and their family, her brother Fergus **MacKenzie**, sister-in-law Caro **MacLeod**, cousin Alex **Fraser**, and all their loved ones are compelled to emigrate from Scotland because of the Potato famine and Clearances.

The story follows these families as they journey from Scotland to the New South Wales colony in the 1850s. Mary struggles to cope with the changes and losses in the first months of settlement. Although the other women rely on her, she is nearly overwhelmed. Mary can't settle in this fierce land and pines for home.

Together, the families endure hardships such as accidents, loss, floods, and relentless work, ultimately forging a strong bond with their new homeland. Trials, tribulations, and triumphs mark their saga as they establish themselves in Australia.

Will Mary ever find peace and contentment where danger and sickness have taken loved ones? Can her love for Murd sustain her through the turmoil of life? And what becomes of the brooch given to Mary as she leaves her mother?

Pacific Wanderland Publications printed by Woodslane Press 9780994578228
Paperback ISBN 9781503251434   ebook 9781923097025   LP ISBN1533473641
D2D ebook 9798223852209

Sara's Author Bio

Sheila Hunter and Sara Powter were a passionate mother-and-daughter team of amateur genealogists. As they collaborated on their family tree, they made many fascinating discoveries. Their most significant finding was the discovery of four convicts whose perspectives on colonial life sharply contrasted with those of the military personnel. Transported to Australia between 1792 and 1814, these four felons lived during the peak of the convict transportation era.

Before her passing in 2002, Sheila adapted some of these histories into enchanting stories, later published as her Australian Colonial Trilogy by Sara. Sheila also left a fourth, unfinished story, inspiring Sara to complete it. Before taking on that task, however, Sara first created the 'Lockleys of Parramatta' series to ensure she could honour her mother's work. She completed the first two books in that series before attempting to finish 'Dancing to Her Own Tune'—for which Sheila had written the first 30,000 words.

Vividly evoking the Colonial Era, these books delve deeper into the theme of overcoming adversity in Colonial Australia, exploring how it emerged, the demise of the Convict system, and the discovery of mineral wealth. Sara skilfully intertwines precise archival data with a captivating narrative to craft a collection of stories about faith, love, loss, and redemption.

Two hundred years after her family arrived in Australia, Sara continues the Australian Colonial stories that start with *Gentle Annie Soames*, a saga about the First Fleet. Her *First Fleet Trilogy* is now complete. Following this chronologically are *The Hunter to Macquarie* Collection, the *Unlikely Convict Ladies* Trilogy, and The *Lockleys of Parramatta*. The *Convict Birthstain Collection*, set in the mid-1800s, follows. All the stories are stand-alone novels.

See Sara's web page to keep up to date with more stories.   Amazon Aus QR
Signed copies are available from:-
https://www.sarapowter.com.au
(Australian Postage only)
Email me at
saragpowter@gmail.com
FACEBOOK
https://www.facebook.com/profile.php?id=100063887262514
Would you like*"Unshackled Lives" for free?*
Download from Book Funnel after you sign up.

FREE Newsletter signup
From my web page.